KU-164-259

'Aline Templeton has been producing quietly intelligent, carefully plotted thrillers for years . . . [She] creates a tight, convincing band of characters and has the ability to spin her story beyond immediate events to paint a picture of a small rural community in crisis. She is good at managing her plot and revealing details slowly . . . She has demonstrated that, just when we thought Scotland was saturated with detectives, a strong woman can elbow her way in and find a unique niche.'
Scotsman

'Aline Templeton anatomises a rural community, provides a contemporary gothic frisson and introduces a strong and sympathetic series character. The result is an unalloyed pleasure – an intelligent, character-driven crime novel.'
Andrew Taylor, author of *The American Boy*

'The backbones of Templeton's plot are innovative and unique.'   *Good Reading Magazine*

'Shivery'   *Herald Sun*, Australia

'The build-up of suspense is terrific' *Women's Day*, Australia

'A long-hidden body is discovered in an area isolated during a foot-and-mouth epidemic. The remote rural Scottish background, a blizzard, a feuding farming family with secrets – all these combine to make this novel a compelling read.'
Margaret Yorke

Also by Aline Templeton

The DI Marjory Fleming series

Cold in the Earth
The Darkness and the Deep
Lying Dead
Lamb to the Slaughter
Dead in Water
Cradle to Grave

About the Author

Aline Templeton lives in Edinburgh with her husband, in a house with a balcony built by an astronomer to observe the stars over the beautiful city skyline. She has worked in education and broadcasting and has written numerous articles and stories for newspapers and magazines. Her books have been published in translation in several European countries as well as in the United States.

ALINE TEMPLETON

Cold in the Earth

HODDER

First published in Great Britain in 2005 by Hodder & Stoughton
An Hachette UK company

This paperback edition published in 2018

8

Copyright © Aline Templeton 2005

The right of Aline Templeton to be identified as the Author
of the Work has been asserted by her in accordance with the
Copyright, Designs and Patents Act 1988.

A CIP catalogue record for this title is available from the British Library

Paperback ISBN 978 0 340 83855 6
eBook ISBN 978 1 848 94751 1

Typeset in Plantin Light by Palimpsest Book Production Limited,
Falkirk, Stirlingshire

Printed and bound by Clays Ltd, Elcograf S.p.A.

Hodder & Stoughton policy is to use papers that are natural, renewable
and recyclable products and made from wood grown in sustainable forests.
The logging and manufacturing processes are expected to conform to the
environmental regulations of the country of origin.

Hodder & Stoughton Ltd
Carmelite House
50 Victoria Embankment
London EC4Y 0DZ

www.hodder.co.uk

To Iain and Clare, at the start of their life together,
with much love

'Cold in the Earth – and fifteen wild Decembers,
From those brown hills, have melted into Spring.'

Emily Brontë

Prologue

Cold, cold, cold. It was the extreme discomfort which penetrated her conscious mind at last and she found she was shivering so violently that her teeth chattered together; her hands were numb, her feet were wet and stinging painfully. Her eyes shot open and she gasped.

It was night and the sky was very clear and black, etched with the brilliant points of a million stars. Over the dark bulk of the house there was a full moon, bone-white against the darkness. The branches of the trees and the leaves of the privet hedges, silver-edged with hoar-frost, glittered in the steely, unearthly light.

She was standing in one of the narrow, overgrown blind alleys of the old maze. She had been dreaming about it, hadn't she, and here she was. Both feet were muddy and one was bleeding from a gash on the instep; the little gold ankle bracelet she always wore was missing too. The jacket of her thick, flannelette men's pyjamas had a tear in one arm and there was a long scratch on the skin below; she must have forced herself through gaps in the hedging. Sleepwalking when she was troubled was a childhood habit, now, she had believed, outgrown. But then of course she had been troubled over these last weeks, very troubled.

Tremors of shock as well as cold shook her as she looked about her in the sick confusion which always followed a rude awakening. Everything felt hazy and unreal to her still. Shaking her head as if to clear it, she turned uncertainly to orientate herself towards the entrance gate.

It was as she struggled to locate it that she heard the click of the gate's latch. She tensed; who else could be about, here in the dead of night? That had been part of her unease, the suspicion that she'd been spied on, followed unseen . . .

Through the sparse, scrubby privet bushes at the end of the long alley came – something. It was swathed in black and its head was a silver bull mask with sharp, sweeping horns that glinted in the moonlight. It capered towards her, tossing its head as it came. A figure of nightmare.

She shrank back into the corner of the blind alley, her heart beating so frantically that she thought it might leap from her chest. She could make no sense of this . . .

It wasn't real, was it? She was still dreaming, in that hideous, persistent way which had been another of her sleep-curses all her life, when you knew you were asleep but still were helpless to rouse yourself from the night terror which had you in its grip. And she was terrified now, in that state of dream-paralysis when your legs feel too heavy to run away and there is no point in trying to scream because your voice is frozen in your throat.

It had stopped capering. It was cantering, lowering its head. She was trapped; even if she could force movement upon her leaden limbs the hedges here grew densely, a solid barrier on three sides that seemed almost to be closing round her. She could hear the animal snorts and the heavy breath as it gathered speed.

Once the horror happened, the shock would wake her as usual and she would fling herself upright in bed, gasping and sobbing and soaked in sweat. *Please God, make it soon!* She was actively willing the final charge when it came.

It was only when one of the pointed silver horns, razor-sharp, pierced her through to the heart with exquisite agony that she understood this was no dream, for the brief moment before she fell into the sleep that knows no waking.

I

The hens, newly released from overnight protective custody, were picking their way down the henhouse ladder with a sort of dreamy deliberateness, blinking in the watery sunshine of a January morning which was surprisingly mild even for this mild south-west corner of Scotland. The sound of their reflective crooning filled the damp air, punctuated by an occasional squawk of indignation as some giddy young thing jostled the dowagers in her unseemly haste.

Watching them, the woman's hazel eyes warmed in amusement as they tittuped fussily out across the sodden grass under the old grey-lichened apple trees, sharp yellow beaks stabbing hopefully for worm delicacies or beetle treats. The woman was tall, only a couple of inches under six feet, with a boyish, athletic build; she was wearing blue workman's overalls and gumboots and her hair, chestnut-brown with only the first traces of grey showing, was cut in a short, practical style. Her countrywoman's complexion showed tell-tale signs of exposure to the elements though her hands were curiously smooth and well kept: nicely shaped hands, large and capable, with neatly manicured nails.

'Off you go, chookie chookies!'

She shooed the laggards out of the little hut, checked with swift efficiency for night-laid eggs which she put into the bowl she had brought, then set it down outside while she fetched the pail with the morning mash from its place of concealment behind the henhouse. It was never wise to provoke the frenzy of shoving, flapping, bullying and shrieking which the sight of this induced until the hens were safely out of the hut's confined space.

She liked hens. She liked their plump, red-brown, compactly feathered bodies on those improbably slim legs; she liked their clockwork movements and the comfortable sounds they made and their silly social squabbles. She liked the rusty throat-clearing of Clinton the rooster – so-called from his ruthless predation on the younger, fluffier members of his entourage – before he produced his crow. And there he went now, shaking his magnificent red comb and stretching out his plump neck.

Tipping the mash into the trough, she watched the mayhem for a second or two, then with the empty pail over her arm collected the bowl of eggs and went through the wicket gate in the dry-stone wall enclosing the old orchard towards the farmhouse. It sat nestled into one of the green Galloway hills, built out of the local stone so that it looked almost like an astonishingly convenient geological formation rather than the work of human hands. In the style of a child's drawing it had a window on either side of the door on the ground floor, three windows above and a grey slate roof which was glinting now in the morning sun, crowning the house with silver.

The sound of a quad-bike's engine made her turn and across the valley on the hillside opposite she could see her husband Bill taking a trailer of feed out to the pregnant ewes which were bundling along behind him as fast as their woolly bulk permitted, the collie Meg rushing round importantly at their heels although in fact no herding was needed. Bill stopped the bike and jumped off, a big man, solidly built, though he had kept himself fit and still looked too young to have just celebrated his forty-third birthday.

There was a thick ground-mist which suggested that the sunshine wouldn't last for long, but it gave an unearthly beauty to the landscape where the shoulders of the soft hills seemed draped in glistening gauze and the tops of bare trees emerged spikily from a swirling lake of vapour. She allowed herself a moment to admire the place she had known and loved all her life – 'God's private backyard', as her father described this tranquil corner of Scotland, bypassed by the busy world.

'Mum! Mum!' Her reverie was broken by Catriona's agitated shout from the farmhouse door. 'Hurry up! We're going to be late!' A conscientious eleven-year-old, Cat lived in a state of permanent terror that she might make herself conspicuous by some appalling transgression like being a couple of minutes late for school.

'Just coming,' her mother called over her shoulder. 'Round up Cammie, will you?' Cameron would no doubt have to be prised away from his GameBoy; at nine, his mind was untroubled by any tedious considerations of duty.

Putting two fingers to the corners of her mouth, she emitted an ear-splitting whistle which echoed across the valley. Bill looked up; she waved goodbye and as he sketched a salute in response, turned and plodded back to the house. She wiped her boots on the hedgehog scrubber by the mud-room door, then went in to pull them off and stack them on the wire shelf which ran along one wall. Cammie's boots were, of course, lying on the tiled floor; she tidied them automatically as she passed, padding in her thick woolly socks through to the kitchen.

Cammie was sitting in the sagging armchair beside the elderly Aga, the inevitable GameBoy in his hands. Cat was trying without success to pull it away from him; she had her father's fair hair but was slim and long-legged, while Cammie, big-boned, tall for his age and already a star in the local mini-rugby team, certainly took his build from the paternal line although he had dark hair and eyes like his mother's.

'Geroff!' he was complaining, shrugging Cat away. 'I'm just finishing this one game, so chill, OK?'

'We'll be late! Mum, make him—'

'Cat, it'll be quicker to let him finish. Cammie, see you're at the front door, ready, in three minutes or you don't see that thing again for twenty-four hours.'

'Sure, sure,' he grumbled, getting up and walking towards the cloakroom, still clicking, while his sister sighed dramatically.

Upstairs, their mother rapidly unzipped her heavy overalls as she made her way to the bathroom to wash her hands, then hopped along to the bedroom, pulling off her socks as she did so. The overalls came off; underneath them she was wearing a smart grey trouser-suit with a V-necked white sweater. She slipped her feet into a pair of low, classic black court shoes, tugged a brush through her hair, put on a slick of lipstick, then checked her appearance in the long mirror on the door of the wardrobe. She settled the lapels and gave a tug to the bottom of the jacket.

Fine. Detective Inspector Marjory Fleming was ready to go on duty.

Laura Sonfeldt closed the main door with its chipped and battered paint, then the metal security door, and walked slowly down the steps outside the Women's Refuge.

It was bitterly cold. A piercing wind whipped driving rain down the narrow New York street, sending litter skittering across the sidewalk. A sauce-smeared fast-food carton blew against her camel slacks but she barely noticed, blinking back tears as she tucked her blonde hair inside her striped woolly hat, pulling it down over her ears, turning up the furry collar of her coat and gathering it tightly about her slight frame.

She was suffering agonies of guilt. It had been such a touching farewell, there in the shabby common room with its motley collection of begged and borrowed chairs and tables, where the walls and floor bore the scars of careless living, spilt food and children's mess and no amount of disinfectant could disguise the smell of soiled diapers and kids' sick. The women themselves were stick-thin with living on their nerves and their drug of choice, legal or otherwise, or else obese from comfort-eating to blot out the fear which had eventually brought them to the shelter, but all had the same haunted and watchful eyes. They had said goodbye to Laura with speeches, hugs, tears and a garish plaster figurine of a mother and child which was in her tote-bag now.

Abandoning them had been a hard decision, even if she'd never been sure how much good she'd managed to do in these past five years of being a listening ear to a never-ending succession of desperate women, most of whom carried the sort of personal baggage that doomed them to be perpetual victims. Counselling always seemed a bit like offering a sticking-plaster for an amputated limb; to have any sort of chance of straightening themselves out they needed intensive psychotherapy, and even then ... Well, she'd found herself becoming more and more cynical about her profession, even if – or perhaps because – her own sessions with spoiled and wealthy socialites had funded her *pro bono* work here at the Refuge.

If it hadn't been for her mother, she'd probably have drifted on like this for years without subjecting her own generalised dissatisfaction to proper analysis, shoemakers' children being notoriously ill-shod. But when the transatlantic phone call came from her mother's next-door neighbour – 'Jane will probably kill me for this, but I thought you ought to know she's had a mild heart attack' – along with the pang of fear had come clarity: she was an exile in a foreign land with a misleadingly similar language, and she was desperately, intolerably homesick.

It would have been different if it had worked out with Bradley, but it hadn't. The Rhodes scholar she had fallen in love with at Oxford and married in a romantic ceremony in the college chapel two weeks after her graduation had turned into a merchant banker back home in New York. As her experience of the Bowery and his of Wall Street diverged further and further, the marriage died by slow and wretched degrees until it was a positive kindness to put it out of its misery.

Even then, she hadn't thought about going home. She had good friends and the exhilaration she'd initially felt in New York hadn't altogether disappeared. She couldn't really complain about her job with a large firm offering designer therapy mainly to women whose child-like frames gave their disproportionately large heads the look of potatoes on sticks; it paid well and made few demands beyond the ability to stop yourself telling them to get a life and a square meal. She'd justified its triviality by her work at the Refuge, sometimes feeling guiltily that she got more out of the arrangement than they did.

Now, though, she could only think how tired she was of city life, weary of its noise and its smell and its polluted air, its intractable problems and its belief that perpetual motion was the same as progress. As she dodged the dirty spray thrown up by a car going through a flooded pothole, she thought longingly of the quiet green English countryside and of her mother who despite having lost one daughter had never so much as hinted that the other had a duty to return. With one last, guilty look up at the grimy windows Laura tramped off up the sidewalk. That part of her life was over. All she had left to do now was to go back to her apartment, get on with booking her flight, and break the good news to her mother; her lips curved at the thought of hearing the pleasure in her mother's voice. And she'd stop being Laura

Sonfeldt; that wench belonged in the foreign country which felt like the past already. She'd go back to being Laura Harvey, a woman at home, at peace.

When she let herself into her rented third-floor walk-up the red light on her answering machine was winking. She pressed the message button without foreboding, pulling off her gloves as she listened and tossing them on to the couch beside the telephone table. It took a moment for the sense of it to sink in, then she froze in the act of unbuttoning her coat, as if the chilling words had turned her veins to ice. She heard her own voice cry, like a child's, 'Oh no, no! It isn't *fair*!' before she fell on to the couch, sobbing as if her heart would break.

Marjory Fleming set down her pen, rolling her head to ease the stiffness in her neck and shoulders and cupping her hands over eyes which were smarting from the strain of peering at the figures on the computer in front of her. She yawned hugely.

It was late January, a Monday afternoon, and the rain was battering the windows of the Galloway Constabulary Headquarters with what seemed like gratuitous violence, blotting out the view – such as it was – of the roof-tops of the market town of Kirkluce, midway between Stranraer and Newton Stewart. The lights in DI Fleming's small fourth-floor office had been on for much of the day and she had spent most of it compiling statistical returns.

Was it really worth the work she'd done to get herself promoted – the studying, the exams, the courses, the interviews? To be fair, she enjoyed her CID responsibilities and she had no problem with the management element: having kids gave you all the experience you needed in adjudicating squabbles, negotiating, motivating, and when it came to the crunch putting your foot down. She knew that her nickname – Big

Marge – while on the whole affectionate, indicated a certain wary respect and she didn't mind her reputation. She wasn't immune to the pleasures of power and the money didn't come amiss either, with farming in the state it was in at the moment.

But the paperwork! More by the month, it seemed, never mind the year. Down at the charge bar it took thirteen separate forms just to admit a drunk to the cells to sober up. And try that in triplicate for the work up here on the fourth floor.

She hadn't really analysed at the time why she had felt so driven to get first her sergeant's stripes and then promotion to inspector. It had taken Bill to suggest, with his usual shrewdness, that it might have something to do with her need to prove to her father she could do just as well as the son he'd always wanted. But it hadn't worked, had it?

Angus Laird, 'Sarge' to generations of Galloway police officers, had made himself a legend in the Force, as much by length of service as by his abilities. He had stayed on long past the time when he could have collected his pension because in his own eyes he *was* the job; he saw himself as an old-fashioned copper, keeper of the flame, a one-man bastion against the touchy-feely revolution which had ripped the guts out of the Force. The top brass said all the right things, but with a certain relief, when he went at last into bored and frustrated retirement.

Marjory didn't tell him when she applied to join, but on her first day in the job had presented herself to him in uniform, much as a labrador puppy would hopefully offer a trophy to its master. She might have fared better with a half-chewed slipper. He made it clear she was only a token woman who would never make more than a second-rate contribution to a man's world.

Her elevation to sergeant and her impressive work in the

CID didn't change his mind either. 'Whatever you do, it won't be enough,' Bill always warned her when she agonised over it, but somehow she couldn't just let it go. Her promotion to inspector followed in record time.

'He can hardly say I haven't done well now,' she had said triumphantly to her husband as she prepared to go and tell her parents of her success at their retirement bungalow on the outskirts of Kirkluce, about five miles from the farm.

Bill was a quiet man who weighed his words. He hesitated now, before saying gently, 'You do realise you've totally blown it? He'll never forgive you for achieving what he failed to achieve for all his years' service.'

She stopped, stricken. Of course he wouldn't.

Still fiercely erect at seventy, with a shock of pure white hair, Angus Laird's eyes had narrowed with what she recognised in dismay as jealousy and even hatred.

'It's a sad day for the Force I was always proud to belong to, when they're stopped from appointing a man to do a man's job. Or it would be, if it was a man's job any more.'

That was all he said, while his wife Janet, plump, warm-hearted and uncritically admiring of both members of her family, had exclaimed at Marjory's extraordinary cleverness and said how proud she was. Which, unfairly, had meant very little to her daughter.

Marjory sighed. Today was one of her days for looking in on them on the way home; her father, as always, would be sitting watching television while complaining that there was nothing worth watching these days, and her mother would ask her, just as she had done when Marjory came home from school, 'What have you been doing today, dear?' She knew better than to mention paperwork, which would only provide a focus for her father's scorn.

Anyway, sitting brooding wasn't going to get it done. She was reluctantly picking up her pen again when there was a tap on the door. 'Come!' she called, setting it down with alacrity and looking up expectantly.

'Got a moment, ma'am?' PC Sandy Langlands was a young officer with dark curly hair and a cheery countenance and Fleming's face brightened.

'Come away in! You're a welcome sight.' As he took the seat on the other side of the desk, she added, indicating the disorder of papers on her desk, 'But don't let it go to your head. Hannibal Lecter would be a welcome sight right now. If we put in the hours we spend number-crunching to keep civil servants sitting on their fat backsides drawing their fat pay-packets we could get the crime figures down without any daft government targets – but don't get me started. What can I do for you?'

Big Marge was famed for not mincing her words. Langlands grinned. 'Mostly social, actually.'

She took note of the word 'mostly' as he went on, holding up a wodge of tickets. 'Burns Supper. It's on Saturday . . .'

She looked at him with narrowed eyes. 'Did DS MacNee put you up to this?' she demanded.

He was taken aback. 'Well, yes, he did, right enough.'

Fleming groaned. Tam MacNee was her senior sergeant in the CID who quoted Burns in and out of season and treated as heresy her low opinion of the man who was the locality's greatest son. Allegedly. She leaned back in her chair.

'Listen, laddie, I've nothing against haggis and neeps and tatties. I've even got nothing against the man's poetry. It's this mindless praise of the man himself sticks in my craw. If he'd been writing today he'd be working for *Loaded*. He's got that phooarr! love-'em-and-leave-'em mentality and schmoozing was his other favourite activity – specialised in sucking up to the toffs and then stabbing them in the back when they got tired of being exploited. You'd have to put me under restraint to get me to sit and listen to that hypocritical bastard being drooled over by maudlin honest men and simpering bonnie lassies.'

'I'll take that as a no, then, shall I?' he said demurely.

'With those powers of deductive reasoning we should have you in the CID. Right, we've sorted that. Now, what was the other thing?'

Langlands looked startled. 'The other thing? How – how—'

It did her no harm to have a reputation for mind-reading. 'The thing you really came in to see me about.'

Flustered, he said, 'Well – it's a bit tricky. Off the record, if you don't mind, ma'am.'

Fleming grimaced inwardly. The 'bricks without straw' game, as she called it privately, was one of the curses of police work, when you were expected to take action without using the evidence you'd been given to justify it. 'Mmm,' she said, not committing herself. 'As long as you understand that if it's unofficial it may tie my hands.'

'Yes, ma'am. It's just – well, it's a problem with one of the DSs and I thought a word from you could maybe stop it ending up a formal complaint to the Super.'

'Fair enough. I appreciate that, Sandy.' She did, too. A formal complaint about a subordinate was a procedural nightmare. 'Let's have it, then.'

The constable cleared his throat nervously. 'It's – it's DS Mason.'

Not the biggest surprise since her Christmas stocking. 'Oh aye?'

'PC Jackie Johnston – do you know her? Just started three weeks ago.'

'Can't put a face to her, I'm afraid.' As DI her responsibilities were on the crime side, and she didn't have a lot to do with officers in training.

'Right enough, she's a quiet wee lass and just between ourselves I'm not sure she's cut out for the job. She was about hysterical after he'd finished with her, just because he asked her to administer the caution and she hadn't got it off pat. She's never going to win through if someone with fifteen years' seniority on her and fully twice her size loses it and yells at her.'

Fleming sighed. The Mason temper: she could think of three generations of that family who'd had it, and it wasn't the first time Conrad had indulged the family vice. He wasn't all that popular with his colleagues anyway, but as MacNee had once said, 'He's maybe gallus but at least he's got smeddum,' and she couldn't help but agree: there was a bit too much of Jack the Lad about him, but he had that spark of lively energy called in Scots by the name of an ancient insecticide, guaranteed to make fleas jump. She was reluctant to lose him for the sake of a lassie who, to use another Scots word, was so fushionless that she wasn't effectual enough to have mastered a basic professional requirement. Still, harassment was harassment, especially in modern employment law.

Langlands was waiting expectantly. Fleming made a pyramid of her fingers and propped her chin on it, considering. Then, 'Right,' she said. 'He's due for appraisal soon and we'll talk anger-management courses. I'll warn him now that if there's any formal complaint his career's on the line. That'll put his gas on a peep and I think you'll find he's sweetness and light to your baby copper. Will that cover it?'

The constable's face cleared. 'Sort of "deferred sentence to allow him to be of good behaviour"? Thanks very much, ma'am.'

He was on the way out when she said, 'Fancy her, do you?' and had the satisfaction of seeing his cherubic face turn bright scarlet.

Once he had gone, though, Fleming grimaced. They were an odd lot, the Masons. Grandfather had gone off to join the Republicans in the Spanish Civil War and got in tow with Hemingway – all that Thirties stuff with bullfights and roistering and Being a Man. He'd come back obsessed, called his son and daughter Jake and Brett after characters in one of the novels and set up a pedigree herd of Welsh Black cattle. Brett was Conrad Mason's mother and to this day you heard of them going off to Spain for the *corrida*. Marjory's sympathies were all with the bull, and she couldn't hack it with Hemingway either. She'd had to study him for Higher English and had got into terrible trouble for writing that his women were so compliant they might as well be inflatable.

She could remember hearing about incidents involving the Mason temper – there was something about Conrad's Uncle Jake at the bull sales once – but the details escaped her. She knew her patch, was famous for it even, but her father still had the edge; she could ask him about it this evening. He always enjoyed the chance to show off his vast local knowledge – and pathetically, perhaps, she still found herself anxious to please him.

Marjory picked up her pen again, though her mind was running on the Conrad Mason problem. She'd been there before and it was a bit like domestic abuse; he was apologetic, self-abasing and totally plausible in his promises never to do it again. Until the next time.

And she didn't have much time for psychology generally. Anger management, counselling, personal development – they all seemed to her scams designed to keep more people in comfortable desk jobs. Still, she'd recommend Mason for the course since that was what you were supposed to do. She just wouldn't be betting her hen-money on a successful outcome.

2

'Oh, my dear, I shall miss her so terribly! She was never too busy, always had time to listen . . .'

'I simply don't know where the choral society will be able to find another pianist like her!'

'Did anyone ever have a better neighbour?'

The ladies with their soft, pink, crumpled faces and pastel tweeds clustered round like a swarm of cooing bees. Laura, too thin in black wool challis, smiled and smiled and pressed the gnarled, wrinkled hands. They patted at her with nervous good-will and then at last set down the sherry glasses meticulously on coasters protecting the French-polished furniture and began to drift away, still murmuring their gentle lamentations to one another as they went down the path in the grey drizzle.

The woman who still lingered had a sharper face; her long nose quivered slightly as she spoke and behind gold-rimmed glasses her eyes were bright with intrusive curiosity. She indicated a photograph on the grand piano, an informal shot of a laughing young woman, her profile with its chisel-tipped nose and her blonde hair very like Laura's own.

'*Such* a pity your sister never came back – well, your half-sister, I suppose I should say, only I expect it was much the same thing really, wasn't it?' Her gums showed when she smiled.

'Yes,' said Laura.

'It would have meant so much to poor Jane. You never hear from her, I suppose?'

'No.' Laura felt the eyes scan her face with a sweep like a searchlight, registering the dark circles, no doubt, and the puffiness of recent tears about her grey-blue eyes. In a calculated gesture, she held out her hand decisively. 'So good of you to come, Mrs Martin.'

That left the woman with no alternative but to accept the hand and her dismissal; being a psychologist did have some practical uses. Mrs Martin set down her sherry glass reluctantly, directly on the rosewood surface of the piano, and then she too was gone.

With a tension headache pounding, Laura closed the door behind her, thankful to have the ordeal of the funeral formalities over, yet when she returned to the empty sitting-room it seemed oppressively quiet without the hum of hushed voices. She could hear the wheezy tick of the grandfather clock in the hall, the whisper of flames from the fire in the basket grate which she'd lit in a vain attempt to lift the gloom of the weather and the occasion. Listlessly she cleared away the sherry glasses, her own untouched; she'd never so much as taken a sip of the stuff since she was eight years old when Dizzy, having smuggled a bottle out of the drinks cabinet, gave her a couple of glasses. Laura had been so sick that her mother had sent for the doctor, but even then she didn't tell. She'd always kept Dizzy's secrets.

The kitchen was neat, orderly, just as her mother had left it. She washed the delicate cut-crystal glasses carefully, polished them with a glass-cloth, then carried them back to the sitting-room and put them away in their allotted space in the cupboard, just as if the next person to handle them wasn't going to be a dealer, clearing the house.

Tick, tock, tick, tock. Seconds. Minutes. Hours. Years. Wasted years. As Laura sat in her mother's favourite Victorian tub-chair, looking round the sitting-room with its evidence of a pleasant, tranquil life filled with friendships and hobbies

– the piano, the tapestry frame, the invitation cards still tucked into the mirror above the fireplace – she knew it for a sham. Her cultured, elegant mother had lived with a hell of inner despair as agonising as that of any of the desperate women Laura had counselled in New York.

Not knowing for all these years, that was the awful thing. She could see herself now, a leggy, skinny eleven-year-old, sitting miserably on the stairs, her arms wrapped round her bony knees, eavesdropping as best she could because her parents were in the sitting-room talking to a strange man about trying to find Dizzy. It hurt badly that her sister hadn't told her where she'd gone; she knew she could have trusted Laura not to give her away.

She'd adored Dizzy. Dizzy – Diana – was nine years older than Laura, beautiful and zany and casually affectionate to her little half-sister. Her father had abandoned his wife and child for a career as a professional hell-raiser, drinking himself to death not long after; Dizzy was sufficiently his daughter to want to raise a bit of hell on her own account, doing wild things which drove their mother and Laura's solicitor father into fits of grown-up rage and anxiety and which, as recounted by her idol in whispers later, made Laura laugh so much that she cried.

Dizzy had done all the exotic things Laura longed to do – and still hadn't, somehow. Equipped with a secretarial diploma and the ability to fry an egg, she'd gone off to back-pack her way round the world, picking up casual work on Australian cattle farms and South American ranches. She'd swum with dolphins and run with the bulls in Pamplona. She'd even joined a circus for a bit, until she got alarmed about the ringmaster's intentions – men always fancied her – and came home only when the money finally ran out.

It hadn't been easy for anyone, having an adult, fiercely independent Dizzy living at home. Then one day there had been the row to end all rows, with shouting and slammed doors and tears of rage. Laura had kept well clear, waiting for the storm to blow over; she never remembered one quite as bad as this, but sooner or later everyone would presumably calm down. Even when they discovered she'd gone, leaving a note saying she was going to live her own life, thank you, Laura hadn't worried – and nor, she thought, had her parents, really. There had been a phone call three weeks later, a brief phone call saying that she was fine and she had a job, then ringing off without giving her mother time to say more than 'Darling—'

It was the last word she spoke to her. Jane Harvey had died after fifteen years of living with the dreadful alternatives that her daughter was dead or that she cared so little for her mother as to let her spend the rest of her life in that anguish of uncertainty.

And there was worse. As she sat on the stairs, six months after Dizzy had gone, Laura had heard them talking about her to the strange man. She was old enough to guess he was a private detective; the police had taken no interest in a twenty-year-old who had quarrelled with her parents and left home. She heard him ask if he could have a photograph and her mother saying she would fetch one; guiltily, Laura fled to the upper landing as the door opened and her mother went to the study where the photo albums were kept.

Then Laura heard the man say, 'While her mum's out, just between ourselves – try something on with her, did you?'

Laura couldn't see her father, of course, yet when she thought of it now she could picture Geoffrey Harvey's face as clearly as if she had – his austere, scholarly face set in lines of shock, eyes wide behind his horn-rimmed spectacles. '*I*, Mr Wilkinson?'

Wilkinson jerked his head to a framed photo on the piano. 'A looker, isn't she? Can't say I'd blame you—' She could remember the man's hateful, suggestive titter, a fraction of a second before her father's uncharacteristic roar of rage.

'Get out of my house, now, this minute! I won't sit here to be insulted by your vile insinuations—'

'Have it your own way,' Laura heard the man saying, and leaning over the banister railing saw him come out of the sitting-room, smirking, unhurried. Then she saw her mother in the doorway of the study, standing transfixed, and knew that she too had heard it all.

Her father slammed the front door behind his visitor, then turned and saw his wife. The angry colour was still in his cheeks. 'I'm sorry, my dear. I found him very unpleasant. I'm afraid you'll have to find someone else if you think it's worth pursuing.'

'Yes, of course,' her mother said, her voice a little unsteady. 'He – he didn't give me much confidence either.' They went back into the sitting-room and shut the door; Laura suspected it was never mentioned between them again.

Yet, looking back, it was after this that their marriage – happy enough, in Laura's childish estimation – began to drift slowly, almost imperceptibly, as her mother seemed no longer able to bring herself to make the gestures of intimacy which hold any marriage together. They had lived almost estranged under the same roof until her father died, uncomprehending and sad, eight years later.

Laura hadn't believed the accusation then, of course, and even now, looking back with the suspicious eye of a professional, she thought it was most unlikely. Dizzy had borrowed her mother's car without permission and stayed out all night; the violent row which followed was a perfectly plausible explanation for her flinging out of the house in a fury, even if not for so cruelly disappearing out of their lives for ever. What her mother believed – well, again as a professional Laura could recognise a subconscious temptation to lay the blame for such a catastrophic estrangement on someone other than yourself, and she did remember her mother saying hopefully, when Geoffrey Harvey died, 'Perhaps Dizzy will see the notice and get in touch.' She hadn't, of course. How sad to think that Laura's father's death might have meant to his wife only a barrier removed!

Had there been later attempts at tracing her? Laura didn't know: certainly during her brief visits home from the States Jane Harvey had never mentioned Dizzy's name, and neither had Laura, shrinking from the thought of upsetting her. She was ashamed now of her moral cowardice, of never having defied the comfortable conventions of their relationship to talk about things that mattered. For instance, had Laura's decision to live in New York been seen as another loss, another rejection? They hadn't discussed it. Her mother had never complained, never been other than bright and brave, and Laura had never actually said, 'I love you, I miss you, I wish I wasn't so far away.' If only she had perhaps she wouldn't feel quite so guilty now.

But then, of course, suffering from guilt was one of Laura's personal vices. Had her sister been immune to such qualms of conscience? Had she simply put her family firmly out of her mind? Had she seen the notice of her mother's death and ignored it, telling herself perhaps that it was too late now? There were so many questions unanswered, unanswerable.

There was no record of her death, in Britain at least; lawyers were checking registers overseas while advertising for Diana Warwick now in all the major world newspapers. The executors had agreed with Laura that the house should be put on the market immediately. The estate, divided equally between the sisters, was a very substantial one and with her share Laura could take her time to work out what to do with this new, empty life. She had come to feel an exile in the States;

it was a bitter irony that having returned she should find herself rootless, a displaced person in what she had thought of as home.

If only Dizzy had been here! Faced with the grim task of sorting through their mother's intimate possessions, they could have cried and laughed together over the memories they invoked – though of course that was an idealised picture. She couldn't really remember much of her sister, beyond her glamour and her careless kindness.

She'd been self-centred without a doubt. Thinking about it now, it was possible too that her parents' divorce had made her to an extent self-destructive like her father. With that heredity, she could have been vulnerable to alcohol abuse and her daring, try-anything mentality might have led her into drugs – into prostitution, even. Yet somehow Laura couldn't see Dizzy as human flotsam. It didn't fit: she'd been tough-minded, a rebel, not a drop-out.

So where was she? Happy, busy, absorbed in her own life and indifferent to the havoc she had wrought in the lives of her mother, her stepfather, of Laura herself? Even now, all those years later, she still dreamed of Dizzy – sometimes vibrant, exciting as she always had been, sometimes in a context of horror from which Laura would wake sweating and with her heart pounding. Always, afterwards, there were tears.

There had been one of those dreams last night, not surprisingly: she was sleeping in her childhood bedroom where so often she had lain hopefully awake for Dizzy to push open the door and tell her of her latest escapade, putting her hand over Laura's mouth to stifle the giggles. It had been what Laura privately called one of the black dreams, full of threat and ill-defined horror. Dizzy was in danger and it was cold, cold; Laura had struggled awake to find her covers on the floor and, shivering, pulled them up again.

Oh yes, they had all suffered, as people in their situation

always did. Grief and loss caused such waste, such distortion of people's lives.

Resentment grew in her, resentment and anger. It gathered as tension in her throat, half-choking her, so that she snatched at the grey and black silk twill scarf at her neck to loosen it. She jumped up from the chair and went over to her mother's pretty walnut bureau where in Laura's childhood writing materials had always been kept. They were there still: headed cards and notepaper, envelopes of all sizes, in their little pigeonholes. She tried not to read the pad headed, wittily, 'Chopin Liszt' with its poignant domestic entries – coffee, butter, cornflakes – and picked up some sheets of ruled foolscap and a ballpoint pen.

'*To Dizzy, Address Unknown,*' she began.

'The Masons?' Angus Laird said. 'Oh aye, the Masons of Chapelton!'

It sounded as if he was savouring the name. Perhaps his daughter was being over-sensitive in thinking that what he was truly savouring was her deference to his superior knowledge.

He even switched off the television set. Janet, pouring tea from the big brown china pot which had either survived since Marjory's childhood or been indistinguishably replaced, caught her daughter's eye with a little smile and nod which suggested two women sharing a benevolent conspiracy to keep their man happy. Marjory smiled back non-committally as she took her cup.

'Did they have some sort of charity do at Chapelton once?' she asked. 'I seem to remember playing in the garden – there was a sort of maze—'

'Gracious me, fancy you remembering that!' Janet exclaimed. 'You can't have been more than eleven or twelve. It was for the Lifeboat – Mrs Mason was on the committee,

you see. And you were all very excited about this maze – a
bit overgrown, I seem to recall, and someone got lost and
then there were tears, well, there usually are, when bairns
get excited, aren't there! But it was a funny kind of a thing
to have in a garden, I mind myself thinking, far too much
work—'

Angus cut ruthlessly across his wife. 'I was under the
impression, Marjory, that you were asking for background
information. Of course, if all you want is to listen to your
mother clattering on—'

'No, no, of course she doesn't.' Janet turned pink with distress. 'There I go again – my mother always used to call me
a wee clatter-vengeance! But I'll hold my wheesht now and
not say a word.'

Angus fixed Marjory with a hard stare, as if daring her to
go to her mother's defence, but having long ago accepted
that her parents' relationship – which had, after all, lasted
for well over forty years – was their own business, not hers,
she too 'held her wheesht'.

Appeased, her father went on, 'More bawbees than
brains, that family. It was old Edgar Mason bought the
farm after the war – sold some big company down south
somewhere so he could raise pedigree bulls and play at
being a farmer. He'd a bee in his bonnet about bulls after
being off in Spain with thon writer fellow. That maze you
were on about – that was something to do with bulls too
– there's some stupid carving about them in the middle of
it . . .'

'I remember!' Marjory interrupted. 'The Minotaur – there
was a picture of it, half-man, half-bull.' Then, seeing her
father's expression, she said, 'Greek mythology. Sorry,' and
subsided.

'The old man was off his head by the end. There were
rumours – mind you, folk in these parts'll say anything, but

it's true enough they'd to call us out a couple of times to restrain him, bellowing like one of his own bulls. Blamed it on that foreign muck he'd been drinking when he was young, but if you're asking me Jake's not a lot better. He was in the papers thon time he went at one of the judges at the Royal Highland Show because his bull didn't win. And the sister too – her with the daft-like name—'

'Brett?' That was Conrad's mother; Marjory's heart was sinking as she listened to this recital of hereditary dysfunction.

'Daft, like I said. Ill-natured too, that one. Lost a husband with her screaming and carrying-on, just the way Jake lost his wife, and a proper lady she was too. Beats me what she saw in him.'

'That's right!' Janet was never repressed for long. 'Rosamond – she was a real nice woman. Then she just walked out on him and I never heard of her since. And after, of course, Jake's boy fell out with him too and left home – Max, his name was, but I don't know what happened to him.'

Angus snorted. 'Good riddance. Spoiled rotten. There was a business with drugs – got off with a slap on the wrist, but if I'd had my way he'd have been locked up.'

That could mean Max Mason was mainlining heroin, or that he was a teenager who'd taken a puff on a spliff. Given Angus's attitude to drugs of any kind, Marjory found it hard to tell. 'What's the situation at Chapelton at the moment, then? Conrad Mason – you remember he is in the Force? – gives Chapelton as his address.'

She hadn't declared her reason for wanting to know about the Masons; at the mention of Conrad's name her father's face brightened. 'Now *that*'s a good lad!' he said approvingly. 'Though what he's doing still tied to his mother's apron strings I don't know. The old man divided up the house when Jake got wed and of course when the daughter's man threw her out she came running home and changed her name and the boy's back to Mason—'

'As if the father had never existed,' Margery murmured. That explained a lot about Conrad.

'Aye, right enough. And that's where she stays now. Jake's still running the farm – he's as daft as his father was about his blessed bulls. But Conrad, now – made of the right stuff, you could see that, even when he was wet behind the ears. He'll be looking to make rank soon, no doubt.' Then he added spitefully, 'That's if they're still allowed to make up real men these days, instead of women and pansies.'

Marjory had heard all she needed and she'd had enough. She got up to go, feeling proud of her own maturity in disengaging rather than becoming locked into a bitter and pointless argument. 'Thanks, Dad, it's always useful to get a bit of background on these things. I'd better be getting back to make Bill's tea.'

Angus hesitated, obviously longing to ask why she wanted to know but reluctant to risk the humiliation of being refused on grounds of professional discretion. Instead he grunted, 'So well you might. About time too.' Then he picked up the remote control to flick on the TV once more and Marjory noticed, with an involuntary pang, how the animation left his face and his eyes, fierce and challenging a moment ago, went blank.

Janet escorted her daughter out of the room. 'Wait a moment, dearie. I was baking today and I just made an extra sultana cake for Bill. I'll pop it in the Tin.'

The Tin was a well-travelled receptacle making regular journeys, empty, from Mains of Craigie to Kirkluce and back again, full.

'His favourite. You spoil him, you know.' Smiling, Marjory followed her mother through to the kitchen where the warm, sweet, homely smell of baking still lingered.

'There's some scones too, and a few wee chocolate crispies for the bairns.'

'They make a beeline for the Tin whenever it appears. Thanks, Mum.' She dropped a kiss on her plump, cushiony cheek as she took it from her.

Janet beamed. 'You know it's my pleasure. I may not be awful clever like you and your father but if I say it myself I make not a bad scone.'

Marjory laughed. 'The best. I just never had the courage to compete, that's what made me join the police instead.'

Janet lowered her voice. 'It was nice to see your dad so bright today, wasn't it? He still misses the Force, you know, though it's ten years come the summer. And he still minds all the local stories. Those Masons – there was one time when—'

Recognising one of her mother's lengthy reminiscences coming on, Marjory said hastily, 'I really do have to go. Cammie has rugby practice tonight—'

'Of course, of course.' But as they reached the front door Janet went on, 'Mind you, what your father didn't mention is that good looks run in the family the same as temper. Jake Mason, when he was a young man . . .' She giggled girlishly and Marjory caught a fleeting glimpse of a pretty, flirtatious young woman somewhere underneath the wrinkles and the tightly permed white curls. 'Well, none of us ladies would ever have wondered why Rosamond Mason married him. To tell you the truth, I'd have had rather a notion for him myself, if I'd been a few years younger. Only don't you go telling your father!'

The fire had gone out by the time Laura had completed her therapeutic task and it had long been dark outside. She straightened up painfully, almost dazed from the effort of hours of concentration, and shuffling together the untidy pile of paper read it through. It was good: professional but personal too, hard-hitting. A pity Dizzy would never see it.

She paused. She'd written articles occasionally for newspapers in the States; why shouldn't she knock this into shape on her laptop and try it on one of the London broadsheets? It would strike a chord with other estranged families, might even shame someone into relenting, into picking up the phone . . . There would be a chance, however slim, that this someone might be Dizzy.

Suddenly exhausted, she dragged herself to her feet. Tomorrow; she'd sort it out tomorrow. Meanwhile she'd get a sandwich and a glass of wine and take them up to her bedroom where she couldn't hear the relentless *tick, tock* which was again sounding so loudly through the silent house.

3

When the phone rang for the fifth time within two hours, Laura very nearly didn't answer it. Her ability to refuse invitations gracefully and with apparent regret was starting to show the cracks of excuse fatigue.

Mercifully, they'd left her in respectful isolation the day after the funeral. She had time to write up her article, strong-mindedly suppressing the misgivings which the cold light of day had awakened, and send it off to the *Sunday Tribune*. What, after all, had she got to lose?

After posting it, she'd taken herself for a long walk along the right-of-way through the parkland of the local manor house. It was a pretty walk, with drifts of snowdrops under the grey boles of the beeches and glimpses through the bare branches of the mellow golden stone of the Georgian house. It would be going too far to say the sun was shining but the clouds had a tinge of matching gold and somewhere in a bush a bird was chirping in tentative anticipation of spring.

It felt, Laura thought fancifully, like a draught of pure, cold spring water after the stale, over-chlorinated stuff she had been used to, and she returned refreshed to tackle the task of sorting out the house. She was dreading it, even though she knew that like everything else in Jane Harvey's life, her mother's affairs were well organised. Documents the lawyers would need were filed and labelled and she had kept few personal papers.

Apart from letters from her daughters. As she opened one

of the long drawers in the bureau the sight of Dizzy's flam-
boyant scrawl with its flying 't' strokes and the circles above
the 'i's, made Laura catch her breath, but they all had foreign stamps and pre-dated Dizzy's leaving home. She pulled
one out of its envelope, then thrust it back unread, reluctant
to fall again under the spell of her sister's charm. It was just
too painful. She'd been given those breathless, ungrammat-
ical effusions to read at the time and they could have nothing
new to tell her. Anyway, they were worn with constant
reading; her mother must have combed them again and again
for clues which weren't there. Laura sighed. The lawyers
could have these too.

Her own letters, with their American stamps, she dumped
unceremoniously in a black plastic bin-bag. She had no wish
to come face to face with that younger Laura either, bub-
bling with enthusiasm about her new husband, her new
country, her new life. All of them, now, consigned to the
mental bin-bag which holds discarded dreams.

Bleakly she climbed the stairs to her mother's bedroom.
This, with its intimate evidence of an interrupted life, would
be the hardest part; the perfume she always wore, Estée
Lauder's White Linen, still hung on the air and a choking
lump came to Laura's throat. She wouldn't give way to the
disabling tears, though, busying herself with collecting,
tidying, slowly obliterating the personal so that strangers
should not paw over her mother's life.

She hesitated over the clothes – expensive, some of them
almost new – and wondered whether her mother would have
wished them to be given to friends. But then, of course, that
would open up a whole 'who-got-what' can of worms; Laura
seized them ruthlessly and put them into the bags. It would
be a good haul for a charity shop.

Jewellery: that could go to the lawyers too, meantime.
Furniture: her eyes lingered on the bow-fronted Regency

chest, the pretty Venetian mirror. The house was full of beautiful things her parents had collected over the years, but she had decided it must be sold and with that decision had effectively rendered herself homeless, so they had better go too. She would have nowhere to put them until she found herself somewhere to live and she had no idea as yet where that would be – the country, probably, though definitely not here where she would be haunted by memories round every corner. The problem was that without roots or constraints it was hard to know where to start looking.

She had been very tired when she had finished and it was late, but at least the most painful tasks were behind her now and she could look to the future. She went to sleep considering a half-formed idea that perhaps she might rent somewhere in London for a bit, look up a few old friends while she worked out her next step.

By lunchtime the following day the tentative plan had become an imperative. She'd had visits from four of her mother's friends, three offering affectionate support and the fourth, the long-nosed Mrs Martin, offering 'help' in disposing of her mother's wardrobe ('I know how distressing these things can be for the family, dear') and proving unable to conceal her disappointment at being told that it had been dealt with already.

The phone went all day with offers of hospitality as well as business calls from lawyers and accountants. Laura had collapsed again into bed, even more exhausted than she had felt the day before, with a priority list on her bedside table headed 'Find Flat'.

This morning had started in just the same way ('Now Laura, my dear, I want you to come to lunch on Sunday. My grandson's popping down from London – *such* a nice boy, doing so well with KPMG. I'm sure you'd have a lot in common and I simply won't take no for an answer . . .')

and by the end of the fourth call Laura was feeling persecuted.

She eyed the phone with loathing as it rang for the fifth time, had a brief wrestle with her conscience, then picked it up. She found it hard to keep the terseness out of her voice. 'Yes?'

There was a slight, surprised pause, then a pleasant male voice said mildly, 'I was hoping to speak to Laura Harvey, if it's convenient. This is Nick Dalton – I'm Features Editor of the *Sunday Tribune*.'

'Oh!' Taken aback, Laura sat down heavily on the little tapestry chair by the phone table. With her other problems, she'd put the article completely out of her mind; now she rapidly tried to gather her scattered wits. 'Sorry, yes, Laura Harvey speaking.'

It was a very flattering phone call. He was impressed with the article, thought it might well strike a chord with readers and wanted to run it in a couple of weeks or so. He even hinted that, dependent on reaction, there might be the possibility of an occasional series on what he called domestic psychology and mentioned a fee which would have made Laura sit down abruptly if she hadn't been sitting already.

'Now, you're down in the country somewhere, aren't you? I wonder if we have a photographer anywhere near you?'

It was a sign. 'I'm going to be in London within the next few days,' Laura said and promised to contact him, but her first thought on setting down the phone was not that here was a possible new career opening up. It was that at least she had a genuine excuse to escape Sunday lunch. She'd always been a rotten liar.

The dress agency was a small, single-fronted shop, flanked on one side by the lavish plate-glass expanse of an estate agent's and on the other by the primly frosted windows of a solicitor's office, in a side street off Gloucester's main shopping centre. The name above it, The Band Box, was painted in elegant gold script on black and in the simply dressed window a dusty-pink suede suit was artfully displayed to emphasise the lines of its expensive cut.

Inside, it was no more than a large room, with one end partitioned to provide a small back office and two changing rooms behind grey velvet curtains. The carpet too was soft grey and long mirrors reflected the rails of clothes arranged in blocks of colour and the shelf above where hatstands flaunted extravagant creations.

Its owner, currently reassuring a customer of the fit of a DKNY trouser-suit, was a slim woman, fine-boned and a little above medium height. Her hair, done in a French pleat, was natural blonde; she was discreetly made-up and unobtrusively well dressed in a pale caramel jersey suit with a cream shirt in heavy silk. Her manner, too, was quiet, as if not drawing attention to herself was a considered policy.

Over the years she had built up a loyal and extensive client base, on the one hand of ladies who came in twice a year to sell last season's designer wardrobe, on the other those who had the aspirations but not the clothing allowance. She had at one time or another passed most of them in the street unrecognised, yet if she had chosen she could have been very striking with her blue-grey eyes and refined bone structure. But there were lines of sadness about her mouth, and around the eyes where laughter lines usually show, her fine pale skin was curiously unmarked.

She packed up the trouser-suit, layering it carefully with tissue paper and carrying out the credit card transaction with quiet efficiency, responding with a smile to the customer's confidences about the job interview for which it was being purchased. She saw her to the door and wished her luck, then returned to her desk in the back office with the label to credit the sale to the appropriate account. She enjoyed her work, was proud of the business she had managed to build with a minimal bank loan. It gave interest and definition to a life which held very little else.

January was always a slow month for clothes sales and it had been a quiet day. It was dark outside and in another quarter of an hour she could shut up shop and return to her comfortable rented flat; she had planned a pleasant supper and tonight there was a good drama series on television. She was contented enough with that and her books for company and barely noticed the solitude any more.

Mechanically she tidied her desk and took the keys to lock up. A newspaper lay beside them, neatly folded in the buff wrapper in which it had been posted. She picked it up with a sigh, looked at it as if the act of tearing off its covering would be an ordeal. With a paper-knife from the desk she slit it slowly, then unfolded it.

It was a local newspaper with only half-a-dozen double sheets and it didn't take long to scan. Nothing in particular caught her attention but when she put it down her mood had changed. The quiet evening at home didn't seem so attractive now; perhaps she'd check if there was something she'd like to see at the cinema where she could sit in the warm dark surrounded by people instead of the ghosts of her past, and with the most highly paid entertainers in the world up there on the silver screen doing their best to take her mind off all the things she didn't want to think about.

Marjory Fleming wasn't exactly dragging her feet over setting up an interview with Conrad Mason – not exactly. But when he turned out to have a couple of days off, and then she did, and then there was a conference she had to attend and the statistical return had to be completed before the deadline, she wasn't particularly sorry to have an excuse for putting it off. It was only when she passed PC Langlands in the corridor a week later that her conscience pricked her into action.

When Conrad Mason came into a room, you knew he was there. He had the sort of presence which is a professional asset for a policeman: he was tall and broad with it, possessed of an uncompromising cast of features which suggested hitting first and answering to the complaints panel afterwards. He'd been known to break up a brawl just by coming into the bar and looming.

He was looming now. 'Sit down, Conrad,' Fleming ordered. 'I always feel like a stick of forced rhubarb under a flowerpot when you're standing over me.' He obeyed, smiling.

With her mother's remarks about his uncle in mind she looked at him with fresh interest and was forced to acknowledge that he too was actually a bit of a hunk. His hair was short, very dark and curly, and he had the sort of craggy face which might no longer be fashionable in the age of the New Man and the sarong but which would certainly appeal to any woman whose favourite fantasy involved caves and clubs and a bit of chest-pounding.

She only became aware that she was staring when he shifted uneasily and put a hand up to his face. 'Have I a smut on my cheek, or something?'

'No, no,' she said hastily. 'I was just in a dwam. OK, do you know what this is about?'

He shook his head, puzzled but not troubled.

'If I say the name "WPC Johnston" would it ring a bell?'

'Jackie Johnston. Yes, she's new, started a few weeks ago.' He still looked perfectly relaxed.

'Do you remember shouting at her ten days ago?'

That was a shock. His face darkened. 'Did she tell you that?'

'No, she didn't. It was reported by someone else, and let's get this straight right now this minute,' her tone was steely, 'if I hear even a wee suggestion that you're taking it out on her you'll be in the sort of trouble that will make you wish you'd taken a job cleaning public toilets instead. You and I both know it's not the first time we've had to have this sort of conversation and I'm trying to make up my mind where we go from here.'

She expected him to apologise, make excuses as he always had before. Instead he said, tight-lipped, 'Is the verdict in already before the trial? Or am I to be allowed to put my side of it?'

A muscle at the corner of his mouth was twitching and his brows had drawn together; he was staring directly at her in a way which made Fleming wonder if he was daft enough to think he could intimidate her. She leaned back in her chair and met his challenging gaze squarely. 'Yes, of course.'

'We were about to detain a suspect. I told her to give the caution and she had three attempts at it and then I had to prompt her. Maybe we should use her all the time – they'd all be so helpless with laughter we could throw away the handcuffs.'

'Do I take it you felt she'd made you look in some sense ridiculous?'

'Too bloody right I did.'

'Watch your tone, Sergeant.' Fleming spoke sharply, concerned at his belligerent attitude. 'You felt, did you, that the constructive thing to do about a professional failing on the part of a new recruit was to frighten her into hysterics? That this would make it more likely that she would be able to cope next time?'

'No, but it certainly showed the bastard we were arresting who was boss.'

Fleming said nothing. Loudly. The pause lengthened

uncomfortably until at last he burst out, 'Oh, I suppose you're going to say it was inappropriate and unprofessional behaviour. I suppose I should have said it didn't matter and patted the little dear on the head – oh no, of course not, I'd have been reported for sexual harassment instead, wouldn't I?'

'Yes, you certainly would. And you don't seem to realise how lucky you are that no formal complaint of bullying and harassment has been lodged.'

'Then what the hell is all this about?' He was on his feet, his face suffused with dark colour, his eyes wild and his huge fists tightly clenched. 'If I'm just here to jump through hoops—'

'Stop right there, Sergeant. That's an order. And stand to attention.' Fleming jumped up and came round the desk to within a foot of him. She was not that much shorter than he was; she held his gaze relentlessly, hoping that he couldn't hear the pounding of her heart. The silent struggle continued for a few seconds, then like an animal subdued he dropped his head. A moment later he straightened up, hands by his side, feet together, as the tide of angry colour ebbed from his face.

'Sorry, ma'am,' he mumbled.

'Oh yes, I should think you are. And it's just a question of how much sorrier I'm going to make you.' She went back round the desk, glad to sit down before her shaking knees betrayed her.

He stood in front of her, rigidly at attention, his eyes fixed somewhere above her head. She sighed. 'Oh, for God's sake, Conrad, sit down and stop being such a fool. You're a good detective but you've just demonstrated a lack of control which would make you a total liability.'

He almost collapsed into the chair, as if someone had hit him behind the knees. He was sweating; he was taking out a handkerchief to mop his brow as she went on, 'That, plus the business with Johnston – I have to ask how long it's going to be before you lose it completely and take someone out. What on earth is going on?'

'Sorry,' he said again, still speaking thickly. 'Personal problems. I shouldn't have let them get on top of me like that. It won't happen again.'

This wasn't the moment to point out that this was what he'd said last time. 'Do you feel like telling me about them?' Fleming said gently.

Mason bit at his lip, his head again bowed. He looked up at her fleetingly, then down again, as if trying to make up his mind. Then he started: his mother – she was so demanding, claiming he neglected her but it was only because he was going on training courses and anyway he'd a right to live his own life after all, hadn't he, and most men wouldn't put up with it . . .

Eventually he trailed into silence. Fleming hesitated, weighing her words, then said, 'Tell me to mind my own business if you like, but why don't you get a place of your own?'

'It's – well, it would be difficult.' But he was recovering visibly, as if what he had said had released some almost unbearable tension. He shrugged and smiled. 'I certainly couldn't afford the Jag on what they pay me at the moment.'

Conrad Mason's XJ6 was celebrated throughout the Galloway Constabulary and was held to explain his success with a string of very flashy young women, though none of them lasted long. Not the type, anyway, that you would take home to a possessive mummy, his superior officer reflected.

'I suppose I thought if I got promotion it would make it possible to get my own place,' he went on. 'But after this – there's no point, is there? Well, the only good thing about it is I'll have more time to spend with Ma. She'll like that.'

After what he'd said about his mother, this response was so false that alarm bells jangled in Fleming's brain. He was no fool; she'd given him a clue that she thought it would be good for him to have his own place and he was implying that a stop on his promotion would prevent this desirable outcome. He was trying to manipulate her.

'I'm going to have to think this one through,' she said coolly. 'I'm sorry to leave it unresolved but you must see that you have brought it on yourself.' She trailed the remark provocatively – hoping, perhaps, that another outburst would bring things to a head.

If so, she was to be disappointed. 'I know I have. I'm sorry to have placed you in this position, ma'am. Thank you for not condemning me unheard.'

He went out. It was an entirely appropriate, indeed commendable reaction. Why, then, did it make her more, rather than less, uneasy?

Marjory had stayed for the late shift and it was after nine o'clock when she hurried across the car park in the teeming rain to head for home. The kids would have come back on the school bus; Bill would have forced Cammie to do his homework and Cat to stop doing hers, given them their supper and with any luck got them to bed so that their parents could have a quiet dram by the fire in what was left of the evening before the early night a farmer's routine demanded.

They were, in a sense, in the calm before the storm at the moment. The black-faced ewes in lamb had been rounded up and brought down from the hills where they lived in all weathers to the luxury of the maternity suite, as Bill called the lush pastures close to the house. Once the lambing started he would barely see his bed. Marjory always tried as far as possible to work child-friendly hours for a few weeks, though in fact her mother was more than happy to help out with any problem.

As she drove the six miles home in the darkness, wipers switching in the persistent downpour, she thought lovingly of the man waiting for her at home: kind, humorous, hard-working, with the gift too of a solid sense of proportion. She relied on him to talk her down if she looked like getting her knickers in a twist over something insignificant and tonight she was planning to get his perspective on the Conrad Mason problem.

That was the Mains of Craigie sign now. She turned in and as her headlights swept round, dozens of eerily glowing eyes were picked up in the beam. Some of the sheep were restless and she could hear their plaintive bleats. They came from a 'hefted' flock – one with a homing instinct for its own particular territory, taught by ewe to lamb down the gener-ations so that they never stray – and they were uneasy in this unfamiliar place. Marjory had a particular affection for the black-faced breed, the leggy, thick-coated ewes and the rams with their magnificent curly horns, hardy and unde-manding creatures which even in harsh winter conditions would scrape down through the snow to find their own forage.

As she bumped up the stony track and over the brow of the last rise the farmhouse came into view, its welcoming lights glowing soft gold against the dark mass of the hills behind. Coming back to it at night, its promise of warmth and comfort always made her think of 'The Last Homely House' in *The Hobbit*: a bulwark of sanity against the crazy world of drugs and crime and personal disaster where she operated. How lucky they were, despite the problems of modern farming, to have all this and the bairns and each other!

The lights were on in the children's bedrooms. That was a promising sign: all that stood between her and the fireside now should be a recap of any triumph or disaster their day might have held and a couple of goodnight hugs.

At last, with maternal duties discharged, Marjory sank into one of the deep-cushioned armchairs beside the hearth, kicked off her shoes with a sigh of content and wiggled her toes to the blaze. Meg the collie was blissfully stretched out on the rug and thumped her tail lazily when Marjory pointed out to her that she was a spoiled dog and other collies lived in kennels outside.

'What other dogs do is wholly irrelevant to her,' Bill said, handing Marjory a heavy tumbler with a measure of straw-coloured liquid in the bottom. 'She knows she's really a person with a furry coat. *Slainte!*'

He took his place opposite, a big man, broad in the shoulder and deep-chested, so that his tall wife was able to feel agreeably dainty beside him. His fair hair was receding rapidly now but his blue eyes still held, she always thought, the innocence of a good man who looks out on the world and finds that goodness reflected back.

'*Slainte!*' she responded, tilting her glass to him, and sipped, feeling the golden fire burn satisfyingly down her throat.

His day had been uneventful; she told him her worries about Conrad Mason and he considered what she had said in silence. She had learned long ago not to interrupt the process; if she tried to hurry a response, '"*The mills of God grind slowly,*"' he would quote provocatively, '"*yet they grind exceeding small,*"' and go back to his contemplation. Tonight when she was weary it was pleasant just to sit and watch the coloured flames, orange and scarlet and green, and the logs glowing red-hot. One collapsed into grey ash with a gentle sigh.

Eventually Bill said, 'You've three problems, haven't you? One's the staffing angle – you've always said he's one of your most effective men and you'd be hard pushed to find anyone as good again. The second is whether, if he doesn't get his cards, anything can be done to stop him going "aff his heid" and hitting someone. And the last one, my lass, is covering your own back. What'll happen if you go to the Super?'

'Mmm.' Bill was spot-on with his analysis, as he usually was. 'It depends. He won't care about Johnston and to tell you the truth, I know I should but I'm not sure I do – she's kind of a feeble creature and I'll be surprised if she doesn't jack it in anyway. But if I tell him I felt threatened – you know what a stickler for protocol Bailey is. Mason would be out so fast his head would be birling.'

'Do you know what you want?'

'Oh, I know what I *want* right enough. I want Mason to keep a civil tongue in his head and I want everyone else to behave so well they won't provoke him. Oh yes, and I want world peace and us to win the lottery and Scotland to get the Rugby Grand Slam this year. And I wouldn't mind just once having Cammie choose to read a book instead of zapping aliens on his GameBoy.'

'Well, I'm jake with all the rest but I think you're reaching a bit with Cammie.' Bill finished his whisky and got up. 'You'll have to work it out for yourself, lass. I'm just away to let Meg out and check on the sheep.'

As he moved, Meg was instantly at his heels. Marjory drained her own glass. 'You did remember to shut in the hens, didn't you, love?'

'Would I forget your precious chookies?'

Master and dog went out together. Marjory stood up, yawning hugely, put the fireguard in front of the fire and switched off the lamps. She'd think about what to do in the morning, but at least now she had the problems clearly articulated in her head.

4

With a cup of coffee, a road map and a *Good Pub Guide*, Laura Harvey was attempting to plan her future.

The one-bedroom flat she was renting had been a lucky find. It was tastefully furnished in neutral colours and the big windows and cream walls made the living-room with a kitchen area at one end feel quite spacious. It had a good central location too, within walking distance of Oxford Street.

She'd been here for two weeks. London was full of seductive attractions, her friends were hospitable and it would be easy just to drift, filling her days with pleasant, purposeless activities until it became a way of life – easy, and self-destructive. In the aching emptiness of her loss, she felt a fierce need for somewhere to call home and it wasn't going to be in another restless capital city. She was in danger of making her grief a prison; planning a physical escape had a symbolic attraction.

She'd been very disciplined, each day choosing a different route out of London, only to return depressed each night by country roads choked with traffic and pretty villages which were no more than urbanised commuter colonies. She would have to go further afield, she realised now, find a pleasant country pub and spend a night or two over on the borders of Wales, perhaps, or down in Devon. The map was spread open now on the coffee table and she was surveying it helplessly.

Yesterday's edition of the *Sunday Tribune,* also on the

coffee table and folded open at the page with her article, distracted her attention and she looked at it again with the pride of authorship. '*Dear Dizzy . . .*' was the headline and below, '*Laura Harvey anatomises the psychology of loss.*' The small photo of Laura at the head of the column, she had noticed wryly, made her look strikingly like Dizzy herself. She was pleased with it, though. It read well and she was hopeful Nick Dalton might think so too and ask her to write something else. If she was lucky, it could be a new direction for her career – once she found somewhere to pursue it from. She went reluctantly back to the map.

Her house-hunting research was in want of focus. She needed a practical itinerary, clear, ordered objectives, systematic planning. With a pad balanced on her knee and pen poised, she turned to the map of the whole country. Wales, Devon, East Anglia, Cumbria . . . where to start? She sighed, twisting a strand of hair escaping from its clip at the back as she always did when trying to concentrate.

At last she did the only logical thing. She shut her eyes and was just describing circles with her forefinger prior to stabbing the map at random when the phone rang. She suspended the operation, opened her eyes again, feeling foolish, and answered it.

It was Nick Dalton's secretary. They had, she said, received a lot of e-mails about Laura's column; would it be all right to forward them to her, once they'd weeded out the cranks of course? Nick himself would be phoning in a day or two, but he was very pleased.

Glowing with pride, Laura agreed and hurried to plug in her laptop. Imagine – fan mail! She was, however, quite unprepared for what came through: there must have been at least seventy e-mails. Feeling stunned, she settled down to read them.

They varied enormously in character. Some were short

and gratifyingly appreciative of a good professional job. Laura enjoyed those. Others were less complimentary and she was mature enough to stop reading when she recognised their tone. There were some making helpful suggestions ('Try the Salvation Army' was the usual one – as if they hadn't!) and still more expressing sympathy. She came across two which claimed to know where Dizzy was, but the context made it plain that these were either naïve or malicious nonsense. A small number were encouraging, telling of the unexpected return of a prodigal son or daughter and urging her not to give up hope, but the vast majority were heart-rending cries of agony, hundreds of words describing unremitting grief and pain for someone who had walked out, last week in one case, more than twenty years before in another.

Laura felt emotionally battered before she was half-way through them. She forced herself to stop – they had a horrid fascination – and make a cup of coffee while she took time to think.

She didn't have to read them all, couldn't possibly reply. She wasn't strong enough, just at the moment, to bear the weight of other people's despair. Perhaps the newspaper would help; it was bound to know of counselling services they could recommend and have secretaries to deal with this volume of correspondence. She would switch off the laptop now and go back to her blind selection of an area to visit.

Her finger was poised to click the mouse-button when her eye caught the subject of the e-mail she had stopped at. 'Was Dizzy Di?' it said. She caught her breath, clicked on it and scrolled down with a shaking hand.

'Yo! Laura Harvey,' it began. 'Did your sister look like you? There was a gorgeous Di who looked like that, way back in the bad old days when we were in the power of the Minotaur. I would have played Theseus to her Ariadne but she escaped first and I could only follow. Call me to hear more.' It gave a mobile number and a name.

Laura's hand was stretching out to the phone when she had second thoughts. Struggling to keep calm, she read the message on the screen again, more carefully this time. It had a very strange tone; had the sifting process let one of the crazies through?

On the other hand – yes, Laura looked like Dizzy; yes, Dizzy did call herself Di outside the family. And for all she knew this sort of cryptic style might be no more than a common affectation in chat-rooms on the Net.

It still made her feel uncomfortable. She frowned at the screen. What sort of person had written this? It shouldn't be impossible to tease something useful out of the evidence in front of her.

He wasn't very sensitive, for a start – that jaunty 'Yo!' wasn't an appropriate response to an article which had been serious, even moving. A young person, perhaps, or at least someone trying to appear trendy.

Then there was the reference to the Minotaur, Theseus, Ariadne – what on earth was that about? She'd had the Ladybird book of Greek myths when she was small – there'd been a labyrinth, hadn't there, and human sacrifices to a monster, half-man, half-bull, until Theseus killed it. There was something else she'd read too, a book by Mary Renault expounding some theory about it all being to do with some ancient Greek fore-runner of bull-fighting. Ariadne, she seemed to remember, scrabbling in the rag-bag of recollection, was the customary simpering supportive princess. Not exactly a role she could imagine Dizzy performing – but then he said that she hadn't.

So what did it have to do with her sister? And why should – she squinted at the name – this Max Mason have wanted to put it in his message?

The most obvious answer was, to get attention. But just saying he might have known her sister would have had that effect – so what did this do that the plain facts wouldn't? Well, it caught her off-balance, intrigued her, whetted her curiosity. And curiosity was like an itch you just had to scratch, driving you to impulsive, unconsidered behaviour.

Laura felt the tingle of anxiety. She would have called her-self streetwise after her years in New York; this was a rather strange individual she knew nothing about, yet she'd been on the point of grabbing the phone and opening up a channel for him into her life without giving a thought to her own security. Not very smart!

She couldn't possibly ignore the message, even though it didn't sound as if he and Dizzy were still in touch. She could e-mail back, of course, which would keep him at one remove, but then he'd have her e-mail address and she wasn't at all sure that she wanted him to be able to contact her at will.

A 'number withheld' call was probably the best thing: he'd have no way of calling her back if he proved to be some sort of weirdo and she put down the phone on him. And as a plan, it had the merit of satisfying her impatience to find out what he had to tell her. She reached for the phone again, dialled the privacy number carefully, then the number she had been given. She drummed her fingers nervously as she heard it ringing.

The voice that said, 'Max Mason' didn't sound weird. It was a pleasant voice with, Laura thought, the faintest hint of a Scottish accent. When she announced herself he said, 'Hey, that's great! I was afraid the message would get, maybe, snarled up in the system.'

Laura said cautiously, 'The girl you knew – she looked like my photograph?'

'Spitting image. Were you alike?'

'Yes, oh yes!'

'I reckoned you had to be her sister. I knew her as Di – Di Warwick.'

At the name, Laura's throat constricted. 'That – that was her name. Oh, do you have any idea where she is?'

Max sounded regretful. 'Not a clue. Sorry if I raised your hopes. Like I said, it was way back – fourteen, fifteen years ago, it must have been.'

'I didn't really think you would,' she said dully. 'Where was that?'

'Up in Scotland. In Galloway where I – where I used to live.'

There was, Laura thought, bitterness there. 'Scotland! Why on earth – what on earth was she doing in Scotland?'

'My father' – she hadn't been wrong about his tone – 'employed her as a sort of Girl Friday. He has a pedigree herd of Welsh Black cattle and she did the office stuff for the farm and saw to it he wasn't bothered with details like cooking his meals or ironing his shirts – you know the sort of thing.'

'Tell me about it. Everything you can remember.'

'Everything! Well, that's some story. It would be better to meet up. Where are you?'

Laura hesitated before admitting that she was in London.

'That's no sweat, then. I could do lunch tomorrow, if you can.'

She felt pressured. 'Perhaps we could talk a bit more—'

'My battery's low,' he said. 'There's so much to tell you . . .'

It was an artful thing to say. She wasn't sure it was true, but she had to talk to him: it was possible he might know more than he realised . . . Covent Garden, she suggested, the pub downstairs at one o'clock.

She could feel quite safe there; even in February there would be tourists and buskers, probably. She had no reason, no reason at all, for feeling a terrible reluctance to go, as if this were something much, much more momentous than a meeting with a stranger who had once known her sister, a long time ago.

The warehouse, on the outskirts of Newton Stewart, was a seedy-looking breeze-block building, but its doors stood open on what looked like some sort of eccentric department store. Nicked tellies, DVDs and car radios were laid out together in one corner, smuggled cartons of cigarettes piled up in another. A grandfather clock dominated a collection of antique furniture and silver and beside a couple of weathered garden statues a gnome with a leer and a fishing-rod peeped out of a classical stone urn.

DS Mason showed DI Fleming round with a proprietorial air, drawing her attention to the more choice pieces like a salesman. 'That sideboard – looks like it's the Regency one they said was worth five figures. And there's a painting at the back there fitting the description of the one that went in the break-in at Knockhill House . . .'

'That's been a very nice piece of detective work, Conrad. Very nice indeed.' Fleming was generous in her praise and listened attentively as he detailed his plans for follow-up arrests. She gave the operation her blessing and then with a final, 'Well done!' went back to her car, where DS MacNee was waiting to return to headquarters with her.

She started the engine and the wipers – had there ever been a wetter spring? – and said wryly to the man at her side, 'All I ask is that you don't say, "A man's a man for a' that."'

Tam MacNee had spoken up for Mason when she had canvassed his opinion before; now he gave his gap-toothed grin. He was short and stocky with swarthy, acne-pitted skin, and in his regular plain-clothes uniform of jeans, trainers, black leather jacket and white T-shirt looked nothing like the conventional image of a policeman. When he and Marjory had worked together as partners, some years before, a suspect they'd lifted – clearly aggrieved that pigs working under cover weren't obliged to wear diced caps – had snarled, 'You're nothing but a wee Weegie hard man,' and she could find no fault with the description.

The first twenty-five years of Tam's life had indeed been spent in his native Glasgow where Marjory guessed he'd been on the lawless fringes of society. Like many another man, he'd been saved by the tough love of a good woman; behind him – indeed, towering over him – was Bunty MacNee, a comely Dumfries lass who could give her husband, at a conservative estimate, a couple of stones and when necessary the sort of flea in his ear which would have a lesser man whimpering for mercy. He adored her, though, and had put up no resistance to her determination to return home and remove him from the companions of his misspent youth.

As poacher turned gamekeeper Tam was a first-class detective, with a near-uncanny knack of second-guessing the criminal mind and no ambition for any promotion which would take him away from down and dirty operations. Fleming still relied on him more than anyone else despite their cultural disagreements.

'Too obvious,' he scoffed. 'No, no, I was just going to say Jackie Johnston was a "wee, sleekit, cow'rin', tim'rous beastie" –'

'And that isn't obvious?'

'– and about as much use to us as a chocolate fireguard. But Mason, now – he's the wee boy!'

'He's certainly got better timing than Fred Astaire,' she said dryly. 'He was needing the Brownie points after the way he's been carrying on.'

'Och, if he just keeps a civil tongue in his head he'll do fine.'

'Mmm.' She was still far from certain that he would, or could, even, but there was no doubt that Mason's coup in mopping up the house-breaking gang which had caused them endless hassle – particularly from middle-class house-holders, every copper's nightmare – went a long way towards justifying the softly-softly approach she had decided on, with Tam on the watch for any further trouble.

'How's the "hardy son of rustic toil"?' MacNee asked idly. 'Busy with the lambing?'

Fleming nodded. 'Poor Bill – this rain's been a problem. They can cope with snow all right, but they don't like the wet. Still, there's been a good few twins and no orphans yet. Cat's very disappointed. To tell you the truth, I'm a wee bit disappointed myself.'

A fair number of lambs owed their lives to the warm bottom oven of the Aga, and she loved their quavering bleats and the eager butting of the little, hard, black woolly heads as they scrambled for their bottle. It was time-consuming, though, and then it was always tough persuading the chil-dren that come the day they'd to go off to the market like any ordinary sheep.

'Bunty's always at me to get you to give her one to raise, but I'm not that daft. I'd end up living ten years with a bleating hearthrug. Her and her waifs and strays!'

The MacNees had no children and Bunty's kind heart was legendary. Marjory had lost count of the three-legged dogs and one-eyed cats that called the MacNee villa home, and asking Tam for a reprise on the numbers wasn't tactful. She changed the subject.

When they got back to Headquarters MacNee went to give warning to the dungeonmaster of the likely influx to the cells while Fleming sought out Superintendent Bailey to give him the good news, then briefed the Press Officer. It was a good day; the mood of satisfaction spread through the building as word got round and a couple of personnel problems Fleming had thought might be tricky sorted themselves out in the general atmosphere of good-will.

For once she managed to knock off in time to pick up the children from school. As usual, they were bickering; to avoid having to listen to them she switched on the car radio and caught a news summary which had just started.

'. . . suspected case of foot-and-mouth disease at Cheale Meats Abattoir in Essex. Tests are being carried out . . .'

Marjory caught her breath. It happened every so often, a scare about foot-and-mouth, and even though it regularly proved to be a false alarm a shudder would always run through the farming community. It was a virus that spread like wildfire.

She was too young to recall the '67 outbreak in detail but she could remember the terrible newspaper pictures of burning cattle and the disinfectant mats at all the farm road-ends. Farming had taken years to recover from it and blood-lines established over long years had been ruthlessly wiped out. She could only hope that this was the usual alarmist nonsense. Anyway, Essex was a long way off and surely, more than thirty years on, better processes would be in place to contain an isolated pocket of the disease. She decided not to mention it to Bill; he seldom heard the news and there was no point in worrying him unnecessarily.

But when she parked the car and the children tumbled out, still squabbling, she saw Bill coming across from the stackyard in the rain, his oiled jacket glistening, and from the grimness of his expression it was obvious that the story had reached him.

'You've heard the news,' Marjory said. 'But even if it's true, it's Essex, Bill – that's not exactly on our doorstep.'

'I wish it was Essex. Hamish Raeburn phoned me,' he said heavily, mentioning their neighbour who owned a dairy herd

on the adjoining farm. 'He's on the NFU committee, you
know. It's a farm in Hexham the animal came from.'

'Hexham! Oh no!' That was seriously alarming; the
Farmers' Union would have reliable information and that
was too close for comfort.

'It's worse than that. They send their beasts to the market
at Carlisle as well.'

That was where they sold their own stock. Marjory swallowed hard. 'Maybe the tests will prove negative,' she offered.

'It's a bad farm. There were complaints months ago and
they didn't take any action. There could have been infection
there for weeks without anyone noticing.'

She felt sick. They were so vulnerable: a small mixed farm,
with sheep spread out across a couple of hillsides, some
arable land and a herd of stirks bought in to fatten for the
beef market. They were only just recovering from the problems of BSE; it would be too cruel . . .

There was no point in agonising. 'Do you want a cup of
tea?' she asked, but her husband shook his head.

'I'm just away down to check on the ewes. Another five
lambs today – two sets of twins.'

'That's good. No custom for Cat's "cuddle-a-lamb" service, then?'

He shook his head, smiling, but as he turned the smile
faded. She watched him head off down the path in the
unremitting rain, then went into the house with a heavy heart.

In the Band Box dress agency, the fair-haired woman had
also heard the alarming news. The shop radio, always kept
tuned to Classic FM, at a discreet volume, broadcast the
item on the four o'clock news bulletin.

As she heard it, she became very still, listening intently.
She barely heard the Litolff *Scherzo* which followed and a
sturdy matron, optimistically holding up a size 10 Frank

Usher evening gown with a query as to whether it might fit, was at first gratified by the proprietor's, 'Yes, yes of course,' then later, in the privacy of the changing cubicle, rather indignant.

In her little office the other woman sat on, a furrow appearing between her finely pencilled brows.

5

There were no buskers braving the elements when Laura came down into the courtyard outside the Covent Garden pub; there was a chilly wind driving the rain under the glass roof and she hurried into the dark, fuggy warmth of the bar.

She was deliberately early, feeling it would give her a chance to scan people as they arrived and see if she could spot Max Mason; he knew what she looked like and somehow she felt that put her at a disadvantage. She'd given some thought to her appearance, gathering her hair into a neat knot and putting on one of the dark trouser-suits she had worn for work. It was a calculated distancing technique: formality as self-protection.

There was a fair number of people inside already, spread about among the irregular nooks and bays, but the pub wasn't busy. Laura collected a glass of Rioja, then found a round table in the corner of the window which gave on to the courtyard and commanded a view of the entrance as well.

Outside, a toddler caught Laura's eye, descending the steps very carefully hand-in-hand with her mother; a trendy tot wearing a pink coat and a purple hat with a shocking pink flower, and a distinctly yummy mummy. She was watching them with some amusement; the voice that spoke quietly at her ear gave her a shock.

'Laura.' It was a statement, not a question.

She turned sharply. A man was standing at her elbow, a

man with fairish hair and dark blue eyes, a little over medium height. He had neat features and a full-lipped mouth which somehow suggested petulance or even weakness; he was wearing a beige jacket over a brown polo-neck, stylish but not expensive, in contrast to the heavy gold watch on his wrist. She hadn't seen him come in; had she been so absorbed in watching the child that she had missed him, or had he – uncomfortable thought – been in the pub already, watching her these last ten minutes?

She was startled. 'M-Max Mason?' Her stammer betrayed her; she was irritated that he should have seen this sign of nervousness, especially since she thought she caught a glint of satisfaction in his smile. He had an expensive-looking smile, with very white and regular teeth, and he was holding out his hand.

She shook it. He kept hold of her own rather too long as he studied her face. 'Hey, hey! Di's kid sister! And you can't be a lot older than she was, last time I saw her. Swear to me that while I get a drink and the menu you won't do a runner like she did?'

Laura snatched her hand back, then was annoyed with herself all over again for making her discomfort apparent. She didn't reply, giving him only a tight-lipped, unamused smile. He had caught her off-balance again, just as he had done with his message.

She made her voice chillingly polite when he returned. 'Thank you for taking the trouble to get in touch with me. Do you work in London?'

It had no effect. Sitting down, he said as if she hadn't spoken, 'It's kind of weird looking at you.' He had the irritating mannerism of making a statement sound like a question. 'It's like something's gone out of focus. The eyes, a bit bluer, the nose – yeah, sure. But . . .'

He was fixing his gaze on the different areas of her face

in turn, as if calculating proportions. 'A tad too much chin, not quite enough cheek—'

The disregard for social conventions might be entirely innocent – or not. Laura didn't know whether to feel angry, amused or threatened.

'Talking of cheek . . .' she said lightly, and saw his face change on the instant. The corners of his mouth turned down in a rueful grimace and he slapped the back of his left hand. 'Sorry. Rude. Naughty. Let me buy you a nice lunch and I'll be good and mind my manners. We've got lots to talk about.'

Laura chose a salad more or less at random. While he queued at the bar she stared out into the courtyard, biting her lip, conscious of having been out-manoeuvred. It was unnerving that her attempts to keep him at a safe psychological distance had been so ineffective; she couldn't read him and it piqued her professional pride. He must have been in his thirties yet his behaviour was almost childlike. Was that calculated, an act put on for his own purposes, or was it really some curious kind of naïvety?

There was money there, or at least there had been at one time, but somehow Laura suspected he wasn't making it himself. A spoiled child, perhaps, who had never seen the need to grow up? The manner of his apology, as if his charm could broker forgiveness for any misdemeanour, suggested he'd been accustomed to indulgence.

But she hadn't been charmed, had she? He'd left her feeling uneasy, so it hadn't worked. Perhaps it never did; perhaps he was just a poor little rich kid with hang-ups that condemned him to go on repeating the mistakes of the past. She'd met a lot of those, become almost a connoisseur of the variety of fronts which could be constructed to suggest a non-existent confidence – one of which, of course, was undermining the confidence of the other person.

That made some sort of sense: after all, she'd been considering how to shield herself too. At least it was a working hypothesis.

Like a karate expert making use of his opponent's body weight, she turned his own technique of surprise against him when he returned. 'The Minotaur,' she said without preamble as Max sat down again. 'Tell me about the Minotaur.'

She could be confident, this time, that his response wasn't calculated. It was ludicrously transparent: his face darkened, his mouth became a thin line and his hands clenched involuntarily into fists.

'Jake Mason. My father – he's a bastard.'

How many times had Laura heard this tone of raw anger – even this phrase – during therapy? It had been her practice to say nothing in response, only to look an enquiry and she did that now.

As if she had opened a sluice gate, the disjointed story came pouring out. His affectations of speech vanished as he painted an emotional picture of a tyrant, a darkly powerful man with a towering temper, obsessive about the bulls he bred and his own money and importance, indifferent to the feelings of his wife and son.

'He – he drove her away, my mother.' Max's voice was thick with rage and hatred. 'She just vanished one day, when I was seventeen. I've never heard from her since. And he did the same to Di too, when I was eighteen. When she left I walked out and I've never spoken to him since.'

Laura drew a shaky breath. 'How – how did my sister come into all this?'

The waiter brought the food. Max had ordered a beef stew which he ate absent-mindedly as he talked. Laura toyed with her salad, too tense to eat more than a few mouthfuls as she listened.

They'd met, apparently, at the Sanfermines Festival in

Pamplona the summer before Dizzy vanished, at the famous running of the bulls when the half-dozen selected for bull-fights that night are loosed into barricaded streets leading to the bullring; young men historically display their courage by running with the dangerous, volatile creatures.

Max's eyes were dreamy as he talked. 'Di was amazing. Braver than most of the men – braver than me or my father, come to that, for all he always talked big. She actually touched one of the bulls, do you know that? It's the craziest thing you can do. People die that way. I can still see her – the white shirt with the red scarf and the red sash round her waist, blonde hair flying . . .'

Laura's eyes prickled with tears. Dizzy had told her about it when she came home, talked of the strange madness that seized you, the terror, the absolute joy.

Max was going on. 'They fire a rocket, you know, when the first bull leaves the corral, then another when the last one goes. If there's a long gap it's a danger signal – probably means one's got left behind the herd and it'll be panicky, getting spooked by everything. This was on the third morning and there was a long, long break before the second rocket.

'I'd done the run along with the first bulls and reached the barricades at the bullring end. The other five were inside by the time the last one appeared and it was going crazy, pawing the ground, charging everything. You ever seen a fighting bull? No?

'They're – well, fantastic. Black, wicked creatures, all bunched muscles and power and cunning. Every one thinks differently and you've got to get inside their heads to stay alive – that's what makes a great matador. When he kills the bull – the moment of truth – it's an act of homage to the most amazing animal in the world.'

'Hmm.' Laura wasn't entirely sure the bull would see it that way.

'That day, there was a group of about thirty running around the last one – ahead, alongside. One guy had fallen – there'd been rain that night and the cobbles were slippery – but he'd the sense to lie still and the bull ignored him. He'd got the scent of his mates ahead, probably, and he was heading for the bullring pens.

'Then suddenly this girl appeared out of the group. The rest were all men. She dodged to one side till the bull passed, then darted round behind and touched its flank. Everyone gasped. The bull wheeled on its haunches and charged in one movement, the way they do – so fast you can't believe it. If she'd lost her footing on the cobbles he'd have gored her to death, but she vaulted over the barricade and the crowd caught her.' His face was alight with remembered excitement. 'God, you should have heard the cheers!'

That hadn't been when he'd met her, though. That had happened later, when with the rest of Pamplona he'd gone after the evening bullfight to the Plaza del Castillo. Max described it as if it had happened yesterday: the seething crowd inside the famous Café Iruña with its mirrors, its glass chandeliers and its nicotine-darkened walls where Hemingway had got drunk on absinthe along with, Max claimed, his own grandfather.

'They've kept it the way it was, you know, very Thirties with the marble bar and the bentwood chairs. I saw Di at a table in the middle with all these guys around, everyone a bit drunk, talking and laughing. My father was at the bar with a lot of old bores he met up with every year – still does, probably. I haven't been back.

'I sort of drifted to the edge of the group round Di but I couldn't get near her. I was only a kid and they elbowed me out.'

It still rankled. 'How old were you?' Laura asked gently.

'Seventeen – eighteen, almost.'

Seventeen, and Dizzy would have been twenty. He had clearly thought himself in love with her, with that first fervour of a boy worshipping at the goddess's shrine.

Max barely noticed the waiter taking the plates away. 'It got a bit late and eventually she left with some of the young men. I followed her out. They were all a bit drunk – she probably was too. The roads out of the square are quite narrow, alleyways really, and by now most people had gone home. She was on her own with about four of them. I followed, a bit behind. They went out of sight round a bend and when I heard her call out I started to run.

'She wasn't laughing now. They were all very lairy and they'd probably just wanted a kiss to start with, but it was getting out of hand. She was struggling and lashing out at them, but one was behind her pinning her arms and the others were laughing and grabbing at her feet as she tried to kick them.

'I put my head down and charged them like one of the bulls. They were pretty drunk and I must have looked pretty scary coming out of the darkness. I landed a few punches and then they scattered.'

'Pretty impressive!'

Laura hadn't meant to betray her scepticism, but he flushed. 'Well, my father came up just at the end and they probably thought there were more of us coming. She was certainly grateful. We sort of acted as bodyguards for her for the rest of the festival.

'My father said if she ever wanted a job to let him know – we were always needing people after my mother left. None of them lasted long. When he discovered you only got a slave by marrying one he'd lose it with them and then they'd leave.'

The tables around them had emptied and the waiter had

brought them coffee. At last they were getting to the point where he might have useful information for her.

'So when Dizzy – Di – got fed up with living at home, she called your father to ask for a job?'

'That's right. She came in – oh, October, November, was it? I know she left in January.'

In her eagerness, Laura leaned forward across the table. 'Look, I need to know every single tiny detail. There may be something you saw, something you don't even know you know, but that might give me a lead to follow on what she did next.'

It was a mistake. She could see his withdrawal immediately. He had been facing her squarely, meeting her eyes as he talked; now he shifted to sit sideways at the table and he looked past her as if his attention had been caught by something in the empty courtyard.

'Well, hey, that's a pretty tall order. We're talking fifteen years ago here.' His voice was once more rising at the end of the sentence. 'Glad to be of service, like they say, but total recall's a bit off the scale.'

He'd slipped behind the shield again, as uncertain people, too directly challenged, tend to do. Laura tried to regain lost ground.

'Was she a good Girl Friday?' she asked, smiling. 'I don't remember her being very domesticated.'

'OK, I guess. She got across my aunt, though – they'd a couple of up-and-downers. She's always sticking her nose in.'

'Does your aunt live with your father?'

'Not exactly. It's kind of weird – there's the farm office and the study and the main kitchen and so on, then the rest of the ground floor is our flat – my father's, I should say – and my aunt and my meathead cousin live upstairs. Enough to drive anyone to leave home, don't you reckon?'

Laura had spent enough time listening to his family problems. 'If you can't remember anything, do you think your father would?'

Max laughed, shortly. 'You'd better give him a miss. Women seem to have a habit of disappearing around him.'

But his father, perhaps, might have a different version of the story Max had told her. Laura persisted. 'Can you give me his phone number?'

'I think it's changed since I left home. I could try and get it for you, I suppose. Give me yours and I'll call you.'

She'd be moving shortly anyway; with only slight misgiving, Laura gave it to him, then got up to go. He was staring at her again. 'So like Di,' he murmured. 'Really takes me back.'

They climbed the steps from the pub together. He was going back to work; he did something vague as a broker, putting companies and investors together. He went on to the Tube station while Laura walked more slowly along the rows of shops. There was something comforting about the brightly lit windows, the scent of toiletries, the elegant, expensive nothings on display. She felt she had walked long enough with the ghosts of her sister's past today; she needed to escape that twilight world.

The temperature had dropped overnight, low enough to bring a powdering of snow to Chapelton, three hundred feet above sea-level on the exposed uplands where stunted trees grew with flattened tops as if they had been trimmed by the cutting edge of the wind. The wide arch of the sky was still cold and clear but over in the east a red winter dawn was firing clouds massing on the horizon with a muddy, sullen glare.

Conrad Mason pulled the collar of his thick navy peajacket closer about him as he came down the front steps of the big Victorian house. He was theoretically on the early shift today but before he checked in he would be making a couple of calls on one or two people who wouldn't be expecting a personalised waking-up service. They weren't early risers and he wasn't in any hurry.

He lit up a cigarette – the first of the day was always the best – and on an impulse strolled off down the gravel drive which led to the fields, the smoke and his breath making clouds of vapour on the chill air. It was a habit with all the Mason men when they had something on their mind to go and – well, if not exactly talk to the animals, then contemplate their problems in their presence. And he had a lot on his mind.

He ought to have been feeling pretty good. The Super had been seriously chuffed with him and even Big Marge had been forced to grit her teeth and give him a pat on the head for his triumph over the burglaries. It had cost him, of course – there was no way his 'squeak' would have coughed for the measly £50 he was authorised to offer – and he'd had to find another £50 to get himself off the hook.

That was all it had done, though, and the euphoria had quickly worn off. Even though he'd shown them what a good man could do, even if he slogged his guts out passing exams, promoted posts as DI were few and far between. Big Marge had the job he wanted, and she wouldn't be going anywhere. He drew fiercely on his cigarette and expelled the smoke through tightened nostrils. Women! He was balked at every turn by bloody women.

And this foot-and-mouth business – it was a crisis rapidly being converted to a major catastrophe by the bungling idiots in charge. Well, 'in charge', as long as you'd use the term to describe someone clinging to a juggernaut. He had a bad feeling in the pit of his stomach about it: the epidemic was spreading like wildfire and the Chief Constable, no less, was pulling in police from all over the district to address them on it this afternoon.

His feet crunched on the gravel as he walked on past the straggly eyesore of the old maze and the open gates of the stockyard. No one was about: the stockman they had at the moment was a lazy sod and the curtains of his flat above the pens were still drawn. There was a housekeeper's flat there too but it was empty at the moment. Thanks to Jake being too mean to pay proper wages and his mother's incurable habit of detailing any failings with more energy than tact, no one stayed long and the house got dirtier and the food more disgusting with every passing year.

Living at home was getting to him more and more. He felt stifled by it, imprisoned as if he were locked into a bad marriage. If his mother found out he had a girlfriend, however casual, she behaved like a betrayed wife. If he took a holiday, other than the traditional one to Pamplona each year in homage to her bloody father, who'd been an evil old sod, she made him pay for it with sulks, tantrums and a multitude of personal inconveniences like forgotten messages and ruined laundry. Everything she did now affected him like fingernails being scraped across a blackboard and she manipulated the purse-strings like a puppeteer jerking around a marionette. It was lucky he'd decided seven years ago to bail out of the farm; at least he had his police wages, even if they came nowhere near to giving him the standard of living he was entitled to expect. If he'd stayed he'd have been forced to exist on what his uncle chose to pay him – minimum wage, probably, mean old bastard – and what Conrad could wheedle out of his mother.

He daren't leave home, though. If he did make his escape, he had little doubt that she would cut him off in rage and spite and he'd have to kiss goodbye to any chance of getting his hands on the farm, which he lusted after with a passion. He'd never met a woman yet who inspired anything approaching what he felt for the vast upland acres in this quiet, beautiful countryside, and he loved the great black beasts they bred which were such a part of his childhood, loved their size and their power and the sweet, heady smell of their grass-fed breath. But working here would have meant taking his orders from Jake and then – the ultimate indignity – from that wimpish little sod Max when his turn came to crack the whip, because though Brett had a half-share of the inheritance she'd been left with no status on the business side.

Oh, it was reasonable enough. Grandfather Edgar might have been barking but he'd have had to be baying at the moon to let his daughter within a mile of an executive decision. He might have considered her son, though. Surely Conrad could have expected a guaranteed future in the farm or at least a trust fund to let him walk away to set up his own? No such luck.

Still, he was pinning his hopes on Max's long absence, his silence, even, since as far as Conrad knew he hadn't communicated with his father since he left home. Surely Jake must have disinherited him by now: the dynasty of the Chapelton Welsh Blacks was important to Jake and Max would barely know a stirk from a heifer. Conrad, on the other hand, had always been careful to show his interest, taking leave for the Royal Smithfield Show and getting himself known in the Welsh Black Society. He didn't have to fake it; bull-worship was orthodoxy in the Mason family and the romance of it was deep in Conrad's soul.

He had reached the solid metal bar-gate to the nearest of the in-fields and stopped to lean on it, a habit which had started when he was barely tall enough to see over the top bar. And there, cropping at the tufts of grass rising clear of the snow with that familiar, rhythmic, tearing sound, was the bull Conrad had watched more than twenty years before, when this was the most promising bull-calf they'd had in years. They'd honoured him with the name Minos, held by the first Chapelton Champion, and he hadn't disappointed.

Champion Chapelton Minos II, commonly known as Satan, was still a superb beast though long retired from stud duties and on Jake's orders living out an honoured old age. A hardy breed, brought inside only in the most extreme of winter conditions, Welsh Blacks are large, solid beef cattle and Satan's size was at the upper end of the standard, well over four feet at the withers and not far off a ton in weight. His horns were forward-pointing, sharp and widely placed, and he had a nature as evil as his nickname suggested. He'd killed his man once, years ago – 'Stupid bastard,' had been Edgar Mason's only reported comment on the tragedy – and they'd had to buy off another stockman too, more recently, who'd only just escaped with his life. But Edgar, Jake and indeed Conrad himself would have paid whatever it took to protect this living proclamation of raw, untamed brute nature.

Satan was looking at him now, blunt, powerful head raised, eyes small with suspicion as his jaws rotated. Conrad finished his cigarette and threw away the butt. 'Satan!' he called. The bull stopped chewing for a moment as if assessing the voice, then dropped his head to graze with what almost looked like calculated contempt.

Conrad hadn't really expected recognition but the animal's magnificent indifference irked him. 'Satan!' he called again. This time the bull did not even raise his head.

Why was it that being ignored always got to him, made him feel young, small, a nothing, of no account? Conrad felt the flush of rage mounting to his face. As he rattled the gate, yelling a string of obscenities, Satan's head did come up, but with what looked like only mild curiosity, his jaws still moving

rhythmically. Still in the grip of temper, Conrad swung himself up on to the gate.

That was different. He had placed himself within the bull's
established territory and Satan was suddenly, dangerously
still. Then he snorted, turning to face the challenge squarely,
his eyes fierce with baffled courage, the mark of the bull's
uneasy relationship with man down the centuries, from
ancient Greece to modern Spain.

At least Conrad had been acknowledged as an adversary.
That was all he'd wanted – wasn't it? He wasn't angry any
more, except with the Fates wearing official faces who might
at any moment dictate the destruction of a relationship that
went back over twenty years – a relationship of challenge
and response.

For a moment Conrad held back. The grass was slick with
the snow which was just starting to melt. Satan was, what,
sixty, seventy yards away across the field? It would be insane,
of course – he wasn't twenty now and it must be ten years
since their last encounter . . .

Conrad had played the game first in his early teens. Edgar
had caught him once and thrashed him to within an inch of
his life, not because of the danger to himself but because the
effort of charging took condition off the bull. It hadn't stopped
Conrad, though, and he'd had a couple of narrow shaves
when Satan was in his prime. Surely the beast would be
slower now?

In a matter of weeks, days even, there might be no Satan,
no Chapelton herd, if the white-coated men came bent on
genocide. His throat constricted at the thought and in the
grip of some sort of nostalgic madness, Conrad jumped
down into the field and stepped slowly towards the bull,
every muscle tense with concentration.

Satan snorted once more, tossing his head the better to
catch the scent of the intruder, his enemy. He pawed the

ground as the man took another few, measured steps towards him.

The charge, when it came, was as always with bulls sudden and implausibly fast for such a bulky creature. The game was to hold your ground for as long as you dared before you fled: Conrad stood still for the first five seconds, retreated for two more, then turned and ran for his life as the ground began to tremble under his feet.

It came close to a fatal miscalculation. He had trespassed fewer than ten yards into the bull's territory but he had left his escape dangerously late. As he turned his foot slipped on the treacherous ground and he all but fell; only a desperate effort saved him and he could actually feel the panting breath on the back of his neck as he flung himself over the gate to safety. A fraction of a second later, Satan's head connected with the stout metal, rattling its poles.

He must have been mad. Despite the cold, sweat was pouring down Conrad's face as he fumbled for another cigarette, then needed three attempts to light it. He was getting an unnervingly close look at those sharp, wicked horns as Satan directed them at the gate yet again.

Gradually Conrad's racing heart slowed. That must have given it a better workout than half an hour on the treadmill at the gym. He grinned shakily and touched one finger to his forehead in a mock salute as the bull raged to and fro, eyes rolling white, nostrils flaring, shaking his nose-ring and blowing clouds of steaming breath into the cool, damp air as he patrolled his boundaries.

Conrad's grin faded. It was all too hideously likely that the next challenge would come from the men with needles carrying death, and no proud defiance from one of the lords of life would move them either to fear or to pity.

6

The black crow was flying slowly, coasting on the currents of buffeting wind under a lowering sky. Sated on carrion, it had flown further than usual, unimpeded by the need to scan the ground for food, and beneath it now were acres of ever-green forest, bleak moors, an isolated farmstead. Then the hilly ground flattened and fields of rich green pasture appeared where black cattle browsed. The ruffling surface of water in a makeshift cattle trough caught its eyes and it descended in leisurely sweeps to perch on the edge of the rusty old bath. It dipped in its beak, once, twice, three times, and then with thirst as well as hunger satisfied took off again.

For a brief moment, a red stain showed on the water, then dispersed.

There was an air of unreality about this whole business, Marjory Fleming thought, or was it just that she was light-headed from worry and lack of sleep?

The Major Incident Room at Galloway Constabulary Headquarters had been opened up and rows of plastic chairs were now squeezed between the banks of desks where computers flickered as officers from all over the region gathered to be briefed by the Chief Constable on what had been flagged up as the 'worst-case scenario'. Unfortunately, Marjory reflected grimly, 'worst-case' looked like being the only game in town.

Like the bubonic plague, the foot-and-mouth epidemic

was spreading at the speed of a galloping horse: Moffat three days ago, Gretna two, Whithorn yesterday. Paths and lay-bys had been closed, animal movements halted, local events cancelled, and there were disinfectant baths at every farm road-end, even if that was pretty much like superstitiously carrying a St Christopher medal in your car for protection, more in hope than expectation. No one really believed these were anything other than cosmetic measures when you were dealing with a virus – five microns in diameter, they said, whatever that might mean – which could be transmitted by wind, birds, animals, feet and tyres, could travel up to thirty miles, could be swallowed or inhaled and could survive in pastures for months. As she went about Kirkluce these days Marjory could almost sense a collective holding of breath as its inhabitants waited for certain calamity to strike, as if they were watching the line of a forest fire racing towards them or could see a wall of water building to a tidal wave, ready to break and engulf them in disaster.

Tam MacNee slid into the vacant seat beside her and seeing her expression gave her a consoling nudge. 'Cheer up, hen. You never died a winter yet.'

She managed a man smile. 'Burns?'

He shook his head. 'My old mammy was always saying that. Daft, if you ask me, but there you are.'

Chief Constable Menzies' arrival at that moment meant she could do no more than mouth, 'Get raffled!' as they stood up. Though it was only three o'clock the sky outside was dark with heavy cloud and the lights were on; Superintendent Bailey's bald pate glistened as he reverentially ushered his superior officer to the desk at the front. Menzies looked imposing beside his shorter, plumper colleague: he was a tall, distinguished-looking man with well-cut iron-grey hair. Police officers tend to be dismissive of those who sit on their backsides and bark instead of getting

their hands dirty, but the word on the beat was that Menzies
was no worse than most.

Sick at heart, Marjory listened as he characterised this as
the worst crisis to hit rural Britain in more than thirty years.
Their job here in Galloway, he pointed out, would be even
more difficult because of the close links which so many officers would have with the farming community; there must be
no personal favours, no bending of the rules, whatever their
private opinion might be. 'It's in every farmer's interest to
get this thing stopped in its tracks,' he pointed out. 'Think
of it as tough love.'

That produced a few wry smiles, but Marjory sat stricken.
She'd been so busy worrying about their own situation, emotional and financial, that she hadn't even begun to consider
the professional implications. Of course, the police helping
to enforce the official destruction orders would be the enemy
to any farmer, unless he was fully in sympathy with government policy. And precious few of them were, always supposing they could work out what it was from the conflicting
signals coming out of Downing Street. Blair's incompetence
would be farcical if it wasn't tragic.

'It's no part of our job to judge the rights and wrongs of
MAFF policy,' Menzies was reminding them now. 'We're
not the makers of the law, we're its servants, and it will be
our duty to protect government vets and slaughter teams as
they go about their grim but necessary business.'

Even as Marjory was consoling herself with the thought
that enforcement was the responsibility of the uniforms, he
went on, 'There will be, I have no doubt, organised protests
and this is an area where I will expect good intelligence from
CID. We must be pro-active not reactive.'

This was a favourite catch-phrase, much mocked by his
subordinates. MacNee sighed elaborately, with a sidelong
look at Fleming, but she barely noticed. Act as a spy on her

own community? How could she? And if she did, would she ever be forgiven? In the country memories are long, with grudges handed down from one generation to the next.

'We've been given unprecedented rights to enter private property without a warrant. I stress that these must be exercised with extreme sensitivity. Remember that you will be dealing with people in a highly volatile emotional state and I don't want any of the tragedies which may well occur to be laid at the door of police brutality. Remember, too, that you have the power to confiscate shotguns . . .'

Marjory had to suppress a gasp; it felt as if someone had taken a grip on her heart and squeezed it tight. In normal times, farmers had twice the normal risk of suicide anyway and in the last epidemic it had been a serious problem. Bill was a sensible man, but . . .

They'd talked last night about what they would do if a D notice was served on them, which would effectively quarantine them on the farm.

'You need to take Cat and Cammie and go and stay with your parents before it happens,' he pointed out. 'You've got your work and they can't afford to miss school. And even if we're not officially quarantined, we'd stand more chance of escaping it if no one was going to and fro. I could stay here and you could leave supplies at the road-end so I don't starve – and see your mother keeps the Tin full!'

The logic was inescapable but even so she had protested about her own banishment, if not the kids', until Bill said gently, 'It'll only be for a week or two, probably, and surely you can stand it for that long?' And of course she'd had to give in; she was after all an adult with a responsible job and it was pathetic to be making a fuss because she hated the idea of going back to living under her father's roof. She'd agreed they'd pack up and leave that night.

She was having second thoughts now. Bill would be so

isolated! They'd had to let the farm-worker go a couple of years ago when the dairy herd stopped being profitable and had to be sold. It was hard enough for him to manage now; imagine how it would feel to go on working these punishing hours tending livestock which might well be doomed, then going back to a silent, empty house.

If it was just the fattening cattle, she wouldn't worry. Losing them would be a financial blow but they'd weathered set-backs before and no doubt there would be compensation eventually. But the sheep – the sheep were different. They had colonised Mains of Craigie land even before Bill's grand-father bought the farm and Bill's pride in and, yes, love for his heritage went deep. How would he deal with strain and anxiety and perhaps, in the end, despair, if she was banned from his side? She couldn't bear it if anything happened to Bill.

By the time the Chief Constable had wound up his per-oration, she had made up her mind. She would see Bailey and ask to take leave – call it compassionate leave, if neces-sary – and it was as if a burden had been lifted. She and Bill would be together, and together they could face whatever the fates had in store.

She was humming 'Stand by Your Man' as she made her way to the Superintendent's office half an hour later.

'No,' Donald Bailey said flatly.

Fleming stared at him. 'I'm asking on compassionate grounds, Don. Surely you can understand my position?'

She was taken aback. Bailey was inclined to be pompous and to stand on his dignity but he was in general a good boss and they'd always had a good relationship. She'd been, she thought, eloquent about her situation, both domestic and social; she'd expected him to try to talk her out of it, then, however reluctantly, to agree.

'Of course I bloody understand!' He spoke with a bluntness unusual for him. 'It's a hellish position for you, but then it's not a bed of roses for anyone. People like you with good links to the farming community are particularly valuable just now, and anyway we're going to be at full stretch over the next few weeks.'

She said stubbornly, 'Surely it's going to be mostly a problem for the uniforms? In fact, I'm expecting crime figures to drop. Having everyone staying in of an evening's fairly going to cramp your style if you're into housebreaking or pub brawls.'

Bailey shifted uncomfortably in his swivel chair, which gave a protesting squeal. 'I'll be brutally frank. We're expecting trouble of a kind which may well involve the CID.'

'Like suicides, you mean,' she said flatly.

'We-ell . . . Violence against the person, anyway, whether that person is someone at the other end of a gun or the man holding it.'

'And what if Bill's one of them, left on his own?'

Bailey pursed his lips. 'It's not very flattering, is it, to suggest that Bill might be selfish enough to inflict that on you and the bairns?'

She'd have liked to have an answer to that. There wasn't one, though; winded, she subsided and he went on, with evident reluctance, 'I'm afraid it's an order, Marjory. I need you.'

'Sir,' she said automatically, then paused. 'I could resign . . .?'

It was gesture politics and they both knew it. She'd get no support from Bill, who would have every right to feel insulted at the implication. It would certainly be crazy for her to throw away their only certain source of income because she was feeling neurotic. And she could almost hear her father's voice – 'Well, I could have told them they were daft to put a woman in a man's job.'

She didn't meet his eyes. 'Sorry,' she mumbled.

Bailey's brow cleared. 'I always knew I could rely on you to conform to the highest standards of the service,' he said.

It was only as she heard the familiar orotund phrase that she understood how anxious he had been, and realised that, perhaps, he had stuck his neck out in backing her promotion and would suffer for it if she let him down with a response which would definitely be judged feminine and neurotic. Which might – she was nothing if not fair-minded – even *be* feminine and neurotic.

'Thanks, Don,' she said with genuine gratitude, getting up. Then, at the door, she turned. 'But how would you like to have to go home every night and hear from my father what a balls-up the modern police force is making?'

He'd been a constable when her father was a sergeant. He laughed. 'Rather you than me, right enough. Thanks, Marjory.'

'What are you saying? Are you trying to tell me that after Papa slaved all these years to breed the best pedigree herd of Welsh Blacks in the country, they could just march in here in their jackboots and slaughter them all? Wipe out his life's work, the heritage he left us? And you would just let them do it, just stand by and do nothing – nothing?'

The woman's voice rose dangerously. She was pulling a long chiffon scarf through her hand with sweeping, theatrical movements and her heavily jowled face was mottled with patches of dark red. Her histrionic behaviour was in marked contrast to her overweight frame, with its broad bosom and wide hips. Only her style of dress, shapeless layers and wispy scarves, gave a hint of the Isadora Duncan within struggling to get out.

She gestured dramatically towards a row of leather-bound ledgers in a bookcase to one side of the elaborate Victorian fireplace. Above it hung the dusty, mounted head of a magnificent black bull with sweeping horns, a silver plate underneath declaring its champion status. Round about were mementoes recording triumphs at the Royal Smithfield Show: rosettes, certificates, framed newspaper cuttings.

'Look at those records, Jake! Meticulous records of every cow, every bull, every pedigree, right back to nineteen forty-seven. That's more than fifty years!' She glared at him: her eyes were a curiously opaque grey-green which at school had earned her the unkind nickname 'Goosegogs'.

'I can count, Brett.'

The man who spoke sounded exhausted. His head was propped in his hands as he sat at a Regency partner's desk facing a tall bay window which gave on to a gravel drive and a lawn beyond. The wall behind him displayed a montage of bullfighting posters, ancient sepia photographs and, in pride of place, a silver mask of the horned head of a fighting bull, superbly moulded but tarnished from neglect.

He had a marked family resemblance to his younger sister: the same heavy build, the same strongly delineated features, which, though clumsy on a woman, were striking in their male form. The years had been much kinder to him too and his thick black hair, curling and cropped short, showed no trace of grey. The contours of his face might have blurred and his eyes, dark blue where hers were green, were set in sclerotic whites which suggested too many evenings spent with a whisky bottle as sole companion, but he was certainly still an attractive man.

'Do you think I haven't flogged my guts out trying to find a way round this?' he said tautly. 'Foot-and-mouth isn't even that serious, and you can vaccinate against it – but the Government won't authorise the vets to prescribe it. Yes, yes, I know,' as she made to speak, 'I've thought of that – give me some credit!'

He glared at her and when she subsided went on, 'I've tracked down a supplier in Spain and he's sending me some so I can do it myself – oh, there's a nonsense about vaccinated herds being less valuable, but who's to know? I can protect our own cattle, but it wouldn't make a blind bit of difference. If just one of the farms on the Chapelton boundaries has just one infected animal the men from the sodding Ministry of Agriculture, Fisheries and Food are entitled to walk in here and slaughter everything that moves.'

His anger mounted as he spoke; he brought his clenched fists down on the red leather desk-top with a force which indicated the level of his frustration.

Brett swooped over to take the chair opposite and covered her brother's hands with her own. 'Jake, you're getting too emotional,' she said infuriatingly. 'You need to calm down and think this thing through rationally. Now, who's in charge of making the MAFF decisions? We probably know them, or at least know the person who tells them what to do. If it's a question of money – well, I know you're always boring on about times being hard, but to save the herd—'

He stared at her, rage swamped by astonishment. 'Are you really suggesting trying to bribe officials? Are you mad? Or do you want me to end up in jail?'

Brett tossed her head and laughed, in a parody of the girlish gesture someone had once, long, long ago, described as attractive in the days when her hair wasn't grey and straggling. 'Don't be silly, Jake. I wasn't suggesting anything crass, that goes without saying. There must be subtle ways of approaching these things.'

He groaned, sinking his head into his hands again. 'Oh, shut up, Brett. Just shut up, would you?'

She burst instantly into noisy tears. 'Shut up? How can you say that, when all I want, all I've ever wanted, is the best for you and Conrad, and to preserve Papa's legacy . . .'

Jake sat in dull despair as the self-indulgent lamentations continued. He was trapped in a relationship more permanent than any marriage with this woman who owned a half-share of his business, his house and the family money and was bound to him by the ties of blood and the needs generated by her own failures. She was demanding, extravagant, possessive and becoming more neurotic with every year that passed. As if his anguish at the thought of losing his own life's work – the superb black bulls with the same ancient Celtic lineage as the glorious fighting bulls of Spain – weren't enough, he would no doubt have to cope with what Brett termed 'one of my *petites crises de nerfs*'.

The first of these had been when her husband, a transparent chancer she'd insisted on marrying against all advice, had decided there must be less costly ways of earning money and walked out. The second was worse, when Jake had signed the papers committing her adored papa to a discreet private nursing home when age had compounded the ravages of absinthe abuse to the point where he was actively dangerous. There had been others over the years, though latterly Jake had come to suspect they were manipulative contrivances directed at ruthlessly forcing her brother or her son into compliance with her selfish demands.

The sound of a car being driven a little too fast, spurting gravel, cut off Brett's sobs as if it had triggered a switch. She jumped up, dabbing at her eyes with the end of her scarf.

'That's Conrad back. He's the very person who can tell you what to do. I'll fetch him now.'

Her departure was a relief. The headache Jake had suffered all day was pounding now and he reached into the desk drawer to take another couple of painkillers, though it was only two hours since he'd taken the last dose and they didn't seem to be doing much good anyway.

All day the news had been getting worse. He'd tried telephoning MAFF to point out that the Welsh Black was a rare breed and to offer to put the herd in quarantine along with everyone coming into contact with them, but the only person he had reached was some underling who had just parroted the regulations, then when he lost his temper put the phone down on him.

And the herd, really, was the only thing nowadays that gave Jake anything recognisable as pleasure – his magnificent beasts, majestic, simple in their needs, honest to their own brute natures. Human relations were ugly and sordid by comparison, a maze of complicated and dangerous paths where you could see no way through – like the maze there at the foot of the garden which he had so deliberately neglected for so many years. He didn't often allow himself to contemplate the grim wreckage of his life, the failures, the disasters, the terrible secrets, but in the apocalyptic light of present events he found himself contemplating them more and more often. He groaned, shut his eyes and leaned back in his chair, digging his fingers into the base of his skull to try to ease the pain.

The sound of Brett's whining tones as she complained her way down the corridor with her son was almost a relief, though there wasn't much love lost between Jake and his nephew. True, Brett was an unduly possessive mother and far from easy to live with – who knew better than he did himself? – but Conrad treated his mother with cruel impatience and blatant contempt, and even Jake too, in the unguarded moments when his temper got the better of him. Afterwards, he was always obsequiously and unconvincingly apologetic

Jake was no fool and Conrad's strategy, in any case, was hardly subtle. He was desperately hoping to inherit control of the farm – and he probably would, when Jake got around to remaking his will. Conrad had the true Mason feel for the beasts, a good eye for selection, and he'd carry on the tradition of Chapelton champions. Max, though . . .

It was like pressing on a painful bruise. As always, his mind slid away from the thought of his son.

He could hear his nephew's voice now outside the door. At least Jake could trust him over this: the prosperity of the family business was dear to Conrad's mercenary little black heart. Certainly, as a policeman, he'd be in the best position to know what, if anything, could be done, and perhaps, after all, media reports were exaggerated – they usually were.

One look at Conrad's sombre expression as he came into the farm office behind his mother was enough to disabuse Jake of any such comforting delusion.

'Does my bum look big in this?'

The large, jolly young woman who had squeezed herself into a short, tight, orange Max Mara skirt had to say it twice before the fair-haired woman, sitting in her office with newspapers bearing lurid pictures of cattle pyres open in front of her, reacted.

'Sorry?' she said. She looked up, her grey-blue eyes wide and expressionless, then realised what the question had been. For a terrible, unguarded moment the thought, 'Your bum would look big in anything,' almost reached her lips. She fought it back. 'Well . . .' she murmured diplomatically.

'It does, doesn't it?' The woman turned to squint over her shoulder at the pier glass in the corner under a strong spotlight, and shuddered. 'Oh dear. No wonder you were struck dumb. Never mind – back to the drawing-board.'

'What about this – or this?'

After quarter of an hour's hard work evangelising for the slimming virtues of black, she was able to see her customer leave with a larger, longer, slightly draped crêpe skirt in that useful colour and only a brief, longing glance at the orange creation, now back on its hanger.

Shutting the door behind her, she returned to her desk and the newspaper she had been studying with such painful attention. It wasn't one of the garish tabloids; it was a sober production with the masthead the *Galloway Globe*, though its headlines were in the largest point available and its pictures of the pyres – livid smoke, sullen red and orange flames and the black, twisted limbs of burning carcasses – were as shocking as any. She read on, unconsciously wringing her slim hands, as she scanned column after column in a painful search for the information she hoped, yet feared, to find.

'Are they going to come and kill all the sheep? Even the *lambs*?' Cat was sitting up in bed, her eyes bright with tears, when Marjory came in to say goodnight.

The little wooden bed, tucked in under the eaves, had been painted white by Marjory herself, and Grannie Laird had stitched its patchwork quilt. These days Cat was starting to make noises about the room being babyish but at the moment the pink-shaded bedside lamp was bathing in its rosy glow the relics of childhood – the doll's house, the soft toys which were almost if not quite outgrown – and creating an idyllic picture of comfort and security. Only the faint moan of a rising wind hinted at a bleaker world beyond the pink gingham curtains.

It had been a lot easier to deal with Cammie, whose main preoccupation was the cancelling of the mini-rugby tournament next week. Marjory had to swallow hard.

'Not necessarily. If everyone is really careful and sensible it might just fizzle out and anyway our sheep might not get it.' But Cat was entitled to an honest answer: she went on, 'Though yes, of course they might.'

The tears spilled over and Marjory gathered her daughter

into her arms with the meaningless reassurance mothers have murmured down the ages. 'It's all right, pet, it's all right . . . Have you got a tissue? Here. Now listen – you're a farmer's daughter. You know what happens to sheep anyway.'

Sniffing, Cat nodded.

'So it's sad and we're upset this is happening, but it's not as if they were going to live happily ever after, is it?'

Fair-minded like her mother, Cat acknowledged the justice of this. 'And at least there haven't been any pet lambs this year.'

Marjory had thought of that; it was one of the few 'well-*that*'s-a-mercy' aspects of the whole sorry situation. 'And you'll have fun staying with Grannie and Grandpa. She's going to give you cooking lessons and you'll be much better than I ever was.'

'And I can walk round to Flora's after school.' Her daughter brightened. 'They've got satellite, you know . . .'

Having given her daughter's thoughts a more cheerful direction, Marjory kissed her goodnight, but as she walked downstairs she was close to tears herself. Oh, what she'd said to Cat was sensible, but all the same it felt as if a whole ordered way of life was being torn apart by the forces of anarchy and chaos. She could almost see them, wolves prowling round the fold, grey menacing shapes in an outer, impenetrable darkness.

Had her parents, she wondered, felt similarly helpless as they waited for the outbreak of war? Of course it wasn't the same – no one was going to come and bomb their farm-house – but even so, it was a war of sorts, not only against the virus but against the bureaucratic powers of a government which either didn't understand or didn't care. Or both.

She would be obliged to help support its edicts, then she'd have to go home at night to her father who would have his own views and wouldn't hesitate to express them. It was an indefinite sentence, too, the sort Human Rights legislation wouldn't allow to be imposed in a courtroom. Cruel and unusual punishment.

'Bill?' she called as she reached the hall, but there was no answer. He must still be out with the sheep and anyway she had a pile of clothes that needed ironing before she could pack them. She set up the ironing-board in the kitchen and switched on the portable TV.

The news was on, full of more and more depressing stories about the progress of the disease. Marjory watched till she could bear it no longer, then channel-hopped between a soap, a quiz show and a sit-com, each of which seemed even more irritatingly stupid than usual, and she switched it off. She was ironing with only her own gloomy thoughts for company when she heard the door of the mud-room open.

A few moments later Bill appeared in his stocking soles but still wearing his wet oilskins. Meg the collie, soaked and shivering, slipped past him to press herself against the warmth of the stove.

In Bill's hands was a tiny lamb, legs swinging from the sad, inert little body. 'The first of the orphans. It's a bit of a bugger that this is the best lambing season we've had for years, despite the rain. Do you suppose there's any point in trying to revive it?'

Marjory set down the iron. 'Oh, Bill – a little black one!' She came over, touched the soft, damp fuzz of its fleece. 'Poor wee thing – we should give it a chance, surely?' Then she thought of Cat and grimaced.

'Cat.' Bill read her expression. 'She'd fall apart.'

The little creature's eyes were shut tight, its life almost perceptibly ebbing away. Marjory hardened her heart against sentimentality; they might, after all, only preserve it for a more miserable end.

There was a huge lump in her throat. 'Let it go,' she said.

Miserably Bill nodded, then trudged out cradling the dying lamb, back into the wind and the rain.

7

It had all happened with such agonising suddenness and speed. Jake Morgan read it in the eyes of Willie Strachan the stockman as he stood in front of the desk, pleating his tweed bunnet in his labourer's hands, black-seamed and cracked and split with outdoor work. He was a tall, wiry man in his thirties with a two-day growth of stubble, a hard man whose daily business was handling the dangerous unpolled cattle of the Chapelton herd, but he was clearly afraid to speak. As if the drooping lines of his body weren't shouting the news so loudly that it was all Jake could do not to put his hands over his ears to shut it out.

Jake had believed that here on these upland acres they were isolated enough to be protected. Conrad had been banished already to find digs in Kirkluce; the farm-workers and their families had been banned from leaving. The vaccine from Spain should arrive in the next couple of days; he'd reckoned that if the worst came to the worst, with the contagion in a neighbouring farm, he could disclose his precautions and demand special consideration. He'd prepared himself for a long-drawn-out agony, watching as the flood-tide of the virus lapped the shores of his island of security, wondering if his strategy would work. He wasn't prepared for a lightning strike.

'Yes?' he said dully.

Lesions, the man reported, on the lips of three of the cows. They seemed listless, too, hanging their heads and off their feed.

'I – I see.' Jake tried to clear his head, to think calmly, but the headache which was never far away these days had returned with excruciating force and there was a singing in his ears. Perhaps if they isolated these cows they could manage to contain it. No one need know; there wouldn't be the usual to-and-froing to the village with gossip. They'd lose a few, obviously – could kill them and dispose of them quietly themselves – but once the vaccine arrived there would be a chance to save the nucleus of the herd if they acted fast enough.

'Bring them into the stockyard, Willie,' he ordered. 'In fact, bring in all the cows from that field. Strict isolation – don't let them near any of the others.'

'Aye, I did that, sir, right away.'

'Good man, good man. Now, what next?'

'Well, I phoned the vet—'

It took a second for the significance of the words to strike Jake. '*What?* You did *what?*' Leaping to his feet, Jake yelled the word; the man recoiled, taking a couple of nervous steps backwards.

'I thought—'

'You thought? You thought? You know what you've gone and done? You've signed the death warrant of every animal on this farm! You've wiped out fifty years of work, mine and my father's. You imbecilic, moronic bastard!' Flecks of foam were gathering at the corners of Jake's mouth.

The door flew open and Brett Mason stood in the middle of the doorway, in a dramatic pose. 'How can anyone in this house possibly be expected to live a normal life when—'

Then, sensing for once a tension in the atmosphere which she hadn't generated, she stopped. 'Jake, what's happened?' she demanded sharply.

Her brother spun round, his face suffused with alarming colour. 'Meet the man who's decided to destroy our lives,' he said thickly. 'We've got a couple of infected animals and he phones the executioners so they can come and massacre the Chapelton herd!'

Her eyes widened. 'The bulls! Oh no, Papa's bulls! They can't do that, they can't, they can't!'

She began to scream hysterically, shriek after shriek. It seemed almost practised: performance art, perhaps. Strachan stared at her in alarm, unconsciously removing himself to a less exposed position between the desk and the fireplace.

Jake, however, found himself unmoved. His sister's over-reaction seemed, oddly enough, to make him feel calmer; he said coldly, 'It won't work this time, Brett. It's too serious for your little games. If we can't think of some way out, we're finished.'

She stopped, with bizarre effect, in mid-scream. Jake stood still, his hands to his aching temples. His companions were silent, although Brett's bosom was still heaving with emotion and Willie Strachan's eyes were wary.

At last Jake sighed. 'Right, I've got a plan. It probably won't work, thanks to your little bit of personal initiative,' he shot a smouldering look at the stockman, 'but it's all I can think of. Strachan, you can go back and phone the vet again immediately. Tell him it's a false alarm, that you've had another look at the cows and they're fine now. You can say you had a bit of a night last night and weren't seeing straight this morning. I'll make it worth your while.'

But Strachan's face had taken on a stubborn cast. 'I'll do no such thing. The fancy beasts you've got out there are no different from the sheep on Dougie Duncan's wee hill farm that got culled last week – they're out there, spreading what they've got. The law's the same for the toffs as for the rest. of us and you'll not buy me to break it when there's poor folk could lose their living because your cows were treated different.'

At first Jake's face showed incredulity and then it darkened into a mask of rage. 'You impertinent – impertinent—' Almost blinded by his furious despair, he blundered across the room towards the younger man who was standing with his arms folded and his stubbled chin stuck out truculently. Jake tried to swing his fist, but somehow his arm had no real strength in it. The rage seemed to be exploding inside his head, bringing with it a searing pain like none he had ever experienced before. Then everything went dark.

He keeled over like a felled tree and landed heavily face down on a Persian rug, right at the feet of his horrified employee.

'Oh, my God!' Strachan dropped to his knees, took Mason's shoulder and turned him on to his side. His mouth had fallen open and his eyes were almost closed, with an alarming rim of white showing.

'You've killed him!' Brett's voice rose to a shriek. 'You've killed him, that's what you've done. Jake! Jake!'

The screaming began again. Shaken to the core, the man scrambled to his feet. 'Don't, woman, don't!' He seized her arms and shook her gingerly. 'Look, he's not dead, he's needing an ambulance instead of you skirling in his ear.'

It was, in one sense, effectual. She stopped instantly and sprang away from him, her eyes glittering. 'Take your hands off me, you peasant brute! Isn't what you've done to him, done to us all on this farm, enough without assaulting me as well? But you'll pay for it, oh yes, I promise you, you'll pay for it.'

Strachan stepped back, his face expressionless. Then he shrugged. 'What's the use?' Going to the phone on the desk he dialled 999. 'Ambulance,' he said. 'Quick's you can.'

Brett had shrunk back against the shelves by the fireplace in the attitude of a woman at bay, her hand to her throat, histrionically panting for breath. When Strachan came off

the phone she said with icy hauteur, 'May I have your permission to go to my brother now, or will you attack me
again?'

'Please yourself,' he said gruffly. 'I never touched you,
except to stop you getting wrochit up into the state he's in
now.'

She subsided on to the rug next to her brother's inert
body, patting at his face, holding his hand, sobbing, but quietly. Jake's colour was an unhealthy greyish-purple now and
he was breathing stertorously.

Strachan perched himself on the end of the desk, his arms
folded, staring at the floor. Not a word was exchanged in
the long twenty minutes until the wailing of a siren announced
the ambulance's welcome arrival.

With swift efficiency the three paramedics went about
their business. Brett, dry-eyed, watched in brooding silence
until they loaded her brother on to the stretcher. Then she
walked across to the telephone, close to where Strachan was
standing looking awkward and out of place.

With her eyes fixed on him, she too dialled 999. 'Police,'
she said. 'This is Mrs Brett Mason, Chapelton Farm near
Glenluce. I wish to report that my brother and I have both
been assaulted by Willie Strachan, the stockman on our farm.
I was afraid to call for help while I was alone with my attacker
and my brother was unconscious but now the ambulance
men are here to protect me and I will go to the hospital with
them. I am the mother of Sergeant Conrad Mason and I
want him to be informed immediately. Thank you.' She set
down the phone without waiting for the operator's response.

'You ill-hearted besom!' Strachan exclaimed. 'I've done
nothing—' He swung round to appeal to the other men.
'Here! You'll bear witness there's not a mark on the old bitch,
nor on him neither—'

One of the paramedics put a restraining hand on his arm.

'Calm down, laddie. She's in shock, that's all. Now, madam, if you'd just like to come and sit down a minute, I'll take a few details while they get your brother settled in the ambulance. We'll look after you both – don't you worry.'

Brett, drooping artistically, allowed herself to be supported to a chair. She didn't look shocked to Willie Strachan; it seemed to him that the expression on her face was one of vindictive triumph.

To her intense irritation, Laura found that her encounter with Max Mason had unsettled her completely. She was suffused with a sense of urgency which would have been more appropriate if Dizzy's trail had been days rather than years old. Being reluctant to give Max her mobile number, but equally reluctant to miss his promised call with Jake Mason's phone number, had meant that she was trapped by the phone and had to spend a bored and frustrating day in the flat, waiting.

Of course she'd tried phoning him herself, only to be fobbed off with an answering service. She'd tried Directory Enquiries in the hope of getting in touch with Jake and had been dealt with by a young man who expressed a conventional willingness to help her but, when she had no address to back up the name, showed a reluctance verging on hostility to the suggestion that he might explore the possibilities of Masons living in Galloway.

When Max phoned at last, in the early evening, only to ask her if she fancied going clubbing with him, Laura found it hard to be civil. 'Not totally my scene, dude,' she said with icy sarcasm. 'What about that phone number? Did you get it for me?'

As before, she had cause to regret a blunt approach. 'Oh, my father's?' He sounded defensive. 'Well, not in that sense.'

'And in what sense, precisely, did you get it then?' she

thought but managed not to say, though with difficulty,
instead summoning up her best couch-side tones. 'Problems?'
she murmured sympathetically.

Max seized on that. 'It's Ex-Directory, OK? And I didn't
keep a note of it. It's back in the dark ages, after all . . .'

He was stalling, for whatever reason. Clearly, though, he
wanted to pursue the acquaintance, which should give her
a bargaining counter – if someone fancied you, it always did.
She persisted. 'But don't you still have contacts who might
know?'

'Wo-ho! So many years back, what do you think?'

'What a shame,' she said sweetly. 'Thanks, anyway, for
contacting me. Pity there's no way forward. It was good to
have met you.'

'Hey, hang about! There might still be someone I could
dig out—'

Taking candy from a baby, this was. Laura had to conceal the smile in her voice as she said, 'Really? You mean
you think you could?' Yes, surprised, impressed – that was
good.

'Oh, I guess. Sure to be somebody, if I put my mind to
it. But listen, what is your scene if you don't do clubbing?
Eating out, theatre—'

She sounded, she hoped, transparently honest. 'Max, to
be absolutely straight with you, I can't think about anything
else at the moment.' Well, that was true, wasn't it? 'Why
don't you call me again when you've got your father's
number? Then I can talk to him and get it out of my system.
He might give me the brush-off, I suppose, but—'

'Oh, I think you'll find he will. He doesn't really do helpful.
But you'd feel you'd given it your best shot and then—'

'Absolutely. And then – Speak to you soon.'

Laura put the phone down with some satisfaction. Max
might do a good line in cynical manipulation but he wasn't

the only one who'd read the manual on playing power-games. She'd put money on getting a phone call tomorrow night saying he'd quite unexpectedly found the number in an old diary or some such face-saving excuse. It did cross her mind that she could be storing up a certain amount of trouble for herself in encouraging Max to think their relationship might have some future, but she didn't want to think about that now.

She didn't really want to think, either, about the dangerous vacuum in her life which, following the rules of nature, was being filled to the exclusion of everything else by this enquiry, but she recognised the unhealthy signs of obsession. So the following morning after breakfast, telling herself sternly that she couldn't afford to put her life on hold for a glimmer of information which might all too easily be a will-o'-the-wisp, she poured another cup of coffee, fetched the road-map and the *Good Pub Guide* and prepared to give her housing dilemma her best shot. She'd been thinking about Wales, hadn't she, and Devon? Yet somehow, she found she was leafing through towards the back of the road atlas to where she could find the maps of Scotland, inexorably drawn to the one which showed the south-western corner which had occupied her thoughts since the day before yesterday.

Laura had never really studied a Scottish map before. Why would she? She'd been to Edinburgh a couple of times, holidayed once in St Andrews, but that was the extent of her experience of the northern kingdom. Certainly, no mental picture had been conjured up by Max's mention of Galloway.

Looking at the map now, the most noticeable thing about the area labelled 'Dumfries and Galloway' was how cut off it seemed to be from the rest of Scotland. The sweeping motorway from Carlisle to Glasgow seemed almost to mark out a boundary; from it, a single road wound its way west to Stranraer with its ferry links to Ireland. Other roads, twigs of the main branch, led to towns and villages with intriguing names – Beeswing, Kirkgunzeon, Palnackie – all thickly clustered to the south and along the coastline of the Solway Firth. Moving north, there were fewer names, further apart, with blank tracts of land in between, seamed with a river or a lake or two – or lochs, she supposed they must be called – and forests. Then, to the north-west, not far from the Irish Sea coast, there was an area where there seemed to be nothing at all.

Even without the Dizzy connection, it looked intriguing. It promised beauty, with its seascapes and low hills, empty moors and great forests. There was nothing at all to stop Laura going up there to have a look – just a look.

Except, of course, for the foot-and-mouth epidemic. It was, she remembered suddenly, one of the places which had been hardest hit, like Cumbria, and they were talking about the countryside being 'closed'. She'd seen what was happening on the news – the sad, sickening evidence of an epidemic raging out of control, whatever spin government officials might attempt to put on it. She switched on the news at lunchtime with a renewed and personal interest.

Marjory Fleming was preoccupied as she walked through the entrance hall in Kirkluce Police Headquarters. A farmer near Bladnoch had barricaded himself into his farm with his infected cattle; he was known to have licences for three shotguns. He was someone Marjory and Bill had known since they all went to Young Farmers' dances together, and Superintendent Bailey, aware of their friendship, had called her in to see whether she thought she could talk him down before they put in the heavy mob.

Marjory's heart sank as she listened to him; she had been astute enough to ask for time to think it over before she gave him her response, which basically meant phoning Bill. Apart from the fact that he would have a useful opinion on whether the personal touch would do more harm than good, she welcomed an excuse to speak to him when there was actually something to talk about. They spoke every night, of course; he sounded exhausted but calm and so far there had been no disasters to report, but there never seemed to be much they could talk about. Once she'd said that the children were fine and checked that he'd picked up the supplies from the road-end, any news she had to give him was bad news and he didn't need that. He didn't ask the questions that would have forced her to tell him the terrible news of farms and farmers' lives being destroyed on every side; she thought she sensed a superstitious fear of talking about it, in case it might attract disaster to him too.

Perhaps he wouldn't even want to discuss the problem about poor Bob Christie which had just been dumped in her lap. Lost in thought, she almost bumped into DS Mason who was crossing the hall at speed. He stopped sharply and apologised.

'My fault, Conrad. An emergency?'

'Yes – well . . .' He was frowning. 'There's been a weird message from my mother – something about an assault by our stockman and she's gone to hospital with my uncle.'

Fleming was startled. 'That sounds bad!'

Mason hesitated. 'Yes – but when I ran a check on it to see what had happened there'd been an ambulance call earlier. I contacted the paramedics and they seemed to think there's nothing in it, except that my uncle's had quite a severe stroke. Which is bad enough, of course,' he added hastily.

His final remark, Marjory noted, was very much an afterthought. 'Of course. Don't let me detain you anyway. Keep me in the picture, if you would.'

'I'll do that. Thanks.'

Marjory watched him go, her mind distracted from her

own problems for the moment. There was no doubt about it, the Masons were a weird lot. What normal son, on hearing his mother has complained of being assaulted, runs a check on it to see whether she's telling the truth?

'Don't be ridiculous, Mother, he didn't assault you.'

The relatives' waiting room at the hospital was fortunately empty, so that Conrad Mason had no need to consider the sensibilities of strangers in giving his reaction.

Brett sat in a red moulded-plastic chair, ignoring the polystyrene cup of pale grey tea placed beside her by a solicitous nurse, with the air of a duchess inexplicably forced to accept hospitality in a pig-sty. 'Of course he did, dreadful man. I've made a complaint to the police so you can see to it that he's properly punished.'

A muscle twitched in Conrad's jaw. 'Can I explain to you the laws of evidence in Scotland? You can't convict on one person's unsubstantiated word against another's. There has to be what's known as corroborating evidence – the tiniest bruise, perhaps? But there isn't a sign of one, is there, and as far as Uncle Jake is concerned, he had a stroke, that's all.'

'But you don't understand *why* he had a stroke!' Brett cried. 'That – that creature decided there was something wrong with a couple of the cows and phoned the vet. And now they're going to come – come –' her eyes welled up – 'and simply *obliterate* your grandfather's memorial!'

Conrad went very still. 'Do you mean – foot-and-mouth?'

'Well, of course. Only he's so stupid it probably isn't – and the whole herd, and Jake too, most likely, are going to die because of that man. If you don't call that assault, what is it?'

The vision came before him of Satan, old and fierce and proud, reduced to nothing more than a tonnage of dead meat, his progeny slaughtered with him so that the line he had perpetuated would simply vanish, tipped on to a pyre or into a pit. Conrad felt sick, dizzy. There seemed to be a sort of roaring in his head.

'Got to get out of here,' he said thickly, pushing roughly past his mother who had jumped up anxiously. He hurried blindly past the sympathetic stares of staff used to seeing distraught relatives, and somehow got himself outside into the open air. He lit up, dragging the smoke into his lungs as if it were as necessary as oxygen.

It was some time before he came back. He was pale but calm and when his mother started to fuss round him he shook her off unkindly.

'Stop pawing me. Now, there's no point in discussing this. You can stay here; I'm getting back to the authorities to see if anything can be done.

'But as far as Strachan is concerned, drop it. All you're doing is making a fool of yourself, and while you're entirely at liberty to do that I won't have you making a fool of me as well. You'll withdraw the charges, and then you'll keep your big mouth shut. Is that clear?'

Brett's eyes had been fixed on her son's face. She began to smile, almost to simper, fluttering her short, stubby eye-lashes.

'Oh, Conrad, you are *so* like your grandfather! Sometimes I almost think it's him speaking to me. As long as I have you, I feel I haven't altogether lost him.'

Before she had finished the sentence her son left the room, as if he were afraid of what he might do if he stayed.

Laura's phone rang at half-past four. She picked it up, expecting it to be a call from a friend who was arranging theatre tickets; instead she heard Max Mason's triumphant tones.

'Laura? I'm just phoning to say goodbye.'

'Goodbye? You're going somewhere?'

'Home – I'm going home. It's the most extraordinary thing. After I'd talked to you, I suddenly thought of the local store where we'd always had an account and phoned to ask. The woman who runs it – she's a miserable old cow, I could never stand her – just said,' he put on a comic Scots accent, '"You needna' fash yersel', he's in the hospital wi' a stroke!" I couldn't believe it – the Minotaur's had a stroke!'

It was hard to know how to respond. Given the jubilation in his voice, 'How very sad for you' was clearly inappropriate. On the other hand, in these circumstances, you couldn't exactly say, 'Great news!' either.

'Your father? Is it bad?' That seemed safe enough.

'Oh yes. I called the hospital, and he's in intensive care. They're not even sure he's going to pull through. So of course I've got to head right on back to Chapelton to take up the reins before my cousin gets in on the act.'

'Chapelton?'

'That's the name of the farm. We've a thousand acres up above Glenluce. But look, I'm not signing off. We'll get together soon, OK? Once I've sussed out the situation, maybe you could come up and stay.'

Being in close contact with Max and what was clearly a dysfunctional family was almost the last thing she wanted – except losing her only line to Dizzy. 'That would be wonderful,' she said hollowly. 'Thanks very much.'

'Oh, sure, sure. I'll be in touch.' Then he added with a short laugh, 'You could chat to my cousin about Dizzy – he always fancied her.' The phone went dead as if he were in too much of a hurry to say goodbye.

Laura set it down slowly, uncertain what to make of what she had heard. She was chilled, certainly, by the callousness with which Max had reacted to the news of his father's illness and possible death. True, he'd described him as a monster, but in her experience sons in that sort of relationship often suffered abnormal devastation when the object of their professed hatred died. Perhaps Max was covering up his feelings, even from himself? If so, there would be a price to pay later and she could only hope it wouldn't be any of her business when the bills came in.

There was no knowing how long he would take to get back to her – if, of course, he did. Promises were easy to make and easy to break; she could imagine that Max might well be prey to changeable enthusiasms.

She knew where he lived now, though, and where Dizzy had spent that winter when she was twenty. She got out the road-map again and looked it up; she thought she'd seen the name Glenluce this morning and yes, there it was – over to the north-west in the area that looked almost bare of settlement.

So why should she wait for Max's unwelcome invitation? Chapelton was obviously a large farm and in a country place like that would be well known; there would be people, too, who had lived in the neighbourhood for years and someone might, just might, if she jogged their memory, remember a pretty blonde who had worked there fifteen years before. In the middle of February, with a foot-and-mouth epidemic raging, it wouldn't be hard to find accommodation and she could pursue her enquiries at leisure.

And there was another thing, too. Nick Dalton had invited her to come up with another psychological slant on something which would have wide popular resonance. Could anything be more suitable or topical than the impact of a disaster like this on a rural community – and it would give her the excuse, too, to go around and talk to the locals.

Best of all, she wouldn't be forced into close proximity with Max, or find herself intruding on a household where surely someone must be upset about what had happened to the head of the family.

When the phone call she had been expecting came, it was her friend to say ruefully that she hadn't been able to get tickets.

'It doesn't matter,' Laura said. 'I'm going to Scotland.'

A small, quiet professional voice in her head was still murmuring about obsession, but she talked it down. By its very definition, an obsession seemed irrational to the person having it and this was entirely rational – wasn't it?

It was after nine o'clock when Margery Fleming got back to her parents' house that night. She'd worked a twelve-hour shift – not particularly unusual, except that this one had imposed an emotional strain which had left her feeling so drained and exhausted that she barely felt able to get out of the car.

Six hours of it had been spent at Bob Christie's farm, shouting at first through a loudhailer, an operation which had left her throat raw. Eventually, she'd persuaded him on to the phone, then at last got him outside to talk. He was defiant at first, defeated at last after hours of patient discussion. They had confiscated his shotguns, escorted the slaughter team in to do their work, and she had seen the bluff, cheery farmer she had known since he was a cheerful, thoughtless youth – an unreflective man, she would have said – reduced to a sobbing, shivering wreck by the agents of the state, of which she was one.

Marjory hoped her presence had been helpful – Bill, sounding worryingly listless when she spoke to him, had thought on balance that it would be – but feared that Bob would never forgive her, not for what she had done professionally but because she had seen him a broken man.

What she needed now was her own fireside, with Meg the

collie asleep on the hearthrug, a dram in her hand and Bill in his armchair on the other side, dispensing his unique blend of sound common sense.

Well, she wasn't going to get it, was she – not even the whisky, since her father was notoriously abstemious. And sitting feeling sorry for herself wasn't going to help either. She had a job she loved which was difficult at the moment, that was all, and she despised whingers. With that thought she found the energy to get herself out of the car.

The hardest part was getting herself ready for the onslaught – the children, uprooted and unsettled, her mother fussing because she hadn't been home to supper, her father wanting to know too much about what she had been doing all day. Well, she might as well flick the upbeat switch right now.

She let herself into the house, calling brightly, 'Hello, I'm home!'

There was no reply. The hall was in darkness; Angus Laird did not believe in having lights on when there was no one there to see them, though it would have grieved him to find himself on the side of the Greens. There was only a line of light under the sitting-room door and through it Marjory could hear the sound of voices and laughter.

After a moment's fumbling for the handle, she opened the door, and four startled faces looked up from a table by the fire where playing-cards were set out.

'Goodness gracious, is that you?' Janet Laird exclaimed. 'I didn't hear the car – I was just fair away with all this nonsense.' She glanced at the clock. 'Quarter past nine! I don't believe it! Cammie Fleming, it's high time you were in your bed.'

'I'll go when we've had one more game of Racing Demon,' Cammie bargained. 'Just the one.'

His grandfather said gruffly, 'You'll do as your grannie tells you. But one more maybe wouldn't do much harm.'

Cat, who had been tidying the cards into neat piles, said, 'Hello, Mum! Grandpa's been teaching us how to play but he keeps winning.'

Marjory stood in the doorway feeling disowned, surplus to requirements. She heard herself saying to her father childishly, 'You never taught me to play Racing Demon. I didn't know you could.'

'There's a lot about me you don't know.' He didn't even turn to look at her. 'Well, if we're having another game, you'd better get on with it, laddie.'

'And then *straight* to bed,' Janet added with mock severity.

'I'll just make myself a cup of tea and a sandwich.' Marjory had deliberately not eaten in the canteen; she hadn't wanted to upset Janet by refusing the meal that would have been saved for her.

'Fine, dearie,' her mother said absently. 'Oh, now see what your grandfather's done!'

Upstairs, in the little single bedroom Janet had sentimentally kept as a shrine to her daughter's girlhood, untouched apart from the poster of Alice Cooper (representative of defiance rather than homage), taken down the day she left home, Marjory set down her mug of tea, a slab of cheese and an apple on the dressing table. Faded photographs were still tucked round the rim of the mirror – old schoolfriends, family pets, a young and improbably tidy Bill scrubbed up for some important event she had now forgotten.

She caught sight of herself in the mirror. There were shadows round her hazel eyes and deepening lines between her brows and on her forehead; her skin was showing evidence of the ravages of time and she was pale with tiredness. It was the face of a middle-aged woman but the mouth – oh dear, she recognised the sullen downturn she had seen in that same mirror so often, so many years before. It was the 'think-I'll-go-and-eat-worms' expression of the misunderstood teenager she had thought gone for ever, long ago.

At her age! And when she had been all prepared to resent the demands and the fussing!

The ridiculous side of it struck her. The drooping mouth in the mirror quirked up at the corners and then she and her reflection were laughing together, laughing till the tears ran down their cheeks in twin rivulets – a little hysterically, perhaps, but with therapeutic effect.

8

It all looked just as it had when he had left the place fifteen years before: the same rolling hills carrying stands of trees on their crests like horses' manes, the same grey dry-stone dykes with the grey clefts above which were their source, the same scrubby whin bushes lining the roads, mud-spattered by the passing cars. The same weather, even: a blustering wind, squally showers and a heavy sky hinting that worse might follow.

Max Mason floored the accelerator on the beaten-up hired Peugeot, overtaking a sedately driven Rover dangerously close to a bend in the road, as if speed could outdistance memory. He'd left London in a mood of savage triumphalism the moment he could get his hands on something – anything – that would get him up to Scotland; he'd driven all through the night on only a couple of hours' sleep in the car park of a service station and a cup of black coffee. He'd seen a grudging dawn as he crossed the border but now, on the sweeping road which led to Glenluce and beyond that to Stranraer, he could feel the elation draining away. In its place there was an uneasy churning in his gut and his head buzzed with a confusion of conflicting emotions and uncertainties. He'd forgotten how that felt after all these years in London being his own master, clear-minded, controlled, controlling. Now . . . Families, there was no doubt, were seven sorts of hell.

He needn't have come. Indeed, he might have been wiser

to stay in London and let the unspeakable Conrad run the show until the curtain came down. The best ending for the drama would be the Minotaur dying, leaving Max as his heir with full executive powers and the ability, at last, to pay back a few old scores by telling Conrad to jump. The worst would be Max wasting his time running the farm while the Minotaur lingered inconveniently on, then died leaving everything to Conrad – but, Max recalled suddenly, you couldn't do that in Scotland. Your children had to get 'the bairns' part' of your estate and frankly, with business the way it was at the moment, anything would be better than nothing. So scrub that. It would be a tragedy if the Minotaur made a full and rapid recovery and young Theseus went back to London empty-handed. Theseus loses again.

The memories Max had so deliberately stifled for years were surfacing now, along with the bitterness, the anger and that hideous feeling of helplessness which was worse than anything. But he'd been here before, often enough, and he knew what to do. He was good at it and it worked, mostly.

Shaking his head as if that could dislodge the thoughts, he turned his mind very deliberately to other things – a bit like steering a juggernaut lorry on a roundabout, feeding the wheel through his hands until the exit he was looking for appeared.

Laura! He'd think about Laura instead. Max didn't quite know what to make of her. Her likeness to Di was unsettling; perhaps that was what intrigued him – that, and her cool elusiveness. Usually he could be sure of having the upper hand in any relationship he chose to pursue but she'd led him on so skilfully to talk about himself that he only realised afterwards how little he knew about her. And knowledge was power.

Was she in a relationship – married, even? She must, he supposed, be a journalist, and on the phone he'd caught a hint of a North American twang, but that was all he'd picked up. Now she was calling the shots and he was uneasy. He'd have to call her soon, redress the balance. Have her up to stay, perhaps, all being well – or rather, all being very far from well as far as the Minotaur was concerned.

And there was his mind again, swerving uncontrolled back to the prohibited subject. Strange how much easier it was to think of the Minotaur, felled by a thunderbolt from Jove, than about his father, stricken, enfeebled, no longer a worthy adversary in the war of hate . . .

That, thank God, was the Glenluce turn at last. He indicated and moved across into the turning lane, yawning as he did so. It had been a punishing journey and the toughest part of it, dealing with his aunt and his cousin, still lay ahead.

He glanced across the fields as he started on the Glen road and it was only then, with a shock, that he realised what was different, what was, indeed, very, very different. Where were the sheep and cows grazing in the roadside fields? Where were the dots of white on the hillsides, the flocks which were so much a part of the landscape? The fields were empty and great tracts of the hills were bare, a lush, green, uncanny desert.

In London the foot-and-mouth epidemic had seemed irrelevant, the sort of thing you tutted about over a pint before you got back to the serious topic of football. The real world, fast-moving, metropolitan, was where Max belonged now, the world where meat came from plastic trays, not carcasses. It was with a growing feeling of dismay that he pressed on, through the narrow village street of Glenluce where regimented modern houses outnumbered the cottages now, through New Luce with its church and its shop, on over the hump-backed bridge and across the rattling cattle-grid protecting the unfenced road where sheep had right of way because you couldn't explain to them that they didn't. Where were they now?

The road was rising now, potholed and narrow, with passing-places. The wind was ripping the clouds apart so that there was even a blink of sunshine as Max reached the higher ground where Chapelton land began. A tiny loch, with the sky reflected in its peaty waters, showed dark navy blue and a dozen tiny rivulets trickled down into the broader shallow burn running brown and stony beside the road. And the sky – he'd forgotten that wide, wide sky and the feeling it gave you of the globe curving away beneath you.

The fields his grandfather had nurtured into fine pasture stretched on either side, emerald-green in contrast to the rust-red of sodden bracken and the brown clumps of dead heather. Driving slowly now, Max put down the window and let in the fresh, damp air; he could hear the wind rushing through the roadside trees, already wizened and contorted by its power. Somewhere there was a curlew, giving the melancholy cry which is its name in Scots: 'Whaup! Whaup!' His throat tightened with some sort of atavistic emotion. It spoke to him, this countryside, in a language he'd all but forgotten at a level too deep to explain even to himself, but suddenly his life in London seemed insubstantial, shadowy.

It was an unwelcome thought. Max drove on again, recognising familiar landmarks now: the old rusty bath in a corner of the field which acted as a drinking trough for the cattle, the rock outcrop that looked like a frog. But surely he should have been seeing some of the cattle by now, the great horned black cattle which were part of the landscape of his dreams to this day. There was no sign of them.

There was the sign over the entrance to the farm, though, boasting proudly in blue and gold, 'Chapelton. Pedigree Welsh Blacks. Champion herd.' And there, stepping forward to block the way as he made to turn in, were two men in dark blue with diced caps.

'Morning, sir. Heading for Chapelton?'

Did the police run special courses in stating the bleeding obvious? 'Self-evidently,' he said acidly. 'It's my father's farm. I'm Max Mason. All right?'

The two men exchanged glances. The shorter, stouter one with sergeant's stripes on his arm spoke this time. 'Er – I don't know if you've heard, sir—'

'About my father? Yes, of course I have. That's why I'm here. Now, can I go in and find out what's happening?'

'Well – I'm afraid there's been an A notice served on the farm.'

'Unfortunately, Sergeant, I'm not really up to speed on police jargon. Perhaps you could indulge me by explaining what that means in plain English?' Good God, he sounded exactly like his father! Five minutes back and he'd slipped into speaking Landed Gentry. Why hadn't he said, 'Hey, man, what's going down?'

The sergeant cleared his throat portentously. 'It means that the existence of foot-and-mouth disease has been confirmed on the premises and as a result teams from the Ministry of Agriculture, Fisheries and Food are engaged in an operation at this present time under the emergency powers. Anyone entering said premises at this moment in time would not be permitted to leave until such time as it is pronounced free from infection by the appropriate authorities.'

Max gave a gasp, as if the air had been forced out of his lungs by a punch to the solar plexus. 'You mean there are men in there right now, slaughtering the cows, the *bulls*—' He choked on the word. 'And there's nothing I can do to stop it?'

It wasn't really a question. The policemen remained impassive, as if fearing a 'No' would be provocative.

Swearing, Max slammed the car into reverse, shot backwards and spun it round so close to the men that they had to jump back for their own safety. Then he slammed on the brakes and leaned across to open the nearside window. 'Is my cousin Conrad Mason in there?' His teeth were clenched so that he could hardly articulate.

Glancing at his sergeant, the constable said, 'No, sir, he's staying in Kirkluce I believe. Er – you've had quite a shock. Should you be—'

Max didn't wait to hear the end of the sentence. He was off down the narrow road at a crazy speed.

Watching him go, the sergeant shrugged. 'Och well, he'd be hard put to it to find a sheep to hit. And with the postie past and the mobile shop not due till eleven I can't mind of anyone else who might get in his way this hour of the morning.'

'Except maybe some more of thae MAFF inspectors, Sarge.'

'Oh aye.' His superior sniffed. 'Well, if he wipes some of them out it'll give the buggers a taste of their own medicine, won't it?'

The Glen Inn was a small grey building on the outskirts of New Luce, little more than a pub with rooms. An undistinguished glass extension at the side revealed tables with orange cloths and cream napkins optimistically set for service and window-boxes on the stone ledges of the deep-set windows at the front suggested an attempt to prettify the bleak exterior, but empty as they were they only added to its dilapidated appearance.

Brett Mason eyed the place with distaste as she got out of the car in the deserted car park at eleven o'clock. Hardly what she was accustomed to! But then, the whole world had turned itself upside down in the last twenty-four hours: the farm, the cattle, Jake . . .

She daren't think about the cattle, or about Jake. She'd checked out of the more comfortable hotel in Dumfries where she'd spent the night; there was no point in staying when it was just too harrowing for her to go and see him lying there with tubes everywhere. He wouldn't have wanted her to be upset.

And now there was the farm. She'd been told, quite brutally in the circumstances, that she couldn't go back to her own home – her only security – without being imprisoned there for days, weeks even, amidst the sort of butchery that would give her nightmares for years afterwards. 'Has Britain become a police state?' she'd demanded of the hapless official, shaking with fury. The answer seemed to be that it had and owning property conferred no rights over what happened on it.

She had been, quite simply, thrown to the wolves, with no home, no Jake to protect her and Conrad flatly refusing to deal with that wretched man Strachan and claiming that he couldn't be at her side where he was needed because of his duties. Well, she'd remember that the next time he came asking for money.

So this – this hovel was what she was reduced to. At least it would give her well-placed headquarters for a campaign of harassment to make sure of getting back to the farm as soon as possible. They'd get tired of her turning up three times a day to check on progress and it was her lifetime's experience that the squeaky wheel did indeed get the grease.

And however angry she might be with Conrad at the moment, she was still determined to see to it that they were both securely established at Chapelton if – well, if anything *happened*. She couldn't be entirely sure that Jake had actually changed his will as she had instructed him to, and if Max hadn't been cut out – as he so richly deserved to be – it would be a disaster. But they said, didn't they, that possession was nine-tenths of the law, and she was confident that she could make Max's position completely intolerable if he tried to assert his rights.

Brett picked up the case she had packed so hastily yesterday before following the ambulance to Dumfries and walked across the car park to the hotel, noting with some disapproval that the window-frames needed painting.

She felt a certain proprietorial interest in the Glen Inn; after all, Scott Thomson would never have been able to find the deposit for a mortgage if it hadn't been for the compensation he'd extracted from Jake a couple of years ago. And it wasn't as if the man didn't know all about Satan's little ways; it was pure incompetence for a stockman who'd been with them all these years to let himself be cornered, and frankly he was lucky to have escaped with only a crippled arm when you considered what had happened to Satan's previous victim.

With the smug air of a benefactress Brett entered the narrow hall and looked around. It was the first time she had set foot in the place: there were chips in the cream paintwork and she dismissed as 'petrol station flowers' the bunch which had been placed rather than arranged in a vase on the reception desk. There was a little brass bell beside it; she pinged it once, then a moment later twice more.

A door at the back of the hall opened and a woman appeared, looking flustered and smiling nervously. She was pale and very thin, with bruise-coloured circles under her eyes and the lines of a frown between her brows. When she saw who stood there she stopped, standing very still, her smile fading, but she said, politely enough, 'Good morning, Mrs Mason. Can I help you?'

'Indeed you can.' Brett eyed her pityingly; really, it was quite depressing the way some women let themselves go. Lisa Thomson had been a pretty enough girl with her dark curly hair and big brown eyes but now the hair was dragged

severely into an elastic band at the back and with not a scrap
of make-up on her face she looked like a woman of forty
when she couldn't be thirty yet. She'd lost weight, too, which
didn't suit her – subconsciously Brett smoothed down her
skirt over her own solid thighs – and she looked as if her
dress shop was Oxfam in Kirkluce. It was sad to see her so
lacking in self-respect – and that sour expression didn't help
either.

Brett took particular pains to smile graciously herself.
'Now, Lisa, you've probably heard of the sad problems we've
been having at Chapelton.' She paused for the appropriate
expressions of sympathy but when they were not forth-
coming went on with a sharper edge to her voice, 'I want to
be on the spot until I can get back into my home, so I shall
require a room here – your best room – for a few days. And
of course it would have to be at a very special price – you
must be desperate for custom at the moment.' She looked
pointedly at the full complement of keys hanging on the
board behind the other woman's head.

Lisa's dark eyes narrowed and for a brief, uncertain
moment Brett had the crazy idea she was going to say no.
She didn't, of course; she looked down at the ledger open
in front of her and said in a colourless voice, 'Certainly, Mrs
Mason. That won't be a problem.'

She named a figure which Brett of course ridiculed,
offering a much lower price which was, naturally, acceptable. She handed her case to her hostess and followed her
up the narrow stairs to the landing which had five num-
bered doors opening off it. After insisting on viewing each
of them, with unfavourable comments, she settled for the
one she had been shown first with a grudging, 'I suppose
this will have to do.'

Gesturing to Lisa to put the case down, she collapsed into
an upholstered chair with wooden arms which stood beside

the disused fireplace, now filled with a bunch of dusty silk flowers. 'Oh dear!' She heaved a theatrical sigh.

She got no response. Lisa left the room, closing the door so firmly that it almost sounded as if it had been slammed. Brett was alone, with nothing to do but consider her emotions.

She didn't like being alone. She never had. There was something unnerving about no one being there to react to you, as if you were looking in a mirror and there was no reflection. There had always been someone when she needed them, up till now – darling Papa, Jake, Conrad . . .

Now what was she to do? Lisa, ungrateful madam, had shown not the smallest interest, despite Brett having been like a mother to her when she'd married Scott and joined the Chapelton community nine years ago.

She could feel the familiar tension rising. This was when she would normally have announced that one of her nervous attacks was threatening, but now there was no one to hear her say it, soothe her, arrange for the problem to go away. She felt abandoned, even betrayed all over again, as she'd felt when Papa died and left her, when Eddie had walked out on their marriage . . .

What if she had an attack here on her own? What if she wasn't strong enough to beat it by herself? It was frightening, terrifying, a great big black thought like a cloud blotting out the sun.

It mustn't happen, that was all. Despite all they had done to her, despite Jake's illness and the tragedy of the farm and her son's unfeeling attitude, she must put herself first for once, stop thinking of others and keep calm. She found a handkerchief, blew her nose, then sat up straight in her chair, rearranging the scarf round her shoulders.

The remote control for the small television in the corner was lying on a shelf beside her. She clicked it and the room was instantly full of company and laughter. She settled back in her chair to watch; after all, there was something terribly unsatisfying about being distraught if there was no one to see how distraught you were.

Back at the reception desk in the hall, Lisa Thomson looked down despairingly at the register where she had just recorded the unwelcome guest. How was she ever going to tell Scott that she hadn't told Brett Mason where she could go, sailing in here as if she owned the place?

They'd had such a fight to get the money out of the Masons for Scott's arm. He could never work as a stockman again, but he wasn't in a union so they'd had to employ a lawyer to make Jake pay up. And that was only because he was scared there'd be an order for his precious bull to be destroyed if it got to court. It should have been, when it killed one of the stockmen before Scott, and it was an evil beast, Scott said, just biding its time to do it again.

The pay-off, though, had been pretty good in the end. In fact, they'd talked about it being kind of a blessing, you could say. Well, you wouldn't be able to buy your own home, even, on a stockman's wages, let alone a nice wee business, and it had just seemed meant when the Glen Inn came up for sale. It had been their local; a bit spit-and-sawdust, a bit run-down, but they'd reckoned all it needed was a bit of TLC. There were disused rooms upstairs they could do up with en suites and then they could make their fortune with the holiday market and weekend breaks. Donna and Kylie were out at school all day; Lisa would have time on her hands when she wasn't having to go up to the big house to clean and it would be rare to be her own mistress instead of having Mrs Mason yakking on at her all the time.

The bank manager had said to her the other day that they'd set out with 'the fatal combination of optimism and inexperience' – well, why couldn't he have told them that at the start instead of now? She kept her mouth shut, of course, because she'd to keep on his good side, but it made her sick to her stomach when she thought back.

The improvements went way over their budget; they'd had to borrow extra to pay for them but even so when the inspectors came round from the Tourist Board they only gave them one star – 'acceptable' – when they'd been counting on three stars – 'very good'. And Lisa's cooking was only 'acceptable' too – well, she'd never thought she'd be in *A Taste of Scotland* right off, but she'd shed hot tears over the insult. Advertising was something they hadn't allowed for properly either, and since they couldn't afford a computer they weren't on the Internet, which didn't help. They'd got by last year, just, on casual visitors for overnights and meals, along with the bar profits.

That was before Scott began drinking them. He'd missed the outdoor work and the beasts at Chapelton – he'd been there a long time – and once the first excitement of being his own boss wore off, he hadn't enough to do. His drinking had started during the long, dreary winter months when he'd have a dram with the regulars, just to be sociable, he said. Then, as the business failed to meet its targets and the bank got restless, he began to match them glass for glass. Now, with the locals staying at home and the countryside officially declared closed, he was seldom sober.

Lisa had never dreamed that she'd have to take on such an awful lot of responsibility. Scott was nine years older, an old-fashioned husband who in their nine-year marriage had never expected her to do more than look after the house and the weans and have his meals ready for him when he came in. He'd lifted his hand to her once or twice recently – but then, she tried to excuse him to herself, it was really hard on him when what mostly needed doing was stuff he called 'woman's work' and he felt he was lowering himself if he did it. He hated taking orders from people too, even if they were the paying customers.

Lisa's eyes filled with tears as she looked down at the name on the register. They needed the money so badly! Foot-and-mouth had been the last straw for their ailing business, and they wouldn't be in line for fat compensation cheques like the farmers, like the Masons. Repossession was staring them in the face and then what would she do with two children and a crippled husband? Then she sniffed and wiped her eyes fiercely with her fingers. She hadn't time to waste fussing about the past – or even about the future. What she had to do at the moment was to work out a lunch for Mrs Mason that wouldn't have the old bag demanding a refund. Oh, and how to break the news to Scott so that he wouldn't set about their much-needed guest, even verbally, let alone – she felt sick at the thought – physically.

At least she'd been smart enough to overstate the price of a room so that even after she'd let herself be beaten down she would still be getting £10 a night over the normal rate. At the memory of Brett Mason's satisfaction at the bargain she had struck, the faintest ghost of a smile crossed Lisa's lips, though it didn't last long.

9

The police, arms linked, had formed a solid, double-banked line across the road and were gradually but inexorably pushing back the struggling, shouting protestors. They made an unlikely mob, with tweeds and oiled jackets predominating, but anger thickened the air like fog as they found themselves forced to retreat down the narrow walled lane, away from the junction where a line of vehicles had drawn up: 4x4s with officials and government vets, a van with equipment, police mini-buses and escort cars with their lights flashing. Breathing heavily, Tam MacNee pushed forward. He hated being drafted on to uniform duties, hated wearing the bloody thing, come to that. And the waistband wasn't as comfortable as it used to be; he'd need to have a word with Bunty about her high teas.

'Remind me,' he muttered to the officer on his left, 'what was it about being a uniform that made me go for the CID?'

The man, breathless himself, grinned mockingly. 'Not hard enough, eh? I'm telling you, this lot's frigging amateurs. All they've thrown is tatties and there's not one on their backside in the road. I've seen worse at a Women's Guild outing.'

With a final push they cleared the road-end. The crowd gave a last, despairing heave, then as the waiting cars swept by a groan went up. There was the sound of sobbing, but the pressure on the police line eased.

The gate was shut across the farm drive and in front of it a man and a woman stood, his arm around her shoulders, blocking the way. The leading police car stopped and four officers, one female, jumped out. A conversation ensued; the crowd, their view of the proceedings blocked by the dark blue phalanx, surged restlessly forward and again were forced back.

At last the woman, breaking down in tears, stepped aside, violently shrugging off the policewoman's attempt at comfort. Her husband put up no more than a token struggle and as the police restrained him, gave up. The gate was opened for the vehicles, then shut behind them, and he turned away, head down, broken.

The second line of police moved back to block access to the gate and with that secured the order came for the front row to stand down. As the police broke ranks the crowd, subdued now, pushed sullenly past them. Many of the women were in tears; a young man, fair-haired and fresh-complexioned, his face contorted with rage and grief, lunged towards MacNee, drawing back his fist, but an older man restrained him.

'Don't sully your fists, laddie. Scum like them isn't worth it.'

MacNee, tensed for evasive action, dropped his eyes. It was a dirty business, this whole thing. It really got to him and he was a townie. What must someone like Marjory be feeling now? He could see her, a tall figure in a belted trench-coat, standing beside one of the cars at the back.

A group of women had reached the farmer's wife by now and she was the centre of a huddle of concern as they tried to coax her away. Suddenly the sound of sheep bleating in alarm filled the air and the mood of the crowd, which had been dispersing hopelessly, turned ugly.

'Proud of what you've done?' a man's voice yelled. 'No guts, no decency.'

All at once the situation was tense again. Unbidden, the police immediately drew closer together, but these were

law-abiding citizens, unused to confrontation with the
forces of order they had respected all their lives. They
looked about them uncertainly and the moment passed.

Just then, as he was heaving a sigh of relief, MacNee
noticed that the farmer's wife, with her friends, had drawn
level with Fleming, saw too with dismay that they obviously
recognised her.

'Marjory Fleming, I can't believe you're standing here, letting them do that.' Her voice was shrill.

MacNee began shouldering his way to her side and heard
her say quietly, 'I'm sorry, Susie, I've no alternative. It's my
job.'

'Get a better job then,' another woman shouted. 'If you
all resigned, they couldn't do this to us, could they?'

'Rather have the army instead, would you?' The bulky
figure of Conrad Mason, made even more intimidating by
the uniform, loomed up out of the crowd. He was scowling.
'Move along now, madam, you're causing an obstruction.'

Drunken football hooligans seldom fancied their chances
when Mason flexed his muscles; the women, exchanging
uneasy glances, did as they were told and he turned away,
satisfied. But as the farmer's wife drew level with Fleming
she turned to look at her stonily, then very deliberately spat
straight in her face.

MacNee was there in two strides but Fleming's hand shot
out, restraining him with an iron grip. 'Leave it, Tam.' She
stood impassively, the spit trickling down her cheek until the
women had passed, her jawline and her shoulders rigid, her
hands clenched so that the knuckles showed white. Then she
took out a handkerchief, wiped it carefully away and without
speaking turned to get back into her car.

MacNee caught her arm. 'You're a professional, Marjory,'
he said, the roughness of his tone concealing his concern.
'You've been spat at before.'

'Not by someone who's had coffee at my kitchen table,' she said dully.

'Och, don't take it to heart. She's not herself, that's all. She'll be round to say her "sorry" in the morning.'

'I won't be holding my breath.' Fleming opened the car door, then, as he made to follow her in, said, 'No, Tam. I've got to handle this on my own. It's my job and I wanted it.'

'Away and have a chat to Bill on the phone,' he urged.

She looked at him stonily. 'You're joking, of course,' she said, climbed in and drove away.

In the gathering dusk, Laura might almost have missed the Chapelton sign, if it hadn't been for the police car parked across the entrance and the pitiless illumination of arc-lamps which silhouetted a group of buildings against the skyline. She caught her breath; here she was seeing the harsh reality of foot-and-mouth, hinted at before by the greasy smuts on her windscreen, the oily, acrid smell and the wreathing black smoke of pyres which she'd noticed on her journey north.

She had formulated no particular plan in taking the narrow road up over the moors beyond Glenluce where Max had said the farm was situated. After a long drive up from London, with the early darkness of a Scottish winter evening, nowhere booked to stay and more hope than expectation of even locating Chapelton, this wasn't exactly a rational thing to do. But she had felt all day that she was retracing Dizzy's steps and there was a sort of romance about that which had gripped her, even as an inner voice howled: *What do you think you're doing? Latching on to someone else's adolescent rebellion to compensate for your own low-key, conventional life?*

Well, she'd located the farm, and it was obviously in a state of siege. Was Max inside there, she wondered, presiding over a macabre slaughter of his father's treasured cattle? And if so, would it seem some sort of symbolic catharsis as the lives sacrificed atoned for his own losses – his mother, his home? Perhaps, even, the loss of a father's love?

Anyway, driving aimlessly on in drizzling rain and growing darkness wasn't constructive. She'd noticed the lights of a small hotel just outside the last village she'd gone through; that would do for the night, might even if it was half-way decent prove quite a good base for research for her article.

She'd been considering that on the way up; she needed to talk not only to farmers who were clearly suffering what could only be called bereavement but to people working in the infrastructure of small businesses – shops, restaurants, little hotels like that one – who were dependent on tourism in countryside which had been officially declared closed, without any hope of the compensation for lack of livelihood which would be available to the farmers.

There was a passing-place at a point where the road was a little bit wider too. She turned the car and set off back down the road she had come. As she turned a corner, a big black bird rose, startled, from where it had been tearing at some unidentifiable road-kill and flapped off towards a Forestry Commission plantation, dark against the sky.

> 'Light thickens, and the crow
> Makes wing to the rooky wood,'

Laura found herself muttering. That was *Macbeth*, wasn't it – the Scottish Play, you were supposed to call it to avert bad luck. And the speech went on to say something about 'night's black agents'. She shuddered involuntarily; not a pleasant thought, out here in the wilds where you might almost be the only person on the planet.

But in fact, there were the lights of the hotel ahead, and she turned into the car park, suddenly bone-weary. She got out, fetched her suitcase and walked towards the building, then hesitated on the doorstep. There was a dispirited air about the place, indefinably depressing; perhaps it would be better to look for somewhere else? But she was very tired, and after all she needn't commit herself for more than one night. She opened the door and went in.

The woman who appeared in answer to Laura's tentative ping on the bell looked even more exhausted than Laura felt, heavy-eyed and with a tiny muscle jumping above dark brown eyes which looked too big for her thin face. She seemed surprised, as if the request for a room was unusual, but yes, she certainly had one available.

'I hope this'll suit.' She was looking anxious as she unlocked the door to a room at the back of the house. 'The two biggest rooms are taken.'

'I'm sure it'll be fine,' Laura said soothingly, then, as she saw the simply furnished room with its cheerful curtains and bedspread, added, 'This is lovely – very comfortable.'

The woman's tired face lit up with an unexpectedly sweet smile. 'I'm awful glad you like it. It makes a real difference.'

There was an unspoken suggestion that not all guests were as appreciative. Not an easy job, running a hotel!

'Yes, lovely,' Laura repeated. 'And that's the bathroom?'

'Just a shower-room.' The anxious look reappeared. 'I'm sorry, I know a lot of folk like a bath, but we've not a lot of space, you see—'

'Don't worry. That's fine, honestly. And I'll be able to have supper here?'

'Yes. Well, it's nothing grand, just two choices. But the fish van was round today and I've some real nice fish that were out there swimming around this time yesterday.'

Laura laughed. 'That sounds wonderful. And I can get a drink in the bar?'

'Yes. Er, yes, of course. My – my husband does that. It'll be open at six. Probably. And the meal's at seven.'

Laura noted the nervous hesitation but said only, 'That's

fine. I'll have plenty of time to have a shower and change. Thanks very much, Mrs—?'

'Oh, Lisa. Lisa Thomson.' She looked down at her watch with a harassed, White Rabbit expression. 'Sorry, I'll need to be getting on. There's the bairns' tea, you see—'

'Of course. Don't let me keep you.'

Laura unpacked, her mind on the woman who had just left. People's lives always intrigued her and there was a lot of harsh experience written on Lisa Thomson's face. It had a look that reminded her of the women she had known in New York: what sort of man was the husband, when talking about him made Lisa so nervous?

Still, she would have plenty of time to find out and, it struck her, Lisa and her husband were just the sort of people she needed to talk to for her research. Even if they had three rooms let tonight, she doubted if that was the norm, and it must be a real struggle to keep an enterprise like this afloat. There would be bar trade too, of course, and that would be a good way for her to meet the locals. Feelings must be running high just now; she suspected that it must be hard for a government whose major concern was all too obviously their urban power-base to convince a rural population that it wasn't either cavalier or incompetent.

How long, she wondered suddenly, had the Thomsons been running this place? It was the nearest pub to Chapelton and it was hard to imagine that Dizzy wouldn't have been a regular. Certainly, it was a long time ago and Dizzy had been there for a very short time, but she had the sort of personality that made people remember her. It was exciting to think that here might be another source of information. She might even have made friends, kept in touch . . .

It was unlikely, sure. But Laura went to have her shower in a mood of defiant optimism.

*   *   *

The meal was surprisingly good, the ambience distinctly less so. The orange tablecloths with their cream napkins were a brave attempt but clearly the money had run out when it came to the cost of curtaining the extensive windows round three sides of the room. There were orange pelmets across the top but the strips of matching fabric down the sides of the windows were only for show. It let such heat as there was escape and it was somehow unnerving the way the darkness outside seemed to encroach on the room, making it feel bleak and unwelcoming.

Its only other occupant was a large, florid woman at a table next to the only radiator. She was unwisely arrayed in a series of layers and scarves which only added to her bulk and she had cold, pale green eyes; she nodded stiffly and unsmilingly in response to Laura's 'Good evening' as she passed on the way to her table.

Fortunately Laura had thought of putting on a few layers herself – a thick black mohair tunic over a white silky poloneck – but she wished she'd brought a book. It was disconcerting, eating in a chilly silence broken only by the clink of cutlery on plates and a short fit of coughing by her companion, except when that lady was complaining to Lisa Thomson about aspects of her meal which weren't perfect and the service which was undeniably slow – although considering that Lisa was obviously cooking as well, it was unsurprising. Laura found herself childishly raising her voice as she handed back her plate with thanks, so that her praise for what had incurred the other's condemnation should be clearly and, she hoped, irritatingly heard.

The bar, when she had looked through the glass doors earlier, had been empty. Summoning Mr Thomson to perform his barman's duties might get her off on the wrong foot, she thought, and anyway there might possibly be more people to talk to in here later. When she left the dining-room, having received only the stoniest of stares in response to 'Good night', she went back to the bar.

It still wasn't busy. In fact, there was only one customer, a weather-beaten old boy with a growth of grey stubble and rheumy blue eyes, sitting at the bar with an almost empty pint mug and an empty shot glass in front of him. Laura smiled at him as she took her seat on one of the bar stools; he greeted her with, 'Aye, aye,' said with a nod and a wink. At least the natives were friendly.

She wasn't so sure about the man behind the bar. He was of middle height, harsh-featured, with a shock of red hair and an expression which would make Gordon Brown in one of his more professionally dour moments seem positively vivacious. In his mid-thirties, Laura guessed, but beginning to run to seed with a sagging jawline and an incipient beer-gut. One arm seemed to sag awkwardly and he didn't use it to prepare the vodka and tonic she ordered.

'Could you put it on my bill, please? Oh, and one for yourself?'

'Thanks.' That was very nearly a smile. He put a glass to the whisky optic and uninvited poured himself a double; Laura looked at him sharply. His eyes were dull, the whites muddy, and she realised this was certainly not the first drink of the day. That explained poor Lisa's anxiety, at least partially.

The sound of a glass being set down in a marked manner called her attention to her neighbour. The faded eyes had a hopeful expression and his ingratiating smile was so broad that she could, in the unlikely event that she should wish to, have counted the yellowed stumps in his gum, like memorial stones marking a battle lost to age and decay.

She said gravely, 'Could I offer you a drink?'

'Aye, could you!' The ancient cackled with pleasure. 'Nip 'n' a chaser, Scott.'

A pint of beer and another whisky – a single this time – was set in front of him; the whisky vanished in one gulp, chased by a deep swallow of beer and followed by a satisfied smacking of the lips.

Laura prepared to capitalise on her investment. 'Do you live near here?'

The good news was that he was more than willing to chat to her and he had plenty to say. The bad news was that she could barely understand a word of it. She listened with a glazed expression, nodding sagely in what she hoped were the right places, while behind the bar Thomson watched with sardonic amusement.

Her elderly friend was making short work of his pint. Laura was just considering how to disengage herself before she became responsible for a refill when she heard someone open the door to the bar. She had her back to it; not wanting to turn and stare, she didn't realise who it was until a familiar voice spoke.

'Good God, Laura!' Max Mason said blankly. 'What in the hell are you doing here?'

She spun round, feeling her cheeks turn crimson in embarrassment. What a fool she was! The nearest pub to Chapelton – she'd thought about that in connection with Dizzy but not Max. Now he'd think she was pursuing him and she'd been caught on the back foot again. She could only say feebly, 'Goodness, Max!'

Under the interested eyes of the other two men he pecked her on both cheeks. She could almost see him preening.

'Hey, hey! This is some surprise! I always knew I was a babe magnet but this sort of pulling power is awesome!'

'Don't get the wrong idea,' she said tartly. 'I'm researching an article on the effects of foot-and-mouth and up here I thought I could kill two birds with one stone and do a bit of digging about my sister as well.'

'Sure, sure.' His tone was mocking. From the jauntiness of his body-language and the brightness of his eyes it was clear he was on some sort of high. 'But come on, it's good to see you. Let's hack into a bottle of something.' He leaned his elbows on the bar. 'Got up to speed with wine yet, Scott? Or are you still more comfortable with cattle cake?'

Laura had thought Thomson's expression dour before; now it was so black that she was afraid he might turn violent. He said nothing, though, merely producing a couple of glasses and a bottle of red wine and opening it when Max had approved it with a careless nod.

'He was our stockman at the farm when I left,' Max said, taking the bottle and glasses over to a table in the farthest corner of the bar. 'Had some sort of accident a couple of years ago, his wife said.'

Laura followed him, making a note of the information. If Thomson had been at Chapelton when Max left he must have been there with Dizzy, though she'd better put in some practice at getting blood out of stones before she progressed to pumping him for information.

'There's foot-and-mouth at the farm, did you know?' Max was pouring out the wine, hardly expecting an answer; not wanting to admit to her reconnaissance, Laura said non-committally, 'I'm so sorry – that's awful.'

She couldn't read his expression. 'They're killing them now. They've been at it most of the day – I'm expecting a call from them any time now to say they're finished.' He fished out a mobile phone from his pocket and set it between them.

'Are you alone at the farm?' she asked.

He looked puzzled. 'Alone – oh no, I'm not at the farm at all. If I'd set foot in the place they weren't going to let me leave until it was declared free of infection, and God knows when they'll get round to that. No, I'm staying here.'

As Laura's heart sank he went on, 'And you are too, obviously. Brilliant! You can hold my hand when my wicked cousin comes in breathing fire. My aunt's summoned him. She's staying here too and when I drifted in this afternoon I thought we'd have to book another hospital bed beside the Minotaur.'

'That must have been the lady I saw in the dining-room this evening.' For once Laura felt some sympathy for Max. 'How is your father? Have you been to see him?'

'Not good, but still hanging on. No, I haven't visited. Have to give the old bastard a sporting chance and the sight of me would probably carry him off.'

He changed the subject. 'Still, I'm in the driving-seat at Chapelton. I went in this afternoon to check it out with the lawyer. Stuffy old sod – he wouldn't tell me a thing about the will but since he agreed I should take over day-to-day admin I think I can take it I haven't been bumped off the beneficiary list.

'That was what nearly finished Auntie off – she was sure her dear little Conrad was right in there. He's a policeman now, apparently, of all bizarre things. So I'm scared he's going to have me arrested on some trumped-up charge when he comes roaring in tonight. You will come and vouch for my good character, won't you, if I'm hauled off to the Tolbooth in Kirkluce?'

He had glanced at his watch and now he was drumming his fingers on the table; he was, she realised, genuinely nervous about the confrontation ahead. The last thing she needed was to get herself involved in a family fracas. She stood up.

'I will, I promise. But I'm sorry, I'm going to abandon you now. I've driven eight hours today and I'm bushed.'

'Laura, you can't—' As he spoke, the phone on the table rang and he reached for it, saying hastily, 'Wait just a minute, I want to say something – hello? Max Mason speaking.'

She could, of course, leave anyway but it would be gratuitously rude. She hovered, in the awkward position of trying not to eavesdrop while being unable to avoid hearing every word.

They had finished the slaughter, it appeared. They were moving out tonight and tomorrow the disposal of the carcasses would start.

Max seemed surprised, if pleased. 'I was told this afternoon that it was likely to take some time?'

There was some lengthy conversation, then he gave a tight-lipped smile. 'Nice to have friends in high places, then. I'm glad my cousin's useful for something.'

He listened again, then said, 'I don't see why it shouldn't be there. We won't be needing the ground for cattle for quite a bit. If ever. Go ahead, dig your pit.'

He rang off. 'Sorry. Well, at least they're getting on with it. They've decided pyres are too risky now – wouldn't you think they could have worked that out before they contaminated half the farms in the country? So tomorrow they're digging a pit in Satan's field—'

Laura had been conscious of a door slamming a moment earlier; as Max started speaking the door to the bar had been flung open and a man strode in, tall, broad and good-looking in a brutalist kind of way.

'*What?*' he bellowed. 'What did you just say?'

Max looked up with elaborate unconcern though Laura noticed that his defensive body-language – rigid shoulders hunched, fists clenched before him on the table – betrayed his anxiety. 'Well, well, well! If it isn't my cousin Conrad!'

'You can't dig up Satan's field!'

'Wanted to keep it as some sort of shrine, did you? You and my father were always besotted with the animal – nasty-tempered brute, as I remember.'

'Don't – don't be ridiculous.' Conrad spat out the words;

the hatred between the cousins was almost tangible. 'It's some of the best pasture we have – we'll need it when we restock.'

'*If* we restock.' Ignoring his cousin's stunned expression, Max got up. 'Come on, Conrad, I know we can't expect civilised behaviour from the Filth, but you might at least say hello to a lady.'

Conrad half-turned, then at the sight of Laura, gaped. '*Di?*' he stammered, then, 'No, no, of course it isn't.'

Max's smile was malicious. 'This is Laura Harvey, her half-sister. It's a remarkable likeness, isn't it – like a ghost of time past, coming back to haunt us?'

It took only a moment for the man to regain his poise. He smiled, very charmingly, and held out his hand. 'Do forgive me. I didn't mean to insult you – you must be years younger! How is she, by the way?'

'I'm – I'm afraid we've lost touch.' Laura, too, had been thrown by the introduction. It was what Max liked to do, his standard power-play, but she wasn't about to accept his direction. 'You two obviously have a lot to discuss,' she said firmly. 'I'm off to bed.'

She ignored Max's protest and walked out, aware that Conrad's eyes were following her. But she was more disconcerted when, as she closed the glass door, she realised that Scott Thomson, too, was staring after her, with an expression on his face that she could not read.

It was, perhaps, unsurprising that Laura slept badly. She woke fully at around three o'clock, that time of the morning when, viewed through the prism of tiredness, the world seems a cruel and hopeless prison. Her grief for the loss of her mother, suppressed by activity during the day, welled up now and she turned her face into her pillow to stifle her sobs.

At last she got up and went through to the little shower-room to splash her face. She could hear the moaning of the wind; she switched off the light and pulled back the curtain to look at the weather.

It was pitch black outside. There was no moon and no sign of stars; after living in towns and cities this deep darkness was almost shocking. It wasn't raining, but there was a strong wind blowing and she could just see bushes being whipped about in the garden below. She dropped the curtain again. As she was turning away, she heard a noise from somewhere not far away. It sounded like a bull, or a cow, perhaps, bellowing. She didn't know much about animals, but it sounded as if it was in distress.

They'd slaughtered all the Chapelton cattle, hadn't they? And there certainly wasn't another farm between here and there. Could they have missed one, left it wandering alone and terrified among the corpses of its herd?

Laura looked out of the window again, but apart from wavering, indecipherable shadows she couldn't see anything. She was getting cold now too. Trying to put the thought of the wretched creature out of her head, she got back into bed and tried to compose herself for sleep.

IO

'Good morning, ma'am.' PC Langlands was at the reception desk the following morning when DI Fleming came in. Instead of calling her usual cheerful greeting, she looked straight through him, leaving him searching his conscience for a reason and nervously anticipating a summons to account for whatever it was.

Oblivious to the trouble she had caused, Marjory Fleming plodded up the stairs to her office, her whole body heavy with the weight of her misery. Perhaps, she reflected briefly, it just showed what a cushy life she'd had that she'd never before felt wretched like this.

She'd never been at odds with Bill before, for a start. They'd had the odd quarrel, but until yesterday they'd always been on the same side. It hadn't been easy recently, with all that was going on, and the lengthening pauses in their evening conversations had been thick with unspoken thoughts. But Bill was a reasonable man and after all it was at his insistence that she had gone to stay with her parents precisely so that she could carry on her job.

Still, his sympathies were naturally with his friends and colleagues; hers were too, only she did feel a certain resentment that while she was understanding about their difficulties, they seemed entirely unprepared to make allowances for her own. Did they think she enjoyed this, for heaven's sake? She didn't say that to Bill, though; for days now they had talked stiltedly about the children, her parents, anything but what was uppermost in both their minds.

Yesterday, when he picked up the phone, she knew from his voice that he had heard about the day's events. Tired of papering over the cracks, she said abruptly, 'Have you been talking to Susie?'

Yes, he had, and it was clear where he stood. 'It's been a bad business. It's an awful pity you had to be involved.'

'You *know* I haven't any choice,' she cried, feeling betrayed. 'You know I don't like it any more than you do. None of us wants this—'

'But it was so badly handled! Couldn't you have intervened, worked at persuading them to accept the situation instead of putting in the heavies?'

'You think we didn't? Perhaps you can suggest the easy way to make someone who's barricaded themselves in and whistled up a protest mob comply with the law?' She was angry now. 'I can promise you we tried everything else – it's too expensive to mobilise that number of people unless there's no alternative.'

'Oh, if it's a question of *money*, of course—' There was pent-up rage in his voice.

'Your money. Their money.'

'If it's our money, it's not how we'd choose to spend it.' Then Bill stopped and she heard him take a deep breath. 'Look, Marjory, we're getting into a quarrel over this and it's not constructive. You have your point of view and I have mine. It's just I was very upset to think that you'd lost a good friend.'

Good friend! 'Did she tell you what she did to me?' Marjory's tone was dangerously quiet.

'Did? No.'

'She spat in my face.'

It silenced him and she enjoyed a moment of bitter satisfaction. When he spoke again his voice was softer.

'I didn't know that. I'm sorry, love.'

She hung up on him. She knew it was stupid. She had waited for him to ring back. He hadn't.

This morning she was suffering for having taken an olive branch and trampled it underfoot, and she was worrying about the children too. Cat, under Janet's influence, was rapidly becoming a Fifties throwback: Marjory rarely saw her without a pinny on and she had even said reproachfully, 'Mum, why don't you pull out all the beds to clean behind them every week? You can't have a clean house if there's dust under the beds.' Like her grandmother, she'd taken to waiting hand and foot on the menfolk and her brother was rapidly becoming a male chauvinist piglet.

But last night, when Marjory had got home late, lacerated after the day's problems and her conversation with Bill, Cammie was still awake and in tears when she went into his bedroom. Playing Racing Demon with Grandpa had palled; Cammie had made the mistake of saying it was boring and his grandfather had taken his revenge by confiscating Cammie's beloved GameBoy.

The child put his arms round his mother's neck and sobbed. 'I don't like it here any more. I want to go *home*.'

'I know, I know. It's a bit tough, isn't it? But maybe it won't be long now.'

She managed to soothe him, kissed him goodnight and went wearily downstairs trying to work out what to do.

It wasn't that she had any brief for the GameBoy – just the opposite – but Cammie was, after all, a kid who'd been uprooted from home and this was just plain bullying. How typical of her father to react with vindictiveness to any slight, real or imagined! What was so sad was that he and Cammie had been developing quite a good relationship and this had created a no-win situation. If Cammie went on feeling unjustly treated it would sour his affection for his grandfather, but if Marjory waded in and forced the return of the stupid thing, her father would never forgive Cammie for causing him to lose face. It was Angus who would be the principal loser: it was his problem, his choice . . . Still, it was a shame.

She could hear the sound of the television as she came downstairs; it had barely been on since the children arrived. There was a light in the kitchen, though, so her mother must be working there. She could go and talk to her about it.

It didn't, of course, come as news to Janet. In her own inimitable way she managed to be sympathetic to everyone without taking sides; after listening patiently she had told her daughter not to fash herself, that it would all be fine in the morning and why did she not get herself off to bed for a good sleep because she was looking real peelie-wallie?

Marjory had agreed, but it was still one more reason for feeling depressed. She let herself into her office and sat down at her desk to check her e-mails, hoping against hope that there wasn't another exercise like yesterday's on the agenda. For once, the thought of paperwork was positively inviting.

She found nothing too alarming: the tasking group anticipated no serious disturbances over the next twenty-four hours, she had a debriefing appointment with the Super, a planning meeting, a request for permission to go on a training course and there was a circular about planned alterations to the canteen. And a note, unsigned, which said in quotation marks,

> 'For the future be prepar'd
> Guard whatever thou canst guard:
> But thy utmost duty done
> Welcome what thou canst not shun.'

She read it with a wry smile. No prizes for guessing who'd sent that one.

Marjory was in the middle of a report when the man himself knocked on the door and came in.

'Tam!' she said. 'I got your note – appreciated the support if not the message. You bloody try welcoming—'

Then she noticed his expression. 'What's happened?' she
said sharply.

He sat down. 'We've maybe a wee bit of a problem on
our hands, boss. We've just had this call from the guys digging a burial pit over at Chapelton. They've found a body.'

Laura began her research in the morning in the offices of
the local weekly paper, the *Galloway Globe*, and found that
the editor, a round, cheerful man rejoicing in the name of
Neil MacSporran, was delighted to be helpful. He set her
down with back copies of the newspaper and even recom-
mended a few people he thought would be happy to talk to
her.

By eleven o'clock she was drinking coffee and eating feath-
erlight oven scones in the kitchen of a farm near the coast
towards Wigtown which had lost its stock in the first week
of the epidemic. The place was eerily empty and silent; the
farmer's wife talked incessantly while her husband said
nothing but paced like a caged animal, often stopping by the
window to look out over the deserted fields. She talked, he
didn't, which worried Laura: he was in a high-risk profession for suicide and a reactive depression, left untreated, was
a recipe for disaster.

As she rose to go, she said to him, 'Have you been offered
counselling?' and at last saw him animated.

'Load of blethers!' he snorted. 'My certies, lassie! If you
caught me having any truck with a daft-like notion like yon,
you'd know I'd gone clean gyte!'

The vocabulary was obscure but the meaning was plain
enough and perhaps he knew his own business best. Laura

grinned, agreed that he might not be the ideal subject and left, promising to come to see them again.

She had lunch in a cosy café in Wigtown and a useful chat with its proprietor, then after a browse through a couple of the bookshops for which the town is famous and more conversations, she had pages of notes to write up and she headed back.

She'd booked in to the Glen Inn for another couple of nights. It would give her a chance to find out if the Thomsons remembered Dizzy and she might even pluck up the courage to ask the unpleasant Mrs Mason for her recollections, though these were unlikely to be positive; Max had said the two women had been at loggerheads.

Lisa had clearly been pleased about the extra business even though she had looked this morning as if the strain of catering for several visitors single-handed was almost overwhelming. She confided that she and Scott had been very late to bed; they couldn't lock up until the cousins left the bar and they'd stayed up till all hours quarrelling. 'Bellowing like two of their own bulls,' she said with a nervous giggle.

'Oh! I wonder if that was what I heard last night,' Laura had said, though on reflection she was fairly sure the sound had not come from inside the hotel. If it was a lone animal she could only hope they had found the poor thing today and put it out of its misery.

Driving back over the now-familiar territory to New Luce, Laura planned the rest of her day: she should write up her research on her laptop while it was still fresh in her memory, and she'd bought a copy of *The Thirty-Nine Steps*, with its Galloway background, which would keep her comfortably amused in her room and out of Max's way at least until dinnertime.

Just before she reached New Luce she realised there was a police van behind her and she slowed down to let it overtake. There were two police cars in the car park of the hotel too; it must be something to do with the slaughter at Chapelton.

She was completely unprepared for what awaited her. As she opened the front door, Max emerged from the dining-room at the side of the hotel, looking white and shaken.

'Laura!' He pounced on her, grabbing her arm so hard that it was painful. 'Where have you been? I needed you!'

'Max, whatever's wrong?'

He gestured behind him to the open door of the dining-room where Laura could see uniformed police and two or three other people sitting at one of the tables. 'They came this morning – they've found a woman's body in the field they were digging up. It's been there for years. Laura, it's my mother, I know it is! I always thought my father might have killed her – why would she have gone away and never got in touch with me?'

He began to cry, great tearing sobs. Laura, dumbfounded, put her arm round his shoulders and looked helplessly round for somewhere he could sit down.

'Here – take him through here.' A woman had emerged from the dining-room and was holding open the door to the small residents' lounge on the other side of the hall. She was tall, with an air of easy authority; she had reddish-brown hair, neatly shaped, and a wide, good-humoured mouth but, Laura thought, her hazel eyes were cool and watchful. She wouldn't miss much.

It took a few minutes for Max to regain control. Visibly embarrassed, he fumbled for a handkerchief. 'I can't think why I did that. Sorry. Not my style.'

Before Laura could speak, the other woman said, 'You've had a considerable shock, Mr Mason. You were extremely helpful to us this morning, helping us to deal with your aunt until DS Mason could get here, and this is a very natural delayed reaction.' She turned to Laura. 'I'm Detective Inspector Fleming. And you are . . . ?'

'Laura Harvey.' A raised eyebrow invited her to elaborate and she added, 'I'm here doing a piece for the *Sunday Tribune* on the local effects of foot-and-mouth.'

She felt, rather than saw, the woman stiffen. 'You're a journalist?'

'A psychotherapist. It's a feature article.'

It didn't look as if DI Fleming's opinion of psychotherapists was a lot higher than her opinion of journalists. 'And your connection with Mr Mason?'

Laura had no intention of going into that. 'We know each other in London.'

'I see.' Fleming was clearly putting two and two together and making about twenty, but if she chose to jump to conclusions it wasn't Laura's job to stop her. She said nothing, and Fleming turned back to Max.

'Are you all right now, Mr Mason?'

'Oh, sure. My father's murdered my mother, but hey! I'm cool with that.' Max was recovering his composure.

Colour rose in Fleming's cheeks. 'I didn't mean—'

'Yeah, fine. But look, I've had about as much as I can take for today. Leave me with my friend, OK?'

'Of course. But perhaps I could send someone to talk to you tomorrow, Ms Harvey? Nine o'clock?' She went out.

'Tell me about it, Max,' Laura said gently and again prepared to listen. She hadn't done this much listening in the course of a day since she was in New York.

'He's upstairs with his mother, ma'am. The doctor's just arrived to give her a sedative.'

'Let's be thankful for small mercies,' Fleming said with feeling. 'Look, when DS Mason comes down again, tell him to stop by my office. I'm going back to HQ now with MacNee.'

Her jaw aching with nervous tension, Marjory went back out to the car. And she'd thought she'd had problems when she got up this morning! She'd only dealt with a murder once before, a domestic where the victim's husband phoned the police to tell them what he'd done, which wasn't exactly like being Senior Investigating Officer on something like this.

'Right,' she said to MacNee as she drove out of the car park. 'Tell me what I've forgotten.'

'Lunch,' her companion said bitterly.

'Oh, for heaven's sake! I think there's a bag of apples in the back there if you're desperate.'

'I'm desperate.' He leaned over to scrabble in the back seat, found two apples and handed her one. She shrugged and bit into it, though she was too strung-up to feel hungry.

'Secure the site. I've done that. Have the police surgeon pronounce death officially.'

MacNee snorted. 'Not hard to tell, when the body parts aren't actually connected.'

She gave him an impatient look. 'This is a checklist. I like putting in things I've done so I can cross them off. Notify the Chief Constable and the Procurator Fiscal. Open a policy book to record why I made every decision to make it easier for the defence to take me apart in court. How am I doing?'

'Alert the Press Officer? They'll be over us like blow-flies.'

'They were seeing to that at HQ. But for any favour don't mention blow-flies. When I get back I'm going to put a bomb under MAFF and make sure they remove all the carcasses today and get on with disinfecting the place. With us all tramping around and vehicles going back and forth we'll be spreading the virus everywhere we go. Let alone the smell . . .'

Fleming shuddered. When they had arrived at the farm it had been like some scene from Grand Guignol. There were the bodies of slaughtered cattle everywhere, beginning to bloat as the stomach gases fermented. Foxes and crows had been at them already, tearing at the carcasses and pecking at the dead eyes. A black miasma of flies kept up a low, sinister buzzing.

The stench was nauseating; the constable with a clipboard logging all visits to the scene was looking green and trying to find a position upwind. He pointed them down the drive from the house, past the maze which Marjory remembered from her childhood, even more overgrown now. A feeble sun was struggling to find its way through the clouds and a fresh wind was blowing in from the sea, mercifully in the right direction, clean and salty, and Marjory drew in deep breaths to clear her lungs.

As they entered the field, it all seemed surprisingly tranquil. A flock of black and white oyster-catchers had alighted there to feed, strutting about on their red stilt-like legs and probing the grass with long red beaks, but as the metal field-gate clanged they swirled up in alarm with raucous cries.

A screen of polythene sheeting had been erected already and Fleming and MacNee made their way towards it. A big yellow digger was parked nearby; its operator, leaning against it and smoking nervously, stubbed out his cigarette and stood up expectantly, then, as they went into the shelter, sighed and lit up again.

Marjory braced herself. Like every police officer, she had experience of road accidents and the horror of tangled metal and fragile human flesh. But this . . .

Curiously enough, it was less disturbing, not more. What was in the pit, three feet deep, was not immediately recognisable as a body; disturbed, apparently, by the claw-bucket of the digger, the skeletal parts, caked in earth, had been dispersed, dehumanising them. What tissue remained, mainly on the torso, was black and leather-like, reminding her of ancient mummified bodies seen in a museum, the sort they found in peat bogs – and, of course, the soil around here was damp and peaty. There were a few grey, rotting rags of what must have been clothing but there was only one thing to suggest a person who had lived and laughed and suffered: a long strand of earth-clogged hair still clinging to a patch of shrivelled scalp. Marjory turned her eyes hastily away and went back out with some relief into the cold fresh air.

The surgeon had been, the SOCOs were on their way. They would need to establish an incident room and the Glen Inn, handily placed just a couple of miles away, was the obvious place. Under a certain amount of pressure the proprietor agreed that they could have the dining-room; it was an added bonus when they discovered that two of the guests about to be displaced to the bar for meals were Max Mason and his aunt. Max Mason's reaction to the news of what they had found at Chapelton and his aunt's subsequent hysteria had been a rich source of information, or speculation at the very least.

'Do you reckon the guy's right? That his dad killed his mammy?' MacNee's utterance was somewhat impeded by a mouthful of apple.

'It's possible. I remember my parents saying she just walked out on him, but you'd think she'd have relatives asking questions if she just disappeared.'

'Have to bring in the old boy, won't we? Where is he?'

'Didn't you know? He's in hospital with a stroke. I asked Conrad about him yesterday and apparently he's stable but he can't move or speak.'

MacNee groaned. 'That's all we need. A defence agent's dream – won't even have to warn him to say nothing under questioning.

'Still, at least if it's her we'll know when it happened, for a start. Sixteen years ago she disappeared, the son said. So Conrad would have been – what? Twenty, maybe? That'll be useful. Not often you get an inside track like that working on a case! Get him to deal with his mother – anyone else would ask for danger money.'

Fleming looked at him sideways. 'Aren't you forgetting something?'

'If it's not her, you mean?'

'If it is her, Conrad's a suspect. He's close family. I'm calling him in to tell him I'm taking him off active duty as of now.'

II

When Laura came down the stairs at nine o'clock the following morning, there were two people waiting for her in the hall of the hotel: a short, dark man wearing a black leather jacket and a laconic expression, and a young, nervous-looking policewoman in uniform. The door to the dining-room was open on a scene of considerable activity; the front door was open and a man in workman's overalls was bringing in rolls of cable.

The man came forward. 'Ms Harvey? Detective Sergeant MacNee.' He flipped open a plastic wallet to give a glimpse of an identity card. 'This is Constable Johnston. We won't keep you long – just a brief statement, that's all.'

Laura followed them through to the dining-room. It wasn't an ideal place for an interview. It was very noisy with computers being carried in, telephones being installed and somewhere someone using an electric drill. Uniformed officers and detectives were going to and fro, having discussions and giving instructions; in the car park outside there seemed to be constant arrivals and departures of police vehicles and other cars.

The questions were fairly perfunctory, like ticks being put in boxes so that it could be said to have been done. Sitting at a table in one corner, she told the police when she'd arrived at the hotel and how long she planned to stay, that she was researching an article on foot-and-mouth and that she had never been here before. They didn't ask her how she knew

Max and she didn't volunteer the information; there seemed little point in introducing irrelevant complications.

The policewoman said nothing, confining herself to laboriously recording Laura's answers in her notebook. MacNee glanced at her irritably once or twice, giving Laura the impression that she must be falling down on the job of asking routine questions and he didn't like having to ask them all himself. Was this an etiquette based on seniority, or was it perhaps to leave him free to assess her guilty reaction to such penetrating questions as 'What is your home address?'

Certainly, as MacNee had promised, it didn't take long. A statement would be prepared and brought to her for checking and signing, he told her, and thanked her for her cooperation.

A young man in jeans and a dark green fleece had been hovering nearby. He moved forward as Laura stood up to go, but the policewoman spoke for the first time. 'Sorry. I didn't get your address down. Sorry.'

There was a 'Tchach!' of impatience from MacNee; he turned to his waiting colleague. 'Were you wanting something?'

The man held out a transparent plastic package. 'DI Fleming asked me to bring you this. The SOCOs found it yesterday at the site and she wants you to show it to the son to see if he can identify it.'

'Right.' MacNee took it from him and set it on the table. 'I've to see him at nine-thirty. It'd be useful if he could give us something definite to go on.'

The policewoman was experiencing some difficulty with 'Marylebone'. As Laura spelled it for her, her eyes went to the package on the table. It held a thin chain, still looped through a pendant, grimy with the earth which still clung to it but recognisable as gold. The pendant was in the form of a prancing bull.

Laura stared, feeling the blood drain from her face. Her knees turned weak and there was a ringing inside her head. The policewoman was staring at her stupidly as Laura groped blindly for a chair and collapsed clumsily on to it.

The two men broke off their conversation. She heard MacNee say sharply, 'For God's sake, she's going to faint!' and then a grey cloud smothered sound and feeling.

When she came to, she was stretched out flat on the floor; Lisa Thomson, holding a glass of water, was kneeling anxiously beside her in front of a huddle of awkward-looking men. MacNee, standing at the table where the policewoman was still seated looking bemused, was berating her.

'Could you not have seen she wasn't well, woman, instead of sitting there looking glaikit? She could have hurt herself if I hadn't caught her.'

Laura struggled to sit up. 'I'm so sorry! I don't know what—' Then recollection came flooding back and she put her hand up to her head.

Lisa put her arm round her shoulders. 'It's all right. Take it easy now, and have a wee drink. Then we'll get you upstairs for a lie-down and you'll be fine.'

Obediently Laura sipped and MacNee came over to help her up. 'Dearie me!' he said jocularly. 'We don't usually get witnesses fainting until after we've brought out the thumbscrews.'

Then he noticed that Laura was looking towards the table, her lips quivering. He followed the direction of her brimming eyes. 'The necklace!' he exclaimed.

Silent tears welled up and spilled, unheeded, down her cheeks. 'My sister's,' she said brokenly. 'She bought it in Spain after she'd run with the bulls. She said she would always wear it because it was – it was the most wonderful experience of her life.'

*   *   *

According to the tasking group, there was another foot-and-mouth protest scheduled for today. Thanking whatever gods protected deserving police officers – even if in any profession other than divinity they'd be done for dereliction of duty – Marjory Fleming reflected that challenging though the role of Senior Investigating Officer in a murder enquiry might be, at least it meant she wouldn't be assigned to other duties.

She'd had to fly by the seat of her pants yesterday but she hadn't made any major blunders, which was a good confidence-booster. Then she'd burned the midnight oil to put herself through a refresher course on procedure – always a life-jacket in stormy seas – and this morning she felt much more in control. She'd had a very helpful meeting with the Super, too; Donald Bailey had been SIO on a murder case in his time and she'd been able to talk through some of her concerns.

Not the least of these was the problem of a trail gone cold. Where did you begin to investigate a crime that was, if Max Mason was to be believed, sixteen years old?

Bailey put his fingers together in a contemplative pyramid and pronounced, 'In exactly the same way as if it happened yesterday. You search the scene, you question the suspects, you talk to witnesses, you commission the reports. And you look for the same old things: means, motive and opportunity.

'And in this particular case, it appears at the moment, you have the considerable advantage of knowing not only who the victim is – which is so often the most difficult thing to establish – but you also have a very plausible prime suspect.'

Fleming grimaced. 'Try proving it, though, when he can't even answer the charges. I phoned the hospital and Jake Mason's condition is not only unchanged but unlikely to change. Ever.'

'Imprisoned already, in his own body, without so much

as a trial,' Bailey mused. 'Let's hope he's guilty. You know, Marjory, this may well turn out to be one of those cases where we can't close the file but we NFE it.'

She wrinkled her nose in distaste. 'No Further Enquiry's never a very satisfactory outcome, is it? Cheaper, though – that can't be bad.'

'Indeed. By the way, what's the situation vis-à-vis DS Mason? I gather you've taken the precaution of suspending him meantime?'

Fleming sighed. 'He wasn't happy about it, and that's an understatement. Perhaps I could have assigned him to other duties but in the circumstances it seemed a bit risky having him on the premises with possible access to information that some smartass lawyer could claim later he shouldn't have had, and I certainly don't want accusations that we assumed he was in the clear because he was a copper. I'll probably lift the suspension if everything points to Jake Mason, but at least we'll have shown willing.'

'That seems like good thinking. Try and speed it up, though – we're overstretched already.'

'I know. Speaking of which, I'd better get back to my desk. Thanks, Donald.' She got up and he rose too and went to hold the door open for her in his old-fashioned way.

'A final piece of advice,' he said. 'As SIO your primary task is coordinating and directing. And budgeting too, of course – our masters never let us forget that.

'Your detectives are your eyes and ears on an investigation. It's your job to be their brain.'

'Will you tell them or shall I?' Marjory's response had been flippant but she took the advice to heart. She couldn't waste her time flat-footing it around, but had to be sure of getting every scrap of relevant information from interviews, without being inundated with details about the witness's mother's maiden name. She'd called a briefing meeting for later this

morning when she would spell it out and by then she hoped
to have Max Mason's identification of his mother's pendant
to give the direction of the enquiry some immediate legiti-
macy. Unless, of course, like most men he never noticed
anything a woman was wearing.

DNA tests were the next step; she was just making a note
to get one set up for Max Mason when MacNee came in
and the whole thing went pear-shaped.

Fleming listened in stunned silence as MacNee recounted
the morning's events.

'So then Max comes in just as the wifie's taking Laura
upstairs for a lie-down and she tells him what's happened
and then we have him going doolally too,' he finished. 'I tell
you, it fair takes it out of you.'

Her eyes narrowed. 'I thought yesterday there was something else about that girl being there besides the research,
something she wasn't mentioning. From what she said it
sounded as if she and Max were an item but the way she
reacted to him didn't back that up.

'Did you find out what the sister was doing at Chapelton?'

'It was kinda vague. He said she was a Girl Friday or something for a few months, but we couldn't question either of
them, with Harvey looking as if she'd collapse again any minute
and him glaring at us as if it was all our fault. We'd have had
complaints of police brutality before you could say *skean dhu*.'

'So it's probably nothing to do with the mother's disappearance at all. And what does that say about our chief suspect? There's no more reason for it to be Jake than it is for
it to be Max or Conrad, or anyone else who might have been
around at the time, if it's not his wife.'

'Unless,' MacNee volunteered helpfully, 'she's there too.'

Fleming stared at him in horror. 'Oh, God. Serial murderer – that's all we need. We'll have to dig up the whole
field, won't we?'

'Maybe she's got family who know where she is.'

'If she has we'd better find them right away before we blow the budget looking for non-existent bodies. Get the Press on to it – they love being offered a cloak of social responsibility as a cover for the usual muck-raking.'

'Right, boss. I'm on my way.'

'The girl.' Fleming was tapping her teeth thoughtfully with a pen. 'How soon is she going to be fit? If we could just get a DNA sample from her today and compare it to one from the body we could have the results within twenty-four hours – forty-eight at worst. It wouldn't have to be anything fancy – they'd have enough material to run the standard test.'

'I'll find out. She'll be as anxious as anyone to move things along. We'd better leave interviewing her till tomorrow though.'

'Bring her in here. Nicely, of course, using your unique brand of persuasion – and I don't mean the Glasgow Kiss.'

MacNee gave his gap-tooth grin, making a head-butting gesture. 'You're just a wee spoilsport, so you are.'

'I want to sit in on this one,' Fleming said more seriously. 'I need to get a handle on the case. She was pretty economical with the truth when we spoke to her and I want to see to it we get the whole story this time. She's a psychotherapist – she must have known what she was doing.'

MacNee snorted. 'I think you're reaching, there. Most of the ones I've come across have been raving nutters.'

She smiled. 'Well – you know my views. Thanks, Tam.'

When he had gone she went back to her computer, highlighted all she'd written this morning and pressed delete. She'd have to start again from scratch with notes for the conference. And she'd have to see Conrad Mason.

If the victim was a young woman, that put both Mason cousins squarely in the frame along with Jake. She wanted to tell Conrad herself before he went to see his mother at

the Glen Inn and heard what had happened; seeing a reaction was always useful. She was picking up the phone to
arrange it when she remembered – Bill!

She'd tried to phone him yesterday to tell him what was
going on and do her best to make her peace but she hadn't
got through and then with the demands of the day she'd forgotten about it until she was leaving the office at half-past
eleven and it was much too late.

She dialled the number but when he answered he sounded
totally unlike himself. For a moment she wondered if she'd
got a wrong number.

'Bill? Bill, is that you? Are you all right?'

Marjory heard him sigh. 'They're coming today. There's
nothing wrong with the sheep, nothing at all. But they've
got it over at Windyedge and their boundary touches ours.
So they're going to kill dozens of healthy animals. And there's
nothing I can do to stop them.'

He spoke in a flat monotone, as if showing any emotion
at all would make him fall apart.

'Oh, Bill,' she faltered. 'That's – that's awful!'

'Yes.'

She didn't know what to say. What could she say – and
what use were words, anyway? She should be beside him,
to hold him, to give him the strength to cry if that was what
he needed to do. 'When will they let me back home?' she
asked.

'Well . . .' The heaviness in his voice lifted slightly. 'You
could come back now, Marjory. It doesn't matter if you bring
in infection – the poor beasts are doomed anyway. You'd
have to stay until they gave you the all-clear, but it wouldn't
be more than two, three days maybe. They could spare you
that long—'

She closed her eyes in despair. How could she tell him?
And what would it do to their marriage, when she did?

'Bill, you probably haven't heard, but yesterday they found a body buried at Chapelton. It's a murder enquiry and I'm Senior Investigating Officer. There's no way I can get leave at the moment.'

His silence was long and eloquent. Then he said, 'No. Of course not. Fine.'

'Oh, darling—'

'By the way, I'm sorry—'

Marjory wouldn't let him finish. 'About the other day? I should be apologising. I can't think what made me put the phone down like that. I'm sorry, I'm sorry—'

'No, it wasn't that.' He sounded cold, indifferent. 'I'm apologising because I forgot to shut up the hens last night and the fox got them. Sorry.' The line went dead.

Her precious chookies! Marjory buried her face in her hands. She had seen before the wholesale slaughter which was the fox's sickening trademark. It was all the more obscene because somehow there was something so innocent about hens, their squawking silliness and their crooning contentment, their simple needs and petty squabbles, and the thought of such savagery made her feel physically sick.

Her own happy, loving, secure and yes, in its way, innocent home life had been savaged too, by dislocation and misunderstanding and tragedy and cruel, ugly death.

And she still had a murder investigation to conduct and a briefing meeting in half an hour, and Conrad Mason to see before that. She swallowed hard, squared her shoulders and went back to her computer.

DS Mason had managed not to lose his temper yesterday when she had told him her decision, but only just. Today he looked completely self-possessed, upbeat, even, as he came into DI Fleming's office. She suspected it was because he thought she had summoned him to put him back on duty;

how, she wondered grimly, would he take the news not only of indefinite leave but the shortening of the odds on him in the suspect stakes? Well, she could only hit him with it and find out.

'Sit down, Conrad. I'm afraid I've got bad news about your return to active duty.'

She saw his brow darken but when he leaned forward in his chair it was to make a sweetly reasonable appeal. 'Look, you must see that this is ridiculous. We're badly under strength at the moment and here I am going stir-crazy sitting in someone's front room. Of course I can see I couldn't have anything to do with investigating my aunt's murder, but—'

'It seems that it probably isn't your aunt. We're working at the moment on the likelihood that the body is that of Diana Warwick who was, I understand, employed for a time at Chapelton some years ago.'

Watching him closely, Fleming tried to read the flickers of reaction crossing his face. Shock, certainly, but that could be for all sorts of reasons. Alarm? Perhaps. Then he bowed his head, which could be emotion but could also be the calculation of an experienced interrogator who knew how easy it was for your expression to give you away.

When he looked up his face was blank. 'Diana Warwick,' he said soberly. 'Di. I remember her quite clearly – she had the sort of personality you wouldn't forget. Oddly enough, her sister's staying at the Glen Inn at the moment – did you know that?'

'She identified a necklace found with the body as being her sister's.'

'I see. Yes.' He wasn't about to elaborate.

Fleming glanced at her watch. 'I've got a meeting in five minutes. I'll get someone to take a proper statement from you – everything you can remember, you know the form.

And don't decide to go and top up your sun-tan in the meantime.'

She tried to deliver the prohibition lightly but he had no illusions as to its implication. 'I'm a major suspect for this one, inevitably. A real suspect, not just a theoretical one.' He looked up to meet her eyes squarely. 'I didn't do it, of course.'

'Can you think of anyone who would have had reason to?'

'My mother!' He gave a sharp crack of laughter, then added hastily, 'I didn't mean that. It was a joke. It's just she was the only one who famously didn't get on with Di. To be honest, my mother doesn't really get on well with anyone.'

'Why Di particularly?'

'Oh, mostly house stuff. Di was a decent enough cook but she wasn't so hot on the cleaning side. My mother doesn't like to lift a finger but she has high standards and a Victorian attitude to staff. Di would give as good as she got when Mother yelled at her, which was *lèse-majesté* or something. And then of course . . .' He hesitated. 'I don't want this to sound as if I'm boasting or anything, but Di did have a bit of a crush on me at the time and Mother's always been very possessive.'

Recognising false modesty, Fleming made a non-committal sound. He went on hastily, 'But we're not really talking a motive for murder here. Anyway, you've met my mother – can you see her out in a field in the dead of night digging a shallow grave?'

Certainly, it conjured up an interesting picture. Fleming glanced again at her watch; she had to leave it there.

As she went along the corridors to her meeting, she tried to sort out her immediate impressions.

The news had undoubtedly shaken him, but that was to be expected. He had been almost immediately on his guard; again, any policeman would not be slow to understand what

was at stake and she'd seen evidence before of a strong element of calculation in Conrad Mason's make-up, except
when he lost his temper.

That stuff about his mother – what was that about? She'd
asked him what he would certainly recognise as a very standard 'whodunit' question; had he reckoned that turning it
aside with a preposterous suggestion was a good way of
playing for time while you considered who you could most
plausibly finger to further your own interests?

Always supposing you were guilty, of course. Fleming
found that she had no difficulty with that concept. But then,
his cousin Max – there was something about him that rang
wholly false too. This one could run and run.

12

Laura Harvey's eyelids were thick and heavy, her nose was red and swollen and her eyes so sticky with tears that this time cold water had little effect. She had wept through the hours of darkness, as if the death of the sister she had still in her heart believed was alive had released grief for other deaths, insufficiently mourned: the death of her father, her mother, her marriage, her career. Her life.

The police had talked about counselling, had suggested that the ineffectual young policewoman who had taken down Laura's statement should stay with her, but she had refused both offers. She didn't want professional hand-holding, although later, alone in her room when she'd managed to get rid of Max, she had tried to think of someone she could talk to who would not be embarrassed by her extreme distress. Her friends in London? New York? There wasn't one who wouldn't be bewildered, lacking the explanations she was too distraught to give. Since her marriage ended, she couldn't think of a single person with whom she had shared her innermost thoughts and fears.

You didn't need a training in psychology to realise that it was unhealthy to have, among a host of pleasant acquaintances, not even one close friend, especially when you had no home or family. If she had been looking at her own case professionally, she would have concluded that the obsessive nature of her hunt for Dizzy had been less about finding the sister she hardly knew than about attempting to establish some focal point in the desolate emptiness of her life.

It was a weary night. She found herself longing for dawn with the atavistic instinct which associates a lightening sky with a lightening of sorrow or pain, and drew back her curtains hopefully, but the winter sun rises late in Scotland. It was only just up when there was a tap on the door and Lisa Thomson appeared with a tea-tray.

She looked at Laura's ravaged face with sympathy but said only, 'Here's a wee cuppie for you. And you'd maybe like your breakfast up here? It's not awful comfortable in the lounge anyway and there's policemen all over the dining-room.'

'You are kind! Tea's just what I need, but I don't want anything to eat, thanks.'

'You'll be needing your breakfast before the day's over.' It was an instruction, not a suggestion. 'I've some nice morning baps the baker's just delivered and there's my mother's home-made marmalade too.'

Laura was touched. 'You've enough to do without having to go up and down with trays. I'll get something later—'

'Och, it's no bother. With them all needing snacks and coffees all the time I've been able to get Dawn up from the village to help, a real sensible lass, and I'm fine now.' And indeed, she did look much better this morning, busying herself in pulling over a table to put the tray on. 'You just enjoy your tea and she'll be up with your breakfast in a wee while.'

The kindness of strangers! Laura found her eyes filling again with weak tears but she blew her nose fiercely, determined not to lapse back into misery.

After tea and a shower she felt much better. She would, as Lisa had pointed out, need all her strength for the day ahead and when she tasted the freshly baked rolls with pale farm butter and dark, bitter, chunky marmalade she found she was hungry after all.

They had taken a DNA sample from her yesterday but clearly there was little doubt in their minds that the body so long interred was Dizzy. She mustn't let herself dwell on the ghastly realities of that horror; how merciful that her mother had been spared it! How sad, though, that she couldn't have known it wasn't lack of love on her daughter's part that had given rise to those cruel years of silence.

Today Laura was to be collected to go into the police headquarters in Kirkluce, 'just for a wee chat' as the detective with the broad Scots accent had said, but for all he made it sound innocuous, she was worried about it.

She was well aware that, while she had told them the truth in answer to their questions, it had been very far from being the whole truth. It had seemed at the time unnecessary, indeed distracting, to involve her whole family history.

Max had been so certain! And might there have been an element of subconscious denial, too, because she so wanted Dizzy to be out there somewhere, alive? Or perhaps it was simpler than that: she had gone to bed late and exhausted, with her head full of Max's problems.

He had talked for hours about his dysfunctional family, about the difficulties there had been, about his father's autocratic bullying. 'She probably stood up to him for once and he lost it with her,' Max had said. 'The Mason temper. It's a curse in our family.'

And, from the way he spoke, a source of pride as well, which was most likely what perpetuated it. And certainly, the vast majority of women murdered were killed by their partner, often in a fit of uncontrollable rage.

'How did you get on with your mother?' she asked.

As always, when she faced him with a direct question, she sensed withdrawal. Then he shrugged. 'Hey, I was a teenager!

But she loved me – I never had the faintest doubt about that.'

It had interested Laura that he said, 'she loved me' not 'I loved her', which would have been the appropriate answer to the question asked. She didn't miss the implication that she would never have left home and abandoned the son she loved.

Women did, though, and now it looked as if this woman had. Which meant that in failing to tell the police about Dizzy Laura had withheld vital information. Was that an actual offence? She couldn't remember and even if she had been able to, the laws here in Scotland were different. She felt distinctly uneasy.

She hoped it wasn't the woman inspector who wanted to see her today. She'd felt skewered by her uncomfortably shrewd gaze the last time; this time she was afraid she might be barbecued as well.

There were sixteen e-mails Marjory Fleming hadn't opened yet this morning and it was eleven o'clock. She'd had constant interruptions, phone calls, summonses to meetings, and she had the uncomfortable feeling of being strapped to a bolting horse.

Last night she'd made a point of going back to her parents' house for supper to touch base with her children; she hadn't seen them at all the previous day and she was still worried about Cammie. But when she went in, to her astonishment, she found her father with the GameBoy in his hands and Cammie sitting on the arm of his chair urging, 'Go on, Grandpa, collect your ration pack now!' When Marjory appeared, he barely took time to say, 'Hi, Mum,' and tell her that Cat was at hockey practice before he went back to his excited encouragement.

Smiling and shaking her head, she went through to the

kitchen where Janet was engaged in the intricacies of making a pastry rose for the top of the steak pie. 'I see diplomatic relations have been re-established,' Marjory said.

'Och well, you know men,' Janet said comfortably. 'Often they're just needing a wee excuse not to go on being daft.'

'That's pure domestic magic! How on earth did you do it?'

She dimpled demurely. 'Did you not know a magician's never allowed to let on to anyone how the trick's done?'

So that was all right, then. Marjory's phone call to Bill, though, had been brief and entirely unsatisfactory. There was really nothing she could do at the moment except keep phoning until he told her the farm had been cleared. Then she would simply move herself and the children back in, whatever he said, and start making some sort of pretence at normal life. As normal, anyway, as it could be, in the middle of this investigation.

The result of the DNA tests was expected in the afternoon and after that she would have to give a statement to the media; so far, the discovery of the body had been an inside-page item, only a few lines in the tabloids, but this – a blonde, glamorous young woman missing for fifteen years and found in a shallow grave – would promote a feeding frenzy.

Fleming was determined, though, to sit in on the interview with Laura Harvey, scheduled for half-past eleven. Her first impression of her had been of someone very cool, very controlled, calculating, even; surely someone like that would have worked out that another missing woman would have, at the very least, been of interest to the police? Tam was interviewing her along with DC Charlotte Nisbet; he was always reliable and she didn't miss much – a quick-minded, able young woman with a can-do attitude and a good sense of humour, working already for her sergeant's exams – but even so, if Harvey was holding out on them, her own formidable presence could make a significant difference. With a hunted glance at her watch she began popping open e-mails as if she was shelling peas.

Despite her best efforts, the interview was well under way before Fleming arrived. At the sound of the door opening behind her Laura Harvey turned her head.

It was a shock. Fleming had pigeonholed her as the typical English rose: fair-skinned, blonde, good-looking and very self-assured. Today her blue-grey eyes were swollen to half their size and her skin was puffy and raw from the salt of tears; she was obviously in a fragile state. You could not doubt the genuineness of her grief and there was no sign of the cool control which had made Fleming suspect calculation. Indeed, a look of definite alarm crossed her face as she recognised the new arrival.

Fleming had come with the express intention of using her presence to apply pressure; it was a bit like lifting a sledge-hammer and looking down to see the hapless nut in pieces already. Unfortunately dematerialising wasn't one of her skills, so she did the next best thing by refusing a chair at the table and standing in the farther corner of the room, just out of Laura's line of sight.

MacNee was positively cooing, smiling benevolently the while – not a pretty sight. 'So this was how it came about that you discovered your sister's connection with Chapelton?' He indicated a newspaper article which was lying in front of him on the desk. 'Max Mason contacted you?'

Laura nodded and MacNee, with a glance at his boss, handed the article to her. As Laura went on to describe their meeting and the story Mason had told her, Fleming skimmed through it.

It was good, quality-feature journalism, given added force by the personal dimension. Fleming looked at Laura with new eyes; it came through very clearly that she had still believed her sister was alive and there didn't have to be any other reason for following up the line of enquiry offered to her. The families of Missing Persons always did, even on slighter evidence than this.

DC Nisbet had been listening intently, her sleek dark head on one side. Now she cut in, 'But you had no suspicion when this body was discovered that it might be the explanation for your sister's disappearance?'

Laura was wearing a black sweater with a turquoise and black silk scarf looped round the neck; she began to fiddle with the fringe. 'Not until I saw the gold chain.' She paused. 'You didn't find her ankle bracelet, did you? She always wore that too – it had a little gold dolphin on it.'

MacNee looked at Fleming, who shook her head. 'Not as yet.'

'It doesn't matter.' Her voice was low and still husky from crying. 'I suppose I should have thought of Di but I – I just didn't.'

Fleming waited for MacNee to pursue that, but he only nodded sympathetically. Reluctantly she stepped forward and saw anxiety flare again in the other woman's eyes.

'Laura, why didn't you mention your sister either to me or to Sergeant MacNee when he spoke to you yesterday?'

'It didn't occur to you, maybe?' MacNee suggested helpfully.

Fleming shot him a look of intense irritation. Laura began, 'Yes, that's right,' then catching Fleming's eyes on her, faltered. 'No, it isn't really. Of course it occurred to me when you asked me why I was here. It's absolutely true that I'm doing an article on foot-and-mouth for the *Sunday Tribune*, of course. But if I'd told you about my sister there would have been questions and questions and questions when it wasn't relevant at all. Max seemed so positive it was his mother—'

Still keeping her gaze fixed, Fleming said, 'It's not that there's something you don't want us to know, is it? Because if there is, this would be a good time to tell us. We'll find out anyway.'

Laura shook her head vehemently. 'I'm sure there must be things I haven't told you – my head feels so thick and stupid this morning – but it's not deliberate.'

This time Fleming allowed herself to be convinced. She moved on. 'So – am I right that your family had no contact with your sister after she left home? No idea what sort of relationships she might have had with anyone up here?'

'There was that one phone call to say she was all right but she didn't even say where she was. All I know is what Max told me. He said his aunt had rows with her and his cousin fancied her, but then I'm pretty sure Max had a crush on her himself. She was . . . very attractive.'

'And Jake Mason? Was he attracted to her?' Nisbet asked.

'Max didn't say so. When they were out in Pamplona – I told you about that, didn't I? – it was his father who told Dizzy to get in touch with him if ever she needed a job. But I don't know.'

'Fine. Now, was there anything else, boss?' The glance MacNee gave Fleming was a little nervous, she thought – as well it might be! 'No,' she said. 'I think Laura's had enough for today. Thanks very much. This can't have been easy.'

With evident relief Laura got to her feet. 'I was afraid you might be going to charge me with obstruction or something.' She managed a shaky laugh. 'I'm sorry if I wasted your time, or if I've been less than completely coherent today. I think I'm probably in shock.'

'I'm sure you are,' Fleming agreed. 'We'll arrange to have you taken back to the hotel and there'll be someone there to control the Press – you'll be under siege later, I'm afraid. Someone will be in touch with you to talk about what to do.'

Laura grimaced. 'It does make bad even worse, doesn't it?'

'Try our job!' MacNee said with feeling. 'Now, if there's anything else you think of, however daft – an impression, even, anything that strikes you as maybe a bit out of kilter – share it, will you? Here's my card.'

Laura took it. 'There is one thing,' she said slowly. 'I don't know if I should even mention it—'

'Yes.' All three police officers spoke at once. 'Definitely,' Fleming added.

'It was just – well, Max told me that Scott Thomson was working at Chapelton when he left home so he must have been there when my sister disappeared – was killed. He was behind the bar when Max told Conrad who I was and when I went out a few minutes later he gave me a really strange look. Not – not pleasant.' She gave a half-humorous shudder. 'That's it. That's all, and it's a pretty subjective judgement, of course, to say it was a strange look. I was very tired and probably making too much of it.'

MacNee scribbled something down in his notebook and Fleming said, 'You can leave the evaluation to us. You've told us he was at Chapelton at the significant time, which will save us having to find out. Keep thinking. Sometimes it's some minute observation that's the key to the whole thing.'

As the door shut behind Laura, Fleming turned wrathfully on MacNee. 'And what the hell was *that* about, Tam? Since when have you started suggesting excuses to someone who's being questioned?'

Nisbet grinned. 'Oh, you missed all the best bits.' She mimicked a Glasgow accent. '"Now don't you worry yourself, we're no' as bad as we look! You just sit down here, Laura – you don't mind if we just call you Laura?" Tam MacNee doing the kid-glove treatment – they'll never believe it down the pub!'

Stubborn under the combined assault, Tam protested, 'You'd only to look at her today to know she was a poor wee soul. "*Then gently scan your brother man, Still gentler sister woman*," as the Great Man says.'

He was howled down. 'I'm setting up a fines box for Burns quotations,' Marjory declared. 'Ten pence for a phrase, fifty pence for a whole verse.'

With a flourish Tam produced a £1 coin and gave it to her. 'There you are. That should cover the next couple of days. Though by rights it should be you that's paying for the privilege – cheap at twice the price.'

Brett Mason's expression, which had seemed frozen in a state of perpetual affront, changed to signal fury. She sat bolt upright, her bulky frame overflowing the small chair which was the only seating in her bedroom.

Forced to perch on the bed, DC Nisbet wasn't happy. She was aware of having been offered up to this interview as a sort of sacrificial lamb and her position did nothing to uphold the majesty of the law which she felt she might be required to invoke at any moment. All she'd asked the woman was whether she'd been at Chapelton at the time Diana Warwick disappeared and you'd have thought she wanted to know her knicker size.

'This is – this is outrageous!' Brett declaimed. 'Has it come to this – that I have to defend myself against a charge of *murder*?'

'No, madam,' Nisbet said patiently. 'This, as I explained, is merely a preliminary enquiry to get as much background as we can.'

Somehow she managed to calm Brett down then lead her through the facts, with only the occasional exclamatory diversion. She even persuaded her to admit she remembered the weekend when Warwick had disappeared, if only because she'd had to start looking for another housekeeper, though she insisted she couldn't remember who else of the household might have been there. Truth or expedient amnesia? Nisbet wasn't quite sure.

It had gone better than she could have hoped so far. Now, unfortunately, she had to move on to the more delicate questions about relationships and personalities. 'She was a very attractive girl, wasn't she?' she began, as she thought, uncontroversially, and was quite unprepared for the vehemence of the response.

'Little tramp! A slut around the house – hadn't the first idea about running a gentleman's establishment, spent all her time throwing herself at anything in trousers.' Tiny flecks of spittle appeared at the side of Brett's mouth. 'The number of times I spoke to my brother about her, wanted to sack her, but oh no! he wouldn't hear of it. I even sacked her myself once and he actually overruled me! And of course, after that there was no holding that trollop, once she knew Jake had taken her part against me, his own sister—'

She stopped suddenly as if she had only just heard what she was saying. She produced a handkerchief to wipe her mouth but her eyes above it were wild and staring.

Nisbet tried not to make it obvious that she was measuring the distance to the door. The woman looked as if she might lose it completely at any moment, but this was useful stuff. She went on carefully, 'Was there a relationship between her and your brother?'

Brett tossed her head and laughed unconvincingly. 'My brother? Have a relationship with a woman of that sort? Certainly not, any more than my son would, for all that she did her best to ensnare him, flashing those big blue eyes, oh-so-innocent, getting him to help her, setting him to dancing to her tune! Oh, I had to put a stop to that, I can tell you!'

She was talking louder and louder, hectic colour appearing in her cheeks and her eyes becoming almost glazed.

Nisbet swallowed hard. 'How did you do that, Mrs Mason?' She put the question as gently and neutrally as she could, but the other woman reacted as if she had been brought to her senses by a slap in the face.

She looked confused for a moment. 'What – what are you suggesting? Young woman, if you are taking my words to be some sort of admission of guilt . . . I spoke to her, that was all. Is that quite clear? Told her to leave my son, and my brother, alone. Told her she should go before she caused more trouble. And I was glad when she did. Glad! Why shouldn't I be?' She glared at the detective; the white foam had appeared again at the corners of her mouth and her impressive bosom had begun to heave.

'I – I see.' A storm was clearly about to break and Nisbet couldn't see how she could avoid it. Oh well – two steps to the door, three at the most . . .

'So you had a row with her, then?'

Brett crumpled dramatically in her seat, then burst into noisy sobs. 'I won't be bullied in this way! You invade my room, you insinuate the most dreadful things, you victimise a helpless woman! Oh, you'll pay for this, I tell you.'

Despite the affecting sounds there were no tears. The handkerchief was wielded to great effect but this time the eyes were hard and spiteful. 'My son is your superior officer – what do you think he'll have to say to this? And your commanding officer too. You'll be the one with questions to answer by the time I finish with you. Now, get out of my bedroom before I summon someone to have you thrown out.'

'Yes, madam.' Nisbet got up and went to the door. 'I shall pass on your complaint to Detective Inspector Fleming.'

Outside, she sagged against the wall of the corridor.

Complaints were always a nuisance though in this context she reckoned she could rely on Big Marge to sort it out.

But that woman really was something else! Were her admissions naïve or was she so totally unbalanced she didn't know what she was saying? There was one thing certain – the next interview would have to be conducted in controlled surroundings. And she'd taken her punishment; someone else's turn next time.

Tam MacNee was interviewing too, in the back corner of the dining-room away from the cameras of the Press gathered outside. Screens had been put around one of the Tudor-style dining-room tables though these couldn't, of course, filter out the constant noise of telephones and conversations.

Across from him, sitting on one of the imitation wheel-back chairs, Scott Thomson's face was pale under the flaming red hair and his disabled arm lay awkwardly across his knees, but he was leaning back in a pantomime of ease, his lip curled in a sneer. 'It's aye the same with you lot – something happens, do you lean on the toffs in the big house? Not a chance. You're away to pin it on the farmhand who has to work for his living.'

MacNee surveyed him without enthusiasm. It was four o'clock in the afternoon and the man had been at the whisky; he could smell it on his breath and hear it in the faint slurring of words and see it, too, in the cocky attitude of the man. Oh well, drunks were never a problem, you just got your retaliation in first.

He leaned across the table, sticking his chin out aggressively. 'See, you, let's get this straight. A girl's dead. Are you saying we shouldn't try to find the bastard that killed her? Or do you just want us to lock folk up because they've got money and you're pouring the money you've got straight over your throat?'

Assailed by raw belligerence, Thomson recoiled, then sat up in his chair. 'I didn't – I wasn't—' he stammered.

'Right. You didn't. You weren't. Let's start again. You were stockman at Chapelton when Diana Warwick came to work there?'

'Aye.'

'What was she like?'

'Just a lassie.' He shifted uncomfortably. 'It was years ago, right? She wasn't there long anyway.'

'Where did she stay? In the big house?'

MacNee saw the man hesitate, as if trying to calculate what would be made of his reply. 'Come on, come on. It's not that difficult,' he hustled him.

'No. There's a flat the housekeepers live in.'

'Whereabouts?'

Again the hesitation. 'Above one of the steadings.'

'And where did you stay?'

He licked dry lips. 'Stockman's flat.'

'Don't waste my time. Next door, was it? Neighbours? Were you married then?'

'So what if I wasn't?'

'Good friends, maybe?'

'What are you getting at?'

MacNee could see he was nervous. That was the easy part – he'd done his best to make him nervous, after all. Working out if there were other reasons too was the hard part and getting him to open up about them if there were was the hardest of all. Intimidation had worked so far. It usually did.

He leaned forward again. 'Will you not take a telling? I'm here to find out about Diana Warwick and the more you jink about trying not to give me the answers the more suspicious I get. Next step's having you in for questioning under caution.'

It was amazing how fear could sober you up. There was

no slurring of the words now. 'OK, OK. She was – trouble. There were always kind of –' he searched for the word – 'goings-on around her. She had something—'

'Sex?' MacNee suggested brutally.

Thomson gave a short laugh. 'Oh aye, sex right enough. But it wasn't just that. She kind of – dodged people, if you get me. Drove them daft, not knowing where they were. There were always quarrels.'

'Who was she sleeping with?'

'Everybody. Nobody. You tell me.'

'You?'

Again he laughed harshly. 'Me? Her and me? See my hands?' He turned his good hand palm uppermost to show the scars of outdoor labouring. 'You think a woman like that would so much as let me touch her – even when both of them worked? His mouth twisted in bitterness. 'But them up at the big house—'

'Jake? Max? Conrad?'

He shrugged.

'Were there comings and goings to the flat at night?'

'Not that I ever saw.'

But. He didn't quite say it; the word hung on the air, though. 'What were you going to say?'

'Say? I said it.'

MacNee changed tack. 'What did you think when you knew who Laura Harvey was?'

He was taken by surprise. 'Think? Well, nothing.'

'Don't muck me about. You were rattled, weren't you? Giving her funny looks?'

'Who told you that? I – I was just interested, that's all.' He had started to sweat.

MacNee moved in for the kill. 'Look, Scott, I'm not wanting to get you in trouble. Did you have a thing going with her?'

'I told you! I'll swear on the Bible . . .'

MacNee laughed. 'You may have to, at that. Your best bet's not to try to be too smart.'

'I know that—'

'So what was it you didn't say just now?'

The man groaned. 'If I tell you, will you believe what I say's all there was to it?'

'I'm not in the guarantees business. Sook it and see.'

'I saw her going out of her flat once or twice, late, just in her pyjamas.'

'Pyjamas? This was – what, December, January? Where did she go?'

'I never saw. It wasn't long – she'd head down towards that old maze then be back just a wee while later. Ten minutes, maybe.'

'On her own? Just in her pyjamas? No coat?'

'That's right.'

'And you never went out to speak to her?'

He shook his head violently. 'So help me God, I never.'

'A pretty lassie, outside alone in her night-things and you never went near her?'

'I knew I should have kept my gob shut!' he cried. 'That's what you've been at the whole time, trying to bloody trap me. I never touched her. But you'll not believe me, will you?'

MacNee's smile was mirthless. 'Oh, don't let it get to you, laddie. We don't believe anyone at this stage in the game.'

Laura stood to one side of her window, screened by the curtains. The car park and the little garden in front of the inn were thronged with cars and people, some police but mostly Press and photographers. She felt, as the inspector had said, under siege.

On the advice of the police Press Officer, she had faced the battery of flashing, rattling cameras – an ordeal in itself

– and read out the banal form of words which had been suggested to her. She had even handed over the photo of Dizzy
– laughing, vivid – which she'd brought with her to jog memories, when she was still so hopeful of finding her.

'They'll maybe leave you alone after that,' the Press Officer
had said, though not hopefully, and of course they hadn't.

It was partly the fact that all the chief actors in the drama
were cooped up in this one place, and the crime scene was
still off-limits, although there was a rumour that by tomorrow
Chapelton would be declared free of infection and the Masons
would be allowed back home, which might take some of the
heat off. Only some, of course; the police operation would
be based at the inn for an indefinite time, and from the questions the journalists had shouted to her – which Laura hadn't
stayed to answer – they wouldn't be satisfied until they had
some sort of 'human story' on her too.

One way and another, living in the hotel had become
something of an ordeal. Despite the pressure Lisa Thomson
was under she'd been very good about bringing meals up to
Laura so that she needn't come downstairs, but the little bedroom was beginning to seem like a prison.

For Lisa, though, it was clear things had taken a turn for
the better. She was looking years younger than she had at
the beginning of the week.

'I'm real sorry about your sister,' she said to Laura when
she came up with her supper tray, 'but I have to say this is
just a godsend for us. I've been that worried about the money
but this'll see us through.'

Laura seized the opportunity. 'I'm glad about that. You
work so hard to make us all comfortable. I hope you won't
mind, but with all this I've been thinking of looking for somewhere else.'

Lisa nodded understandingly. 'If you're having to stay on
a bit there's some nice holiday cottages with no one in them

a couple of miles down the road. Quiet, you know – you'd be private and none of that lot,' she jerked her head dismissively towards the window, 'would know where you were. I know the owners – they'd be glad to have you. I could give them a call if you like.'

It looked like the answer to her problems. Laura didn't want to leave the neighbourhood before she knew more about what had happened to her sister and she had a job to do, too; she'd already got some good material to form the basis of her article. But it would be wonderful to have her own private space where she wouldn't have to spend her time dodging the press and rebuffing Max. He was becoming very tiresome, over-attentive and solicitous in a way that made her uncomfortable.

His latest suggestion was that the Minotaur, as he persisted in calling his father, had killed his own mother, then Dizzy: a convenient theory, since the man couldn't speak up in his own defence. It seemed the police were working on those lines, though: according to Lisa and the new waitress, they hadn't stopped digging up the field.

Marjory Fleming yawned and looked at her watch. Five o'clock – perhaps she'd go down to the canteen and have a cup of tea. And maybe a sandwich; she couldn't remember having lunch so probably she hadn't.

Just as she got up she noticed another e-mail arrive; with a sigh she decided she'd better check it.

It was from the pathology lab, with their post-mortem report as an attachment. Her sandwich forgotten, she clicked it open and scanned it rapidly.

Then she sat back in her chair. 'Good grief!' she said blankly.

13

'It's an absolutely brilliant shop – The Band Box, it's called,' the large, jolly girl said to her companion as they walked along the narrow streets near Gloucester Cathedral. 'Designer clothes, a fraction of the price, and the woman who runs it has perfect taste. She can always find exactly the right thing and she won't let you take anything that doesn't suit you. There was this orange Max Mara skirt I really fancied, quite short and very fitting—'

Her companion, built on rather less generous lines, gave her a candid look. 'If she talked you out of it, she's your best friend.'

'You're not joking. I told Jeremy about it and he said it was a deal-breaker – he's on for the loving and cherishing bit but if tight orange skirts come into it the whole thing's off. Here we are – oh!'

She stopped outside the shop. As usual, there was only one item displayed in the window: a beautifully cut coat in silver-grey wool, edged with misty-grey mock fur.

'Ooh, *lovely!*' the other woman cooed.

'Yes, but it's closed! I don't understand that.' She looked at her watch. 'Ten to ten, and it's supposed to open at nine-thirty, look.' She pointed to the discreet card giving opening hours fixed to the window, then shaded her eyes and peered in through the glass of the door.

Inside the clothes hung on their rails, neatly arranged as always. The door to the back office was standing open; there were no lights on and no one was there. Disappointed, she turned away, pulling a face. 'That's such a shame! You'd have loved it.'

'Perhaps she's just running late,' her friend suggested. 'We could always come back in the afternoon.'

'Why not? I tell you what – let's go on to Cheltenham. There's a really good place in Montpellier. We could lunch there too, and drop in here again on the way home.'

Laura picked up her suitcase and laptop, checked quickly round to make sure she hadn't left anything, then squared her shoulders as she left the room. Getting from the hotel to her car was going to be an unpleasant, even frightening experience. She'd checked from the window and they were still there, several men and a couple of women, some with cameras draped round them, hanging about looking cold and bored.

Inside, it seemed quieter this morning, with fewer policemen around. Lisa had her bill prepared – a very modest one – and Laura was waiting at the desk while her card was processed when she heard a sudden flurry of activity outside. There were shouted questions, the slam of a car door, and a moment later Conrad Mason appeared in the hall, his good-looking face dark with irritation.

Seeing her, he stopped. The black look vanished and a very charming smile took its place. 'Laura! You remember we met, very briefly—'

'Of course.' She smiled back, then jerked her head towards the door. 'How many of them are there out there?'

'Too many,' he said feelingly. 'But then, you know what they say about a thousand journalists at the bottom of the sea – a good start.'

'I'm bracing myself.'

He glanced down at her suitcase. 'You're leaving?'

Laura nodded. 'It's been a bit difficult here.'

'Yes, of course. It would be.' He studied her face; he had hazel eyes with long dark lashes, she noticed. 'You've had a hard time, haven't you? I'm sorry.'

She was finding sympathy very difficult to handle at the moment; it wasn't easy to say lightly, 'Thanks. No, it hasn't been much fun.'

Lisa came back with the slip for her signature; as she scribbled it Conrad said, 'Heading back to London, then?'

'No, I'm staying in the area. I've been commissioned to do an article on the effects of the foot-and-mouth epidemic so I'll be around for a little while yet.'

'Where are you going to be?'

She hesitated; she had had it in her mind not to give out her new address but she'd have to inform the police so it would be simple enough for him to find out. Before she could speak, he laughed. 'I promise not to betray your whereabouts to the Press even for hard cash.'

'I'm sure you wouldn't.' She smiled and told him. Then she paused again. 'Perhaps you would keep it to yourself, though. I – I'd appreciate a bit of peace and quiet.'

The corners of his mouth twitched but he said gravely, 'Absolutely. Changing the subject completely, how's Max?'

She burst out laughing. There was no doubt about it, Conrad Mason was a very attractive and amusing man. Still, she said only, 'I'm sure he's fine,' then thanked Lisa and went to pick up her cases.

'No, no, let me.' Conrad got there first. 'Now, I'll give you an escort out to the car. Stick close behind me – don't get separated.'

Opening the door was the signal for a renewed burst of activity; a dozen people converged on them and once again there was the rattling click of automatic shutters and the glare of flashes. Conrad's big frame sheltered her from the worst;

she walked blindly behind him as they closed in, ignoring questions, offers and even threats.

'Talk to me, Laura – we'll make it worth your while!'

'Where are you going now? You might as well tell us, we'll find out anyway.'

'How do you feel about your sister being dug up? Give us a quote or we'll make one up!'

'We make them up anyway.' That raised a laugh, but Laura was in no mood to be amused.

They reached the car. Conrad opened the door for her, turning so that his bulk blocked the opening. He handed in her luggage then said quietly, 'It looks as if they might follow you. Position your car so it's right in front of mine and I'll tail you out. When we're on the single-track road I'll stop and block it. You carry on to your cottage as quickly as you can.'

Gratefully she nodded and started up her car as he went to his, a silver-grey Jaguar XJ6. A photographer was leaning on her bonnet, thrusting his camera against the windscreen, but she moved off anyway and he jumped back. She could see two or three people hurrying over to their cars but as she drove past Conrad swung the nose of his to within inches of her bumper. He gave her a thumbs-up sign and she accelerated towards the exit. With him right behind her there was no real need for haste but her own sense of urgency prompted her to take to the narrow road at speed.

Even with a nervously churning stomach, it was wonderful to feel she was escaping. It was a cold, bright morning; by the side of the road the grass-blades were outlined by hoarfrost and the edges of puddles crisp with a glassy skim of ice. The low, windswept trees were etched against the pale sky with the clarity and precision of steel engraving.

Behind her she could see a couple of cars following Conrad. There was only about another half-mile to go before they reached the wider road, but he still hadn't stopped; she only hoped he hadn't changed his mind for some reason.

She reached the cattle-grid, glancing anxiously behind her, then realised of course what his plan was. With rough ground on either side, there was the risk that the following cars might go off-road to get round him if they saw her escaping. Instead, he had stopped right on the grid, completely blocking the opening; short of breaking through the fence there was no way round. They wouldn't be pleased, but something told her Conrad would positively relish that. Smiling at the thought, she accelerated away.

Lisa's directions had been clear and she had no difficulty in finding Burnside Cottages. A mile and a half along a tiny side road, it was a long, low building gleaming with recently whitewashed harling, which had been divided into four separate units. It was an idyllic spot, with access by way of a little stone bridge over a pebbly stream and a view of evergreen forest and moorland. When Laura stepped out of the car all she could hear was the steely chuckle of water over the stones of the burn. She drew in a long, deep breath. It felt as if she hadn't been breathing properly for days.

She hadn't realised quite how much she'd been feeling oppressed. Even before yesterday's terrible discovery, the virulent hostility of the Mason family and the unpleasantness of the drunken landlord had poisoned the atmosphere, despite Lisa's kindliness. Laura remembered, with a shiver, the crow which had flapped in apparent warning across her path before she arrived that night at the hotel; here, in this pretty place, there were no such omens.

> 'This castle hath a pleasant seat; the air
> Nimbly and sweetly recommends itself . . .'

She frowned. That was *Macbeth* too, wasn't it, and there was something about that speech . . .

But the owner of the cottages, Mrs MacNab, was coming out to meet her now, a plump and amiable lady who tried for solemnity appropriate to Laura's sad circumstances, though cheerfulness would keep breaking out. Even the disastrous state of the holiday market didn't seem to depress her.

'Och well,' she said comfortably, 'we've had the good times so you just have to thole the bad ones till the good times come back.'

'Thole' was a new one on Laura but she recognised and saluted the philosophy. She'd have to do a bit of 'tholing' herself over the next bit but she could almost believe in that brighter future, here under the benign sway of Mrs MacNab.

The cottage was simple but comfortable with a kitchen-dining-sitting-room, a bathroom and two small bedrooms at the back. There were brightly checked curtains in red and cream, red covers for beds and chairs, and on the pine table a folded tea-towel which exuded a wonderful warm, sweet smell.

'I just put up a few girdle scones when I knew you were coming,' Mrs MacNab explained, 'and there's a few things in the fridge you'll be needing. If you've any messages you just let me know – I'm a couple of miles further on down the road here so I pass the door on my way into Kirkluce. I could easy pick them up for you at the supermarket.'

She trotted off, leaving Laura to wonder vaguely what messages could possibly be waiting for her at the supermarket. She sank down on to one of the chairs which faced a window looking out over the tranquil landscape. She should really unpack, but she'd just relax here for a few minutes first. All those tears must have been cathartic; she felt drained and peaceful now.

Seconds later, she was sound asleep.

*   *   *

'Gored?' MacNee said incredulously. 'Gored by a bull? And I suppose it just dug a hole with its hooves and covered her up so no one would know?'

'Don't think I didn't point that out,' Fleming said. 'I phoned to discuss it and you know how these conversations go with the experts – if you sound doubtful they just shrug their shoulders. All the pathologist would say is that the wound was consistent with the damage a bull's horn – or a cow's – would inflict – sharp at the point, wider at the base, and the diameter measures up too. He'd seen one very recently – you remember there was that tragedy a fortnight ago with one of the government vets – and it looked just the same.'

MacNee was unconvinced. 'Sounds a gey fishy story to me! I wouldn't have thought you could tell, after she'd been in the ground fifteen years.'

'Parts of the body were pretty much skeletal according to the report, but it's peaty ground and the torso was quite well preserved – skin almost tanned, it says here.' She pointed to the print-out on her desk. 'She was unlucky, seemingly – if the blow had glanced off her ribs she might have escaped but it went straight between them at an angle to pierce the heart. So – instantaneous death.'

'And then what?'

Fleming snorted. '"Then what's" aren't his business. Quite trenchant, he was – "not his job to speculate". What he did say, though, was that the position of the wound was odd. I mean, what would you do if a bull was coming at you?'

'I wouldn't stop to ask him what he thought about the next Old Firm match.'

'Exactly. You'd be running away, with your back turned. This was direct and frontal. And the other thing was that with the vet there had been other damage – bones broken by trampling, other goring injuries. He said that the soft tissue had disappeared from other parts of the body so he couldn't be absolutely sure about flesh wounds. But there were certainly no broken bones.'

MacNee seized on this. 'If you ask me, it's just a fancy theory. It's been something that's the same shape as a bull's horn, like a pole or something, and he's linking up the two.'

'Maybe. Still, he's suggested it so we'd better follow it up. Have you spoken to Max Mason?'

'Someone has. There'll be a report somewhere in there.' He indicated the computer.

Fleming sighed. 'There's about a hundred reports in there, most of them completely irrelevant, and I'm supposed not just to read them but remember what they said. Away you go and have a word with Max. It was winter when it happened – where would the bulls have been? You could check with the stockman as well.'

She watched him go with a certain amount of envy. There had been something to be said for the sergeant's job where you got to go out and talk to people directly. Reading reports about what they'd said was a bit like working one of those fairground machines where you have to use a grab to pick up the prize you want but are constantly frustrated by the clumsiness of the implement.

She opened one, an interview with a local shopkeeper, but it seemed little more than 'What I guess might have happened and how I would do your job'. Her mind went back to the report.

Did she believe it could be a bull? The position of the wound was against it, and the lack of any further attack. Though certainly, if there was someone else there they might have intervened, distracted the animal before it could do anything else. And of course someone else had been involved, someone who had buried the body.

Why would you do that, if it was simply a tragic accident? Any serious agricultural injury to an employee had to be

reported, of course, and in the case of a fatality the proceedings were likely to be both worrying and expensive, but
to go the shallow-grave route instead seemed a hugely dis-
proportionate response. And that was leaving aside the whole
question of morality.

She tapped her front tooth with her pen, a habit she had
when she was thinking. Then she reached for her phone.

'Can you try to locate Sergeant Mason, please? He's on
leave at the moment but I want a word with him as soon as
possible.'

'Stuff happens.' Max Mason shrugged. Like Scott Thomson
in the same situation, he was leaning back in the dining-
room chair, though this time it looked like a calculated attitude rather than a gesture of defiance. His facial expression
suggested contemptuous indifference.

The temptation to say, 'Don't care was made to care,' and
wipe it off with a clip round the jaw was strong, but Tam
MacNee said only, 'So the feeling I got that you were knocked
sideways when you heard about it wouldn't be right, then?'

Max's reaction had been a niggle at the back of his mind;
he wanted to prod him about it before he moved on to the
questions he'd been commissioned to ask.

'Well, normally,' Max drawled, 'if I'd been told someone
I knew had been found decaying quietly in one of our fields
I'd have taken it pretty casually. As you do. But you may
recall it happened when I'd thought it was my mother and
actually I was quite fond of her, strange as that may seem.
You haven't found her yet, have you?'

He scored with that one; MacNee gritted his teeth. 'No,
we haven't. You're still claiming she was murdered by your
father?'

Max shrugged again. 'It's more than likely, isn't it? He
killed Diana, obviously—'

'That's rather less obvious to us than it is to you.' The snotty little bastard was taking control of the interview; it was throwing MacNee off his stride. Hoping to swing the balance his way, he hurried into an ill-judged question. 'What if I suggested she'd been gored by one of the bulls?'

There was no doubt that he'd succeeded in taking him by surprise, but not usefully. Max's eyes flickered, but he only said, 'A bull? You could tell that, after all this time?'

'Oh, you'd be surprised what we can find out. Did she help with looking after them?'

'Diana? Of course not.'

'Would the bulls have been out in the fields then at that time of year – winter?'

There was a fractional pause, then he said heartily, 'Oh, certainly. Absolutely. Welsh Blacks are a very hardy breed. That's why my grandfather chose them.'

MacNee was kicking himself now. He should have asked that question first; the bull theory was a nice, convenient one and since Mason had said the girl didn't work with the beasts, the only place she could have come into contact with one was in an open field. Maybe it was a truthful reply – maybe!

Max was prepared to be expansive now. 'The field she was in was Satan's field. He was a big brute with a nasty temper – there was trouble with him before, I'm sure, though I was too young to know the details. Conrad could probably tell you.'

'"Satan" could hardly have buried her,' MacNee pointed out drily.

'But my father could!' Max was leaning forward eagerly now. 'He wouldn't want a fuss—'

'Seems a bit extreme, surely?'

'He *is* extreme – anyone could tell you that! He's not normal – never has been.'

'That's a nice neat theory anyway, isn't it, seeing we can't talk to the man and see for ourselves.' The son's eagerness to condemn his father was sickening. 'So what about your mother, then?'

'My – my mother?'

At last, a chink in his armour of cockiness. 'You said he'd killed your mother, and this girl. If he didn't kill the girl, if it was an accident . . .'

It was obviously an effort to take up his offhand attitude again. 'So? Maybe he just drove her out, after all.'

'But she never contacted you, all these years? Can't have missed you much, can she?'

Max's face changed. 'You can't say that!' His voice was rising. 'She – she would have. I left home myself, she didn't know where I was—'

He'd got him on the raw. MacNee said smoothly, 'A year later, wasn't it? That's a long time for a mother to ignore her only son—'

'Shut up, shut up!' Max yelled. He jumped up, knocking over the chair he had been sitting on, and stormed out.

MacNee stared after him ruefully. There was such a thing as being too successful in upsetting a witness; he hadn't covered himself with glory there. He emerged from behind the screens to an ironic burst of applause from the officers working in the dining-room.

Looking for Thomson, he went through to the bar. There were no lunchtime customers but Thomson was there, reading a red-top newspaper with a glass half-full of whisky on the counter beside him.

At the sight of MacNee he stiffened. 'What are you after now? I've told you everything I know.'

'Are the bulls at Chapelton brought inside for the winter?'

Thomson looked surprised. 'What do you want to know that for?' Then, as he got no reply, he added grudgingly,

'They're not usually. If it went below freezing I'd my orders to bring them in.'

'Right.' MacNee pondered the answer. If they could find out when, exactly, the girl had disappeared there'd be a record of the weather somewhere. 'Do you remember a bull called Satan?'

He wasn't prepared for the outburst of obscenity, but when the reason for it emerged he could only sympathise. It explained a lot, too, about Thomson's attitude to his former employers.

At the mention of an attack on Diana Warwick he only said flatly, 'I don't know anything about it,' and stuck to that.

MacNee wasn't having much luck with his interviews today. He tried another tack. 'Would she have been likely to have any contact with the bulls?'

For a moment he thought he wasn't going to get an answer to that either, then Thomson said, 'She was daft about them, like they all were. Specially that brute. It's like it was a god, or something. I'll tell you what Jake Mason used to say: "He's killed his man." Like he was boasting about it. What does that say about the rotten bastard?'

What indeed? The interviews might not have gone according to plan but MacNee had plenty to think about as he drove back to Police Headquarters.

'Of course!' Conrad Mason had the air of one who has at last seen the obvious. 'Of course, that would be exactly what happened!'

Fleming had explained the goring theory, hedging it about with every sort of caution; she was taken aback to find it hailed with such immediate enthusiasm. She raised her eyebrows. 'It would leave an awful lot of questions unanswered, Conrad.'

'I bet I can answer most of them.' Mason got up as if he

was too excited to stay still. 'You don't understand. If it was Satan – that was the bull that always lived in the field you found her in – he was a thousand kilos of dead meat. He'd killed a man already; somehow or other my grandfather saved him that time, probably with huge payouts to the man's family. But Satan was a champion, a superb example of the breed. He was still a young bull then, worth a fortune in stud fees, but it wasn't just that. My uncle idolised him.'

'Are you really saying he'd have buried a girl's body, taken the risk of a long prison sentence, just to save a bull? Hardly a normal reaction—'

'That's the point.' Conrad sat down again and leaned across the desk. 'Look, he was a risk-taker by nature. You don't do Pamplona bull-runs if you haven't that sort of temperament. And he simply wasn't normal where bulls are concerned – perhaps none of us are. Particularly with Satan – he used to follow Jake around like a puppy when he was a calf and he'd still come up to the rail to be petted, right up to the time of Jake's stroke. You know the way people are about keeping lions and tigers as pets? Well, Jake felt the same about having this incredibly powerful, dangerous animal behaving like a pet lamb. He doted on Satan.'

'Did you say up to the time of his stroke? Is the bull still alive, then?'

'Was,' Mason said bitterly. She saw the grief and anger in his face; his uncle was not the only one who had loved the creature.

'Of course. I'm sorry. I do hear what you're saying, Conrad, but it's not really as easy to explain away as all that. If a bull gores someone, it doesn't stop at that. It follows up the attack, tosses the body, tramples it—'

He frowned. 'Yes, but if there was someone else there to drive it off – and no one better than my uncle, as I said.'

'Mmm.' It was plausible, certainly. 'The other thing the

pathologist flagged up as strange was the wound's position. Right in the front, a wound to the heart.'

Mason wasn't so sure about that. Fleming watched him closely. It was his job to deduce what happened from evidence and he was good at it; in this situation, where there was a solution which would clear him of suspicion, he was more than capable of reversing the process. Come to that, it was hardly unknown for a detective to decide on a conclusion and look for the facts to fit it. She waited with interest to hear what he would say.

'The front,' he said. 'You'd expect her to be running away, wouldn't you? I wonder . . .' Then his brow cleared. 'Oh God, I think I know what this was about! The bull-running.'

'At Pamplona? What on earth has that got to do with it?'

'You know that was where my uncle met her?'

'Yes, I think so. I read it somewhere.' She gestured vaguely at some papers on her desk.

'I didn't go that year. My pathetic cousin Max did, and gave himself airs because he'd been with my uncle when he'd rescued Di from some drunken Spaniards. Anyway, Di was always talking about the bull-run – most wonderful experience of her life and all that. She'd actually touched a bull – that's suicidal. And if she'd tried it out on Satan, thinking that because he was bulky he'd be easy game, she could have got caught out – she'd come up from behind, then he'd whirl round and catch her in the ribs. See?'

He made a magician's triumphant gesture, palms uppermost. Perhaps that was the only reason why Fleming felt she had been subjected to a performance. She said stubbornly, 'It still seems to me an unlikely thing to do. Pamplona's one thing, Scotland in winter's quite another.'

Mason made an impatient movement. 'Look,' he said, then stopped as if he had changed his mind about what he was going to say.

'Yes?' she prompted him.

'I've done it myself. When I was a kid, of course, and I wasn't dumb enough to try to touch him.'

'And you told Diana about this?'

'Yes. Yes, of course. And it's just the sort of thing she would do.'

'Did she ever say she was going to try it?'

The hesitation was fractionally too long. In an interview you could often get more idea of what a person was thinking from the gaps than from what they said; Fleming was almost certain he was working out which would be the safest reply. 'No,' he said at last. 'No, of course not. I'd have tried to stop her. Not that it would have made any difference – she was that sort of girl.

'It does hang together, you know,' he urged. 'And of course,' he gave a rueful smile, 'I really would like to think that even if my uncle was every sort of fool he wasn't a murderer.'

Oh yes, nicely calculated little touch of family feeling there. He was waiting for her response, but she could see that he had decided already what it would be. He was going to be disappointed. 'You've suggested one plausible scenario,' she began, and saw his face change.

'Surely you can see it's the obvious one?' he insisted.

'One plausible scenario,' she repeated. 'There's a lot to consider before it's accepted as the right one.'

'Like?'

She shot him an icy glare and he retracted hastily. 'Sorry, boss. That sounded rude.'

'Yes, it did. As I was saying, until it's accepted you're still a suspect. This isn't a professional conference about the case, Conrad. You've been in a position to give me very helpful information, I'm grateful and I will consider it. I won't discuss any other aspect of it with you, and you are still on leave. Officers working on the case have been instructed that you must not be given information about it, so please don't ask them.'

He was, she saw, very angry. 'You can't recognise the truth when it's under your nose,' he said thickly. 'Or is it just that you can't bear to admit that one of your underlings is smarter than you?'

'Mason—' she said, a threat in her voice.

'Oh, I'm going before I do something I really will regret. You've got all the cards – I'm not going to give you the satisfaction of busting me.'

He slammed the door behind him. Marjory put her head in her hands and groaned. Whatever the outcome of the case – and it was undoubtedly a tidy solution, and a cheap solution too, which would certainly appeal to her superiors – he'd blown it now. He was becoming more and more volatile; he had a lot riding on this, of course, but it was alarming that he hadn't been able to see that she couldn't possibly simply accept his version of events and move to close the file. He was often right in his deductions, but she had been worried lately that he was increasingly showing a lack of objectivity about his own theories, a serious fault in a detective and the quickest way to miscarriages of justice.

She'd have to move him on. All being well, he could return to the Force but she'd suggest he went to Traffic. He wouldn't like that, though – and heaven help the first chippy motorist!

'It's still closed. What a shame!'

It was four o'clock; there were lights on now in the other shops, but The Band Box was in darkness. The two women sighed, shrugged and moved away.

14

The tap on the door startled her. It was almost dark; Laura had the lamps on as she worked at the table on her laptop but she hadn't drawn the curtains yet. To anyone outside, it would be like looking on to a lighted stage, and suddenly she was very aware that there was no one at all in the cottages on either side of her. Looking out from the inside, the windows were black and blank.

The door had small glass panes in the top half and as she crossed towards it she flicked the switch for the outside light and saw that it was Conrad Mason who was standing there. Her face cleared and she opened the door.

It was raining again, soft, persistent, wetting rain, forming a misty halo round the light. He was wearing a thick navy jacket but his curly hair was starting to cling to his head.

'Goodness, you're wet!' she exclaimed. 'Come in quickly!'

He stepped inside, shaking himself like a wet dog. 'Drookit,' he agreed. 'And that's just coming from the car. Still, we should be used to it by now. Just remember to check your feet every night to make sure you haven't started growing webs between the toes.'

Laura laughed. 'There's a peg there for your coat. Would you like a cup of tea?'

'Thanks. I just came to see that you'd settled in all right and that no one had found your hideaway.'

'No, I've had a wonderfully peaceful afternoon. Would you like one of Mrs MacNab's scones?'

He sat down at the table. 'Can you ask? They're famous locally. Women at coffee mornings have been known to come to blows for them at the baking stall.'

The kettle was boiling now; she made tea in a little blue pot and brought it across with a couple of mugs and the celebrated scones, then sat down herself opposite.

'I don't suppose you're allowed to say anything much,' she said hesitantly, 'but can I ask you what's happening now?'

He made no attempt to conceal his anger and bitterness. 'Oh, I'm not permitted to know what's happening in the corridors of power at Kirkluce Police Headquarters. I'm a suspect, you see.'

'A suspect?' She shouldn't have been stunned, but she was. That was Max again; somehow his certainty had fixed in her head the notion that the shadowy Jake was the killer. But naturally, Conrad must be a suspect, and Max too, and Scott Thomson, and even, she supposed, Conrad's mother who had quarrelled with her sister. Suddenly there was a very cold feeling in the pit of her stomach.

'Ridiculous, isn't it?' he laughed shortly. 'You'd think they'd know—'

The hammering on the door was such a shock that they both jumped. 'What the hell,' Conrad exclaimed, jumping up, then, 'Oh God, Max! I might have known.'

The outside light was still on and they could see him clearly, wearing a rakish wide-brimmed rainproof hat and a brown caped Drizabone coat. Laura opened the door to let him in.

He ignored her. '"I'm just going back to Kirkluce now" – oh, sure! I knew this would be where you were going, you lying bastard,' he greeted his cousin, scowling. He took off his hat, throwing it down on a chair as if it were a gauntlet.

Conrad had a considerable advantage in height; he used it now to look down contemptuously at the shorter, slighter man. 'Oh, I think it counts as mere courtesy, Max. The lady didn't want people to know where she was, so how could I betray her confidence? If I'd known you were following me I wouldn't have come here. But what took you so long? Missed me turning off, did you? That would be typical incompetence.'

Max coloured but said only, 'She didn't mean me, did you, Laura?' He put the question with a brief, sideways look towards her but didn't wait for an answer. 'Laura's *my* friend. So why don't you butt out instead of elbowing your way in, trying to ruin everything for me, the way you've always done?'

'I shouldn't think she'll want to be "your" friend, after this display. Most women have a preference for adults, not spoiled children who haven't grown past the toddler tantrum stage. You'll bear me out in that, Laura?'

'You don't know what he's like, Laura. If you did, you'd tell him to sod off—'

It was almost funny. Almost, but not quite. Even when they were addressing Laura, they weren't looking at her, confronting each other with their eyes locked like dogs sizing one another up for a fight. The threat of physical violence was thick in the air.

Defusing explosive situations had been all in a day's work in the Women's Refuge in New York; she'd never had to do it in her own sitting-room, though, and she would prefer not to have to do it now. With some resentment, Laura deployed her professional skills.

She stepped between them, breaking the locked gaze with her body so that no one had to lose face by yielding. 'Let's take this calmly, shall we?' she said, her voice quiet but steely with authority. 'This is my space and I don't choose to have it used for "who blinks first" contests.'

It worked. She saw the rigidity of the men's bodies relax at the same time and Conrad half-turned in a classic 'de-escalation of threat' movement. Max, being the physically weaker, was slower to abandon his defensive pose.

'I'm sorry, Laura,' Conrad said smoothly, meeting her eyes this time. '*I* should have known better.'

The faint, mocking emphasis on the word was deliberately provocative and Max was provoked. 'That's so like him, Laura, the apology that isn't—'

It was unbelievable. They were kids who hadn't left the nursery; they didn't need a psychotherapist's skills, they needed Nanny.

'Be quiet, both of you,' Laura snapped. 'Go and sit down and neither of you say another word. It's my turn now.' *And no kicking each other under the table or I fetch the hairbrush,* she was tempted to add. They sat down, looking sheepish.

'You're both suffering from arrested development. You come in here and behave as if I was some toy you were squabbling over. I shouldn't have to spell it out for you that I'm not a thing for someone to possess. I'm a person. I decide. I choose. And at the moment I choose neither of you.'

She had expected them to be chastened; she didn't expect them to be shocked. Max had turned pale and Conrad's face was slack with astonishment as they stared at her.

'What's wrong? What did I say?'

'How – how did you know?' Max stammered but Conrad was quicker to regain his composure.

'You said what she said. In almost so many words.'

Shaken in her turn, Laura sat down heavily on a dining-chair. 'Why? Why should she say that?'

The men exchanged glances, almost conspiratorially, as if they found themselves however unwillingly on the same side. It was Conrad who said at last, 'It got a bit torrid, when Di was around. She sort of played us off against each other so we didn't know where we were. If she'd preferred one it would have been better, but she didn't. Or if she did she didn't tell us. We were all round the table during the morning break – me, Max, Jake and Scott Thomson – and somehow it all blew up out of nothing.'

'You said—' Max interrupted, but Conrad silenced him with a look.

'Whatever. Anyway, she exploded. Set about us all, gave us our characters and then at the end said just what you did.'

'I hate to agree with him but it's true,' Max said. 'That was the problem.'

Laura seldom lost her temper but she lost it now, seized with a protective fury for a twenty-year-old put in a position like that. 'And you felt she was obliged to choose one of you? What did you think you had – a sort of collective *droit de seigneur*? Didn't it occur to your fat, swollen heads that she didn't want any of you – that your attitudes made you totally repellent?

'Or did it occur to you? Did it so affect one of you that you had to go out and kill her as punishment?'

She found she was crying again. 'Get out, both of you.' She snatched up the mobile phone which was lying on the table by her laptop and stood up. 'For some reason, I don't feel particularly safe in your company. If you don't leave now, I'm going to call for police protection.'

They rose too, Conrad putting his hands up in a placatory gesture. 'Of course we'll go. But may I say one thing? It's not like that. I was just going to tell you before Max came. I don't know if they've talked to him about it, but they've discovered something that could explain it all.'

Max nodded fervently. 'That's right. The bull. Let Conrad tell you about it, Laura.'

She was still clutching her phone. 'All right. Briefly.'

'The path lab report says she was gored by a bull. She

wasn't afraid of them – probably wasn't scared enough – and my guess is she tried bull-running with Satan, our champion bull. Very vicious, very cunning, could turn like a polo pony. So he killed her, OK? Then my uncle found her. He's never been balanced about that animal; he'd have had to have Satan slaughtered if this got out. He couldn't do anything for Di; she was beyond help and she'd always said she had no family so he took a huge gamble and buried her. If it hadn't been for the foot-and-mouth, it would have paid off.'

It was so unexpected that Laura was having difficulty taking it in. Max was backing him up now. 'It all figures, Laura – I can see it happening.'

'And this – this is the official position?'

'Oh, who knows?' Conrad's bitterness surfaced again. 'Big Marge Fleming has it in for me and at the moment she's just enjoying watching me twisting in the wind. But she'll have to accept it eventually – it's just so bloody obvious.'

'It's exactly the sort of thing the Minotaur would do,' Max urged. 'Bull worship, with everything including your own family sacrificed on the altar. Nothing else ever mattered.

'Well, it's all going to be so-o-o different in the future. Farm prices may be depressed at the moment, but they'll pick up before long. When I sell it – sorry, Conrad, when I sell my half—'

'*What?*' It was a bull's bellow. 'You can't do that, you slimy little sod.'

'Oh, I think you'll find I can. If the Minotaur would just be obliging enough to give up the unequal struggle—'

'Bastard!'

Laura had her hands over her ears. 'Shut up! Shut up! Get out, now, and have your puerile family squabbles elsewhere. Go and kill each other, if you like. Just don't do it here.'

Shaking with fury, she went to the door and held it open. Max shrugged and left. Conrad, as he passed her, paused. 'Laura—'

'No!'

She shut the door behind them, locked it and secured it with bolts top and bottom, then drew its red gingham curtain across. She went round the room, shutting out the night and the men who had so disturbed her hard-won peace.

Could what they had said possibly be true? From what she knew of Dizzy, it was far from impossible, and there was some comfort in thinking of her death as an accident rather than the result of a deliberately evil act. Laura knew, too, about obsession, knew how it could distort someone's judgement and even perception of reality.

On the other hand, the sick scenario which had emerged this evening was precisely the breeding ground for the heightened emotions which could lead to murder. And it was a volatile family situation; she'd seen that just now with her own eyes.

It was suiting them very well too that the person to be blamed was unable to speak and was soon, judging from what Max had said, likely to die and take the secret of his actions with him to the grave.

If they were his actions. Even if it was true that Dizzy's killer was now dead, waiting for disposal in a heap of all the other carcasses, who was to say who it was who had buried her?

Suddenly, she remembered the first row between the cousins, in the bar the night she had arrived. Max had been perfectly calm about the proposal to dig up the field where they had found her sister's body. It had been Conrad who was so violently opposed to it. She shuddered.

The sound of their voices outside had stopped and a

moment later she heard the car engines starting up. Then silence shrouded the house once more.

Marjory Fleming set the phone down with a sigh. Bill had been monosyllabic, brusque almost to the point of rudeness, and unspecific about when the farm might be declared free of infection. His voice was flat and listless, almost unrecognisable as belonging to the man she loved.

When she had mentioned her fears about suicide to Superintendent Bailey at the start of all this he had been dismissive and she had accepted his point – that Bill wasn't selfish enough to do that to her and the children. But Bailey had been talking about the Bill he knew, not this man with the toneless voice and the reluctance to communicate.

She had been worried enough to phone Hamish Raeburn, at a neighbouring farm which had so far escaped the slaughter, to ask him to get in touch with Bill to see if he was all right. She had a cool reception; he phoned Bill regularly, he told her, and had met him at their mutual boundary on the day of the slaughter. Yes, he was depressed. They were all depressed. Only an idiot would expect anyone not to be at a time like this.

It was a brief conversation and perhaps she was being paranoid in thinking he had substituted 'idiot' for 'policewoman' for the sake of courtesy. Still, there was nothing she could do about it until she got back to the farm, and that, please God, would be soon.

She had enough to think about without that. Bailey was away at a meeting today and she wasn't sorry to have the chance to sleep on Conrad's theory before she presented it to him. There was little doubt in her mind that the Super would seize on such a neat, swift, cheap outcome; all it would take was a carefully worded statement to the Press and the heat would be off. The file wouldn't be closed but it would be NFE'd, with orders to keep a watching brief rather than to pursue enquiries further.

Unless another body turned up. The diggers had managed to make a serious mess of most of the field without result; there was still one corner remaining which they would tackle tomorrow. And what were they to do after that – dig up the whole farm?

If Rosamond Mason wasn't two feet under, where was she? The appeal had gone out for her to get in touch and there had been a photograph in the national newspapers. It wasn't a very good one, unfortunately; she'd be sixteen years older too, and a woman could change a lot in her middle years, so perhaps it wasn't sinister that as yet no one had come forward.

Then there was Jake Mason, accused and unable to defend himself. She made up her mind to go to the hospital tomorrow to see him for herself. It was looking as if the police would end up being judge and jury on his case and it was hardly fair that he should be condemned unseen as well as unheard.

Her appointment with Bailey was at eleven; she could drive over to Dumfries in the afternoon. She was phoning to have her diary cleared when Tam MacNee came into the room.

'We've just been told they've given the all-clear for Chapelton,' he said when she put the phone down. 'The Masons will be able to get back in whenever they want.'

Fleming made a quick decision. 'Slap an embargo on the information until tomorrow. And get someone to swear out a search warrant for the house. I'd like to go up there myself and try to get a feel for the place without Mrs Mason throwing hysterical fits at me like missiles.'

MacNee grinned. 'She's a piece of work, that one. Young Charlotte's got her knickers in a twist, says you'll be getting a complaint about police brutality because she asked her if she'd had a row with Diana Warwick. She says the woman's either aff her heid or as sleekit as they come and has the whole thing worked out. If you're looking for someone who would have done the girl in before breakfast and still had a good appetite for her porridge, she's your woman.'

'She's not really going to lodge a complaint, is she?' Fleming was always one to go straight to the essentials. 'That would be all I need.'

MacNee shook his head. 'I phoned Conrad. He'll talk her down.'

'You spoke to him, did you? Did he expound his theory?'

'Aye, did he! Wouldn't let me off the phone till he'd bent my ear for ten minutes.'

'What did you make of it?'

MacNee considered his response. 'You can kind of see it, in a way. I mean, the man would have to be daft to do it, but there's no evidence that says he wasn't. It's just a wee bitty convenient, though, to my way of thinking.'

That was exactly what had struck Fleming too, but playing devil's advocate she said, 'You have to say it fits the facts very neatly.'

MacNee sniffed. 'That's what I don't like about it. We both know things like this aren't neat, they're messy. Real messy, when you end up with someone dead.'

Abandoning her brief attempt at impartiality, Fleming agreed. 'Conrad was so keen I should accept it, it turned me thrawn and I just dug in my toes. Not that it's unnatural: if a salmon could speak it would ask you to let it off the hook too.'

'His wee cousin was pretty taken with the idea as well. Now he's one that wants watching. Clever beggar – put me right off at the start of the interview with that sort of smarmy, toffee-nosed stuff that gets any honest Glaswegian's dander up. Then he throws an emotional wobbly when I mention his mother.'

Fleming was interested. 'There's something there, you know. He insisted it was his mother's body we'd found but he seemed quite detached in the morning, helping to calm Brett down, then in the afternoon when Laura appeared he went into complete collapse.'

'She'd probably be able to give you a list of psychological reasons for that, all with fancy names. It's probably a syndrome. It always is, these days.'

Marjory gave him an old-fashioned look. 'Oh aye? You know my opinion of psychology.

'But tomorrow I have to report to Bailey. Guess what his reaction's going to be to a conclusion that would mean the whole operation could be stood down within days. And maybe it's right enough. We've no hard evidence that it isn't.'

'There's just one thing,' MacNee said slowly. 'One of the questions I asked was where the cattle would be at the time. Obviously, if they were penned you'd have to be a maniac to get yourself gored. Now Max said they'd be out in the fields but then I was dumb enough to let him know the context before I asked the question.

'So I spoke to Scott Thomson after – though mind you, he was pretty edgy about it too – and he said he'd instructions to bring them in if it went below freezing. If we can fix the date, we could check with the Met Office.'

'We've got that somewhere.' Fleming turned to her computer. 'There was someone they talked to in the village. She remembered Brett Mason phoning to say she needed her help in the house because the housekeeper had walked out at the weekend. The reason she remembers is because it was the day of her mother's funeral and all Brett said was could she come in the afternoon, then?'

'That sounds like our Brett.'

'Yes, here it is. January twenty-ninth was the funeral so the weekend would have been the twenty-sixth/twenty-seventh.'

'There'd be a lot of Burns Suppers that night,' MacNee said fondly, 'with it being so near Rabbie's birthday.'

'Tam!' Fleming jingled a box on her desk threateningly. It had a pound, a 50p and a 5p in it already.

'No, no!' He hastily constructed a cover-up. 'It's just you might find someone had an alibi, if he was a keen Burns man.'

'It would hardly alibi him for the whole weekend, would it, unless he was so drunk as to be incapacitated. And don't get carried away with the notion that anyone who likes Burns can't be a villain. The man was a ratbag – his own mother was ashamed of him.'

MacNee rose with dignity. 'I shall not stay to hear his memory abused. I'll put the warrant in hand and check up on the weather.'

'Thanks, Tam. And say I have to have it by first thing tomorrow morning, even if they've to drag the Sheriff away from his tea to get it. I want to get up there before I go in to see the Super.'

The cloud base had come down to ground level so that the rain was no longer falling but hanging in the air in tiny droplets which clung to clothes and skin and made breathing like inhaling cold steam. The sodium lights in the hospital car park were fuzzy orange shapes in the grey murk and the windows of the hospital were pale yellow shapes in the dark bulk of the building, its edges blurred by the smoky swirls of vapour.

The woman got out of her car, a Vauxhall Corsa, locked it and set off towards the main entrance with unhurried steps which belied the nervous pounding of her heart. She was bareheaded and within a few steps her blonde hair was covered with a fine, damp film.

She had no idea what might be waiting for her inside, no

idea what forces her return might unleash. She wanted to
see him alone first, see him without having to explain to
anyone who she was or why she was here – wanted, above
all, to see him without Brett, his incubus, at his side. How
different everything might have been for them if Brett hadn't
fled back home from the ruins of her marriage and set about
ruining theirs!

She still loved him. She always had. It wasn't a choice she
had made; indeed, how often she had wished that it was!
Real love is not conditional, she had said to him once, *love is
a condition from which there is no recovery.* That was in the
happy days when they still talked romantically together,
before events, like wedges driven in with hammer blows, split
them apart.

The hospital doors swung open as she approached and
she stepped inside, blinking at the brilliance of the interior
after the darkness outside. She paused, brushing moisture
off her hair and blinking away the droplets clinging to her
eyelashes. A man, on his way out, smiled. 'Terrible night
out there, isn't it?' She smiled back, an unobtrusive figure
in her Burberry raincoat.

There was no general board to give her information, as
she had hoped there might be. She was forced to invent a
friend who was a stroke patient, so that the receptionist
would tell her which ward he might be in, before discov-
ering he wasn't and suggesting he must have been discharged.
Then she hung about looking at the WRI shop, now closed,
until the receptionist was busy with another query and would
not see her going into instead of out of the building.

The ward was on the second floor. She chose the stairs
as being less conspicuous than the lift if someone noticed
her and she changed her mind about going in. Visiting hours
were over now and the hospital should be settling down to
its quieter night-time routine.

The main door to the ward was standing open and she could hear the sound of voices and laughter coming from the office just inside. Setting her feet down quietly to make no sound on the hard floor, she went in. Ahead lay a short corridor with rooms opening off to either side. Some, with long windows on each side of the door, showed double rows of beds; others were obviously single rooms.

Nervously she drew level with the open office door and saw that its entrance was blocked by a policeman, standing with his back to her. He was engaged in banter with women inside; she could hear their laughter.

Holding her breath, she slipped past. She hadn't thought of a police guard, though after what she had read in the newspapers it wasn't surprising. And at least it gave her a clue; only one of the rooms had a chair outside it and a table with a newspaper and an abandoned coffee mug. She scratched on the door and opened it.

The room was dark but there was a light over the bed. He was lying there, propped up a little on pillows with tubes leading between his body and stands with bags of liquids. His arms lay slack at his sides on top of the neatly folded sheet, as if they had been placed there by someone else. His eyes were closed, but his face – oh, slackened and distorted by illness and blurred by age, certainly – was still the face of the man she loved. His hair was still dark, still close-cropped, crisp-curled like a lamb's fleece.

Her eyes filling, she went to the bed. Involuntarily she stretched out her hand to run it through his hair as she so often had; with a shock of remembrance she felt its unexpectedly silky softness. 'Jake, oh Jake!' she mourned.

The eyes opened slowly but he did not turn his head. Choking back her tears, she moved forward to stand in his line of sight.

'Jake, it's Rosamond. How are you?'

There was no response. She had no way of knowing if he couldn't hear or if he had heard but chose to ignore the wife who had thwarted his will and left him all those years ago.

'They were looking for me. I thought it was best to come back.'

Still no reaction. She took his hand; it lay unresisting and flaccid in her own.

'Do you want me to stay? Or should I go and leave you?' She studied him intently. He blinked, but no flicker of emotion crossed his face.

She bit her lip. She had no experience of the victims of strokes and it was hard to know what she should do. She had almost made up her mind to leave as quietly as she had come when the door was suddenly flung open.

'How the hell did you get in here? Stand away from the bed!' The policeman in the doorway was very young, hardly more than a boy, and there was a level of panic in his tone.

She did as she was told. 'Please don't worry. I'm his wife. It's all right, truly.'

'But you shouldn't be in here! No one's allowed in without permission.'

'You were talking to the nurses. I didn't want to disturb anyone,' she lied. 'There's no harm done, I promise.'

He looked a little calmer, but still scared. 'OK, you're his wife. I've seen your picture. But you could have been anyone. This is going to mean real trouble for me when I report it.'

She seized her chance. 'Look, constable, let's do each other a favour. Smuggle me out again and no one will know.'

'But they're looking for you, aren't they?' he said, but she could see that he was weakening.

'I promise I'll come back to do it properly tomorrow.' She sighed. 'It was just that I didn't want to find a reception committee waiting for me before I could speak to him myself. Not that it's done any good.' She looked back at the inert figure on the bed, his eyes closed now. 'I don't know whether he can't respond or whether he's ignoring me deliberately.'

'Oh, I can tell you that.' The constable seemed proud of his newly acquired medical knowledge. 'It's called locked-in syndrome. They think he can probably see and hear but he can't move or speak.'

She stared at him in horror. 'But that's – that's dreadful! He's a clever, active man—'

'Not any more,' the constable said with the callousness of youth which knows itself to be immortal. 'Look, if we're going to do this we'd better make it quick. They'll be round soon to put the lights out.'

He put his head out of the door. 'They're still having their tea-break. Off you go. Remember, tomorrow, you promised.'

She left as quietly as she had come. Outside, a wind had got up and was tearing the mist to rags. She could see a glimpse of the moon, and this time the drops on her cheeks were warm and salty.

15

Tiny stones from the gritting lorry bounced up off the road and pinged against the body of the car as Marjory Fleming drove along the main road in its wake. She had been travelling quite fast; as she turned off on to the untreated road leading up through Glenluce she felt the back of the car start to fishtail. Her stomach lurched, though she steered it out of the skid competently enough.

That was careless! Yesterday evening's fog had left wet roads and of course the hard frost which had followed meant black ice today. They'd be having fun in Traffic this morning – cars in ditches, jack-knifed lorries and complaints from everyone about the gritting being too little, too late.

Becoming a statistic wouldn't do her cred any good. She drove on at a more respectful speed, paying extra attention to the road, though she couldn't get her personal problems out of her mind. How strange it was that at the start of this upheaval she had been worried about all the wrong things! Like her father, for instance: she had expected to have to field constant questioning and comment from him but in fact she'd hardly seen him and when she did he was absorbed in the children and showed no interest at all.

She had a friend who practised what she called prophylactic worrying: her theory was that since everyone knew that what you worried about never happened, you chose the worst thing you could imagine to worry about and then you'd be all right. She claimed it worked, though Marjory had never been totally convinced and certainly in this case could never have imagined anything coming between her and Bill. And yet . . .

In a few days at most the farm would be given the all-clear and she and the children could go home at last. It was a bitter irony that having left so reluctantly she should be so dreading her return: the empty chicken run, the deserted fields and at the centre of it all a disheartened, resentful man who had nothing to do to pass the long days. Even Meg would be low-spirited; collies were highly intelligent, over-sensitive creatures and even a day or two without work was enough to induce a crisis of self-confidence. The children, too, had got used to the freedoms of the town and being the focus of their grandparents' attention; going back to the farm, with no animals, a depressed father and their mother's cooking – correction, make that heating up of ready meals – would be a difficult adjustment. It was all going to be very, very tough.

She sighed as the car rattled over the cattle-grid and glanced round about her. Such a bleak picture! No sheep. No birds that she could see. Pine trees motionless and grey with frost. The little burns all locked into stillness. A nuclear winter might be something like this: a silent, ice-bound landscape with a low red sun veiled in brownish cloud. They were fore-casting snow today and Marjory was keen not to be up on this high, exposed ground when it started.

There was the Chapelton 'Pedigree Herd' sign; she turned in. There was no one guarding the entrance today and she wasn't sure if there would be anyone at the crime scene either. She couldn't see any cars parked outside the imposing Victorian mansion.

There were steps flanked by balustrades leading up to the front door and to one side was a room with a wide bay window which was Jake Mason's study and which, with the smaller farm office, was the only place in the house they were authorised to search. They could also enter the flat in the steading where Diana Warwick had lived, but the Sheriff had been strict and the terms of the warrant were very specific. Human Rights legislation outlawed any sort of fishing expedition and he had considered intrusion on the personal areas of the house unjustified by the evidence. It was for today only; if they wanted an extension he would be prepared to listen to their arguments.

In fact, there was no way that Fleming could have rationalised bringing in extra manpower for a search and it was such a huge place that she'd have time for only the most cursory look round if she were to be in time for her appointment with Bailey – and it was never wise to keep him waiting.

Conrad had supplied the keys with a bad grace and no instructions. She had to try three before she found the one which would admit her to the vestibule – ten feet square, fourteen feet high with a floor of encaustic tiles as its only feature – then pressed down the brass lever latch on the mahogany inner door with its etched frosted glass and went into the hall. It was a huge, sombre space with elaborate ceiling mouldings and a heavily carved staircase going up from its centre to a landing the full width of the hall. There it divided into two flights, rising to either side under three tall arched windows fitted with opaque leaded glass which reduced the amount of light while adding little to the decor. There were no curtains or carpets to reduce the harsh effect of so much dark, highly varnished wood.

Her feet echoing on the parquet floor, Fleming went towards the study and let herself in. Almost the first thing she noticed was the smell of dust, which caught at her throat. She wasn't, heaven knew, the best housewife in the world – ask Cat – but this was the smell of deep-seated neglect, lodged in the heavy, dark red velvet curtains and the upholstery of the button-backed chesterfield. It looked as if when the Masons had bought the property they'd taken over the furnishings as well and they hadn't been cleaned since.

She'd heard that bulls were Jake Mason's religion: this, then, was the Holy of Holies. From the walls, a hundred bulls looked down from posters, photographs, framed newspaper cuttings. There were rosettes, silver cups and statuettes. Above the elaborate fireplace hung the massive head of a black bull, a silver plate below it presumably declaring its champion status though it was too dark with tarnish to read. Its glass eyes were dull under a film of dust and Fleming could see where moths had eaten away at the hide. The horns, though – those sharp, forward-pointing horns – were still undeniably impressive.

She stood below, looking up at them. On their own farm they'd always had polled cattle. Some came that way genetically; some you de-horned because they were dangerous otherwise. Even cows, if they had a calf to defend, could be lethal, but she'd read in one of the reports that Mason refused to poll his herd despite a string of minor incidents and one or two major ones. Demeaning, he had called it. Allegedly.

As a weapon, horns were finely adapted. It was, after all, what they were designed to be and a blow, delivered with the thrust of a powerful neck behind it, could readily produce the injury the pathologist had described.

Right. She glanced at her watch – quarter to ten. If she wanted to look at the flat and the field again she couldn't afford to stand speculating. She took a rapid mental inventory of the room in case a follow-up was needed: the ledgers on either side of the fireplace, the remarkable silver bull mask, black with tarnish, on the other wall, the list of things to do on the desk in the window – phone NFU, phone MAFF, order feed-stuff – which was probably the last thing Jake

Mason wrote before his stroke. And was, by all accounts, the last thing Jake Mason was ever likely to write.

Locking up as she left, she went out, walking down the icy steps with some caution, then headed for the stockyard building. A dozen housekeepers had since passed through the flat Diana Warwick had occupied, but Fleming still wanted to see it for herself, to try to imagine how it would have felt to have been an adventurous girl accustomed to roaming the world, finding herself isolated in this back-water.

The door to the flat opened on to a steep staircase and led into a small sitting-room furnished with what looked like rejects from the main house. In the bedroom, a cheap-looking divan, an old-fashioned wardrobe and a chest-of-drawers took up most of the floor space. The bathroom looked pre-war, untouched apart from its accumulated chips and cracks, and the kitchen was a curtained area with a discoloured sink and two electric rings.

She went to the window with its view of the straggly maze she remembered and stood looking out, as Diana must have done too. Why had the girl come here – and, more impor-tantly, why had she stayed? It was understandable that leaving home in a temper, you might take up the casual offer of a job, but why would you stay in this shabby, claustrophobic place with a thoroughly unreasonable mistress? There were always people who weren't Brett Mason advertising for housekeepers.

You'd stay if you were in love. If you were in love, you were dumb enough to put up with anything – though Fleming had a suspicion that the bathroom might have finished it as far as she personally was concerned.

So who was the man? Diana had met Max and his father in Pamplona, which was why she was here in the first place. In that situation the smart money would be on Jake; what twenty-year-old girl is likely to fancy a seventeen-year-old boy?

She hadn't even met Conrad before she arrived. So she hadn't come here for love of him – although that didn't mean he was ruled out. She might have come because it was convenient, but stayed because she'd fallen for him. The same applied to Scott Thomson, of course, if your taste was for a bit of rough. So where did that get you? Nowhere.

Fleming let herself out of the flat, glancing nervously at her watch. It was after ten now; if she was to be sure of getting back in time she must leave by ten-thirty. Keeping Donald waiting, as he had explained to her at their first encounter, was not so much a discourtesy to him personally as an undermining of the whole structure of the police force. Half-past ten at the very latest.

She walked on down the drive to the field where Diana's body had been interred, a five-minute walk from the flat. The scene was very different today from the last time Fleming had been here; the air was clean again now that the slaughtered carcasses of the cattle had been removed, there was no one about and at the far end of the field a yellow digger stood abandoned in what had become a sea of frozen mud. Where the plastic tent had been only blue and white crime scene tapes strung between metal poles marked Diana's unofficial grave. There was nothing to be learned here. Fleming turned back.

Deep in thought before, she had barely noticed the entrance to the maze as she had passed it, a wrought-iron gate rusting now and listing on its hinges. Beyond it the privet hedges were a disordered tangle, with some bushes overgrown and leggy, some sparse from lack of pruning and some no more than dead twigs. The delineation of the pathways she remembered fleeing down, pursued and shrieking with delicious childish terror, had all but disappeared; you could find your way through gaps to the centre of the maze and that strange monument to the Minotaur – half-man, half-bull. If it was still there.

Prompted by curiosity, she opened the gate. It rasped on its rusty hinges; she had to lift it up to move it and when she let it go again it sank on to one corner at a drunken angle.

Beneath her feet, the ground was uneven and iron-hard. Old dead leaves, blown in heaps against the base of the hedge, were a grey, frozen sludge, but every blade of the rough grass in the alleyways, every leaf of the straggly privet, was separately encased in its pall of frost. There was no colour, no sound; under the threatening, gun-metal sky the maze looked as if it had been ice-bound for a hundred years.

Fleming's breathing seemed unnaturally loud. It condensed in steam and rose in front of her, moving like the only other living thing in this dead landscape. She shivered. Her fingers and toes were starting to sting in the biting cold so she swung her arms and stamped as she set off.

Neglect had blurred the labyrinthine pathways but the maze had not lost its power to mislead. There seemed to be only one way which wasn't overgrown, leading directly from the gate; following it round, Fleming found that it was a blind alley and she was boxed in by a thick stand of privet, through which she could see the centre space but not reach it and was forced to retrace her steps to find a way through.

And there it was, just as she had remembered it, though weeds had forced their way through the stonework as the mortar had crumbled and where there had been smooth green sward were now rough grass and nettles.

The plinth was about three feet square and about four high, built of the local sandstone, and it too showed signs of neglect. Some of the mortar in its walls had crumbled with frost and rain though there had been a clumsy repair to hold in place the large flat stone on top, into which a metal plaque had been inset like a sundial. The engraved image was obscured by a layer of rime; Fleming rubbed at it with her fingers and as it melted the lines of the carving emerged.

It had given her nightmares as a child and she wasn't altogether sure that it wouldn't now. It was brilliantly executed, done in profile and with a certain relish at the brutality of the subject. The dramatic head of the bull wrinkled horribly and realistically at the neck into a powerful human torso; the arms and hands reached forward as if to grasp a victim while the strongly muscled legs and thighs indicated the beginning of a prancing charge.

Max had called his father the Minotaur, according to Laura Harvey. And from what Marjory could remember of the Greek myth, the Minotaur had demanded tribute of youths and maidens; was it possible that Diana Warwick, having been killed by Jake's bull, became some sort of sacrifice linked in his diseased mind with this most bizarre place? Yet the maze had been Edgar Mason's folly, not his son's; surely, if this had been an ancestral practice, someone would have noticed over the years if maidens regularly went missing from the district?

This was ridiculous. She was allowing the atmosphere of the place to cloud her judgement. And that was the first flake of snow; the sooner she got out the better.

She went back, as she thought, the way she had come, but yet again found herself trapped by thick privet. She really had no time to waste; she decided to force her way through, fairly sure that on the other side was the blind alley she had come along before which would lead her to the gate. It wasn't easy; the branches were springy and put up brutal resistance; she had scratches on her hands by the time she reached the other side of the hedge. Stepping out of it, she felt a twig snatch at the fabric of her trousers and with some irritation stopped to release herself.

Bending down, she saw in the heart of the hedge, near the bottom, a small piece of fine chain hanging on a twig. It was black with dirt but when, out of curiosity, she picked it up and rubbed it in her fingers it showed gold. It had a tiny gold charm and a catch but that was still closed; the fragile chain had snapped in the middle. Perhaps it was a bracelet which had caught on a twig, like her trousers, and the owner hadn't noticed at the time. It didn't look particularly valuable anyway.

She was turning away when she remembered suddenly a snatch of the conversation with Laura Harvey: she'd said something about an ankle bracelet her sister had always worn. Fleming fished it out of the hedge and looked at it again.

Yes, it could well be an ankle bracelet. She'd never had one herself – had always thought they were a bit trashy – but wrist bracelets weren't usually as delicate as this. And the minute charm, now she looked at it closely, was in the shape of a dolphin. She turned back, frowning, to look at where it had been. If Diana Warwick had been wandering round in the maze, she'd better check it out more thoroughly.

The slender chain had certainly been there for a long time; the hedge had grown out and round it. And now she noticed too that above, caught in the centre of the hedge, was a small piece of rag, blackened and frayed. Probably a trivial record of some earlier visitor and entirely irrelevant, but given the bracelet, it would be worth following the principle that everything is evidence until you've proved it isn't. She teased it out carefully and folded it in a tissue before putting it, with the broken chain, into her pocket.

The flakes were getting bigger now and it was nearly twenty

to eleven. The maze really needed more thorough checking but she couldn't spare the time; she'd be lucky even now not to find that she was seriously late for her appointment with the Super.

Shaken but mercifully unhurt, Laura climbed out of her car into the steadily falling snow and went round to look at the damage.

Her heart had been in her mouth all the way along the tiny road from Burnside Cottages to where it joined the Glenluce road. It had been like driving on wet glass; she had no experience of conditions like this and she had lost count of the number of times the car had waltzed into the verge so that she had to reverse it out again.

Staying at home would have been wiser, of course, but Neil MacSporran, the kindly local editor, had arranged two useful interviews for her in Kirkluce and anyway she'd finished Mrs MacNab's scones and there wasn't a lot more food in the house.

She'd thought the Glenluce road would have been gritted so she turned on to it with some relief, only to discover that it wasn't. A few yards further on, the road went round a corner; the car didn't, opting instead for the embrace of a ditch and an intimate encounter with a stone wall.

It was her mother's old VW Beetle and its nose, once proudly aquiline, was now distinctly retroussé. It wasn't going anywhere. Dismayed, she looked round about her helplessly. She had her mobile in the car, of course, but what use was that when she didn't know a number to ring?

There was an unearthly hush, the thickly falling snow muffling all sound, and there was nothing to be seen but the huge downy flakes against a purple-grey background. The village of Glenluce was, she guessed, probably a mile uphill, the main road two downhill. Should she head in one direction or the other, or simply get back into the car and hope for rescue before it became a snowdrift?

She glanced down ruefully at her neat fashion boots and her black town raincoat. Flakes were settling on her hair and her clothes and her eyelashes, so thickly that she could hardly see. After only a couple of minutes she was looking like a snowman.

That settled it. She climbed back into the car, brushing off the worst of it, then ran the heater to warm her icy hands and feet. Only for a few minutes, though, then she reluctantly turned it off to conserve the battery. She had no way of knowing how long it might be before the snow went off or help came.

In fact, it was barely quarter of an hour later – though a cold, frightening quarter of an hour, watching drifts build around the car – that she saw the headlights coming up the hill towards her. From the outline of the vehicle she guessed it was a big 4x4; after a struggle with the piled-up snow she managed to open the car door and climbed out.

Her heart sank when she saw the Range Rover's driver. She had vowed last night to have nothing more to do with any of the Mason clan but it was Conrad who jumped down, exclaiming at her plight.

Principles were principles but snow was snow. Gratefully she climbed into the snug interior, her teeth chattering, and made only a token protest when he turned at the road-end and headed back the way he had come. She even endured his lecture about appropriate preparations for a journey in adverse weather conditions which included proper clothing and footwear, a spade, blankets and preferably a flask of tea.

'D-don't suppose you practise what you preach?' she chittered when he mentioned tea.

He grinned. 'Spade, blankets, yes. Thermos, no, but if you look in the glove-compartment you'll find a hip-flask.'

Scotland's national drink had never been a favourite with Laura but she was forced to admit that it was the perfect antidote to the rigours of the Scottish winter climate.

Conrad laughed. 'It's like dock leaves for nettle stings – the local remedy is the most effective.'

He had, he told her, been on his way to Chapelton, having just been told they could return at last. As luck would have it, the Range Rover belonging to the farm had been in Kirkluce for an MOT which had tempted him to try the journey despite the forecast, but with the worsening conditions he'd been thinking of turning back anyway. He promised to use his influence at the garage to get Laura's car priority treatment and didn't mention the scene of the day before, nor the murder investigation. In return she told him about her interviews and her need to lay in supplies, and conversation flowed easily; he was, as she had found him before, good company, pleasant and amusing.

The mechanic at the garage, while ready to be helpful, could only promise that once the snow stopped he'd try to get up to bring her car in before the snowplough came through and buried it – a horror that had not even occurred to her.

As they left, Conrad asked, 'How are you planning to get home?'

She'd wondered that too, but anxious to assert her independence said airily, 'Oh – taxi, probably.'

He looked down at her with some amusement. 'You just don't get it about the weather in the country, do you? You're not going to get a car along that road for another couple of days, if then. Depends what else the snowploughs have to do – keeping the main road clear is the priority and us hicks from the sticks just have to wait our turn.

'I tell you what – you go and see the people you need to see and make sure you've got enough food for the next few days, then meet me for lunch in the Galloway Arms. The snow should have stopped by then. It's getting lighter already and I wouldn't mind having a shot at getting up to Chapelton later, so I can drop you off.'

What could she do but agree? And, if she were truthful with herself, she didn't particularly want to refuse.

Marjory Fleming knew she shouldn't have been late. As she looked at her superior officer, at the pursed lips and the folded hands and the thumbs tapping on his comfortably rounded stomach, she could tell that he wasn't going to be receptive to the note of caution she was sounding.

She had known he would be tempted, naturally. What senior officer, under constant budgetary scrutiny and restraint, wouldn't jump at a solution to a murder case which would mean wrapping it up in under a week, with no more expensive investigation and not even the administrative nightmare of assembling a watertight case to present to the Procurator Fiscal?

Bailey would have forgiven her lateness, if she'd been presenting this as an undisputed solution. And if she hadn't been late, he might have been prepared to listen to what she had to say about the uncertainties: the question mark over the bull's actual whereabouts, the lack of proof that if it was an accident it was Jake Mason who had buried the body. He might even, in an indulgent mood, have allowed her to elaborate on the gut feeling she and Tam MacNee shared that it was all just too bloody convenient.

But she'd committed the double crime of keeping him waiting – which suggested she thought her time more important than his – and voicing unwelcome doubts. So now he was saying, 'Oh, come now, Marjory! You can pick holes in anything if you try hard enough. Can you ever remember a case coming to court where the defence agent couldn't find something to cavil at? It's how they make their living – if we ever put up a completely watertight case they'd be outside the station picketing!'

He laughed, inviting her to laugh with him. It was another black mark that she didn't, saying only, 'Couldn't we hold it for another couple of days? It wouldn't do for it to look as if we'd just picked on a defenceless man. The tabloids could have a field day with that.'

It was the right button to press. His smile vanished. 'You're absolutely right, Marjory. We have to consider the presentational aspect of this very carefully indeed. Well done. But make it twenty-four hours. Money is simply haemorrhaging away and there's a limit to what we can spend for the sake of PR.'

'Thanks, Donald.' She got up. 'I'm going to the hospital in Dumfries this afternoon to see Jake Mason. Not that I'll get anything useful – by all accounts he's in a bad way.'

Bailey nodded. 'Good thinking, Marjory. Wouldn't do for them to pick up that the SIO hadn't even been to see the man.'

He rose as usual and went to open the door for her. 'You know, Marjory, it would be quite a feather in your cap to get this wrapped up now. You'd be flavour of the month with the Chief Constable and that's no small thing!'

'Thanks, Donald.'

Why was it, as she walked back to her office, that she remembered something from the Bible, something about Satan, a high mountain and all the kingdoms of the world being offered for only some minor compromise of principle?

And indeed, what did they have, to set against Conrad's theory? Tam's investigation into where the bull had been at the time of the murder. Max's equivocation. Scott Thomson's 'edginess'. Brett Mason's fevered reaction to questioning. Oh, and a chain which, even if it proved to be Diana

Warwick's, only told you she'd been in the maze once and a scrap of fabric which probably wasn't evidence at all.

In twenty-four hours they would be putting out a Press statement accusing in veiled terms a man who could not say a word in his own defence, on the basis of unsubstantiated testimony given by the two people who arguably had most to gain from this informal conviction. The thought made her acutely uncomfortable.

Sure, further investigation would be expensive, but she'd never heard a definition of justice which featured the words 'financial expediency' and she wouldn't be in the police force if she didn't believe that justice was what it was all about. She owed it to the accused man to pursue every possible line of enquiry until she was directly instructed to drop the case. It looked as if that would only be twenty-four hours.

Back in her office, she arranged for a courier to come and pick up the material to take to the path lab in Glasgow, emphasising that this was a priority request, out of – what? A sense of duty? Sheer bloody-mindedness? She wasn't sure, but she only hoped Donald Bailey's notorious allergy to balance sheets would mean he never found out about such wanton extravagance.

She jumped guiltily, though, when the phone on her desk buzzed and it was her boss at the other end. Trying not to sound nervous she said, 'Yes, Donald?'

'Marjory, I forgot to check with you. Are you back at the farm as of now? I gather Bill got clearance yesterday.'

She had never understood the expression 'pierced to the heart' before; she understood it now. It was only pride which gave her the strength to say lightly, 'Oh, I'll have to prise my kids out of my parents' clutches first! I'll let you know.'

She set down the phone and bent over, her arms crossed about her body to contain the pain.

16

Her emotions still in turmoil, Marjory called in at the Lairds' house on the way to Dumfries to tell them that she and the children were able to return home. Perhaps, if her mother had been alone, she might have confided her troubles, but her parents were together in the lounge, her mother darning socks – who but Janet darned socks nowadays? – and her father engrossed in Cammie's GameBoy.

He glanced up as Marjory came in, grunted, then went back to it. The sound effects were even more intrusive than his eternal TV had been, though Janet appeared oblivious. Marjory's news, however, brought his head up. He stopped playing; there was the noise of an explosion, a dying shriek, then merciful silence.

'That's good news, dear. I'm sure you've been wearying for home, and Bill will have missed you all.' Janet's tone was dutifully bright but she couldn't conceal her disappointment.

Angus said gruffly, 'Oh, you'll please yourself, I've no doubt. You always have. But if you think it's a good idea to take bairns like that out into the country with the weather like this, you're needing your head looked at. Next thing you know they'll be snowed in and Cammie'll miss his rugby practice and get left out of the team. It'll break his heart.'

Marjory had to stifle a smile. 'We'll want them back eventually, you know, Dad.'

He glared at her. 'As I understand it, I was doing you a favour, having them here. But if you're suggesting the boot's on the other foot, you can take them whenever you like – I'll be glad of the peace and quiet.'

She had meant it as a pleasantry; he had taken it as a gibe. The last thing she needed just now was a confrontation, but—

'Och, we've plenty time for peace and quiet when this bad weather's over,' Janet said placidly. 'You said yourself, Angus, it'd be daft to take them away out yonder when it's so uncertain. And anyway, I expect Marjory and Bill would quite like a wee bit time to themselves, wouldn't you, dearie?'

Perhaps they would. Perhaps, indeed, it would be wise to give herself time to cobble their marriage together again before exposing the children to the harsh destruction of their way of life. Perhaps, too, she should be mature enough to show her genuine gratitude – what would she have done without their support? – by letting Angus keep his pride.

'If you're sure that would be all right? I know it's meant a lot of disruption to your routine but it's been brilliant for the kids. Cammie told me you're seriously cool at computer games, Dad.'

His pleasure showed, though he only said repressively, 'I'm supposed to think that's a compliment, am I?'

Marjory and her mother exchanged smiles. '*That*'s settled, then,' Janet said comfortably and went back to her darning while her daughter went upstairs to pack.

Funny, really, that she had never noticed before how regularly her softly-spoken mother achieved precisely what she wanted, leaving everyone else believing their argument had prevailed. Angus had always seemed to his daughter the dominant partner in the marriage, but living at home now as an adult she had seen how seldom his moods and tantrums – so often self-destructive – had any effect. And perhaps there was collusion there: like the dog on the chain who snarls and barks threats, secure in the knowledge that it will be restrained, Angus could rely on his wife to stop him going too far.

Marjorie grimaced ruefully. It was a bit late now to ask her mother for a crash course in how to handle a difficult husband. She'd never had one before; she'd just have to learn on the job.

The Galloway Arms was a cosy, old-fashioned hotel with tables covered with starched white cloths and a fire burning in the hearth. Its menu was old-fashioned too, featuring such homely fare as lentil soup, Scotch broth and shepherd's pie, though it was none the worse for that; as Conrad said, it wasn't really the weather for rocket salad, and laughing, Laura agreed.

Outside the sun had struggled through and a deep covering of sparkling snow had transformed shrubs and bushes into exotic sculptures and embellished every flat surface with a glittering layer of white candy-floss. It gave an air of unreality to everything, making Laura feel somehow that this moment of time was frozen too, dissociated from both past and future.

They talked as normal acquaintances do, of likes and dislikes, books, films, interests. Not, however, about family, background or the tragedy which was in both their minds – Laura couldn't help but notice how gracefully they skated round that. The elephant on the table, in psychological jargon: a huge, major issue which by unspoken mutual consent was ignored completely.

But, she told herself firmly, all that was on the table at the moment was shepherd's pie – and very good it was too. She was actually enjoying herself.

The snow had stopped for the moment at least so there would be no problem, Conrad assured her, about his delivering her back to Burnside Cottages. At the garage, the good news had been that they'd recovered her car, the bad news that it would take two or three days to get it back on the road. Still, she had stocked up with food, drink and reading materials and was looking forward to getting back for a cosy evening with the red curtains drawn, the lamps lit, a glass of wine and perhaps even some pleasantly mindless TV. It was just what she needed – peace and space and time to recover from the bone-deep weariness she still felt from the constant strain of grieving. Even so, she was almost regretful when it was time to go; lunch with Conrad had been surprisingly relaxing.

Yet, as they drove back towards Glenluce, she felt the mood change and conversation faltered and died. The road had been cleared and the verges were piled high with filthy brown sludge; the sun had gone, obscured by thick, dirty-grey clouds, and Laura felt as if the superficial glitter of their amusing lunch had vanished too as dark thoughts gathered again like the clouds themselves. Dizzy was still dead and Laura was in the company of someone who, at the very least, had been there when she was killed. All her uneasiness returned.

When Conrad stopped outside Burnside Cottages she didn't ask him in and when he offered to drop by to see if she needed anything while her car was off the road, she was firm in her refusal. He had been more than kind and she was very grateful, of course, but Mrs MacNab had promised to look in and there was no problem. She was forced to be blunt before he accepted that this was not mere politeness.

After a moment, he shrugged. 'Fine. As you wish. You've got my number anyway.' He didn't look at her as she got out, and drove off as soon as she had shut the car door. He was irritated, obviously; she felt guilty about that but it still wasn't going to change her mind. Apart from anything else, Mason family rivalries were more than she could handle at the moment. She could only hope that he wasn't going to go back and gloat over their lunch to Max.

It was barely three o'clock but with the heavy cloud a leaden gloom had already descended. She set off across the little bridge, clutching her shopping bags.

A lot of snow had fallen since she left. There was no sign of her earlier footprints and in front of the cottages the surface was pristine apart from a track of small footprints crossing at an angle towards the rough ground beyond the low fence – a fox or a deer, maybe, though she wasn't skilled enough to interpret it. There were no friendly lights in the cottages, no signs of human life, and as she walked along where she guessed the path should be she sank in snow over her boot tops. They'd been ruined already, with the wet.

She'd been happy enough in her isolation before and there was no reason, she told herself firmly, to feel imprisoned by it now. She let herself in, turned on every light, boosted the heating and switched on the electric kettle. Then, though it wasn't quite dark, she went to draw the curtains.

There was a strange, purplish tinge to the sky, and as she watched it started to snow again – small flakes, as yet, but after this morning she knew what that could lead to. With a shiver she replaced the view of the brooding desolation outside with the artificial cheerfulness of the red curtains and settled down to the quiet evening she had promised herself.

After a few minutes, though, she got up to switch on the television. Even raucous voices and canned laughter were preferable to the intrusive silence, broken only by the low keening of a rising wind.

Marjory Fleming arrived at the hospital during visiting hours. The foyer was busy, with the WRI shop doing good business, and she had to wait in a queue at the reception desk to get directions to Jake Mason's ward. The receptionist, she noted approvingly, asked to see ID before giving out the information.

When she reached the ward there were several people at the nursing station, deep in conversation with the duty nurse; disinclined to queue again and spotting a uniformed police-woman outside one of the doors, Fleming slipped past. She could have a word later on.

As she approached the constable got up and Fleming saw that it was Jackie Johnston. They'd obviously found her a job where she couldn't do too much harm and was out of the way of Tam MacNee, whose views on her were unprint-able. Johnston was smiling a nervous, ingratiatory smile; if she were a dog, Fleming thought, she'd be rolling on her back and squirming submission. If the sight of an inspector did that to her, you had to ask yourself how she'd handle an armed robbery. Making allowances for her sensitivities, Fleming said in her friendliest fashion, 'Everything all right, Jackie?'

Jackie shrank back as if the innocent question were a threat of violence. 'Y-yes – er, well, I think so.'

There were limits to tolerance when there was a job to do. Exasperated, Fleming said crisply, 'Fine,' and opened the door.

She had expected the tubes, the machines, the charts. What she hadn't expected was the elegant woman with silver-blonde hair sitting by the bedside holding the patient's unre-sponsive hand and talking to him in a low voice. She broke off as Fleming came in.

'Who are you and what are you doing here?' Fleming chal-lenged her. 'There are police orders that no one is to be admitted without authorisation.'

The woman rose and came towards her composedly. 'I'm Rosamond Mason, Jake's wife.'

Fleming stared at her in astonishment. 'But – there's been

a nationwide search for you! Why haven't you made contact to say that you're alive and well?'

A faint flush coloured the delicate skin. 'I'm sorry. When I came to the hospital –' she hesitated for a second, then went on – 'today, I told your young officer who I was and she said it would be all right to go in.'

'Did she, indeed?' Fleming said grimly. 'Of course, Mrs Mason, no one would have any wish to keep you from your husband's side. But you have caused everyone considerable concern and expense.' Thinking with irritation of the digger and the excavated wasteland, she decided not to spare her. 'We thought you might have been buried in that field too.'

'Buried – oh no!' Rosamond was horrified. 'I had no idea – but then I suppose Jake was the only person who could have assured you that I had simply left, and he . . .' Her voice faltered.

We wouldn't have believed him, though. Whatever he told us, he'd have been the prime suspect, just as he is at the moment. Fleming didn't say it, though. Instead, she introduced herself formally, then went on, 'You and I have a lot to talk about, Mrs Mason.'

'Yes, yes, of course. But not here – not in front of him.'

Fleming turned her head to look properly at Jake Mason for the first time. He had been, as her mother had told her, a very good-looking man with his curly dark hair, strong features and the blue eyes which were now staring blankly straight ahead. It was sad to see one side of his mouth drooping and his hands lying in a lifeless position.

Rosamond followed her gaze. 'Yes, I know he looks far away. But they say they think it may be something called locked-in syndrome where he can see and hear and understand, but can't do anything.'

It was a shocking thought. Soberly Fleming said, 'I see,' as the other woman went over to the bed, smoothed the curly hair with a loving hand, kissed his brow and said, 'I'm going now, darling, but I'll be back soon. If that's all right?'

She looked a query at Fleming, who nodded, puzzled and touched by the evident affection. This was a woman who loved her husband: why had she so ruthlessly eliminated herself from his life, and her son's?

Outside, she said, 'I'll go and arrange for a room to be made available. Perhaps you could wait in the sitting-area over there?'

As Rosamond Mason went to sit down, Fleming turned to PC Johnston. 'Explain yourself,' she said shortly.

Johnston looked startled at first, then terrified. 'Oh – Mrs Mason? Shouldn't I have let her in?'

'What were your orders, Constable?'

'Not to let anyone in. But she said she was his wife—'

'Did she produce evidence of identity? No? She could very easily have been a journalist with no respect for his privacy or his dignity, or someone who intended to harm him – even if she was his wife. You were there to protect him against both those things.

'And leaving that aside, didn't you know that police forces up and down the country have been searching for Mrs Mason, and the first thing you should have done was contact HQ and have everyone informed?'

Johnston was sniffing. 'Well, when she just came up like that I thought you must know about her. I thought—'

'Thinking isn't your job. Your job is to follow orders until such time as you have enough experience to make sound judgements. It's not your fault that your temperament isn't suited to police work, but it is your fault that you haven't learned what you've been taught about the basic principles.'

The ward sister was approaching down the corridor. Her face set in lines of disapproval, she ignored Fleming and went to the now-weeping Johnston. 'What's going on here? What's wrong, dear?'

Fleming cut in. 'I'm sorry, Sister, this is an internal disciplinary matter. I'm Detective Inspector Fleming. Can you find me a private room, please, where I can talk to Mrs Mason?'

Glaring at her, the woman led the way to a small waiting-room off the main sitting area; Fleming beckoned to Rosamond Mason and ushered her in. As she shut the door, she heard the nurse say as loudly as she dared, 'Fascist cow!'

Perhaps she was, at that. Sweetness and light didn't cut much ice in police work.

'I wanted to see him first, just by myself.' Rosamond Mason had taken a lacy handkerchief out of her neat black leather envelope purse and was systematically picking it to pieces. 'I didn't realise – I thought he could tell me what was going on.'

'You know what has happened?'

'Only from what I read in the newspapers. I – I haven't really been in contact for a long time. More or less since I left.'

'Why did you leave?' It was the obvious question, but one which had apparently no simple answer. Rosamond looked round the confines of the narrow room as if she were working out an escape route.

'It's – complicated.'

There was a long silence. At last Fleming prompted, 'But from what I saw today, you still love your husband?'

The response to that was immediate. 'Oh yes. Oh yes, I love him. I always have. Too much, perhaps.' She smiled wistfully and Fleming could see how very pretty she must have been when she was younger and happier. 'I think I caught the Mason disease – excessive passions.'

She paused again but this time Fleming said nothing. At last Rosamond began to tell her story, hesitantly at first. 'We were so happy to start with, those first few years. Oh, Edgar was a problem, but that was – that was an *external* problem, if you see what I mean, one we could tackle together.'

What was the problem with Edgar? Fleming wanted to ask, but feared it would break the flow.

'Then Brett came home. Brett—' She stopped. 'It's not my habit to be disloyal or unkind, but I think, in these circumstances, it may be important for you to hear the truth as I see it?'

Encouraged by a nod, she went on. 'She's possessive and extremely vindictive. She'll stop at nothing to get what she wants and when she came home after her marriage failed what she wanted was to be the centre of attention with her father – and Jake.

'Jake shouldn't have let her, of course. He doesn't even like her, but theirs is a very complicated relationship. Their mother died when Jake was ten and Brett was eight and they were left in the care of a father who was, from time to time – well, mad, not to put too fine a point on it.

'Brett uses that to manipulate Jake. He's always rejected any notion that Edgar's problems came from anything other than the absinthe they drank in Spain in the Thirties, but whenever Brett has one of her *petites crises de nerfs* – how I hated that stupid expression – Jake panics. He needs to calm her down, see her normal again, which of course means giving in to her.

'One of her main objectives was to break up our marriage. She didn't succeed; despite the difficulties we were still together, still a couple, until—'

She stopped. The handkerchief was rags now; she looked down at it as if surprised. 'Oh dear, this is very difficult. Could I have a drink of water?'

Fleming looked round. There was a small sink in one corner, beside a tray of tea-making equipment; she filled one of the cups with water and brought it over.

'Thanks.' Rosamond sipped from the thick china cup, then gave a shuddering sigh. 'It was the boys, you see.'

'The boys?'

'Conrad and – and Max. There was a problem, a serious problem, and I could see where it was going to lead.

'They'd never got on. There were constant rows between them. Oh, I know, boys fight, but this went beyond that, way beyond. Brett always took Conrad's side and Jake wouldn't hear a word against Max but I could see there were faults on both sides. I did my best to try to civilise them but Conrad simply despised me and with the atmosphere in that house Max got to the stage where he did too. All any of them seemed interested in was their wretched bulls; the only family holidays we took were to Pamplona and in the end I let them go without me. Those poor, tormented creatures . . .

'By then, Edgar's turns were getting worse, more frequent. He was actively dangerous – Jake had to overpower him physically sometimes – but in between bouts he was still quite normal and Brett wouldn't hear of any sort of serious treatment.

'And the dreadful thing, the horrifying, awful, frightening thing was I could see it coming out in the boys. They needed help to control themselves, maybe even medication – I don't know. But Jake and Brett wouldn't listen; it was just the Mason temper, and they seemed to take a sort of perverse pride in it, as if it were a family talent.

'Then we found out that Max had been experimenting with drugs – oh, the usual teenage stuff, Ecstasy and cannabis. He said Conrad was too, though he hadn't been caught and Brett was adamant that Max was making it up to get his cousin into trouble.

'That was the last straw as far as I was concerned. If, as Jake seemed to believe, it was the absinthe that turned Edgar's mind, what was Ecstasy going to do to his grandsons'? Conrad wasn't my responsibility but Max was. I told Jake he must get him to a clinic, get proper help immediately, but Jake wouldn't hear of it. It would be admitting that there was something wrong in the family and that was against what I used to call Masonic tradition.'

She smiled wryly and took another sip of water. 'We had a terrible, terrible row. It wasn't something we did, really; anger – my own or anyone else's – frightens me and if Jake was angry I gave in. But this time I didn't. I wouldn't yield and neither would he and at last I used my only weapon – I told him I would leave him. By then, I suppose, it had become a trial of strength. He refused, and I left.'

Fleming made her voice carefully neutral. 'You walked out of your marriage and had no further contact for sixteen years?'

'Not quite. He knew he could contact me through my bank and he did, two or three times, asking me to come back, but on his terms. I had to hold out; it was for Max, but I never meant it to be this long. I believed he loved me and I thought he would give in if he truly believed I meant it – and I suppose, eventually, I would have if he wouldn't.

'Then, about eighteen months after I left home he wrote, very briefly, to say that Max had walked out. I phoned him then, offering to come back but – he refused.'

Fleming could see the sparkle of tears. That rejection had hurt; it still did.

'He didn't want me; the marriage was over. I assumed he'd found someone else – he was a very attractive man. So – that was it, really. End of sad, messy story. I always had the local paper sent to me and I would comb it for scraps of information about them all – looking, I suppose, to see if a "companion" was ever mentioned on the social page. I never saw one, but—'

The door opened and the ward sister put her head round it. 'Are you going to be much longer? We've other folks needing this room.'

'I think we're probably finished.' Fleming got up and after a moment Rosamond did too, rising with an obvious effort. She looked very pale and drawn and the nurse gave Fleming another cold, accusing look before withdrawing again.

'Just one final thing. Let me stress that this hasn't been established, it's just a theory we're looking at. It's been suggested that Diana Warwick's death might have been an accident, that she was gored by a bull, the one called Satan, and that your husband might have been so concerned that the animal would have to be slaughtered that he buried her body to conceal what had happened.'

'Oh no.' Rosamond was shaking her head. 'No, no, surely he would never have done something like that. He was certainly foolish – they all were, about that dreadful creature – and it was valuable too, of course – but he wouldn't do that, he couldn't! No, I can't believe he would ever have done anything so wicked. He's a good man, at heart.'

'Sure – certain – wouldn't – couldn't.' The emphatic words only underlined her lack of conviction. She might just as well have come right out and said, 'I don't want it to be true but it's possible.'

'Thank you, Mrs Mason. That's been very helpful. Now, if you can tell me where you're staying someone will come tomorrow to take a proper statement.'

'Can I – can I ask you just one thing? Do you know where Max is? He was quoted in a newspaper report I read, but I thought he couldn't be at home – the nurses said he hasn't been in at all to see his father.'

How typical of Max! Fleming wasn't surprised, but it vexed

her that his cruel indifference would be another sadness for
Rosamond to bear. 'Yes, he's at Chapelton,' she said as
gently as she could. 'Would you like us to notify him that
you're here?'

Rosamond gave a tiny gasp, then compressed her lips as
if willing herself not to show her emotion. When she spoke
her voice was perfectly level. 'Thank you, but no. He'll find
me here when he chooses to come and see Jake.'

The ward sister, standing by the open door, cleared her
throat very pointedly and Marjory left, feeling the hostile
eyes boring into her back as she walked down the corridor.
There was a lot to digest in what Rosamond Mason had
said, but that could wait. There were other things on her
mind; she'd borrowed a police Land Rover and now she was
heading home.

17

'Scott, where are you? You'll need to get down to open the bar.'

Lisa Thomson opened the bedroom door. The curtains were drawn and the room was fetid with stale whisky fumes. Her husband was lying, fully clothed, flat on his back, deep in sottish sleep, his mouth hanging open, and he was snoring loudly. On the bedside table there was a glass with a splash of whisky in the bottom and on the floor a bottle of fifteen-year-old Glenmorangie, three-quarters empty and lying on its side.

At the sight of the bottle her lips tightened. If he was going to get drunk he could at least have chosen a cheap blend – he wasn't even going to taste it after the first couple of glasses. But oh no, Scott had to take the best, as if that proved something.

She'd tried to be a loyal wife, tried to be understanding about the problems: his bad arm, always having business worries, being scared they'd lose everything. But she hadn't had it easy either, and now, when at last they were seeing a good profit . . .

The foot-and-mouth at Chapelton and that poor lassie they'd found had been an awful business right enough, but it had been a blessing for the hotel. With full-board guests and the police camped on the premises, not to mention the bar packed out with folk trying to find out what was going on, they'd got the bank off their backs for a few months at least. She wasn't kidding herself they were out of the woods but at least they weren't finished. You'd have thought Scott could have cheered up a bit.

But he hadn't. He'd been even worse. From the day Laura and the Masons had arrived he'd hardly been sober and she'd had it up to here with his black moods. OK, so he hated the Masons. She didn't take to them herself and the more you saw of them the less you liked them, but acting like a spoiled bairn when you were in business was just daft.

So what was it all about? She'd managed to put it out of her mind – well, she'd had enough to do with making the beds and the meals and the endless cups of coffee and keeping the weans clean and fed until she could crawl thankfully into her bed at night. But it was quieter now . . .

She knew the police had been questioning Scott. She didn't know what they'd asked him, or what he'd said; she knew fine the only answer she'd get if she asked was the back of his hand. She didn't even know how Laura's sister had died, had deliberately not listened to gossip because even thinking about it scared her. It was like looking over the edge of a cliff when everything seemed to tilt and swing away from her. If he'd hit the girl, maybe just that bit too hard . . . It wasn't much of a step from that to wondering if she'd been sharing a bed with a murderer all her married life.

She shuddered, then scolded herself. What on earth was the point of all this daft stuff? What she needed to think about wasn't the past, it was the future for herself and the bairns, for the hotel that could be a really nice wee business.

What would she have done this past week without Dawn to help her? Having another pair of willing hands had made her realise how little Scott had done about the place, even before all this. Dawn was someone she could talk to as well; Lisa had been on her own with Scott and the kids for so long she'd forgotten what it was like to chatter and have a bit of a laugh. There hadn't been a lot of laughter in her life these last few years. Dawn couldn't understand why she put up with him. She'd have put him out long ago, she said, if he went on like that all the time.

Lisa looked down at the figure on the bed. He was unwashed, unshaven, and dribbling from the corner of his mouth. She felt scunnered, almost sick with disgust. His red hair was showing grey at the sides and with the puffy face and sagging chins it was hard to believe he was only nine years older than she was.

The age difference had seemed glamorous when she first met him; he'd been a man, not like the boys her own age. He'd taken advantage of that, she could see now, to bully her, being so possessive and demanding that it was easier just to give up her friendships and stay at home. The only time she'd defied him, to go to a girlfriend's hen-night, he'd slapped her about when she came in – not enough to bruise her but just, as he said, to show her who was boss.

He had been. But now, with all this, she began to think, *Supposing he wasn't here, supposing she had Dawn full-time instead, Dawn being nice and cheery in the bar so people would like coming and stay on for a meal after, instead of Scott drinking all the best whisky and putting them off with glaring at them like it was an insult to be asked to serve them a drink?* It was a dangerous, exciting thought.

There wasn't any point in waking him now anyway. He'd only give her a swearing and in any case from the look of him he'd barely be fit to stand. Anyway, given the weather, there probably wouldn't be anyone venturing out tonight and if there was she could cope herself.

The Masons had checked out, gone back to Chapelton together in the big Range Rover, but not without a lot of shouting and carrying-on. She'd had to listen to them while she made up their bills – discreetly padding them here and there – and Conrad and Mrs Mason had wanted to go off themselves and leave Max behind. But he told them what they could do, said the Range Rover belonged to the farm and he was going to sell up anyway whenever the lawyers allowed him. That got them all going again; they paid their bills without even checking them and she wished she'd slipped in a wee bit more.

The best bit had come when Max had pushed in front of his aunt to go up the stairs and she'd given him his character for having no manners. She tried to remember exactly what Max said: it was really cheeky and funny and she and Dawn could have a good laugh about it later. There was something about it being difficult to know how women wanted to be treated nowadays, but looking at her he could see she must have burned her bra long ago, and then he'd said, 'Not the smartest move, frankly, but I honour your principles and I wouldn't insult you with a patronising, chauvinist gesture.' That was the bit she liked, and Dawn would like that too because they'd giggled about Mrs Mason's saggy boobs before.

So with Laura and the Masons gone there was no dinner to do tonight and with any luck she'd get an evening off with the bairns for once. Just as long as Scott didn't wake up with the hangover he deserved they could have a nice peaceful evening at the telly.

He must have heard the car, heard her coming in. He must certainly have heard her call, 'Bill! Bill, where are you? I'm home!'

Marjory stood in the mud-room and kicked off her snow-caked boots. It was looking unnaturally tidy: the children's boots and shoes were neatly lined up and their coats and jackets still on their pegs, just as she had left them. There was mud all over the red quarry tiles, though; they certainly hadn't been washed recently.

There was no response to her call, no sound of footsteps coming to meet her. It wasn't logical but she had kept a tiny flicker of hope that she had read the signs wrongly, that Bill wasn't angry and would, after all, be happy to see her back. In the continued silence, the flicker died.

It felt strange to be back after all this time, strange to feel the familiar loose handle with the screw that somehow never got tightened on the kitchen door. She opened it and went in.

The man was sitting in the battered armchair beside the Aga, his head back as if he were asleep, but she could see that his eyes were open. The dog at his feet lay, nose on its paws, ears flat, in an attitude of utter dejection. Her ears pricked as her mistress came in and the plumy tail gave a token twitch, then she sighed deeply and the ears flattened again.

They both looked so – so *defeated*. And Bill – she would hardly have recognised the young-looking, vigorous man she had left in this hollow-cheeked shadow with sunken eyes. He looked *old*.

Marjory swallowed hard. 'Hello, Bill.'

He sat up and turned his head, as if only now aware of her presence. 'Marjory.'

It was easier to greet the dog. 'Meg!' she called, bending down and patting her knee. 'Come on, Meggie, what sort of welcome is that? Come and say hello to your mistress!'

At the brightness of her tone, the dog's ears pricked and she jumped up, running across the kitchen with her tail flailing in greeting. Marjory fussed her, pulling the silky ears, patting the smooth head, dodging the ecstatic licks. 'Yes, yes, good girl! That's a good dog. Poor Meggie – did you miss me?'

The dog gave a volley of little, excited barks, then rushed to fetch a half-bald tennis ball and dropped it at Marjory's feet. She laughed, throwing it across the kitchen floor; Meg was off after it at once, her feet skittering on the tiles. Just as they always had, when things were normal.

Bill was leaning forward in the chair now, his elbows on his knees, staring straight ahead. What was he thinking? In the same tone of voice as she had used to the dog, Marjory said lightly, 'And have you missed me too?'

'Yes, of course.' He spoke flatly, as if the words he had said and their meaning had no connection.

She bit her lip. The dog came back with the ball and Marjory threw it again, looking round meanwhile at the state of her kitchen. There was a film of dust over all the surfaces but there was no pile of dishes in the sink, as she had thought there might be; indeed, there was no evidence that the kitchen had recently been used at all. On the scrubbed pine table three bags of groceries hadn't been unpacked, though someone must have picked them up from the bottom of the road. Had he been eating at all, these last few days?

At least the Aga ran on oil and was still putting out its comforting heat. She went over to it, lifted one of the shiny lids and pulled across the big aluminium kettle. 'What I need is a cup of tea. Is there anything left from the Tin?'

'Yes – somewhere.' Bill gestured vaguely towards the table; a Dundee cake, lovingly baked by Janet, stood on a plate with a wedge taken out of it, but judging from the staleness of the exposed crumb, a couple of days earlier. Marjory turned it round and cut into the other side, then brought over the fresh slices, setting one on a plate beside Bill. He looked at it but made no move to pick it up.

Meg had returned to the rug in front of the Aga and lay down with her head on her master's foot. Marjory glanced down. 'Poor Meg! She gets so depressed when she isn't working.'

'Yes. Well . . .' He left the obvious response unstated, his voice trailing away as if speaking was a pointless activity.

The kettle was boiling. Marjory brewed tea, trying not to show her alarm. She fetched the mug that said 'World's Best Dad', a Father's Day present, filled it then handed it to him so that he had no option but to take it. He had a sip, then another, then said, 'That's good.'

'Have some cake. If I tell my mother you haven't finished it she'll be convinced she's lost her touch and go into a decline.'

He picked it up and bit into it obediently as if he had needed to be told to do it, then finished it hungrily.

'I'll get you another slice.' Marjory tried to sound casual. How long was it since he'd eaten? And Meg – Meg, who wasn't usually a cadger, was showing an unusual interest in the crumbs. Had he been forgetting to feed her, too?

She picked up the empty dog-bowl from the floor and filled it from a packet of dry dog food.

When she put down the bowl the dog, normally a delicate feeder, ate ravenously. Marjory had to turn away; as nothing else had, this brought the tears to her eyes. That Bill – *Bill!* – should neglect his dog!

The only way to stifle her rising horror was to be very, very practical. Talking to him, trying to get him to tell her what he had been through to reduce him to this state, wasn't going to work. He had responded to her instructions to eat; perhaps what was best now was to find him things to do, normal, everyday things.

'Bill, I've left my cases and things in the car. Be a dear and bring them in for me, will you? Take them up to the bedroom and I'll sort things out later.'

'Yes.' He got up, moving like an old man, almost shuffling in his slippers. He was on the point of going out into the snow still wearing them; Marjory hurried after him. 'Don't forget to change into your boots!'

She watched him from the kitchen window while he took

out the cases with painstaking slowness – her energetic, impatient husband! – then carry them in and on upstairs. He hadn't changed back to his slippers but she'd rather clean up afterwards than say anything about it now.

Firm ground seemed to be rocking under her feet. She'd been prepared for arguments, recriminations, had come ready to defend herself and hopeful that once they had talked through the difficulties face to face they would weld themselves into a unit again, ready to take whatever the fates had in store together. She couldn't have imagined any other outcome.

She had found instead a monosyllabic stranger, incapable of looking after himself or his dog. What, she wondered, stricken, would have happened if she hadn't come home for another few days?

He was depressed, obviously. It was the most natural thing in the world to be depressed about something so terrible, but – this! Marjory didn't know much about the psychological side of depression, didn't really know much about the psychological side of anything. In fact, she'd always been distinctly scornful of therapies and 'isms' – after all, before Freud people had managed to muddle along talking over their problems with friends and family, then just pulling themselves together and getting on with life. Now, confronted with this, she wasn't so sure. She certainly felt out of her depth.

Bill returned and took his seat again beside the Aga. He'd forgotten to finish his tea; it was cold now with a pale, filmy skin on top. She took it over to the sink and emptied it out.

'You've let that get cold,' she scolded gently, refilled it and once more put it into his hand and stood there till he started to drink. 'Now, what is there for supper?' She didn't expect a response and didn't get one.

In the larder she found some vegetables for soup, and

there was a stew in the deep freeze which could come to gently in the Aga. Bill had always liked stew. And baked potatoes; she scrubbed them and popped them in too. As she bustled round him he sat silent, unnoticing, totally withdrawn.

The comparison struck her suddenly. Here, too, was a victim of locked-in syndrome; though his disability was mental not physical he was at the moment as surely locked in by his total despair.

She had no idea what to do about it. The only consolation was that the murder case was, rightly or wrongly, all but over. Tomorrow night Donald Bailey would declare that Jake Mason was the sole suspect and at that point she could tell him about Bill and ask for – no, demand – compassionate leave. With the case wound up, he couldn't refuse.

Laura wasn't sure what had wakened her. It was cold, certainly, and she had a feeling that she had half-wakened several times to pull the covers more closely about her, but it was the noise outside that made her open her eyes.

She had heard it before, her first night at the Glen Inn – the repeated bellowing of a cow or a bull which sounded in distress or angry, even, though she was no expert. It seemed very loud and quite close at hand, distinct above the noise of the wind which was blowing hard now.

Frowning, she sat up to listen. Surely all the cattle around here had been culled? Conrad had said there wasn't one left, the length and breadth of the Glen. Only a couple of flocks of sheep had been spared, but a sheep would never make a noise like that. It made her uneasy, somehow, though she knew that was foolish. What harm could a suffering animal outside possibly do to her?

Then her brow cleared. She really was a townie! It would be a stag, of course. She'd seen a documentary about it, stags bellowing challenges at one another during the rutting season. But even so, it was strange, surely. It certainly wasn't the rutting season now and she remembered quite clearly that the programme had shown deer feeding in the daytime; why would one be wandering round issuing challenges in the middle of a wild, snowy night? She was cosy in bed and the room was chilly but at last curiosity got the better of her. Without switching on the light, she padded across to the window and lifted the curtain to peer out.

It was pitch dark outside. There was snow being blown against the window, piling up in the corners of the panes, and beyond it she could see nothing at all. She heard the sound again; it seemed to be moving away from her and perhaps it was only her fancy that made her think it had a despairing tone. She waited, but after that there was silence and she was beginning to shiver.

Bending to turn up the radiator below the window, she hopped back into bed to warm up. Foolishly she had left the covers back and the snug nest she had left had cooled down. The hot-water bottle she had taken to bed had fallen out on to the floor; it was stone cold now too and despite some energetic *frottage* her feet obstinately refused to warm up.

She'd never get back to sleep like this! She might just as well resign herself to getting up and refilling her hottie. She could make a cup of tea at the same time. This was where curiosity got you! Heaving herself up with a sigh, she switched on the light – well, pressed the switch, anyway, but nothing happened. She sighed again. Did light bulbs have a special in-built programme that ensured they always went at the most inconvenient possible time?

This time she was wise enough to grope for her dressing-gown and slippers before she embarked on the adventure of finding the light-switch by the door so that at least her toes were protected when she blundered into the chest-of-drawers.

It was only when this switch, too, didn't respond that she understood. Snow, high winds – there must be a power-line down somewhere. Stories appeared every year in the papers about the snowbound countryside and people without electricity for days on end. You shook your head sympathetically when you read them but it didn't prepare you for the reality of being alone in a snowbound cottage without light or heat.

No cup of tea, then, and no comforting hot-water bottle either. But no light! All at once the darkness seemed so thick as to be positively oppressive. She couldn't even see what time it was, to know how long it would be before daylight came.

There must, surely, be candles or a torch somewhere. But how could she find them, when she didn't know where to look and would get colder and colder as she searched? No, however uncomfortable it might be, the most sensible thing to do was find a pair of socks and another sweater and get back into bed. Perhaps, by morning, the power would have been restored and she could feel in control again instead of like a child, frightened of the dark.

18

Laura had lain awake for a long time but when she fell asleep at last she slept deeply, only waking when the sun came through the curtains, shining with unusual brilliance. Groggily, she fumbled for her watch and blinked to focus on it. Half-past nine – that was a surprise! She'd been sure she wouldn't be able to get back to sleep at all.

The room, which had seemed chilly last night, was now icy cold. She could see her breath forming on the air, which didn't bode well for the power problem, and sure enough, when she clicked the bedside light experimentally nothing happened.

Pulling on her dressing-gown on top of the jersey she had been wearing in bed, she went to the window again and opened the curtains. The white light hit her like a blow, making her eyes water.

It was a clear blue day and the snow had drifted, whipped up by the wind. In the reflected sunlight it was dusted with diamond sparkles and there were long blue shadows from the fence-posts and the low trees which darkened to violet in the deeper shade of the house, while the distant pine trees were stark black against the white backcloth. It looked like a Whistler *Nocturne* and when Laura's eyes had adjusted to the intensity of the light, she gasped at the beauty of it all.

With the darkness, her mood of last night had vanished. Looking out this morning, the lack of electricity felt like a bit of a joke, an adventure. There should still be enough warm water in the tank for washing and if she had to have bread instead of toast and orange juice instead of tea for breakfast, it wasn't exactly a serious hardship. She could search the cupboards for candles; there might even be lamps and a primus stove for just such emergencies.

But there didn't seem to be. And it really was very, very cold; she'd have sold her soul for a cup of tea. She began to feel indignant; surely someone who lived here should know what could happen! Certainly, Mrs MacNab had said she didn't usually have bookings before Easter, but even so . . . It was nearly ten o'clock; you'd have thought at least she'd have come along to see how her tenant was faring by now.

She couldn't even work on her article. She'd tried, briefly, even taking it over to the window in the sunshine where it was a little warmer, but her fingers were so cold she couldn't type properly and anyway the battery would probably run out before she could finish. Even if it didn't, she'd have to get out to find a terminal since there was no phone-line to the cottage; she'd a couple of facts to check on the Internet and she'd promised to e-mail the article to Nick Dalton at the *Sunday Tribune* within the next couple of days too and it wouldn't be clever to let him down. It was all very frustrating, particularly when you had no idea how long this might go on.

There certainly wasn't a lot to be gained by sitting here with nothing to do except get colder and colder. Mrs MacNab had said she didn't live far away and Laura had taken the precaution yesterday of buying some sturdy walking-boots; the exercise would do her good and warm her up and perhaps there was an open fire at the other end. Or an Aga, with scones baking . . .

She put on another couple of layers, then her raincoat on top, and looking like the Michelin man set off. The wind had scoured the garden, stripping the snow almost bare in some places and piling it up to two or three feet against the walls and in the ditches. The little hump-backed bridge was fairly clear but below it the snow had accumulated between the banks of the burn and only the merest trickle of running water was visible.

Once she was on the road walking was a little easier. There were even some blurred tracks from a vehicle which had gone past the house then turned in a field gateway further along – or perhaps those were just Conrad's tracks from yesterday. It was certainly a lovely day to be out. The air was like champagne, deliciously cold and refreshing, and somewhere a bird was singing loudly. She looked round to track the sound and saw a robin sitting on a snow-capped fence post, red chest puffed out and beak open, looking as if he'd heard he was in with a chance of a starring role on a Christmas card and was giving it his best shot.

It was all very, very beautiful. This place had a lot of the qualities she'd been looking for in her search for somewhere she could put down roots and feel at home: she loved the tranquillity of the countryside and the busy, friendly little towns where passers-by smiled at one another. The people she'd met were lovely too, with an old-fashioned warmth and courtesy she thought had vanished long ago, and she loved the soft accent and the vivid Scots expressions they used. But could she ever think of it as anything other than the backdrop to her sister's tragedy?

Deep in thought, it took her a moment to notice that the snow was getting deeper underfoot; there was a corner ahead and as she reached it she realised that the fence posts marking the lines of the fields had disappeared. She stopped.

There must be a dip in the road here. You wouldn't know, though, because it was a solid, level sheet of white. The wind must have whipped snow off the fields on either side to collect in the hollow here and there was a drift which must be four feet deep at least. Even if she had a four-wheel drive, Mrs MacNab wouldn't be coming this way today and Laura certainly wasn't going to make it through to the farmhouse of her imagination with its snug kitchen and the smell of home baking.

Absurdly disappointed, she turned back. She'd just have to go home and wait till the power came back on again. She had a roof over her head, lots of clothes she could pile on and food to eat even if it couldn't be heated up; she wasn't going to die of starvation or hypothermia. But didn't these power cuts sometimes go on for days? Last night had probably brought dozens of lines down and with snowdrifts like this all over the area the linesmen would be finding it hard even to get about.

That could mean another night of darkness like the last one – and a long night too when the sun disappeared in the late afternoon and rose late. Anything but that!

Galvanised by the thought, she set off in the opposite direction, back past the house, in the direction of the Glenluce road. It wasn't so very far, and then it was only a couple of miles to the main road. She and Brad had done a lot of hiking when they were first married; even given the snow, that distance wasn't a problem and she reckoned that here-abouts, in weather like this, you could be pretty sure someone would stop and give you a lift into town. The Galloway Arms with its blazing fire and nursery food seemed a very appealing place right now.

Half a mile on, the snow got deeper again. There were tyre marks, only just visible – Conrad's again? – but to go on, she'd have to wade through a foot and a half of snow, with no guarantee that there wouldn't be a worse drift round the next corner. The sun had gone in now too and even her thick clothing wasn't protecting her from the bitter cold. Miserably, she turned back to plod slowly home.

Flakes of snow were drifting down again; the landscape
had lost all its colour and looked bleak and sombre. The
back of the row of cottages, broken only by the narrow windows of the bedrooms, looked forbidding too. It was set back
a little, so that there was an expanse of rough ground between
the building and the road.

Walking along with her head bowed, Laura noticed, as she
had not noticed before, that there was trampled snow all
across this space. The bellowing animal! It must have been
just outside her window – no wonder it had wakened her.
She went to look, hoping that even she might be able to
guess from the tracks what it had been.

Like the tyre marks, the prints had been blurred and distorted by the action of the wind, but the evidence was unmis-
takable. These were human, not animal. Someone had been
prowling backwards and forwards outside her window last
night. Someone bellowing like a beast.

She gasped. Whoever it had been was long gone, but fear
transcended logic. She fled, slipping a couple of times but
managing to save herself; inside, with the door locked and
bolted, she slumped against it, breathless and with her heart
racing in terror.

What was she to do now? Already the sky was grey and
the light seemed pallid, unearthly. How could she cope with
hours of pitch darkness and terror?

There was only one thing for it – swallow her pride and
ring Conrad. She hunted in her bag for her mobile phone,
clicked it on and waited impatiently for a connection, waited
and waited, then stared in horrified disbelief at the terse message: 'No signal.'

It was after ten o'clock when Marjory Fleming got in to
Police Headquarters. She didn't feel guilty about that; she'd
every intention of leaving early too, once she'd spoken to

Donald Bailey. In terms of overtime (unpaid) she was well ahead of the game.

She'd had to stand over Bill this morning to make sure he ate a proper breakfast, and poor neglected Meg had to be given a good walk too; she rushed around, barking joyously in the snow. Then Marjory had to embark on the uncomfortable business of phoning round farming neighbours she would once have called friends, to be greeted with polite hostility. There was huge sympathy for Bill, though, and she'd arranged for a steady stream of visitors. Surely that must cheer him up? And Janet had promised to brave the tricky roads to go out and give him his lunch; having had experience of her mother's gently implacable tactics during episodes of childish faddiness, Marjory could feel confident that Bill would eat it up like a good boy and have a nice clean plate.

She made her appointment with Donald Bailey for later in the day. She wanted to clear her desk and have detailed plans in place for covering her absence before she saw him. Fortunately, being SIO for the murder meant she didn't have any other on-going cases, but even so she'd have a powerful amount of work to shift, just tying up the loose ends.

She'd have to see Tam MacNee and she wasn't looking forward to that. She told herself she had no need to feel guilty; it wasn't as if there was any hard evidence that it hadn't happened in just the way Conrad Mason had suggested. She'd need more justification for sacrificing her personal duties to her professional ones than a couple of question marks and a gut feeling, but she wasn't entirely sure that Tam would see it that way. Still, her mind was made up.

As usual, there were e-mails waiting. She sat down to flip through them for anything urgent before she phoned to summon Tam and get it over with. Most seemed to be internal memos and reports: those could wait.

Then one appeared which caught her eye, from the path

lab in Glasgow, and she remembered the funny scrap of material she'd sent them – had that only been yesterday, when she'd been in such a bullish mood? She could only think it was lucky it had come in now instead of later, when whoever took over from her might well query the expense.

She opened it. It was an informal report, headed 'Interesting!' and as she read it she went very still. The sample she had sent, it said, under a comparison microscope had been found to match some scraps of rotting fabric found with the remains. Though they still hadn't completed all the tests they were fairly sure it was cotton flannelette with a stripe in it – gents' pyjama material, it suggested.

Fleming was still staring at the screen trying to make sense of the implications when there was a tap at the door and Tam MacNee appeared.

'I hear Bailey's set to pull the rug out,' he said without preamble. 'Just when I'd got confirmation from the Met Office that the weekend we're talking about was in the middle of a cold snap when it had been below freezing even during daylight hours for three days. So there shouldn't have been an animal outside at all, but of course he'll pay no heed. All the man ever thinks about is preserving the budget so there's enough in the kitty to let the high heid yins swan off to the Caribbean on fact-finding missions. He'll never agree to give us more time.'

'He may have to. Look at this, Tam.'

He came round to squint over Fleming's shoulder; his lips pursed in a silent whistle of surprise as he read and she explained what she'd done. 'Though what was the girl doing, out in the maze wearing men's pyjamas, if they're right – does that imply she was taken out of her bed, or even killed there, maybe? Though why the maze . . .'

Thinking aloud, she didn't notice MacNee's uncomfortable silence. 'Er—' he said at last, and she looked at him sharply. 'Does this mean something to you?'

'I'd forgotten about it, to be honest. It was my first interview with Thomson – you've got it there somewhere.' He nodded towards the computer. 'But you maybe haven't had time to read it.'

'I've got upwards of a hundred reports in there,' she said tartly. 'I need a steer if there's something significant.'

'Aye, of course you do. I just didn't think to mention it. Thomson said he saw her going out her flat at night in her pyjamas two or three times. I asked, was she going to meet someone, but he said no, she was always back a few minutes later. Seemed a daft-like thing to be doing in the winter but I just put her down as one of these fey types that go off and commune with Mother Nature. Didn't seem exactly relevant – but with this, now . . . Meeting someone after all?'

Fleming was tapping her front tooth with a pencil. 'Doesn't sound likely, just for a few minutes. But why on earth – oh, you don't think she could have been a sleep-walker, do you? Cat had a spell of that once and we found her outside a couple of times. We need to check that with the sister. Where's she staying – still at the Glen Inn?'

MacNee shook his head. 'No, she upped sticks the other day – scunnered with the Masons, poor lass, if you ask me. DC Nisbet has her address – a holiday cottage somewhere off the Glenluce road, as far as I mind.'

'Not the cleverest place to be at the moment, with the weather. I was listening to Radio Solway on the way in this morning and some of the upland roads are blocked and they've power cuts out there too.

'I tell you what,' Fleming went on, tongue in cheek. 'I'll give you the chance to be her knight in shining armour if she's sitting there all cold and pitiful. Don't say I'm not good to you! You can ask her about the sleep-walking – oh, and show her this.' She picked up the ankle bracelet which was lying on her desk in a sealed plastic bag. 'Ask if she can identify it as her sister's – though I have to say that after this I'm pretty sure it must be. But I'm warning you, if you manage to get yourself snowed in with her, I'm going to clype on you to Bunty.'

Tam took the joke in good part. 'Don't do that! "In hell she'd roast me like a herring!" Oh, all right, all right.' He fished out 10p and put it into the box on the desk in front of him as he got up.

On the way out he turned back. 'Did I hear you're back at the Mains? How's Bill?'

'Don't ask. No, I really mean that. I'm in a mess but I'll have to sort it myself.'

He still hesitated. 'You know where I am, if you're needing anything.'

'Yes. Somewhere in a snowy glen chatting up a glamorous babe young enough to be your daughter. Get on with it!'

Her jaunty smile faded as he shut the door. She'd have to change her appointment and go to see Bailey as soon as possible about this new development. It would mean firing up the investigation again, taking the maze apart to find out what secrets it might be concealing. Finger-tip searches, digging – the whole, let's-burn-money paraphernalia. How could she tack, 'And by the way, I'm demanding compassionate leave,' on to the end of that?

It was half-past twelve when the sound of a car's engine brought Laura leaping to her feet. It was coming slowly and it would have to turn and come back this way once it reached the snowdrift round the corner but she wasn't taking any chances. She flung open the door and skittered along the path to the road without pausing for a coat or a change of footwear.

Her first thought, on seeing the Range Rover stopping by the gate, was that Conrad must have either a very forgiving nature or a particularly thick skin. She was framing an exquisitely abject apology when she realised that it wasn't Conrad jumping down from the driver's seat. It was Max.

She had believed she didn't want to see Conrad; it was only now that she realised how much more welcome he would have been. But right at this moment – and she seemed to be saying this rather a lot lately – beggars couldn't be choosers.

'Hey, Laura!' His greeting was jaunty but she thought he was looking a little shaken. 'Whew! That was a bit hairy! Still, it's worth it to find a reception committee of one – I like a girl who's eager.'

He advanced towards her with his arms outspread; she took a neat step back and grasped his hands, leaning forward to submit to being kissed on both cheeks.

'I hate to disappoint you, Max, but it's the car, frankly. I'd welcome anyone who'd come to rescue me from this Arctic hell.'

'Ah, I was right, then!' He sounded gleeful. 'I popped down to the Glen Inn for a lunchtime drink – had to get away from the house with the old girl stomping round stabbing me with looks of hatred and Conrad behaving like a gorilla with a hangover. They'd had a power cut since last night so I said to myself, Max, there's a damsel who probably needs rescuing. Get in there! So here I am!'

'You haven't had it at Chapelton?'

'We're on the supply from the farther end of the road. So far, so good.'

'Lucky you. Come in, anyway. It's freezing out here – not that it isn't freezing inside too. I'm just going to pack up rapidly, then hitch a lift to the Galloway Arms, if you don't mind.'

Max followed her into the cottage. 'I'm afraid there's a teeny problem with that. The snowplough hasn't come through yet and it was skin-of-the-teeth stuff getting along here – would have turned back, if it hadn't been an errand of mercy—'

Laura turned, dismayed. 'You mean you can't get down to the main road? I was counting on that! I've got an article to finish and e-mail to the *Sunday Tribune* and if the Glen Inn's off too—'

Max raised his hand. 'Chill! Unlikely as it may seem, even at primitive Chapelton we're connected. The office computer is state of the art. Out here in the sticks it has to be. It's the only link to civilisation. Even dear Auntie Brett goes Internet shopping.'

'But—'

'No buts! Run off and get packed, ducky, and I'll take you back to Chapelton for a nice hot bath and a cup of decent coffee. There's even a guest suite, you know, so Auntie can't possibly object to giving shelter to an orphan of the storm.'

Go to the site of her sister's murder and unhallowed grave, where, no doubt, there were still the scars of the investigation, where Dizzy's ghost would be round every corner? It was a horrifying prospect, with the Mason family *en masse* to make bad even worse.

But what were the alternatives? At the moment the snow seemed to be confining itself to occasional flurries and in theory the snowplough could arrive to clear the road at any moment – but even so she'd have to go out and search for someone prepared to take her into Kirkluce. Or then again, it might not. Which would mean another night of being cold, in darkness and alone with the fear of whoever had trodden down the snow outside her window . . .

She went into the bedroom to pack up the essentials, without further argument. She could come back later when the roads were open and her car was repaired to clear the house but she certainly wasn't going to spend another night here, even if the Met Office and Scottish Power gave her signed guarantees that it wouldn't happen again.

Laura finished packing and Max took her case as she came out of the bedroom. She picked up her laptop and papers, then followed him out and locked the door.

It had occurred to her to wonder if his refusal to drive her into Kirkluce had been yet another manipulative device, but after a few minutes on the road she made him a mental apology. Max wasn't confident in these difficult conditions; Conrad was a much better, more experienced driver and she'd felt safe with him even in the blizzard, but with Max driving the heavy vehicle seemed to have a mind of its own, particularly at the corners. There seemed to be a lot of swearing and she could see his knuckles were white as he gripped the wheel. Still, they were going so slowly that she didn't think they could come to serious harm, and she definitely owed him a debt of gratitude for coming to rescue her.

As they lurched at last up the Chapelton drive and on to the parking area outside the house, Conrad appeared down the steps. He was obviously very angry. Max, who had barely said a word to Laura as he struggled with the car, turned now with a triumphant grin.

'*Such* fun to wind him up, I always find! He's jealous, of course, because I thought of rescuing you first, but I wonder what his excuse will be?' He jumped down from the car without waiting for a reply.

Cancel the debt of gratitude, Laura thought. With these two, it was all about a kind of sibling rivalry taken to pathological extremes: they might talk about attraction or friendship where she was concerned but in reality she was nothing more than a grown-up plaything for them to quarrel over.

Conrad, red in the face, was yelling something about Max's incompetence and risking their transport on dangerous roads. Max, smirking, was planting occasional barbs, like a matador with a maddened bull. They paid absolutely no attention to Laura as she got down from the 4x4.

She found she couldn't help looking about her, despite the resolution she had made not to seek out evidence of Dizzy's tragedy. All that was visible, though, was the blanket of untrodden snow which lay all about the house; she could see where a drive went round farm buildings and a straggling hedge but nothing beyond that.

Leaving the men still engrossed in their quarrel, she walked up the steps to the front door, which was standing open. A little hesitantly, she stepped into the huge, bare hall. There was nothing to soften the oppressive Victorian style; such indifference to the impression it must make on a visitor made her feel it had an unwelcoming, almost hostile atmosphere. How had Dizzy felt, coming here as a lively twenty-year-old? Had she too felt oppressed, or was Laura's own response exaggerated by hindsight?

At least it was warm, though. A huge, old-fashioned radiator against the side wall was pumping out waves of heat which drew Laura irresistibly. It was too hot to touch with her bare hands but she leaned against it gratefully, feeling the warmth seep through the layers of her clothes.

'And what, may I ask, are you doing in this house?'

The harsh, challenging voice from behind her made her jump guiltily and swing round. Brett Mason was coming down the stairs glaring accusingly as if she'd caught Laura in the act of putting the family silver into a bag marked 'Swag'.

Fright gave way to annoyance. 'I'm sorry I startled you,' Laura said coolly. 'I'm Max's guest – I was snowed up in a house with no power and he very kindly rescued me.'

Brett had reached the foot of the steps; her eyes raked Laura from head to foot. 'If you imagine Max ever does anything from kindness you are sadly deluded. And if you imagine that this will bring you into closer contact with my son—'

Laura was startled. 'Nothing could be further from my thoughts,' she protested.

The other woman laughed harshly. 'So you say. That's what they always say.' She walked away, vanishing through a door at the back of the hall.

Staring after her, Laura shivered, suddenly cold despite all that the radiator could do.

19

'And how was your wee friend, then?' DC Charlotte Nisbet greeted her sergeant mockingly as he came into the CID room, pink-nosed from the cold, rubbing his hands together and very bad-tempered. 'Suitably grateful, was she?'

'You tell me. If she is, it's to someone who got there before I did. A fair waste of time, that was. It's no joke out there, and I've put a dunt in the side wing of the car from a wall that appeared suddenly in the middle of the road. I'd have turned back if I hadn't thought the lassie was on her own with the electric off.'

Shaking her head, Nisbet said solemnly, 'Terrible. And you all set to do your Good Samaritan impersonation. I bet he'd have been pretty scunnered too if someone had bruised his camel and then nipped in first with the bandages.'

'If you've nothing better to do than sit there thinking up witticisms, so-called, you haven't a big enough case-load.'

She grinned. 'I'm hard at work, Sarge. The word's out we're back in business with the Warwick murder.'

'I was never out of it, me. Far too bloody tidy for my liking, with the Masons all ettling to pin it on the old boy. Any normal family, they'd be dinging on about how he couldn't have done it.'

'You could say. But Tam, take a keek at this.' She swung her chair round to her computer. 'I've been combing the records, here and downstairs in the files. All that we have on the Masons is a slap on the wrist to Max for possession in his teens and a few speeding tickets. But look what came up on Scott Thomson.'

MacNee came round to peer over her shoulder. 'Got form, has he? Breach of the peace? Could be anything – that charge isn't called "the Fiscal's flexible friend" for nothing.'

'Yes, but look.' She punched another few keys. 'It was stalking, basically. Persistent too. He was living across in Lanark at the time – got himself arrested for following this girl, then got bailed with the condition he didn't go near her. By the time the case was called he'd breached his bail and the Sheriff got stroppy – locked him up for a couple of months.'

'Well, well. He must have known we'd likely pick this up – and he was the one who told me he'd seen the girl out at night in her pyjamas. Did he think someone might have noticed him watching her, maybe, and told his Uncle Tam before they could? I think I'm needing to have another wee chat with our Mr Thomson. But it can wait. I'll pass this on to the Boss but you'll not catch me on that road again until it's been cleared.'

Lunch had been a deeply uncomfortable meal. There was a communal basement kitchen, serving both the upper and the lower flats; Laura and Max were sitting at a table in the window of the cavernous room eating a pizza Max had taken from the freezer and heated up in a microwave when Conrad and his mother appeared.

Brett ignored Laura and Max completely, going to the fridge and taking out half a dozen eggs, then finding a bowl to break them into, chopping tomatoes. Conrad's greeting was correct but chilly, leaving Laura in no doubt that he saw her acceptance from Max of the help she had rejected from him as a deliberate snub; she wasn't sure he even knew about the power cut, and would have liked to explain. But he had turned his back on her, busying himself with setting out plates and cutlery on a tray while his mother cooked an omelette.

Max rose, pointedly. 'Let's take our coffee in the flat, Laura. It's getting a bit crowded in here.'

The remark was patently both absurd and provocative. Laura said firmly, 'Thanks, Max, but I'll go to my room if you don't mind. I've got a deadline for my article and I'm seriously behind – with the power cut and everything.' She stressed the final phrase.

'Hey, come on! Ten minutes won't hurt—'

'Sorry, Max.' Picking up her mug, she headed for the door, but not before she had seen Max pouting like a child and Conrad smirking maliciously. A plague on both their houses!

'Never know when to back off, do you, Max? Give the girl a bit of space!'

'She's my friend and my guest. Nothing to do with you.'

They were off again. Laura left the room, shutting the door quietly, but she was aware of Brett Mason staring at her with what could only be hatred in those strange pale green eyes.

The guest suite on the ground floor, where Max had installed her, was surprisingly comfortable. Like what she had seen of the rest of the house, the furnishing and decor were old-fashioned and there was a fine layer of dust on the polished surfaces of mahogany chests and tables, but the sitting-room and bedroom were spacious and blessedly warm and had an internal bathroom between them.

The other thing she liked was the key in the lock of the door to the hall. Turn it, leave it in place, and they'd have to start breaking windows to get to you – though it was an uncomfortable thought that this had been the first thing she noticed when Max showed her in.

There was even an electric kettle with a tray of cups and saucers and a jar of Nescafé; it wasn't exactly fresh but only some of it had coalesced into a lump at the bottom. Laura made herself a cup of what could loosely be described as black coffee, sipped it and grimaced. But at least it was hot; she'd suddenly come to appreciate the virtues of 'hot'. She set up her laptop on the table in the sitting-room and settled down.

Laura enjoyed what she was doing. She even thought, without false modesty, that she was rather good at it. She worked solidly for an hour and at the end of it felt more or less satisfied with what she had written. Her only problem was the facts she needed about the foot-and-mouth epidemic; she had to be precise about these, but fortunately Max had shown her before lunch where there was a small ante-room off the main farm office with a fixed-line computer for e-mail and Internet access. She could check those final details then send on her article to Nick Dalton by e-mail as an attachment.

With her work copied on to a floppy, Laura went out into the hall. It was still light outside but here darkness was gathering already; the heavy chandelier which came on when she pressed the switch had several dead bulbs and produced only a meagre pool of light in the centre of the hall, doing nothing to chase the lurking shadows in the corners. There was no one to be seen, but Laura couldn't help glancing uneasily over her shoulder as she crossed the parquet floor. The clicking of her shoes seemed very loud in the echoing silence.

The cramped office itself was sternly businesslike, lit by a couple of fluorescent strips, with filing cabinets and shelves holding stationery round the walls. The curtains hadn't been opened today; Laura drew them back to catch the last of the daylight. On the desk a computer flickered with a screen-saver where shapes in different colours stretched and tumbled and the swivel chair was pushed back, as if the person who'd been using it, last night probably, had risen in haste or impatience. She swung it back, trying not to wonder if Dizzy, too, had sat in this office, on this chair, while she performed the secretarial part of her Girl Friday duties.

Someone had been using the Internet, she found, and conveniently hadn't shut it down. She keyed in the first of her searches; it didn't take long to find the site but once located it was slow to download and she sat tapping her fingers impatiently on the desk. That was when it caught her eye: the little legend at the bottom of the screen showing the site previously accessed most recently. 'Therianthropy', it said.

She frowned at it, her curiosity aroused. The word rang a faint bell; she'd definitely heard it somewhere before. In a lecture, in a textbook? It had strange connotations . . .

She couldn't pin it down. It was irritating her like an itch she couldn't scratch and when the information she'd been looking for came up on the screen she noted it down automatically, her mind elsewhere.

Was checking out what someone had been looking at on the Internet in the same category as reading a book they'd left open, or was it more akin to eavesdropping or reading a letter someone had left lying around? It was an interesting moral question – but it was so annoying that she couldn't remember what she knew! If she just glanced at it to refresh her memory, then closed it again . . .

She clicked on the icon. The screen went black, then an image came up so startling, and with such shocking implications, that the ethical question was totally forgotten.

'At least we've got the digger on site,' Marjory Fleming said. 'I've spoken to the Roads Department and they'll have the snowplough up there at first light. Tam MacNee says it's dire out there at the moment so it's not worth trying to do anything today.'

'No, of course not.' Superintendent Bailey's tone was snappish. 'It's hardly urgent, is it – we're fifteen years off the pace anyway. But I don't quite understand your theory – I take it you've now decided to discount the pathologist's judgement that she was gored?'

Fleming didn't sigh – she was quite proud of that. 'Not really. I haven't reached the stage of having a fully-fledged theory as yet – not enough evidence and a lot of it contradictory. As you always say, running a theory ahead of the facts is like putting the hounds out ahead of the fox.'

It was a pet aphorism; he was obliged to agree, however reluctantly. 'So what's the point you're making, then?'

'The lab has established that she was wearing what they think might have been flannelette pyjamas when she was killed. According to her sister she always wore an ankle bracelet; I found one in the old maze beside the field where the body was found, along with a scrap of rotting fabric that turned out to be the same stuff. That suggests she was at the very least in the maze when she was wearing the clothes she was killed in.'

'Pyjamas, did you say? What on earth was the girl doing out in pyjamas?'

'She may not have been. She might have had a blouse made of flannelette, say, or she might have been killed in her bed, then moved. But there's eye-witness evidence to suggest she might have been in the habit of sleep-walking – we haven't managed to ask the sister for confirmation yet.

'The reason I want to dig up the maze is to see if anything emerges to tell us where she was actually killed – and if it was there I think we would have to discount the idea of the bull. It would hardly be charging down the alleyways.'

Bailey pounced. 'The bull might be in the maze, but why

wouldn't she have wandered into the bull's field if she was sleep-walking? You can see exactly how it would happen – blunders in, bull takes exception, charges, gores her. There you are – she wouldn't even take avoiding action. Marjory, I think you're getting carried away. Occam's Razor, you know!' He was triumphant.

Of course she knew. Occam's Razor was another of Bailey's favourite principles: some medieval bloke called Occam had said that if there was a simple explanation it was usually right. Bailey liked simple answers – and in this case, how could she say he was wrong? He'd spotted a glaring flaw in her argument which, she had to admit, had not occurred to her; had she, perhaps, allowed her dislike and distrust of Conrad Mason to blind her to the obvious?

But Tam had agreed. She collected her wits. 'There are a couple of other factors. We've established when this occurred – it was in the middle of a cold snap. The stockman has orders to move the cattle inside when it's below freezing and we're talking about several days when there were day-time temperatures of minus two degrees.'

Bailey frowned, then shrugged his shoulders. 'So it was the bull's pen she wandered into, after the maze—'

It was a weaker position and he knew it, but he wasn't going to shift easily. Fleming went on, 'And another thing – the person who told MacNee about her going out at night was Scott Thomson, the stockman, whose flat was next to Diana Warwick's with a window overlooking the yard. DC Nisbet ran a check on police records and found out he had Previous. A conviction for stalking, basically.'

'Stalking!' She'd managed to shake him with that. It was powerful precisely because it chimed with standard police procedure: you didn't sit around thinking up fancy ways it might have happened, you looked for someone with a record of having done something similar. 'Play the man not the ball' was another of the Thoughts of Chairman Bailey, but quoting it at him ran the risk of overkill.

He was chewing at his lip. Fleming waited in silence; she'd learned that the female tendency to elaborate for the sake of emphasis didn't work with men. Nagging, they called it.

'Suppose I see what you mean,' he said gruffly. 'But I'm still not convinced.'

That was the opening. A rat on its way up a drainpipe would have been left standing by the speed of her response. 'Nor am I, Donald. But we can't be seen to be ignoring leads in a murder case, can we? The sister's up here writing an article on foot-and-mouth for the *Sunday Tribune* and I don't want the Galloway Constabulary's failure to investigate properly to be the subject of her next in-depth feature.'

Bailey shuddered visibly. 'Certainly not. All right, Marjory, carry on. But there has to be a limit on this thing – if it doesn't turn up something a bit more concrete in the next couple of days, we go back to the original theory. All right?'

Pleased with the effectiveness of her advocacy, Fleming was walking down the corridor before she remembered that she hadn't even thought about her request for leave, let alone mentioned it.

Tomorrow. She'd do it tomorrow.

It wouldn't turn! Stiff with disuse, the key resisted Laura's attempts to lock the door to the guest suite. Her hands were shaking too, which didn't help. She made herself stop for a deep, calming breath, then took the key out and jiggled it delicately back in again. This time it locked; with a half-sob of relief she went through to the sitting-room and sat down heavily on a sofa. The images she had seen on the screen still tumbled horribly through her mind: the crazed eyes, the fangs, the claws and the hair, the savaged victims . . .

After the first site, she'd checked back through the computer

record: four other therianthropy sites had recently been
accessed, all bizarre, all unhealthy. With her ears straining for
the sound of footsteps in the hall, she'd taken the risk of running a Google check on the word and found thousands of
entries; the ones you stumbled on easily came into the 'wacky
but normal' category. The four which someone in this house
had sought out last night most definitely did not.

She'd realised instantly what she knew about the word. It
was the broader term, derived from the Greek for 'wild
beast', for the condition known to psychiatrists as lycanthropy.

Were-wolves. These had been the images displayed, but
the text had reminded her that there were many forms of
were-creatures: were-bears, were-leopards, were-bats . . .
Were-bulls?

Laura wasn't superstitious. Certainly not! These were
pitiable, delusional people and she was a rational scientist –
but it was easier to be rational when you weren't imprisoned
by the elements in the wilds of Scotland in a house with a
dysfunctional family, one of whom might have killed your
sister.

The huge sash windows gaped at her blackly, great sheets
of glass which a tap with a stone would shatter. And she had
locked herself in; it had occurred to her at the time that
unlocking the door again might prove even harder than
locking it had. It wasn't paranoid to try to work out a strategy
for security, she told herself; it was purely common sense.

Then Laura noticed the shutters – solid, Victorian shutters on either side of the window. They didn't look as if they
had been painted since the pine had been varnished when
the house was built and sure enough when she pulled them
they creaked open. The backs were thick with dust and cob-
webs but for once she didn't care about spiders as she
unhooked the solid iron bar and swung it into position to

secure them. She breathed a quick prayer that the bedroom was similarly untouched.

She was lucky. It too had working shutters, so here in her self-constructed fortress no one could reach her. She even felt secure enough to feel ashamed that she'd allowed the power of myth to spook her. Especially since the psychological reality was probably more scary still.

That story the Mason cousins had told her, about Dizzy's death being a terrible accident, covered up by Max's father – the Minotaur, as Max called him – didn't ring true. Who would take a risk like that for the sake of a bull – unless, of course, he believed himself to be that bull, believed rightly or wrongly that in his altered shape he had committed murder?

Shape-shifters – that was another term for them, a name that ran through the history and mythology of a dozen different cultures. And from the evidence she had seen this afternoon there were still plenty of people out there who believed an animal spirit to be an integral part of their being. For some it was an affectation, for others a sort of spiritual, New Age-style identification with the favoured beast.

For others, like the originators of the sites which had so recently been accessed, it was a darker belief altogether. These were people who believed they changed physically, who externalised violent internal conflict by projecting the guilt for their actions on to the animal which 'took over' their personality. Three of the sites that Laura had seen celebrated savage crime allegedly committed while in a state of metamorphosis; the fourth, sad and sick, talked of a struggle against an irresistible compulsion.

It wasn't Jake Mason who'd been looking at these last night. And, she thought suddenly, it wasn't Jake who had been bellowing and trampling the snow outside her window last night, either. What would have happened if she'd gone outside to investigate? Was that what had happened to Dizzy?

Conrad had definitely said that the pathologist's verdict was that she had been gored by a bull's horn. But surely there were other things which could make that sort of wound? Or a horn could be taken from a carcase, perhaps, and used as a weapon in a lycanthropic frenzy?

According to both Max and Conrad, Dizzy had been maddening in her desirability. She'd provoked a frenzy of rivalry and tension; Laura, after her own experience, could readily believe that day in, day out, that sort of atmosphere in this claustrophobic setting might produce the sort of internal stress which could only find relief in an outburst. Jealousy is a powerfully destructive emotion in any of its forms: it wasn't hard to construct scenarios leading to murder.

'*If I can't have you, no one else will.*'

'*If I kill you, he will suffer.*'

'*If my son chooses you, I will lose him.*'

She could hear them saying it, could almost imagine one of them saying it now . . . She went very cold. This wasn't speculation about something that had happened fifteen years ago. The same pressures were present, the same people were within these four walls.

Except the Minotaur. Max's monster had been trapped, if not slain, but somehow the maze of human relationships and emotions here at Chapelton seemed as dark and as dangerous as ever.

20

It was the grinding sound of heavy machinery that woke her, followed a moment later by the loud and persistent ringing of a doorbell. Laura opened her eyes to total blackness; with a sense of panic she sat bolt upright, unable to work out where she was or what time it was, aware only of the pounding of her heart and some unspecific fear.

She had been very deeply asleep. Last night, she had refused to leave her rooms on the pretext of having a headache; she had gone to bed hungry after a supper of black instant coffee and a bar of chocolate she found in her handbag, prepared for a sleepless and fearful night.

The exhaustion of strain and grief over the past few days had proved her friend, though. Sleep had come with the force of a jack-hammer and as she groped now for the light-switch she realised that she had no idea whether or not there had been bellowing in the night or even whether any attempt had been made to breach her shuttered stronghold. She became aware, too, of a fast, steady drip-drip-dripping from outside, and then of the sound of raised voices in the hall. She got out of bed, went to the window, unlatched the shutters and opening one side a careful few inches, peered round it.

Yesterday's fluffy piles of snow had collapsed like a fallen soufflé in a spectacular thaw. Underfoot was a grey, greasy soup of ice and water and as Laura watched, a huge slab of snow slid down the roof with a sound like distant thunder to explode with a noisy splash on the ground below. Snowmelt was dripping from the eaves above so fast that it was like looking out through a waterfall.

In front of the house there were three police cars parked; the front door was open and two uniformed men were standing talking at the top of the steps. A police Land Rover had just driven up and Laura recognised Detective Inspector Fleming at the wheel.

The machinery noise was coming from a yellow digger which was rumbling up the track towards her from the direction of the fields. It stopped beside a straggling hedge then, extraordinarily, made a 90-degree turn and drove straight through it. Seconds later DI Fleming came past the window in a sheepskin jacket, with her trousers tucked into wellington boots, kicking up spray as she hurried after the digger.

Trying to make sense of what she had seen, Laura closed over the shutter again. There had obviously been some major new development and as she bathed and dressed she tried to work out what it might be, without any real success. It was unlikely that the police would have made the discovery Laura herself had made yesterday, but if there was other evidence which had made them doubt the Masons' favoured explanation, hers could only reinforce it – as long as she could persuade them to take it seriously and not dismiss it as fanciful. She'd have to try to get hold of DI Fleming, who seemed an impressive and intelligent woman.

Certainly her own problems were at an end. She could safely emerge for some breakfast and ask to be taken back to Kirkluce after she'd spoken to the inspector.

Her misgivings about the stiffness of the key proved unfounded; it turned easily enough and she emerged cautiously into an empty hall. A draught of damp air swept in from the open front door and through it she caught a glimpse of the police cars outside. There was the sound of men's angry voices coming from the study.

Laura hesitated, but only for a moment. She was ravenous, and she knew where the kitchen was. With any luck, she would have it to herself.

Marjory Fleming looked on watchfully as the digger flattened a broad track into the maze, leaving a trail of debris in its wake as the uprooted bushes were crushed into the muddy slush.

The driver leaned out of his cab. 'This far enough?'

'Five feet more,' she called back to him. He gave her a thumbs-up, obliged, then clanked back out the way he had come.

A white van nosed in as the digger cleared the space, carrying the men in white paper suits and the pegs and tape and spades and plastic bags they would need for their operation. They jumped out to join Fleming as she stood looking at what was left of the blind alley near the gate; only the back hedge and a few feet of the side hedges remained.

She indicated the area to be dug out by hand and stayed to supervise the pegs being put into place, then she left them to it. She wasn't expecting dramatic discoveries; the soil they dug up would be sent to the lab for analysis and if this was, indeed, where the killing had taken place it might have a story to tell. Blood traces remained in the earth for a lot longer than fifteen years.

It all seemed pretty flimsy in the cold, grey light of the wet, dreich winter's day as Fleming plodded back towards the house. Tam MacNee had gone off to lift Scott Thomson and give him the third degree, in so far as police regulations allowed; perhaps something might come out of that. She was in a pessimistic mood this morning, though – pessimistic about everything, in fact. Bill was still acting like a zombie and Marjory had been forced to endure a phone call from a neighbouring farmer, giving her his opinion of a woman who wasn't there for her husband when he needed her.

She'd wondered bitterly if he'd have thought a man should stay home from his work to hold his wife's hand if she had a problem, but she managed not to say it. This was someone who was concerned about Bill, so they were on the same side, at heart; she'd explained calmly that the murder investigation she was responsible for had reached a crucial stage but would soon be over, when she could take leave.

Did she believe it, though? The picture seemed to be becoming murkier and murkier, the evidence more and more contradictory. She was convinced that the accident theory was pointing them in the wrong direction, but how could she ever prove it? The only person who might know the truth was silent in a hospital bed.

She'd felt very nervous at the start of this, her first real murder enquiry. As it went on, when her planning and organisation proved well up to the task, she'd gained confidence but now again she was being battered by doubt. Torn between her professional and her domestic duties, had she allowed herself to be distracted? Was there something she was missing, something another officer – a *male* officer – would have picked up?

Her father had told her often enough how a man would always outthink a woman. He'd come across the technological term 'fuzzy logic' somewhere and gleefully misused it to describe what he believed to be the state of the female brain. Tiredly, Marjory thought that this morning she could hardly argue with him.

She'd certainly never heard a male officer agonise over his responsibilities or wonder whether he was doing the right thing. It wasn't the culture, of course, and who, after all, had heard Marjory express her fears either? Indeed, suggesting to her subordinates that Big Marge was crippled by self-doubt would be a good way of getting a horse laugh.

The thought cheered her a little. Anyway, there was nothing to be gained by picking over this while there was work to do. She quickened her pace.

As she went up the steps into the house she could hear a woman's voice from upstairs, high-pitched and hysterical. An officer was coming down the stairs; when he saw Fleming he jerked his head upwards and rolled his eyes.

'We've had a right stramash here! Her upstairs is throwing a fit – we've had to send for the doctor – and the men are making a stushie too. The Sarge was saying maybe you could have a word with DS Mason, boss?'

She sighed. 'What's his problem?'

'Seems a wee bittie upset the case is being opened up again. And he's not happy about their precious maze being ruined – talking about family heritage and stuff. And the other one's the same, though from what I saw of it they weren't bothering their backsides about it before.'

'Hmm. Not sure I see the point of talking to him at this stage. I'll think about it.' Fleming glanced round the hall. 'Where is everyone else?'

'The Masons took the sergeant into the study to bend his ear. They're still giving him laldy, from what I can hear.'

'So they invited us in, technically?'

'Pretty much dragged us in, when they saw the warrant for digging up the maze.'

'Excellent. I hadn't enough to petition for a warrant for the house but they'd be on shaky ground for a complaint if I have a look around now.'

The first door she opened led to an old-fashioned sitting-room with a bedroom beyond which showed signs of temporary rather than permanent occupation. Another door, however, opened into a surprisingly modern and attractive flat, where the heavy woodwork and panelling were painted white and the rooms were decorated with a clever sense of style, mixing handsome antiques and modern furniture with classic lines. Remembering Rosamond Mason's quiet elegance, Fleming thought she detected her hand at work.

It would have been interesting to see what Brett Mason had done with her territory upstairs (judging by the rest of the house, not much, was Fleming's guess) but as she came out into the hall a man carrying a medical bag came in at the front door, so she turned her attention to the basement instead.

Here, in what would have been the service quarter of the house, little attempt had been made at updating. Exposed pipes ran along the walls, which were painted shiny dark green to waist level and shiny dark cream above. There was a tide-mark of greasy dust which presumably showed where the reach of the cleaning woman stopped. Fleming opened the first door she came to, then stopped on the threshold.

It was hard to say who was the more surprised, Fleming or the woman sitting at an oilcloth-covered table by the window, a piece of toast half-way to her mouth, but it was Laura who spoke first.

'Inspector Fleming! Oh, you startled me. I was afraid it was Mrs Mason – I've just raided her kitchen for something to eat and I don't think she's inclined to be hospitable.'

'Ms Harvey – what on earth are you doing here?' She was startled and annoyed; the girl had agreed to keep the police informed of her whereabouts and finding her in unofficial residence here made Fleming wonder if what she had said about her relationship with Max Mason had been less than wholly truthful after all.

'It's a complicated story. How long have you got? Sorry, that sounded flippant but I do mean exactly that. There's something very strange I need to tell you about.'

Fleming looked at her sharply, saw her grave expression, and experienced a feeling familiar to her from previous investigations, some serious, some trivial, but always the same instinctive reaction, as if some sixth sense were telling her that this was a defining moment, a turning point.

Irritation forgotten, she sat down at the table. 'I've got as long as it takes.'

This time, Tam MacNee noted with satisfaction, Scott Thomson wasn't lounging in his seat. In the clinical atmosphere of the interview room, with the formal identification of the subject, Scott Thomson, and the interviewers, DC Nisbet and DS MacNee, completed, he was sitting on the edge of his chair ready to sing like a canary if someone would just whistle the tune, as MacNee described it to DI Fleming later.

The man was hungover, his bright red hair in vivid contrast to the greasy pallor of his pasty complexion. The quality of their mercy had strained to a couple of paracetamol and a carafe of water, but that was as far as it went. When he made an attempt to justify his previous conviction MacNee was brutal in brushing it aside.

'Cut the cackle. All we want to hear about is what you did to Diana Warwick. Up to your old tricks, were you – following her, pestering her?'

'I – I never.' Thomson licked dry lips. 'Look, I learned my lesson—'

'You told me yourself you watched her out your window.'

'Aye, I told you! Would I of done that if I'd done anything more?'

'Well, that's an interesting question. I think that's an interesting question, don't you, Constable Nisbet?'

Charlotte Nisbet leaned across the table, her eyes on Thomson, exuding sympathy. 'It's tough for you, Scott, I

know that. Give a dog a bad name. But you can see where
we're coming from too. Here's this girl, bit of a babe, come-
on look in her eye—' She turned over a photograph which
had been lying in front of her and pushed it across the table.
'They're asking for it, girls like that . . .'

Diana Warwick, her head turned, her smile warming the
blue eyes, looked up out of the print. It seemed to shock
him. 'Di,' he murmured, staring down at it. 'She was that
bonny . . .'

The two detectives exchanged glances. MacNee, with a
jerk of his head, indicated that Nisbet should take it on.

'It'd be hard not to be tempted, really,' she said softly.
'Hard to be rejected, because you didn't have money and a
posh accent—'

'No!' he said vehemently, raising his head then wincing
from the pain. His eyes were blazing. 'She wasn't like that.
Di was the only one treated me decent. That other one –'
he pointed contemptuously at the print-out of his record
which lay in front of MacNee – 'was a bitch playing games.
She was asking for it, if you like. Half she told the Fiscal was
lies.

'I've had hard luck, what with her and those bastards
the Masons and now you lot – you've been trying to pin
this on me right from the start.' There was a self-pitying
whine in his voice. 'But get this. They're all mad, the
Masons, from the old man down. When Di was there it
was like she got them into crazy stuff. If it was an accident with Satan they set it up. They were like I'd never seen
them before.

'She never fancied me. I wasn't her kind – I could see that
from the start. But I'll be honest with you – I never fancied
her exactly, except like maybe I'd fancy Britney Spears. And
aye, I watched her. I saw her that first night and I kept wondering what she was at – away out in her pyjamas, then back

a wee while later. If there'd been someone after her I'd have been down to see what was going on.'

'Had you a night off?' MacNee asked suddenly.

'Saturday. I'd be away into Kirkluce on a Saturday for the disco at the Green Cat pub.' He gave a mirthless smile. 'Used to like a bit of action.'

'So can you remember if she was out that night, after you came back?' Nisbet asked.

'Fifteen years ago? You're joking. I'd have had a few bevvies then come back on my motorbike and crashed out. Oh, but officer, I'd be stone-cold sober, mind!'

MacNee barely noticed the gibe. Maybe the man was lying, but he was sounding good. A jury would lap that up. So all they had on him was a minimal record and he'd said nothing today they could use. They were wasting their time.

MacNee got up abruptly and looked at his watch. 'Interview terminated, nine-thirty a.m.,' he said for the benefit of the tape, and walked out.

'*Were-bulls*?' Fleming stared at Laura Harvey. She'd always thought psychologists were flaky but this was something else. Was her sixth sense, after all, as fallible as the other five? She said carefully, 'Are you suggesting that someone turns into a bull? With *horns*?'

Laura waved her hands in frustration. 'No, no! I'm obviously explaining myself very badly.' She paused for a second in thought. 'I'm trying to tell you too much, too quickly. Bear with me while I explain.

'Lycanthropy seems always to have existed, to judge by folk-tales and legends. But even now no one's quite sure exactly what it is. There are theories, of course, but no one definitive explanation – when you're talking about the strange ways of the human mind it's not surprising.

'It could be a hysterical dissociative neurosis, provoked by a deep-rooted sense of inferiority and failure. Taking the persona of a strong, powerful and violent animal could be a form of compensation for the humiliations of ordinary life and even, if it was carried through into action, be a way of projecting guilt on to the animal character.

'Another theory is that it's some form of paranoid schizophrenia. Drug use quite often seems to be a catalyst which could explain the New Age tone of a lot of the websites I looked at.'

Fleming pricked up her ears. 'Or absinthe?'

'Absinthe? Yes, I suppose so, particularly in its old-fashioned formulation. They blamed Hemingway's mental problems on that.'

'And Edgar Mason's.'

'Really? Though of course you have to realise there were plenty of people in the Thirties who drank it and didn't go mad. You're probably talking about a genetic susceptibility.'

Fleming's mind was racing. 'I can believe that,' she said grimly. 'Go on.'

'Either way, the subject often has a problem with relationships and sexuality. If these produced fears which overthrew the normal coping mechanisms, violence could erupt.'

'Are we talking about a psychopath?'

Laura shook her head. 'Almost specifically not. A psychopath by definition knows no guilt. The lycanthrope has to seek out the excuse of an irresistible compulsion to escape his.'

'I see. At least I think I do. Give me a minute.'

It was all so extraordinary, Fleming felt as if someone had been birling her round and round so that she wasn't sure which way she'd be facing when she stopped or more probably collapsed into a dizzy heap. Laura was waiting patiently.

'But surely,' Fleming said at last, 'someone would notice,

if every so often one of their family started behaving like a wild animal?'

'Most of the time it wouldn't arise. There are case histories of lycanthropes leading apparently normal lives until some huge personal stress forces their secret life into the open.' She hesitated. 'But a couple of nights ago, someone was bellowing outside my window. Oh, I know, I know it sounds weird, but I'd heard it before.'

Fleming listened to her account, torn between fascination and disbelief. 'But what on earth would provoke something like that?'

'Frustration? Anger, perhaps, in a context of personal instability?'

'Thinking of the Masons, that doesn't narrow the field a whole lot, does it?'

'That's the thing about psychology. It doesn't give you the answers, only suggests questions it might be useful to ask.'

'Like police work! How extraordinary! It's only rarely that evidence hands you the solution on a plate, it just points you to an area you should take a look at.' Fleming was much struck by this.

Laura smiled. 'Psychology's like most things, because it's about life and observation. It can be useful if you use it properly, pointless if you don't, and dangerous if you're clever enough to exploit it for manipulation.'

Fleming smiled wryly. 'You may not realise you're doing a demolition job on a lifetime of scepticism about psychology and all its works?'

'Oh, for goodness sake, don't land me with that sort of guilt! You know how it goes, "I'm a reputable clinical psychologist, you're alarmingly neurotic and he's out of his tree"?'

Marjory Fleming burst out laughing. Then, suddenly serious, she said, 'Laura, can you do anything about depression?'

*   *   *

'Sorry, sir, no idea where she could be.'

It wasn't often that Superintendent Bailey appeared in the CID room unless he had an official visitor he wanted to impress with his common touch. He was very anxious to see Big Marge; word was that he wasn't best pleased about the return to Chapelton. There was another big foot-and-mouth protest going ahead which was stretching their manpower and he wasn't the only officer on a short fuse at the moment.

'Well, tell her I want to see her if she comes in here. I would have hoped that in these days of modern communications it shouldn't be impossible for me to contact my Detective Inspector when I need to do so.' He marched out.

The three detectives in the room waited decorously until he was out of earshot, then guffawed; one of them embarked on quite a plausible imitation of his pompous delivery and got a round of applause.

'Gone AWOL, has she? That's not like Big Marge – she's the keen type. Wonder where she is?'

'*I* know.' The woman officer spoke smugly.

'You told him you didn't.'

'I lied. The Boss drove off from Chapelton with Laura Harvey. The word was she was taking her back to stay at Mains of Craigie but she was being pretty cagey about it so I reckoned she wouldn't want the Super to know.'

The two men looked at each other. 'Well – kind of dodgy, wouldn't you say, someone involved in a murder enquiry?'

'Harvey was just a wee girl when it happened. There's nothing wrong, as long as Bailey doesn't hear about it and go daft – or the Press.'

'You girls must stick together, eh? Well, I promise I won't squeal to the Super or the *Sun*.'

'And have you ever known me clype? Telling tales was a capital offence where I came from. Mind you,' his colleague added warningly, 'if they offer me a Page Three girl as a bribe the deal's off.'

Acting like a hairdryer, the wind from the south had melted the snow and ice with astonishing speed. The roads were running rivers of water and it was a bleak, grey, miserable day, but Laura felt more at ease than she had been for days. Marjory Fleming had taken her concerns very seriously indeed, keeping quiet about where they were going so that the Masons would have no idea where to find her. Laura was grateful and, especially since the offer of hospitality clearly carried some professional risk for her hostess, she hoped she could pay back the kindness.

She listened sympathetically to Marjory's emotional account of her husband's condition as they drove to Mains of Craigie. In the course of her research she'd become very familiar with the torments farmers had gone through and felt she had quite a good understanding of the horrors which plagued their minds – better, even, than Bill's wife could hope to do, seeing it as she did from the viewpoint of a police officer with a difficult and demanding job of her own.

When they turned on to the rough farm road and the farm-house itself came into view, Laura could well understand Marjory's feelings for her home, so apparent as she talked about it. Its very appearance, simple, four-square and unadorned, suggested security and cosiness.

'How lovely!' she exclaimed.

Marjory smiled, but the smile held a trace of bitterness. 'I used to think of it as "The Last Homely House" – Tolkien, you know – when I came back from work late and tired and the lights were on. It seemed a sort of fortress against the awful things that happen in the world outside. But it wasn't, was it? It's turned into a sort of prison for Bill – and I'm scared I could come to see it that way too.'

Laura was silent for a moment, thinking of the prison of grief she had been living in herself, and when she spoke, she was almost thinking aloud. 'We all live with comforting illusions. We need to allow ourselves to accept them because the people who strip life to its bleakest core and focus only on that become mentally sick. And of course, most of the time the comfort isn't illusory: you've had years of security and happiness and a few weeks of wretchedness and misery. This will pass.'

'Will it? I just can't recognise the Bill I knew – so cheerful, uncomplaining, so – so *solid*.' Her voice faltered.

Laura said again, 'This will pass, I can promise you.' She wasn't only speaking to Marjory.

Ignoring the front door with its porch like a quizzically raised eyebrow, they went round to the back of the house, entering via a glass door what looked like a large cloakroom lined with a clutter of coats, shoes, boots and items of sports equipment, from a couple of mud-splattered mountain-bikes to a pile of tennis rackets of widely differing ages and styles. Marjory, with tension showing in every line of her body, led Laura through it and along a passage, then opened the door on a big, traditional farmhouse kitchen.

It had a red-tiled floor and a slightly chipped cream-coloured Aga at the far end. There was a dog lying on a brightly coloured rug in front of it and a man sitting in an old, sagging chair at one side. He was a big, burly man with blue eyes and cheeks reddened by wind and weather, but the eyes were sunken and the cheeks gaunt under a ragged growth of beard. The dog, a pretty black-and-white Border collie, got up to greet her politely; the man did not even turn his head.

'Bill—' Marjory said on a rising note of anxiety.

Laura put a hand on her arm. 'Just leave us. You've got plenty to do. I'll make a cup of tea – I'm good at strange kitchens – and we'll get to know each other gradually.'

Marjory looked uncertain for a moment, then agreed. 'I'd better switch my mobile back on. I've been pretending to be out of range.'

'Say you were at Burnside Cottages – there's definitely no signal there, as I know to my cost!'

Marjory left. Laura went quietly about the business of making tea, found some biscuits in a big tin, then went over to the man in the chair. 'Tea?' She held it out and he took it from her hand without looking up.

'I'm Laura.' She pulled over a kitchen chair so that she was sitting directly opposite him, but he made no response, staring straight ahead as if unseeing. The dog had settled down again at their feet; Laura leaned forward to stroke it then started to talk to it, murmuring soothingly, weaving a pattern of comforting sound. The dog, its head cocked and eyes bright with intelligence, listened as if monitoring a strange code for a recognisable instruction, and Laura thought its master might be half-listening now too.

She took a sip of her tea, then said very quietly, 'Did the animals suffer dreadfully, Bill?'

For the first time, he raised his head and looked at her. He didn't speak, but very slowly the tears gathered and began to spill down his unshaven cheeks.

21

'Only the Chief Constable, Marjory, that's all.' Superintendent Donald Bailey's colour was high, his mouth pursed into a prune of disapproval.

Fleming's heart sank. 'But the woman's a hysteric, boss!' she protested. 'This shouldn't have any effect on the investigation. Even if you have friends in high places it doesn't mean you can literally get away with murder.'

Bailey bridled. 'I trust you are not suggesting that either the Chief Constable or I myself would be a party to any sort of attempt to pervert the course of justice?'

Glacial pomposity was always a danger sign and this time it was iced, with a wee red cherry on top. Fleming knew she was handling it badly. She just couldn't see how to handle it well.

'Of course not, sir. But I'm becoming more and more convinced that we'd be making a serious mistake if we try to nail Jake Mason for this—'

'Evidence?' he barked, then, as she hesitated, continued, 'I mean hard evidence, as opposed to the prejudice you've shown from the beginning against the solution Conrad Mason put forward?'

Fleming bit her lip. What new evidence did she actually have, besides the websites Laura Harvey had discovered? Not a lot, and she had a nasty feeling that Bailey wasn't going to be receptive to the were-bull theory.

He wasn't. He stared at her for a moment, his eyes almost

popping with disbelief. 'I can really hardly credit that I'm hearing this sort of fantasy from a senior police officer. I'm beginning to wonder if my belief in you has been misplaced, Fleming. There's the Chief Constable waiting for me to tell him the reason for this hounding of the Mason family and I'm going to offer him horror fiction?

'I don't know what's got into you, really I don't. I can see you've been under a lot of personal stress, of course – perhaps I should have made greater allowances for your domestic situation. Given that you're a wife and mother.'

Stung, Fleming retorted foolishly, 'There are lots of husbands and fathers in the service too, sir.'

'None of whom has ever come to me with a farrago of nonsense like this. There's no doubt about it, I shall have to consider taking you off this case. At the very least.' Leaning on the desk, he made a pyramid of his fingers and balanced his chins precariously on top. She could almost see the steam emerging from his ears.

She volunteered, 'We shouldn't need to do anything more at Chapelton until we get a report on the soil analysis. We've no one there now, in fact.'

'Well, that's something, I suppose. And is the girl – Laura whatever her name is – still out there? If she is, she'd better not do any more snooping.'

Fleming swallowed. 'No. No, she's gone.'

Bailey was no fool. He looked at her sharply. 'Gone? Where?'

There was no point in lying. Cursing her own inability to deliver a part-truth without drawing attention to the missing part, she braced herself. 'She's at Mains of Craigie. She was worried about her safety and it seemed the simplest thing to do.'

She'd expected him to be angry, had almost shrunk back in her seat as she told him. Instead, he seemed nonplussed.

'You must have taken leave of your senses, Fleming. You know that having a personal involvement could compromise the integrity of the enquiry. What would the defence make of that particular entry in your policy book?'

She didn't dare to suggest she should leave it out, as she had been planning to do. 'Yes, sir. Sorry.'

'I'll have to give this some thought. I'll send for you later. Meanwhile, I take it I can assure the Chief Constable that the disruption is at an end?'

'Yes, sir.' Like a coward, she didn't add 'for the time being'. She got up; he didn't rise and go to open the door for her as he usually did. Feeling sick with apprehension, she opened it for herself and went out.

After she had gone, Bailey sat lost in thought for a few minutes, his brow furrowed. Then he gave a deep sigh and picked up the phone.

'Could I speak to Mrs Mason, please? This is Superintendent Bailey. Ah, Conrad – that's you, is it? Now, listen, lad . . .'

'You're aff your heid,' Tam MacNee said bluntly, looking at his superior officer with some dismay.

He had realised when he came in that she was distracted, showing little interest in his account of the interview with Scott Thomson. When he'd finished, she'd only nodded then said, 'Let me run something past you, Tam,' before spouting a theory that sounded like something from the Hammer House of Horror Showcase. Which was why he didn't beat about the bush in his assessment of her mental state.

'Look,' he went on, 'just because someone thinks they're a bull, it doesn't make them a bull, right? Wouldn't mean they could gore someone so a path lab says that's what happened?'

She was stubborn. 'They could have a weapon – even a horn from a dead bull, say, that they'd use. Or – wait a minute! Suppose they arranged it so the bull could gore her, sort of in tribute, maybe. Like the Minotaur thing . . .'

MacNee was on shaky ground with Greek mythology, but it was true he'd heard Thomson say if there was an accident with Satan, he reckoned it wasn't one. Grudgingly, he told Fleming.

She liked that. 'So suppose someone puts her in the bull's field. She's sleep-walking – Laura remembered her sister doing that – so he, or I suppose she if you include Brett? God, that woman is a nightmare! – anyway – I'm just thinking aloud here – someone finds her in the maze, leads her to Satan knowing she'd be killed, then digs a grave there in the field—'

MacNee pounced. 'With the bull handing him the spade, I suppose? After three days of hard frost? Anyway, did we not more or less establish the cattle wouldn't have been out?'

Deflated, she took his points. 'So maybe she was put into the bull's pen. Obviously it couldn't have been in the field when she was buried. But that's a thought – of course the ground would have had to be soft enough to dig. Do you know when the thaw came?'

'I'd have to check. It was in the stats I got from the Met Office – off the top of my head I'd say it wasn't long after that.'

'Right. I suppose that's progress: we've established that the body couldn't have been buried the night she disappeared. So, was it stored somewhere? We're not going to know, are we? Especially now we're ordered to back off the Masons.'

MacNee looked surprised. 'Problem?'

Fleming sighed. 'I'd better warn you – Bailey may be going to take me off the case. You know he's been resentful right from the start that we couldn't just go along with Conrad's solution . . .'

She told him the rest of the story. When she confessed that Laura Harvey was even now at Mains of Craigie, MacNee put his head in his hands and groaned.

'Whatever possessed you, woman?'

'She's a nice person, Tam, and she's scared.' Fleming was defensive. 'She thinks she's stirred up the sort of emotions that got her sister killed and this way she can keep her head down and be safe until we get this cleared up. And, well, she's going to see if she can help Bill too.'

MacNee looked at her sympathetically. 'Bad, is it?'

'Very bad.' Her lips tightened; she obviously didn't want to talk about it.

'So,' he said, getting up, 'what's the next step?'

'We're waiting for the soil analysis. It's gone to the labs in Glasgow but I've a mate who's a chemist at the local agriculture college and I sent him some samples so he could have a preliminary look at them today.' She sighed again. 'I'm not hopeful, though, are you? Let me have it straight.'

'No. I have to say, I'm not. But what I do know is that Mason's version stinks. It's minging.'

'Mmm. You know what my first mistake was? Not reporting his lapses of control to Bailey. Conrad's one of his blue-eyed boys and if I say anything now he'll think it's because of this. Oh well . . .' She shrugged, then opened the policy book lying on her desk and looked at it gloomily.

'"Sooner or later, one must pay for every good deed,"' MacNee quoted sententiously.

Only half-listening, Fleming said, 'Box!' pointing to the receptacle labelled 'Burns Fines' on her desk.

'No, no,' MacNee protested. 'Spanish proverb. It's true, too. Look at me putting a dunt in the car when I went out to rescue Laura in the snow.'

As he left, she couldn't help thinking bleakly about what he'd said. Her good deed in offering sanctuary to Laura could lose her this job; she hoped that Laura's good deed in offering to treat Bill wouldn't similarly backfire.

She went back to trying to work out what she was going to write. Five minutes later the phone rang.

Laura sat at the desk in the farm office, with its view out over the farmyard and fields, while she put the finishing touches to her article. She was quietly satisfied that progress had been made this morning. Bill still wasn't talking fluently but under gentle prompting he had given her an insight into the distressing end of his flock: animals suffering fear and pain, lambs killed before their mothers' eyes by insensitive officials deaf to his pleas, carcasses left heaped in stinking piles.

In Bill, the son of generations of farmers, the shepherding instinct which man had developed somewhere around the dawn of human civilisation would be deep-rooted. To have to watch, helpless, while wolves destroyed the fold would have been agony – an agony, too, which he had to bear alone after a demoralising period of solitude and deep anxiety. The protective shutting-down of the system to deaden unbearable pain was hardly surprising. What he needed now was to be convinced that the support was there to let him deal with it safely.

He was still sitting in his chair but when Janet Laird appeared with his lunch – a little surprised to find a strange woman installed – he had muttered a greeting, which was, according to his mother-in-law, a step forward.

In a low-voiced conversation with Laura as she left, she told her how delighted she was not only that Bill was getting help and would have someone with him during the day, but that Marjory would have someone to talk to when she came home at night.

'It's an awful hard job, being in the police,' she confided. 'Angus, my husband – they all thought he was a hard man but I've known him upset many a time even if he didn't say much. And Marjory maybe doesn't think it but she's her father's daughter. She's taking all this to heart and she won't let on, even to her mother.'

Laura sensed the hurt. She said gently, 'It's very common, you know, that people don't want to burden their families with their worst problems. It comes of not wanting to distress them – a sort of protective love, even if it does sometimes warp the whole relationship.'

'Like Bill.' She immediately made the connection; those soft blue eyes were surprisingly shrewd. 'He's *very* protective. He needs to be. Marjory's a clever lass, you see, and she's doing a tough job. Bill's proud of her, right enough, but he's not one of these "new men" they seem to have invented – not that I've ever met one, mind – and he has to feel he's still able to look after her. So he could be not saying anything because she'd have to look after him.'

'You've never thought of being a psychologist, have you?' Laura suggested, amused. 'You'd be very good.'

She got an old-fashioned look. 'Me? Away you go! I'm just a housewife. You know, I'm sorry for these young ones today. It was much easier for us. Angus always knew he was master in his own house.'

'Did he, indeed?' Laura challenged her, but a giggle, showing two still-fetching dimples, was the only response as Janet got back into her car.

Laura smiled now, thinking about it. This was a good, strong, supportive family and she had little doubt that once this terrible time was over the wounds would heal and that essential illusion of comfort and safety would work its magic again, though not immediately and not, perhaps, ever as completely. 'Never glad confident morning again,' as her favourite

Browning had it, but even what remained was well worth having, especially in this lovely place.

She glanced out of the window. The rain was stopping now and a glinting, pale lemon sun was forcing its way through a rift in the grey chiffon sky. She noticed the faint beginnings of a rainbow starting to form its arch across the valley, deepening in colour and strength as she watched. The cliché was inescapable: it suggested all the usual sunshine-after-rain, promise-of-better-times-ahead stuff, but trite as that was she felt her spirits lifting.

And there was a special magic of place here too. There was a particular harmony in the lines of the hills and the angles of their meeting which was as satisfying to the eye as music to the ear. All it needed to complete the idyllic picture was sheep, safely grazing . . .

A movement caught her eye and there was Meg coming out of the back door to race in exuberant circles, barking in excitement. A moment later Bill stepped out too, walking slowly and stiffly. Behind him came the stocky figure of Hamish Raeburn, the neighbour who had called in after lunch, hovering anxiously at his elbow.

Laura had left the men together with a murmured suggestion to Hamish that even if Bill didn't say anything he might be persuaded to take a walk, and she was glad to see it had worked. Fresh air, exercise and a change of scene would probably do him more good than half-a-dozen sessions of psychotherapy. She turned back to her laptop.

She had been working for about quarter of an hour when she heard a bell ringing – a doorbell, it sounded like. She got up uncertainly, then remembered the front door she'd noticed as they drove round to come in at the back. Presumably it must open into the hall at the foot of the stairs.

The bell rang again as she hurried down. 'I'm just coming,'

she called as she wrestled with bolts top and bottom which didn't seem to have been moved for some time.

At last she got them pushed back and opened the door, a polite smile on her face, which vanished as she saw the man who stood on the doorstep, his face black with temper.

'I've got a score to settle with you, you snooping bitch!' he snarled.

It felt as if her heart had stopped. She tried to close the door against him but he put his shoulder to it and with contemptuous ease jerked it out of her hands. He slammed it shut again behind him and stood, a terrifying figure in the narrow confines of the hall.

Laura screamed, but there was no one to hear. Bill Fleming, still silent but walking much more strongly now, was a mile away and to his friend's satisfaction was showing no sign of tiring.

'You mean,' Marjory said stupidly, 'you actually have found signs of blood?'

James Macdonald, her scientist friend, was amused. 'Wasn't that what I was looking for? Only in one of the four samples you gave me, though – the one marked A2.'

They had sectioned the ground into 100cm squares; A2 was nearest the back of the hedge and 100cm away from the left-hand corner. She'd also given him B4, C5 and D1. 'Nothing in any of the others?'

'No. I suggest you direct the lab's attention to the A samples first, when they get round to testing them. They won't have any problem – we're not talking traces here.'

'What exactly does that mean?'

'Someone – or something, I don't have the equipment here to test if it's human or animal – bled quite copiously into the soil. I would guess a severed artery, something like that? Not just a cut finger anyway.'

'I see. Thanks, James – I owe you one.'

'Don't suppose you're grateful enough to dish the dirt on this? No? Oh well, I'll get it out of you over a dram or two later – and you're in the chair.'

She put the phone down, still feeling stunned. It had all been theoretical until now. Under Bailey's inquisition she had been uncomfortably aware that the evidence on which she had authorised the demolition of a historic (if neglected) garden feature was very slender, just a scrap of material and a fragile gold chain. Oh, no doubt if she went to Bailey now he would probably point out that in the countryside small animals died violent deaths at the teeth of predators on a regular basis and it was to be presumed that they bled as they did so. And of course she could see that it would only be after the labs typed the blood and ran DNA samples that they could say definitely that it belonged to Diana Warwick.

But in her own mind, she believed it. The emerging picture satisfied her in a way that the scenario involving the bull and its crazily protective owner never had. She could see the girl, sleep-walking into the maze along the least over-grown aisle, just as Fleming had done herself, then wakening, perhaps, to find herself trapped in a blind alley, turning, befuddled by sleep, to be confronted with – who? Or, she thought with a superstitious shudder, *what*? The A2 sample suggested she had huddled, or been forced, into the left-hand corner formed by the angle of the hedges. Fleming roughly scribbled down a grid, then blacked in squares A and B 1–4. She'd ask the labs to start with these samples.

The big question was, what were her chances of pressurising Bailey into allowing her to pursue the Masons before proper confirmation came through? She knew the answer to that: somewhere between zero and none at all. He would point out, with a certain logic, that in the context

of a fifteen-year-old murder another few days were neither
here nor there.

Looking at it dispassionately, she had to admit that her
sense of urgency had a lot to do with her own domestic situation. She needed time at home with Bill, time to make
contact again with the man she had thought she knew so
well, but given the touchy situation with Bailey, it wouldn't
be smart to push the issue. In any case; she'd her neglected
policy book to write up and thousands of words of interviews to sift through. Doing that, and just taking time to
think things through, would probably be a more productive
exercise than flinging herself on her horse and galloping
madly off in all directions.

As was her habit, she began a mind map, taking a fresh
sheet of paper and writing DIANA in large capitals in the
middle of it, adding the names of Scott Thomson, Jake, Brett,
Conrad and Max Mason round about. For quarter of an
hour she worked, scribbling in evidence, ideas and conclusions as they occurred to her in the appropriate area until
the page was almost covered with her random thoughts.

She sat back to look at the pattern she had created. Around
Jake Mason, comments were sparse. If you accepted that
Diana had been attacked in the maze, it exonerated the bull
and obliterated the motive Jake's nephew had suggested. That
left the sexual motive – the same as for all the men – and
she had noted here Jake's repelling of his wife's offer to return.
What was certain was that he had not accessed the Internet
sites.

Which went for Scott Thomson as well. He had form,
though, and that was often a strong indication. But Tam,
who had a good nose for these things, had thought he was
telling the truth in the recorded interview; she circled that
in red as a reminder to listen to the tape herself.

That left the three Masons. By Conrad she had written

'uncontrollable temper', by Max 'manipulative' and by Brett 'unbalanced and hysterical'.

Could she see Brett imagining herself into a bull and somehow 'goring' her victim? She had a sudden comic vision of her Brunnhilde figure charging down the alleyway with a horned helmet on her head to *The Ride of the Valkyries* – but this was no joke. Jealousy was a powerful emotion and judging by Charlotte Nisbet's report on the interview with her, Brett was a woman consumed by it. Fleming tapped her pen thoughtfully on Brett's name.

Then Max. She had disliked him on sight and Laura, too, had been frank about her distrust. He was almost the personification of the Scots word 'sleekit' – smooth, sly, hypocritical – and Fleming had no difficulty in believing him to be cold and calculating enough to bury his guilt along with the body and walk away. Another of her jotted entries linked Laura's mention of drug-taking in connection with lycanthropy with Max's teenage conviction, but then, against Conrad's name, she had entered Rosamond Mason's statement that Conrad was experimenting too but was lucky enough, or smart enough, not to get caught.

It had been Fleming herself who had broken the news to Max of the finding of the body in the field; she would still swear that he believed it to be his mother's. She had written 'Reaction: immediate – cold triumph; delayed – grief.' He'd said, she remembered, 'I knew he'd killed her. She'd never have left me like that.'

And there was, too, the undeniable fact that Max was the person who had authorised the field being dug up for a burial pit. He could have easily objected without arousing suspicion: Laura had heard the conversation and said he hadn't. Fleming added 'Check with MAFF' and another red circle, but she didn't think they'd tell her anything different.

Conrad was the one who had objected strongly, Conrad

with his moods and his violent temper. She'd seen it herself;
looking back to that extraordinary disciplinary meeting,
remembering the knitted brows, the contorted expression
and the clenched fists, she wondered if he had been struggling then to control one of the transformations Laura had
described, and had only just managed to pull himself back
from the brink. He had been exhausted afterwards, sweating
and strange.

She shuddered, thinking of those powerful hands. What
might have happened to her, if . . .

Yes, there could be no doubt that Conrad fitted the profile Laura had outlined. She'd mentioned problems with
close personal relationships: Conrad was notorious for having
a string of girlfriends and never keeping any of them. And
his relations with his mother, too, were clearly far from easy.

'Faulty relationships' appeared against Brett's name too,
though, and it was hard to imagine that the egotistical Max's
interactions would be anything other than superficial. Which,
of course, brought her round full circle.

Then, too, there was the bellowing Laura had talked about.
Fleming hadn't allocated that to any of the names on the
page. Not that she disbelieved Laura; she was sure she'd
heard something but was sceptical about what it might have
been. A girl who'd never lived in the country wouldn't confidently be able to identify natural sounds; hear a vixen
calling and you'd swear someone was being murdered. And
footprints, in what was more or less a lay-by on a narrow
country road, weren't conclusive either. Still, she added
'Bellowing?' and sat back, tapping her pen against her teeth.

At last she wrote in the small space left at the bottom of
the page, 'Gut reaction: CM. Analyse all interviews. Word-
check reports for mentions.' She outlined it in red, then sat
back. She had enough to be getting on with, and presenting
herself as taking a cool, cautious approach to the informal

evidence James Macdonald had given her might do something to placate Bailey.

After all, with Laura safely at Mains of Craigie and probably doing far more good to Bill than she could herself, there wasn't any reason, either operational or personal, to make waves about a few days' delay on a fifteen-year-old case.

'Will you be wanting to head back now, Bill? We've had a good walk.'

Hamish wasn't looking for a reply; Bill had made no response at all to the other farmer's occasional remarks about the weather and the scenery. The most he expected was a shake of the head or perhaps a silent turn in the direction of home.

But Bill said, 'No.' Then, with difficulty, 'This – is good.'

'Well, that's rare! Good man! On we go, then.'

The sun was making a brave attempt now; there was even a patch of watery blue the size of the proverbial sailor's trousers appearing as they set off again up the stony slope of the hill ahead, Meg describing ever-widening circles around their path.

22

A door to the right of the hall was standing ajar. Laura found herself pushed through it, into the long, low sitting-room which ran from front to back of the house, and flung violently into one of the armchairs by the side of the fireplace. There was a pile of accumulated wood-ash from long-dead fires; tiny flakes rose like a puff of smoke as the air was disturbed then floated down again to settle on the dusty surface of a side-table.

He stood towering over her, not touching her but by his physical presence making it an act of intimidation. He was shouting at her, roaring almost, so that the words were indecipherable, a jumble of sound.

She'd never realised before how bull-like he was. Or – her heart missed a beat – had he *become* more bull-like as she watched? His shoulders seemed to swell as he tossed his head back and forth, his eyes were bulging and his hand went to tear the fabric of the black polo-neck sweater he was wearing, as if some expansion of his massive neck made its constriction intolerable. He opened his mouth wider so that looking up from below she could see his open throat. He bellowed.

Laura had heard that sound before, echoing eerily outside on a winter night. Then, when she was safely behind walls, it had scared her. Now, the power of the sound alone was physically distressing and as he lowered his head and stooped so that his arms, clenched into fists, came below his knees, she gave a sob of terror.

He swung away, breathing stertorously, snorting, almost, as he began to pace up and down the length of the room, faster and faster. He seemed to be working himself into a frenzy, foam gathering at the corners of his mouth. He began to trot, turning at each end with a swivelling movement of his haunches. As a bull would.

Her heart was pounding now. Perhaps she would die of fright before the charge came, before that powerful head smashed the bones of her face – a hundred gothic tales, a hundred horror films clawed at her mind.

But even in the grip of panic, an inner voice made itself heard above the thundering of her heart and the superstitious clamouring of her imagination: *They aren't true. It doesn't happen. He only thinks it does. He's a man with a mental problem, like your patients. You know what to do. It's your job.*

And then there was another voice, repeating the advice she'd been given at the Women's Refuge, long ago in another world: *Make like you're big and calm.* It had worked when she'd braved women's partners who were maddened by drink or drugs or anger, or all three. To look small and vulnerable was always to invite disaster, but even so, standing up now was probably the bravest thing she would ever do.

Keeping the movement controlled and unhurried she raised herself from the chair. 'Conrad!' She spoke in a voice of calm authority. 'I'm calling you back. The bull is leaving you now. Leaving you.'

He didn't react to her change of position or to her voice; at first she thought he was oblivious to anything but his mania. Then his bloodshot eyes rolled towards her and his pace faltered.

Her voice monotonous, hypnotic, she went on talking. 'I can see you again now, Conrad, the bull has gone. It's all right. Gone, Conrad, gone. It's all right.' Again and again, for what seemed an eternity, she repeated the soothing phrases until at last he stood still, shaking and twitching, his head lowered like a bull in the ring, weakened physically and mentally and awaiting the *coup de grâce*.

Still she talked. At last he raised his head and shook it, looking about him as if he barely recognised his surroundings. 'What – what did I do?' he muttered thickly, then he collapsed to begin banging his head against the floor. Laura could smell his acrid sweat – the smell of fear – and he started to cry like a child, huddling himself into a foetal position.

She was aware, suddenly, of sharp pain. She looked down at her hands and saw the half-moon shapes of her nails, dug so far into her palms that some were filling with blood. She took a shaky breath as she looked down at the man who had inspired such fear, pitiable and helpless as he lay at her feet. She wasn't afraid now.

'Conrad, did the bull kill my sister?'

'I – I don't know.'

'Did he want to kill me?'

'You told – you told,' he said brokenly. 'I was angry. You liked Max – you didn't want me. She didn't either. I don't know – *I don't know!*'

The anger was still there. She was taking no chances. 'I'll get you a drink of water,' she said, walking confidently to the door and resisting the temptation to look nervously back over her shoulder.

At last the solid wooden door was shut behind her with the old-fashioned key turned in the lock. There was a phone in the kitchen; she dialled 999, delivered her message with calm precision, put down the phone and realised that her legs were buckling. She collapsed into the sagging chair by the Aga and even when she heard the sirens twenty minutes later couldn't summon the strength to get up.

They found him asleep. They led him past her, hand-cuffed, but he didn't turn his head to look towards her as he shambled out. Laura's eyes followed him with sadness and pity and – yes, even regret.

There was only one thing Donald Bailey disliked more than being wrong and that was someone else being proved right, but even for the sake of diplomacy and their future relations, there wasn't anything Marjory Fleming could do to fudge it.

'We've charged him with assault and breach of the peace for a start. We're not ready to detain him for questioning on the murder charge as yet, because of course the minute we do the clock's running and we've only six hours before his brief can roar in breathing smoke and demand we either press charges formally or drop them. And it's not as if we don't know where to find him.

'He's not exactly denying that he killed Diana Warwick, anyway. He keeps saying he doesn't know, it was the bull not him.'

Bailey groaned. 'Should he be sectioned?'

'The police surgeon's checking him over now, but he's rational enough at the moment and he'd hardly be the first killer to use insanity as a defence. I've put him on suicide watch, though – he's utterly humiliated.' He had presented a pathetic figure when she interviewed him, a bully whose bluff was called, even looking physically diminished as he sat slumped over the table in front of him.

'Dear, dear. It's a bad business. Promising young officer, too.'

She didn't correct him. 'Can I take it we can apply for a search warrant? We'd want to take away the computer, for a start.'

'Yes, yes,' Bailey said testily. 'Obviously. I'd better alert the Chief Constable to the probability of another complaint. I simply shudder to think of his mother's reaction. Has she been informed?'

'Not so far. I gather they're drawing lots downstairs for who's to do it and who's going to ride shotgun.'

This was what was known as the bad method of attempting to lighten the atmosphere, she reflected a moment later, as the joke backfired.

'Yes, it's going to be a very delicate business. In fact,' Bailey said with a wintry smile, 'I think you should go yourself, Marjory. That way, I can assure the CC that we're taking all possible steps to treat this sensitively. All right?'

He rose and went to the door to hold it open for her. As she went out, Fleming consoled herself with the thought that if this was his pay-back for her being right, at least her penance would be over and done with by tea-time.

And she'd take Tam with her. Why should she suffer alone? After all, he'd been right too.

'As a reward, I'll let you have a free quotation, if you can think of one,' Fleming said as they drove along the all-too-familiar road to Chapelton. MacNee, having been lucky in the previous lottery, had been loud in his complaints against the injustice of it all.

He sighed.

> 'May coward shame disdain his name,
> The wretch that dare not die,'

he quoted lugubriously.

Fleming laughed. 'What do you think she'll say, Tam?'

'It's not what she'll *say* that's bothering me. It's what she'll *do*. It's all right for you – you're bigger than me. But I'm only a wee fellow.'

'And delicate with it. Your douce nature's a by-word down the nick. But seriously, it's going to be a terrible shock for her.'

'Unless she knew.'

Fleming shot him a look. 'Knew?'

'Well, you'd think if your son was charging around going off his head and bellowing, you'd maybe notice.'

'Right enough.' She was much struck by this idea. 'But you'd cover up for him, even so?'

'I can't see her being fashed about anything except what suits him.'

'And she'd be bothered about herself too, Tam. I'd a pretty clear impression from Conrad about the demands she made on him. She had the money and she used that to jerk him around.'

'He's like a puppet with his strings cut, the now. I even feel kinda sorry for the guy.'

'Hasn't had much of a life, it seems to me. Laura says people with delusions like his often sort of use the animal personality to express what they daren't themselves. And even now, when he's at rock bottom, you can see how angry he is.'

MacNee shook his head. 'Weird. So – if you were an animal, what kind would it be?'

'A dog. I'd take people in my teeth like rats and shake some sense into them.' It came out without reflection; she was taken aback herself. 'I don't know where that came from,' she admitted awkwardly.

'Aye, well. Not surprising, maybe.' MacNee waited, but she didn't choose to elaborate and a few minutes later they turned in at the Chapelton sign.

As she stood on the doorstep, Fleming squared her shoulders in preparation for the ordeal ahead and she noticed that MacNee, after he had rung the doorbell, did the same. Perhaps, she thought hopefully, it would be Max Mason who would answer the door and they could legitimately delegate the task of breaking the news to his aunt . . .

It wasn't. They could see the outline of Brett Mason's

square frame through the etched glass of the inner door even before she opened it.

She didn't look well. Her complexion, always florid, had an unhealthy, purplish tinge and the whites of her eyes were muddy and bloodshot. Fleming remembered uneasily that her brother had succumbed to a stroke as Brett's face darkened into an expression of fury at the sight of them.

'How dare you!' she shrilled. 'How *dare* you? The Chief Constable gave me his personal assurance that this persecution would cease immediately. I shall report this to him at once.' She made to shut the door.

Fleming stepped forward. 'Please wait, Mrs Mason. We have to talk to you about Conrad.'

'Conrad?' She paused. 'He's not here. I'm expecting him back soon. He didn't come in for his lunch and it's nearly five o'clock.'

'That's right. He's at the police station,' MacNee said disingenuously.

'I see. He could have let me know himself, of course, but I suppose if he's back at his work . . . And at least you've come to your senses at last. You can ill-afford to dispense with the services of someone like my son, you know, and I can tell you after all that's gone on he was contemplating resignation.' Another thought struck her. 'Oh – come to apologise, have you? Well, you'd better come in. Naturally I would prefer that none of this had happened in the first place, but I shall tell the Chief Constable I appreciate that an effort has been made.'

Cravenly, they didn't correct her, only exchanging glances as they followed in her wake into the big study at the front of the house with its trophies and pictures which so eloquently showed the family obsession which had ruined her son.

They sat down, Fleming and MacNee on a leather chesterfield, cracked with age, while Brett sat down in a heavily carved wooden armchair as if it were a throne. Clearing her throat nervously, Fleming began.

It took Brett a moment to realise that this was no apology; she began to protest about false pretences but Fleming talked steadily on until she stopped and listened, looking bewildered and uncomprehending.

They had been prepared for a hysterical, even violent reaction. Instead she sat completely still and silent, seeming to shrink in the chair as the sense of what was being said got through to her. She was wearing a long purple scarf; she began pulling it through her hands more and more frantically. When Fleming finished at last, she said nothing for a second, then whispered, 'You've *arrested* him! You've arrested Conrad? Oh no, no, no!'

The tears came then, floods and tempests of tears, with sobs which seemed almost to be choking her as she clutched at her throat. Alarmed, Fleming went to kneel beside her, offering tissues from her shoulder-bag though she dared not touch her. 'Go and see if you can find Max,' she said urgently over her shoulder to MacNee.

He nodded and went out, but hadn't far to look: Max was at that moment coming across the hall. MacNee explained succinctly what had happened and saw a slow, unpleasant smile spread over Conrad's cousin's face.

'Now fancy that! He always was a sod. Good to know the plods have caught up with him at last, despite him being inside the tent. You don't think I'm surprised, do you? You're talking to someone he bullied for years. Wonder if that's why they call it bullying?'

MacNee looked at him with cold dislike. 'Your aunt's pretty upset. Maybe you could stretch a point and try and calm her down.'

'Me?' Max laughed. 'Oh, I'll give it a whirl if it'll make

you happy. But arrange these words into a well-known phrase or saying: rag, to, bull, red, a. Oops, not perhaps the most tactful thing to say, in the circumstances. To level with you, I'd phone the doctor if I were you.'

'I'll do that,' MacNee said grimly, getting out his phone as Max sauntered past him into the study.

Fleming looked up anxiously as he came in. Brett was still sobbing, her breathing so ragged as to be alarming in a woman of her physique.

'Max – oh good! I'm worried about your aunt. Has she got pills or anything?'

Max strolled over to stand beside his distraught relative. 'Haven't the vaguest.' Bending closer, he said in the tones of one speaking to the profoundly deaf, 'Pills, Auntie? Do you have pills?'

It had an astonishing effect. As if he had pressed a button, Brett's sobs stopped and she pulled herself up in her chair; with the tears still wet on her cheeks, she narrowed swollen eyes and spat out, 'Oh, you're happy now, no doubt. It's all you've ever wanted, to see Conrad and me destroyed. No doubt you had a hand in this, you and that woman – oh yes, I could see how Conrad was looking at her, just the way he looked at her sister. And you brought her here deliberately, that – that Delilah, to bring about his downfall! She lured him to it, I could see that. But you'll both suffer for it, I promise! You'll suffer!'

Astonished at this display of virulent energy, Fleming scrambled to her feet, ready to intervene if the woman showed signs of translating her threats into action. Max, on the other hand, looked amused, standing with his hands in his pockets.

'I seem to have achieved the desired effect, anyway. Perhaps she doesn't need a doctor after all – they can't do a lot about a poisonous personality.' As he sauntered out again, MacNee came past him back into the room, looking surprised to see Brett apparently quite recovered.

'Perhaps you should go and lie down, Mrs Mason,' Fleming suggested, not very hopefully. 'You've had a shock.'

'There's a doctor on the way,' MacNee added.

Entirely composed now, Brett looked icily from one to the other, then rose regally to her feet. 'I shall go to my room. It will spare me the offence of your company. You may tell the doctor where to find me.

'Meantime I shall be phoning my lawyer. You may inform your superiors that we will be pursuing an action for damages against you for these monstrous and totally unfounded accusations.'

She swept out, all injured majesty, leaving the two officers staring after her blankly.

'Well, bugger me!' MacNee said vulgarly.

'She's something else, isn't she? I was worried sick, thinking she was completely out of control on her way to having a fit, and then suddenly – bam!'

'Here – maybe she turns into a crocodile in her spare time. Their tears don't mean anything either – and they've a pretty savage bite on them too.'

'You could say.' Fleming shook her head in wonder. 'Anyway, with any luck neither of us will have to see her again. Whoever drew the short straw last time gets to question her.'

'You're not kidding.' MacNee was looking about him as he spoke; he had never been in the room before and he began to wander around, looking at the photographs on the walls and reading the framed newspaper cuttings.

'No wonder Conrad's like he is,' he observed. 'Get all this! Bulls everywhere you look. Probably thought he was a calf, when he was wee.' Moving on, he stopped in front of the trophy cabinet and gave a low whistle. 'There's a fortune here, mind you! Solid silver, some of these – I can think of a few of the local punters who'd pay good money for a tip-off. And not so much as a security lock on the window snibs.'

He cast a disapproving look at the catches on the big sash windows, then moved on to the huge marble fireplace and stood looking up at the mounted head of Champion Minos of Chapelton, dusty and a little moth-eaten but magnificent still.

'Here – wouldn't like to meet him down a close on a dark night, would you, Boss?'

Fleming didn't respond. He glanced round. She was standing on the other side of the room staring up at the splendidly moulded silver bull's-head mask with its wide, sweeping, sharp horns.

'Tam,' she said shakily, 'I think perhaps I've found the murder weapon.'

Laura slept deep and dreamlessly and very late the following morning. She woke with a start, taking a moment to realise where she was while her mind groped compulsively for the anxieties which had dogged her every waking moment.

They were gone. She flopped back on the soft pillows, looking round the simple, pleasant room with its sprigged wallpaper and soft green carpet, and at one of Janet's celebrated patchwork quilts which was draped over the bottom of the bed. There was even a ray of sunshine shafting through the flower-print curtains.

Stretching luxuriously, she looked at her watch. Ten o'clock – good gracious, when was the last time she'd slept as long as that? Though of course it had been midnight before she and Marjory got up to go to bed, after an evening spent sitting by a delicious-smelling fire of apple logs in the room where she had spent the twenty most terrifying minutes of her life, this time with a glass in her hand and Meg stretched out in ostentatious relaxation at their feet.

Bill had been a silent presence at their evening meal but he had eaten well and, Laura thought, listened to their casual conversation. He'd seemed happy enough to go up to bed when it was suggested, even saying, 'Goodnight,' almost normally as he went.

'Try to get him to shave in the morning,' Laura said as they cleared up. 'It'll be good for his self-respect.'

'I'll do what I can,' Marjory said, attacking a pan vigorously with a scouring-pad. 'Oh, Laura – will he be all right?'

'Of course he will.' She was firm. 'Look how far he's come in twenty-four hours. I wish all my patients had made progress as quickly as that.'

Marjory had allowed herself to be reassured and once she had coaxed the fire into life, settled down with total absorption to talk about the case, a topic they had avoided over supper. As the logs began to crackle with leaping blue and green flames, Laura was impressed by Marjory's ability to compartmentalise, an attribute more common to men than women. Perhaps if you worked in the still male-dominated police force, masculine characteristics were a career advantage, and Marjory, with her height and build, had probably been a tomboy – you could picture her climbing trees but never wearing a pink frilly dress.

The police, Marjory had said, were hoping for a straightforward confession from Conrad, though she explained that this, in Scots law, wasn't enough; they'd still have to find corroborative evidence from at least one other source to make the charge stick.

'I hate to disappoint you, but I don't think you'll get it,' Laura cautioned. 'A confession would mean he accepted responsibility and he's said already he doesn't know, it was the bull that did it.'

'The old excuse – "It wisnae me, a big boy did it and ran away."'

Laura laughed. 'Exactly. Ran away so that no one can ever find him and question him.'

'Like Jake Mason.' Marjory got up to refill their glasses. 'I keep thinking, if only we could talk to him he might be able to explain what happened. But he's apparently suffering from something called "locked-in syndrome" – horrific, you know what's happening but you can't do anything. Imprisoned alive inside a corpse – I'd rather be dead. Much rather.'

Laura frowned thoughtfully. 'I'm sure I read something about them having some success with communication. If they can open and shut their eyes of their own accord – and of course he may not be able to – you can show them an alphabet board and point so that they can spell it out. You start with one blink for yes and two for no.'

'Really?' Marjory was fascinated. 'Of course we'd have to get all sorts of permissions, but it's worth a try. Certainly Rosamond Mason would probably do anything to get a response from him. She still loves him, you know. It's very touching.'

'Has Max been visiting?'

Marjory shrugged. 'He hadn't, when I spoke to her.'

They talked on, about the strange upbringing the cousins had had, the obsessive streak running through the family. At last Marjory said, 'I shouldn't tell you this, but I can't resist. I'm really excited – I think we may have found the murder weapon.'

The silver mask would be taken down tomorrow when the search warrant had been sworn out. Everything, Marjory explained, had to be done exactly by the book if you didn't want the case to collapse in court. But given the nature of the injury, it seemed plausible.

'Yes,' Laura said faintly, an all-too-vivid picture in her mind of Conrad's massive figure, surreally surmounted by a silver bull's head – a Minotaur – charging down the confines of the maze on her helpless sister. Still sleep-walking? Rudely awakened? Dizzy had always been confused and frightened when she'd been sleep-walking . . .

Her eyes filled with tears and Marjory was immediately full of remorse. 'Oh Laura, how stupid of me! Do you know, I'd sort of forgotten . . . I shouldn't have told you that.'

'No, no, it's all right,' Laura said, and not long after that they had gone to bed. But now, thinking about it, she remembered that her sleep hadn't been dreamless after all: there had been something about the mask, something troubling her. The image of the figure in the maze came horribly to her mind again—

She jumped out of bed. She'd have to discipline herself to handle images like these, which could only intensify as the case progressed.

Downstairs, Bill was clean-shaven. He was still sitting in the chair by the Aga but he looked round when she came in and said, 'Good morning, Laura.'

The words were only slightly hesitant and it showed he was reaching out to communicate in a normal way. That was progress, and she was optimistic that he was almost ready to start talking out his problems.

'Morning, Bill,' she said casually. 'Sorry, I slept in. This is a ridiculous time to be having breakfast!' She chattered on as she made herself toast and coffee, planning her day. She'd left a lot of stuff at Burnside Cottages and she was beginning to run out of clean knickers; if she went there and packed everything up she could be back in time for a short therapy session with Bill. Then Janet would be arriving with their lunch, as she'd insisted on doing despite Laura's protests of competence. In fact her cheerful presence would make a good natural break since Laura judged Bill still wasn't ready for anything too intensive.

As she put her breakfast dishes into the dishwasher, she told him what she was doing. 'I shouldn't be much more than an hour. I'll make us a cup of coffee when I get back.'

Bill gave her the ghost of a smile. 'No, I'll make one for *you*.'

'Great!' she said, without too much emphasis, but as she went out to the jeep Marjory had told her to borrow – she really must arrange to fetch her own car – she was grinning. Marjory would hail it as a miracle but in truth there wasn't much wrong with Bill that a few days of good food, cheerful company and unburdening himself to a sympathetic audience wouldn't cure. Still, she'd take a small wager that DI Fleming would never sneer at psychology again.

It was only about quarter of an hour after she had left that the phone rang. At first Bill Fleming paid no attention, then, as it went on ringing, looked round as if expecting someone else to answer it. But there was no one there and at last he went over to the phone sitting on the dresser and picked up the receiver.

He didn't say anything, but when someone spoke he listened, and when the voice stopped he said carefully, 'No, she's not here. At Burnside Cottages.'

He put it down again, then smiled as if pleased by this simple accomplishment. He turned to go back to his chair, then stopped.

'Meggie!' he said to the dog, lying as usual on the rug but, as always, watching her master's every move. 'Coming out, Meg?'

The dog was at his side in an instant, feathery tail signalling ecstatic delight that at last her sadly disordered world was returning to normal.

23

It was only a couple of days since Laura had left the cottage, but how long ago it seemed and how different it looked! Then it had been under snow, the calm beauty of the glistening landscape with its long blue shadows veiling nature's deadly power to make a mockery of modern civilisation. She remembered with a shudder the merciless dark and her own fear, the bellowing in the night and the footprints.

Conrad must have been very angry for a very long time. Perhaps it was only the act of 'shape-shifting' which had allowed him to carry on a life in which he seemed normal and, indeed – she gave a small sigh – charming. But his suspension from work, his constant humiliations at Max's hands – even the belief that she was rejecting him by coming to Chapelton with Max – must have been an accumulation of indignities which brought him close to complete loss of control, even before Laura's discovery of his terrible secret. She could count herself lucky that she hadn't had to deal with his attack here, in night and cold darkness. As poor Dizzy had . . .

But she couldn't afford to let herself dwell on the past. Today, if only temporarily, winter had relaxed its icy grip. The little burn was gurgling cheerfully under the stone arch, there were patches of foolhardy snowdrops on its banks, pushing up slender spears to unfurl fragile, green-white blooms, and even some clumps of crocuses producing bright patches of colour along the path. She sniffed the damp freshness of the air, again murmuring King Duncan's apposite words – although, she remembered now, they had been spoken just as he entered Macbeth's '*fatal battlements*'. Well, the best the cottage could offer in the way of battlements was some rather fancy guttering. She was smiling as she let herself in.

There was a light on in the bedroom. She stopped, alarmed, every nerve jangling. It took her a moment or two to remember the power cut; she had left in daylight before the power was restored so it wouldn't be surprising if she'd left a light on. Even so she waited, straining her ears for any sound of movement before she flung open the door on the empty room and felt foolish.

It didn't take long to pack. She cleared the wardrobe and drawers, cleared the bathroom, then fetched a couple of plastic bags to sort out the food in the fridge. She was squatting beside it, looking for the 'use-by' date on a pot of yoghurt, when she heard the tap on the door.

Seeing Max Mason beaming through the glass pane, her reaction was one of irritation. Even with Conrad safely locked up, she'd been hoping to keep her whereabouts secret. She didn't like Max; she'd hoped to avoid having to tell him to leave her alone. Still, she would if she had to.

'Max!' she said coolly as she opened the door. 'However did you know where to find me?'

'Hey, Laura! Some monosyllabic yokel at Mains of Craigie told me you were here. Need any help?' He stepped neatly past her into the house.

'No thanks, I'm just finished. Once I've cleared the fridge I'll be off.'

'I just came to check you were OK after your ordeal yesterday. Must have been seriously scary!'

Laura wouldn't give him the satisfaction of a reply. He had come to gloat, of course, and the note of false concern barely concealed his glee.

Undaunted, he went on, 'They came and took away a silver mask from my father's study this morning, you know – the murder weapon, is my guess. But you can't say I didn't warn you he was a bad man. And at least now he's where he ought to be at last, isn't he?' He paused again for her agreement; again she said nothing.

Her lack of response was making him edgy. He was wearing a black suede jacket and jeans; he thrust his hands into his back pockets in a macho pose, standing over her as she went back to her task.

'It's very sad,' Laura said repressively, starting to stow food rapidly into the rubbish bag without any attempt at sorting.

'But you were on to him, weren't you?'

She was aware that he was watching her carefully – for signs, perhaps, of regret which would feed his jealousy? She shrugged and carried on with what she was doing.

He strolled over to the table where there was a bowl of fruit and picked up an apple. 'May I?' he said, biting into it. She ignored that too, and after a moment he went on, 'I couldn't get the locking yourself in at Chapelton bit – but you'd figured it out, I guess. Quite a foxy lady, aren't you, under that quiet front?'

The fridge was empty now. She stood up. 'I'm pretty much finished here. Do you want any more fruit, Max, or shall I take it away?'

'Sure, sure.'

She fetched her case from the bedroom and added it to the collection of bags. 'Well, that's about it.' She moved purposefully towards the door but he didn't follow her, making a business of finishing his apple.

'You know, I still can't get over this business of old Conrad.'

Laura sighed, loud enough to be heard. She'd had enough of this. 'Yes, very strange,' she said dismissively. 'Now—'

He'd finished the apple at last; she took the core from him, put it into the waiting rubbish bag, tied it up and pointedly carried it to the door. He showed no sign of taking the hint.

'Bit of a joke when you think about it really. Prancing about the maze with a silver mask on his head and a black cloak, pretending to be a bull—'

'But—' Laura stopped short. That was what had bothered her, the problem she couldn't put her finger on. Conrad wouldn't have to pretend to be a bull; he had no need to. In his mind, he *was* a bull. And if not Conrad . . .

Max's eyes were fixed on her, boring into her. 'But what, Laura?'

Her lips were dry. 'Oh, nothing. Forgotten what I was going to say. Would you be very kind and take my suit-case—'

As she turned away, he grabbed her arm, pulling her round to face him. 'You've thought of something, haven't you? Tell Uncle Max.'

'It's nothing, Max. Let go of my arm – that hurts!'

He tightened his grip. 'I don't know what it is, but you know, don't you? That's what I was afraid of – that despite everything you wouldn't be convinced. You fancied him – I could see that – and you didn't trust me, right from the start. I came ready to test you and you've given yourself away.

'I don't know what warned me – maybe I'm just seriously smart. Lucky for me, not so lucky for you. Sorry about this, Laura. I even quite liked you, really.'

'As much as Dizzy?' Laura's knees were shaking and his hold on her arm was cruelly painful, but talking had worked with Conrad.

Max's laugh sounded positively light-hearted. 'Oh, more, in fact. She was so frigging superior, your sister. She was making a play for my father, right from when she first saw him in Pamplona – treated me like some dumb kid, even though I'd seen her first, I'd been the one who really saved her that night. And he was coming on to her too, though he tried not to show it. Maybe they slept together – I don't know. But he made a favourite of her, took her part against me. She'd no time for me and then she took my place with him. And he let her do it – so Conrad could laugh at me because I wasn't the favourite any more. But I paid the Minotaur out for that – and her too.'

The authentic teenage whine was in his voice, and now she understood. How foolish she had been, and how cleverly he had misled her into thinking he had loved Dizzy and she was a substitute! He had come to hate Dizzy and she, Laura, had been nothing more than the audience for a delicious recounting of the circumstances of his revenge on two people who had humiliated him. And what he had said fitted; his personality had always had the hallmarks of a spoiled child rather than someone with a harsh and neglectful father. And Dizzy, poor Dizzy, had stumbled into this cesspit of madness and jealousy and unbalanced minds.

'Your father – the Minotaur – did he have Conrad's problem, too?' Keep him talking, keep him talking!

Max shrugged. 'Grandad certainly did. I was lucky to be normal, frankly.'

Call this normal? The words almost escaped but she bit them back. 'But why the Minotaur?'

'The monster in the heart of the maze, of course. You'd think you knew where he was coming from, that he was a man, a good father,' she thought she heard a softening in his voice, 'but all at once he changed, he was coming from a different direction. He was a bull, trampling you, putting you down in the dirt . . .'

'It must have been very hard for you, growing up like that.' She made her voice soft, sympathetic.

'Yes—' Then he stopped short, his eyes narrowing. 'Hey,

hey! Whatever gave you the impression I was stupid?
Psychotherapy isn't going to help you now.'

Without warning he grabbed her other arm and twisted it
up behind her, then whipped out a cord from his pocket and
bound her wrists together. A second later, a gag was being
thrust between her teeth. She didn't even have time to struggle
– and anyway, what could she, with her slight frame, have
done to resist a fit young man?

'Shall I explain to you what I'm going to do? I think it's
only fair.' He laughed, enjoying the moment. 'I'm going to
put you in a safe hiding-place I – well, shall we say happen
to know? It's all ready, and then I walk back from Chapelton
and fetch that jeep you came in. Oh, and your luggage, of
course. I've even got a headscarf to put on while I'm driving.
Nice touch, no?

'It would be easier to deal with you now, of course, but
with Conrad locked up it really has to be Brett who takes
the rap this time – bless her, she was such a help, uttering
the most blood-curdling threats with the police right there
to hear them! So she has to be at Chapelton on her own
when the dreadful deed is done.' He laughed again. 'Dear
me, it sounds so melodramatic, put like that, doesn't it?

'I know, I know, it would be kinder to put you out of your
misery now, but with forensics these days you can't be too
careful. I'm afraid you'll have to wait but once I've got her
set up, I promise I'll make it as quick as I can. I've got the
vegetable knife from the kitchen, simply covered with her
fingerprints. Clever or what?

'Now, shall we go?'

He sounded so assured – smug, even. His eyes had glittered with pleasure throughout that recital and there was
nothing Laura could do to stop him, except hope that in this
whole elaborate scheme something would go wrong – and
go wrong in time to save her life.

It was a slender hope, but it was all she had. Stumbling, she was frog-marched down the path to the Range Rover parked at the end of the path. She looked about her hopefully but the landscape was bare and silent apart from the harsh caws of rooks in a tree across the field.

He pushed her into the back space, then pulled over a stiff, heavy tarpaulin to cover his prisoner. She could feel it being weighed down all round, then heard the slam of doors and the engine starting. As they lurched off along the uneven road there was only darkness and terror, the discomfort of her cramped limbs and her face bumping painfully on the floor.

'Someone's squealing to the Press,' DI Fleming said grimly, looking round the circle of innocent faces at the morning briefing, 'and when I find out who it is, I'll have their guts for garters.'

It was an empty threat and they all knew it. There were probably a couple of officers in this very room who acted as stringers for those bastards in the media, and an off-beat story about a cop with murderous delusions, especially with a touch of horror thrown in, was worth good money.

Fleming hadn't enjoyed being doorstepped by a reporter with a furry mike and a camera crew on her way into work this morning, hadn't enjoyed having to say politely, 'Sorry, I haven't anything for you at the moment but there'll be a statement later.' Thinking about her conversation with Tam about shape-shifting, there were a number of people she'd enjoy sinking her teeth into right now. *Grrr!* She hastily changed the growl into a cough and brought the briefing to a swift conclusion.

The good thing was that Bailey, having dragged his heels all through this investigation, was now seized by a sense of urgency, so perhaps the Press had their uses after all. The only problem was that he wanted a neat solution on his plate with a sprig of parsley and a slice of lemon by yesterday at the very latest.

Still, they'd been fingerprinting the silver mask in house so the results should be through any time. And the tip of one horn, on close inspection, even seemed to have a slight stain; if that did turn out to be Diana Warwick's blood – the labs had been paid to give it top priority – and there was any sign of Conrad's prints on it, that might be enough to bump him into a proper confession. They needed it badly; you couldn't make a charge stick on the basis of a finger-print on an object in the accused's house even if it did prove to be the murder weapon – something else that the path lab would have to confirm.

Reaching her office again, she picked up the phone and dialled the number of the fingerprints department. 'Any luck?' she said, without bothering to identify herself.

'Er – Tam's on his way up now with the report, ma'am,' was the answer, and she frowned as she put down the phone. Strangely evasive . . .

When MacNee appeared, she could tell it wasn't good news. 'Why do they always send me to do the dirty work?' he complained as he laid a sheet of paper on her desk.

'Because they think I won't hit someone smaller than me. Wrongly,' she said mechanically as she looked at the paper, her frown deepening.

The mask had been wiped clean – that was to be expected. But more often than not, in circumstances like this, there would be a print, smudged or even partial, on some inner, less obvious surface.

And they'd found one – two, in fact. That was the good news. The bad news was that they weren't Conrad's. They could be anyone's – a cleaning woman's, Brett's, Jake's – but they certainly weren't Conrad's.

Fleming seldom swore; she swore now. 'And where does that leave us? No proper confession, no fingerprints, Press baying at our heels, the Super demanding miracles—'

'Just another day in the life of your average copper, then.' MacNee enjoyed living dangerously. 'We can start interviewing again, see if anyone can remember anything in the light of what we've got now. And if the lab comes back with a positive on blood, at least that'll be a step in the right direction.'

'*If*,' Fleming said bitterly. 'And the mask won't even reach them till mid-afternoon.' She looked with distaste at the paperwork which had been piling up on her desk, then got up decisively. 'I'm going to grab a sandwich in the canteen, then I'll drop in on my folks to try and prise the kids out of their clutches. I'm beginning to forget what they look like. Then I'm going out to the hospital to see if I can get permission to try out that theory of Laura's I told you about on Jake Mason.'

'Why not? "*If it does you no good, it'll do you no harm*," as the Presbyterian said when he got sprinkled with Holy Water.'

'I'm leaving now,' Fleming announced, 'and if you're on a homespun philosophy kick you can eat your pie and beans on your own.'

'Bill's so much better,' Janet said approvingly. 'Quiet still, mind, though of course he was never someone with a tongue hung in the middle and wagging both ends. But he ate a good lunch and we'd even a wee crack about a walk he'd had with Meg.'

Marjory's careworn face brightened. 'That's really good news. You know, I've always thought all this psychobabble stuff was a load of rubbish, but you've only to see how much better Bill is. I don't know what Laura does but she's a wonder-worker.'

'She's a real nice lassie anyway. She wasn't in for her lunch and I was fair disappointed. I was looking forward to a good blether.'

'Oh? She must have taken longer than she expected at Burnside Cottages. Or maybe she took the keys back to Jessie MacNab – and if I know Jessie she wouldn't let her away again without a bite to eat.

'Now look, Mum, I'll come in on my way back tonight to see the kids and talk about when they're to come home.'

Janet sighed, then smiled bravely. 'Aye, that's right. We'll miss them, mind. Your father's a Supreme Master or something, Cammie says. I doubt he'll be needing to buy one of those machines for himself.'

The sound effects of a computer game coming from the sitting-room had been a background to their kitchen conversation. Marjory laughed.

'I'll give him one as a thank-you present,' she promised. 'Now, I'd better go.'

Janet accompanied her to the door. 'What time will we see you?'

Fleming looked at her watch. 'Two o'clock – five, half-past, maybe? You know how it is.'

'Oh, I know, right enough,' Janet said philosophically. This was a mind-set she had to advocate later on to an impatient Cammie, who had a rugby practice at seven o'clock.

How long had she been in here? It was frightening how quickly you lost count of time; Laura had almost no idea whether it had been one hour or five. It would be hard to say which was worse, the painful cold or the cramp in her limbs, and at first she had cried but now she felt oddly calm – almost detached.

When the Range Rover stopped and Max had pulled back her tarpaulin covering, she discovered it was drawn up outside a wrought-iron gate, beside the area roughly cleared by the JCB. He had picked her up effortlessly as she blinked in the sudden light and carried her into the concealment of what was left of the maze before he set her on her feet again.

'Now march!' he commanded.

She turned her head, tried to speak, but he ignored the mumbling sound which was all that emerged. His eyes were cold and dead, as if there was no one behind them she could reach out to for human sympathy. His hands on her shoulders now, he steered her ahead of him, tracking backwards and forwards through gaps in the hedges until at last they reached the heart of the maze with its massive stone plinth. The great flat stone on top was squint, loosened from the base, and there were chips of mortar lying on the steps. She stopped and Max went forward to pick up a crowbar which had been lying concealed in the long grass. He began to lever aside the heavy stone.

It was her last chance. She turned to run, looking for the gap in the hedge, then bursting through it as the sharp twigs snatched at her clothes. She looked wildly round for the next gap but before she could reach it he was by her side, swinging her off her feet with contemptuous ease.

'Don't be stupid,' he said icily. 'It's irritating.'

Back at the centre again he put her down and she watched dully as he continued his task until half the internal cavity was exposed, formed by the walls of the column, about three feet square by four feet deep. As he swung her up she kicked out, but she was helpless against his strength. He dropped her through the narrow gap, forced her down, and then the covering stone grated back into place.

It hadn't shifted, despite the desperate attempts she had made, bracing her feet against a wall and pushing up with her head and shoulders. A little light, and air too, filtered through the gaps between the slab and the walls, but these were the only mercies. Muffled moans were all the sound she could make, and even if she could have screamed, who was there to hear her?

Her shoulders ached with the strain of her pinioned wrists and she could feel her hands beginning to swell. She gave up her struggles eventually, and found the least agonising position, her feet against one wall and her back curved against the other so that her suffering hands could rest on the ground behind. She had begun almost to long for her executioner's return. No one would find her here and at least when he came back it would mean the end of this torture.

He hadn't quite said so, but she guessed he had hidden Dizzy's body here at some point. It still puzzled her that he had so readily agreed to the digging up of what he surely knew was her grave, and she would have sworn, too, that finding it had come as a shock to him – but then, how could she trust her instincts any more when she had freely opened the door to Dizzy's murderer – and her own?

Had Dizzy been dead when he put her into this dank, awful place, or had she still been alive, bleeding to death perhaps as she suffered the torture her little sister was enduring now? Laura found herself talking to her inside her head, just as she had talked to her before in that published letter, when she had still hoped Dizzy was out there to answer her questions.

'Were you in love with him, Dizzy? Was Jake the only decent man in this terrible family? He's a prisoner now too, you know, shut in his own body. It might even be worse than this is – I know this can't go on for ever . . .'

'Tam! Come and take a look at this, will you?'

DC Charlotte Nisbet was staring at the computer screen on her desk when DS MacNee came into the detective room.

She had called up two sets of fingerprints. The state-of-the-art computerised fingerprinting system was the pride and joy of the Galloway Force, the only piece of equipment it possessed which could be described as being at the white-hot end of the technological revolution. Comparisons between fingerprints, once the territory of experts, were now a matter of pressing a few keys – if you knew which keys, and Nisbet, possessed of an enquiring mind, had made it her business to know.

'What's the parlour trick this time? Bunty'd a dog once could balance a sugar lump on its nose then throw it up and catch it. We'll need to get you on to that next.'

She didn't rise to the bait. 'See those fingerprints they got off the mask?' She expanded the two impressions so that they filled the screen. 'Now, see these?' She replaced them with another set, then with a click the screen divided so that they were side by side, enormously enlarged. The match was clear.

MacNee whistled. 'Where did you get those from?'

'I knew he'd a record so I went down and dug his prints out from the files and copied them on to the computer.'

'Doesn't prove anything, mind,' he pointed out. 'Still, it's interesting, no doubt about it. The Boss'll be wanting a word with him.'

'Is she around?'

'She's away at the hospital trying to talk to Jake Mason with sign language or something.' His tone was sceptical.

Nisbet raised her eyebrows. 'Is that maybe her clutching at straws?'

'Whole bloody haystack, if you ask me. Still, keeps her off the streets, I suppose. I'll give her a call now.'

He had no success. 'They make you switch phones off in hospital because of all the electronic stuff,' Nisbet pointed out.

'Right enough. And she was going in to see the bairns after on her way home. Och well, it'll do in the morning.'

24

The ward sister who had so taken against DI Fleming on her last visit was on duty again today, her lip curling as Fleming explained her mission. 'I couldn't possibly give permission for experimentation of that sort with one of my patients,' she said haughtily.

'So who could?' If pleasantness won't work, try the alternative. 'Who's in charge of this case?'

'Well, the consultant, of course—'

'Then perhaps you could find him for me, nurse.' As the other woman opened her mouth to protest that you didn't *summon* consultants, Fleming said implacably, 'Now, if you don't mind.'

Her face as red as a turkey-cock's, the nurse gave her a look which would have reduced a lesser woman to a pool of green slime and withdrew to her office to emerge, tight-lipped, two minutes later. 'He's with a patient. He'll come after that.'

'Good. Is Mrs Mason with her husband? I want a word with her too.'

'Yes, but—'

Fleming walked off down the corridor. The police guard had gone now and when she looked through the window in the door of Jake Mason's room she could see Rosamond talking earnestly to the immobile figure, rendered almost inhuman by the plastic tubes and monitoring instruments.

Was he listening? Fleming noticed that she had positioned

herself so that she was in his line of sight and his eyes were certainly open – you would almost swear, watching her.

Fleming tapped on the door but didn't go in. Rosamond looked up and seeing who it was, said something to her husband, patted his hand and came over to the door. She was wearing silver-grey today, a polo-necked sweater which looked like cashmere with a double string of large pearls which looked real. Greeting Fleming warmly, she agreed to come to the waiting-area and listen to what she was proposing.

Fleming gave her a brief résumé of the current situation; when she heard about Conrad, Rosamond bit her lip. 'I was always so afraid that something terrible would happen, afraid for both of our boys. But poor, poor Conrad – and poor Brett! Whatever will she do, with no one to look after her?'

It was strange to think of Brett, with her size and aggressive personality, as a helpless creature, while this slim, fragile-looking woman obviously possessed a core of tempered steel.

'Have you been in touch with your son?' Fleming asked with some curiosity.

Rosamond hesitated. 'No,' she admitted. 'No. He hasn't come to see his father, and if he doesn't even have that much family affection there isn't much point, is there?' Her eyes were too bright.

But Fleming hadn't come here to speculate about the Mason family relationships. Changing the subject, she went on to outline what Laura had suggested, stressing that it was only a theoretical possibility.

As she spoke, she saw Rosamond start to glow. A smile lit up her face and she was suddenly quite strikingly beautiful. 'If he could speak to me again, tell me he understands that I still love him, that I always did! It might help me forgive myself . . .'

'You did what you believed was right at the time,' Fleming

said gently, and the other woman sighed. Then a frown furrowed her clear brow.

'You know,' she said slowly, 'I've been talking all the time to Jake – someone suggested it was good for him – and of course I've told him everything that's been happening. And when I was talking about that poor girl's body, I almost thought he reacted. His eyes kept moving to and fro as if he was agitated, but Sister said I was imagining things.'

'Really?' Fleming was staring at her with sudden hope when a tall, good-looking black man in a well-cut suit appeared, escorted fussily by the ward sister like an ocean liner with a tug.

'Mr Mbele,' she announced.

He glanced at Fleming, with some disfavour she thought, but Rosamond greeted him with outstretched hands and he took them, smiling down at her.

'Patrick,' she said, 'this is Inspector Fleming. She's come with an idea for Jake . . .'

He listened, frowning slightly. At the end he said slowly, 'This has been written up, of course. Doesn't work a lot of the time and I don't like raising unrealistic hopes.' He directed a challenging look at Fleming, who said nothing.

'But surely it can't do any harm?' Rosamond said eagerly. 'It wouldn't hurt Jake, just to try it, would it?'

Fleming could read in the doctor's face that he thought there was very little that would make a difference to Jake Mason's situation, one way or another. 'Sure we can try,' he said, 'but I'm not authorising a police interrogation.'

'Of course not,' Fleming said hastily. 'Look, if I could borrow some paper I'll draw out the alphabet and you could take charge of it yourself.'

'That would be wonderful, Patrick,' Rosamond urged, and Fleming could see that, almost against his will, he was interested.

'You have patients waiting, Mr Mbele.' The ward sister looked as if she might have bitten on a lemon.

'Of course I do, Sister. Thank you – could you get a message to my registrar to carry on? And find some paper for Inspector Fleming?'

She fetched some, handed it over with the air of one offering a cup of strychnine, then left in high dudgeon. Fleming rapidly sketched out a rough letterboard and they went back along the corridor to Jake Mason's room.

His eyes, which had been closed, opened as they came in. Rosamond went back to her usual seat and took his hand while the consultant stood at the end of the bed with Fleming, holding the paper, beside him.

'Hi, Jake!' he greeted him. 'How's it going? We've got an idea here we want to run past you – don't let it bug you, now, but we thought we'd give it a shot. Do you reckon you could blink your eyes, if I asked you?'

There was a long, long pause. Fleming was holding her breath; she guessed the others were too. Then, very deliberately, Jake blinked.

'Could be an accident,' Mbele cautioned. 'Jake, let's kick off with one blink for "yes", two blinks for "no". Can you hear me?'

Blink. Rosamond caught her breath on a half-sob.

'Am I doing a handstand?'

No hesitation. Blink, blink.

Mbele laughed. 'Brilliant! Hey, man, we've got us a conversation here!'

'Oh, Jake,' Rosamond said softly, tears standing in her eyes.

'Now, this lady here has a paper with letters. She'll point, and if there's something you want to say blink at the letters that spell it. Sound good?'

Blink.

'OK – but whenever you get tired just blink twice and we'll pack it in. Right?'

Blink.

'Maybe we should start with a question. Rosamond, is there something you want to ask?'

'Yes,' she said very firmly, and moved to stand at the foot of the bed while Mbele and Fleming looked on, smiling, both perhaps expecting something very personal. Rosamond surprised them.

'Jake, is there something that's been worrying you?'

Blink.

'Something to do with Diana Warwick's death?'

Blink.

'Did you want to tell the police?'

Even Fleming could see that the eyes, moving from side to side, looked agitated. Blink.

Mbele stepped forward, frowning. 'I don't want him distressed. Jake, shall we stop this?'

Blink, blink.

Rosamond's eyes did not move from her husband's face, that immobile, drooping mask which could not reflect disquiet within. 'This is Inspector Fleming, Jake. I told you about her; she's a good person. Is there something you need to tell her?'

Blink.

With a glance at the doctor, who shrugged his consent, Fleming held up the paper, her hands not entirely steady. She pointed to the letters slowly, one at a time; there was no response under she reached 'I'.

Blink.

It was quicker next time; he blinked at 'B', then all the way through the alphabet to 'U'. It was a slow process.

Mbele had started jotting down the letters Fleming called out as Rosamond watched Jake's eyes for his responses.

Suddenly he said, 'Hold it, this makes sense.' His eyes were wide with shock, the whites startling against the black skin. 'It says, "I buried Di."'

'It's not really possible to sue the police for wrongful arrest at this stage, Mrs Mason. At least, not until it has been established that the arrest is, in fact – er – wrongful.'

The solicitor, who was nervously fiddling with a paper clip, was a small, bald, meek-looking man with gold-rimmed spectacles and a prominent Adam's apple which was going up and down like a malfunctioning lift as he swallowed convulsively.

Across the desk Brett Mason was leaning forward in a threatening pose, her pale green eyes bulging with fury and frustration. 'But I told you! You have my word that these allegations are totally without foundation of any sort. Conrad to behave like that? The idea is absurd.'

'I'm sure it is.' His voice squeaked and he coughed to clear it. 'But this is something you could only pursue at some later date, when matters have been resolved in your son's favour. Do I gather he has been charged with assault?'

'Yes, but they're trying to pretend he *murdered* that wretched girl whose body they found—'

He shrank back in his seat in horror. 'Mrs Mason, our firm does not touch criminal cases. I'm sure your son will have his own lawyer—'

She laughed contemptuously. 'Oh yes! I saw him in court this morning. Some *youth* with a shock of hair and *sideburns*! Conrad seems to think he's extremely well thought of, but he doesn't convince *me*! I shall hold you personally responsible for getting him out of prison and home where he belongs – forthwith!'

'But, Mrs Mason—'

She rose. 'I want to hear no buts from you. Your father,

who acted for my own dear father all his life, would have put his foot down. I expect you to do the same.'

Head held high, she made her exit, ignoring his bleated protests. She paused only to say to the receptionist, on her way out, 'Your employer is a fool and an incompetent,' before slamming the door too soon to hear the girl's muttered, 'Tell me something I didn't know.'

Outside in the street, Brett paused uncertainly. What was she to do now? Despite her bluster, she knew she had achieved nothing, and there was nothing else she could think of to do. She had no one who could take charge and assure her that everything would happen just as she wished. She was helpless, unprotected . . . She could feel the tension building which was usually released in one of her *petites crises*.

But who then would sympathise, comfort her? Strangers would only stare, might even have her taken away, as poor Papa had been once . . .

Brett drew a deep breath, clenched her fists tight to control herself. She owed it to Conrad, to Jake, even, to look after herself when they weren't there to do it. Blinking away tears of self-pity, she looked round and saw that she was outside the Copper Kettle tea-room.

It wasn't dark yet, but inside lamps were lit and there was a fire in the old grate at one end of the room. There were small round tables covered with yellow cloths and set with green china and pots of daffodils. At two or three of them, women with shopping bags at their feet were laughing and talking.

What was there, waiting for her at home? Max, unspeakable Max, who had waylaid her to taunt her about Conrad's misfortune, asking her what she was planning to do today for her jailbird son. She hadn't told him, of course, but she hated the thought of going back with the knowledge of failure, back to the cold silence of her flat. There was the tea-room, a haven of comfort . . .

She turned the highly polished brass handle. The bell above the door jangled as she went in and settled herself at a table close to the fire, lovingly eyeing the home-baking under its glass domes on the counter.

'A pot of tea, please,' she ordered. 'And a slice of mocha cake. To start with.' She could almost taste the soothing, rich, chocolatey smoothness of the buttercream already.

The cosiness enveloped her like a comfort blanket. She picked up a glossy magazine from a basket on a side-table; they wouldn't close until half past five so it was a nice long time before she would have to face up to reality again and make the dismal journey back to Chapelton.

It was beginning to get dark. Laura was so cold it didn't matter that it was still colder now; even her mind felt numbed and clumsy with it. She thought she might have slept but she didn't know any more.

She had dreaded Max's return at first, but now she could only think of what would happen if he didn't come to put a swift end to all this. What if she was left here, cold and in pain, to suffer a lingering death? She kept straining her ears for sounds of movement but there was nothing but the muttering of the wind and a rustling in the hedges beyond the walls that confined her.

She had lived through a lifetime in her mind since the stone grated across this morning: her quiet childhood, her adolescence clouded by the loss of her sister, her failed marriage, her parents' deaths, the awful events of these past days . . .

A sad, sad, summary. If this was indeed the end – and what else could it be? – what had she made of her life? She'd helped people, she knew that, and of course there had been the good times too. But in talking to Marjory Fleming about her work and her home and her family, even as she agonised over her problems, Laura had glimpsed a sort of quiet joy in a busy, cheerful, rewarding life that she had never known and now, unless a miracle happened, never would.

The wind was whistling through the gap below the stone now, a melancholy sound. Tears began once more to spill silently down her cheeks.

Marjory Fleming emerged from the hospital and stood outside for a moment, almost in a state of shock. It was dark and a brisk wind was snatching at her clothes and ruffling her hair. She ran her hand through it mechanically, then buttoned up her jacket as she headed for the car park.

Her brain was teeming. Such an avalanche of information – but was it evidence? The uncertainty had nagged at her all through the last two hours.

It had been an extraordinary experience. Several times Mr Mbele had intervened, but each time the agonised movements of Jake's eyes and his swift negative to any suggestion of leaving it for another day had forced the consultant to concede that it was probably more harmful to stop him than to allow him to go on.

At first, it had been painfully slow, disjointed words and phrases to be pieced together. 'Max – spoiled – wrong' had followed 'I buried Di' and 'he killed'. But as the stumbling process went on, Rosamond, ashen-faced but rigidly controlled, began to help him, intuitively supplying words, asking questions, making statements so that he only had to signal 'yes' or 'no'. Mbele had taken over pointing to letters when it was needed to allow Fleming to take notes.

But what sort of status could this information possibly have in legal terms? Any half-competent defence could drive a coach and horses through it.

Yet in her own mind Fleming was sure now, without any doubt, that she knew what had happened to Diana Warwick. Max, unstable and dangerously indulged, had found himself humiliated and, as he saw it, displaced in his father's attentions by a beautiful and headstrong young woman who had seen no need to pander to his sensitivities. Her death and its manner – a mockery of Jake's obsession with his bulls – was Max's psychopathic revenge on them both.

He had left Chapelton that weekend, leaving a note for his father telling him Di had gone 'where you won't find her'. Jake spelled out the phrase in full.

'Did you know then what he had done?' Rosamond's voice was perfectly steady; Fleming could only marvel at her self-control. There was a long pause, then the slow, definite closing and opening of the haunted eyes.

He had searched the farm. It took him two weeks to find her in the plinth in the maze, under the stone slab with the Minotaur inscription on the top – 'Smell,' he had spelled out, the horror somehow intensified by the enforced lack of emotion.

For the first time, Rosamond was noticeably shaken. But she went on, 'Why did you move her? To give her a decent burial?'

Blink.

Mindful of Mbele's watchful presence, Fleming had said nothing. Now she took the risk. 'Why didn't you inform the police, Mr Mason?' she asked gently.

Jake's eyes closed; Mbele moved forward uneasily, but then they opened again.

There was agonised pity on his wife's face. 'You couldn't do it to your darling Max, could you? And – and you blamed yourself.'

Blink. The eyes slid to the letterboard again.

'Something else?'

She could not interpret this time. The words had to be painfully spelled out. 'N-o f-a-m-'

'No family?'

Blink.

For once, Rosamond didn't understand. Fleming had to step in. 'I think Diana Warwick had told him she had no family. So there would be no one to look for her, no one to mourn her.' She did not add, 'She was lying.'

Blink. The eyelids were drooping now and Mbele stepped forward decisively. 'That's it. You've said all you need to, Jake. It's off your conscience.'

But he wouldn't close them, looking again to the board. 'R-o-s,' he spelled out. 'L-o-v-e. S-o-r-r-y.'

The weary eyes closed. Rosamond watched him for a moment, her face working, then walked blindly past the others, out of the room.

Fleming hesitated. 'Should I go after her?'

Mbele shook his head. 'She's a very private person. Leave her to cope in her own way.'

As Fleming gathered her notes together, he had asked, curiously, 'And where do you go from here, Inspector?'

'I wish I knew,' she told him honestly, and she was still trying to make up her mind as she got back into the car and set off.

She might know the truth about Diana Warwick's murder but formal justice wasn't about truth. It was entirely about proof, and if the evidence of a man who couldn't speak was deemed inadmissible (she'd have to talk that through with the Procurator Fiscal tomorrow) they'd be in the same position with Max as they had been with Conrad – without even the hope of a confession. Max, she judged, would confess around the same time hell froze.

Of course, the forensic team would apply its black arts to the hollow plinth where poor Diana Warwick's body had been stowed. They might even find suspicious fibres from clothing that wasn't hers. That was comparatively likely. What was supremely unlikely was that they could match them with any item currently in Max Mason's wardrobe.

So they'd just have to plod on with the case, leaning on Max in the hope of tripping him up, interviewing people, then interviewing them again. But unless the Fiscal could come up with a legal framework in which Jake could give evidence – or unless, by some miracle, his powers of speech returned – it would become one of those cases which ran into the sand, the cases that were never closed, that officers went back to when they'd a bit of spare time. Older cases than this had been solved that way, of course, and she wouldn't give up on it. But meantime . . .

Conrad had appeared in court this morning and pled guilty to the assault; he was on remand, pending reports. The chances were that when the case was called again in three weeks' time the Sheriff would consider that, given he was a first offender and the actual assault was minor, Conrad had done enough time already and could be released on a deferred sentence, probably with the condition that he under-went psychiatric treatment. But unless Max could be brought to trial, it would always be assumed that he had killed Diana Warwick. Worse still, he would probably believe it himself.

The original accusation against Jake Mason (and it hadn't been far from the truth, had it?) had offended Fleming's sense of justice, even when she believed he would never know. Now, in the face of a much greater injustice, she owed Conrad restitution. She had been foremost in prosecuting the case against him and he was, after all, one of her own officers. She had failed to appreciate the scale of his mental problems and she would have it on her conscience for the rest of her life if Max escaped scot-free. She'd become one of those sad, retired police officers bleating in the Press whenever they did a retrospective – 'Well, I knew who did it of course but I can't say . . .'

Would she, hell! She'd grab it by the throat now.

They knew who they wanted. They knew where to look. They knew the questions to ask. Max might give himself away, might already have done so—

Laura! Fleming thought suddenly. He'd talked a lot to Laura, told her about Diana at Chapelton. She needed to go through it all with Laura, as minutely as memory allowed, to see whether there was a chink in the armour through which they could slip a knife.

She was about half-way back to Kirkluce now. If she called Laura perhaps she could drive in to meet her at police HQ to make a recorded statement. That way, at least when she told Bailey what had happened – which constituted 'let's-not-go-there' territory right now – at least she could show she was doing something.

She pulled into a lay-by and dialled the Mains of Craigie number. Bill answered; she was so caught up in her problems that she didn't even notice that he sounded almost normal.

'Bill, I need to speak to Laura. Is she there?'

'No. It's funny – said she'd be back for lunch but she didn't come.'

'Oh.' Fleming frowned, deflated. Then belatedly she added, 'How are you, love?'

'OK.' She could hear constraint in his voice now. 'Laura was going to have another talk with me before lunch. She promised, but . . .'

His voice trailed off as if talking had tired him.

'I'm sorry, Bill,' she said gently. 'That's a shame. I'll see you later – I shouldn't be too late.'

She pulled back out into the traffic, busy now with people on their way home from work. She was disappointed, first that any questioning would have to wait until she saw Laura tonight, second that Laura would have had such a casual attitude to promises. She wouldn't have read her that way.

It was nearly half-past five. She could drop in at HQ and write up her notes so that she was well prepared for what was going to be a very sticky interview with Bailey tomorrow, then pop in to see the kids before she headed for home.

'I'm afraid we're closing now,' the waitress said politely.

Brett Mason was the only person left in the tea-room. The fire was dying down and they had switched off some of the lamps; it didn't look so safe and cosy any more. She rose with a bad grace, took the chit the waitress had left and paid at the counter without leaving a tip.

She shivered as she stepped into the darkness outside. There was a bitter wind blowing and she pulled her coat closer round her and turned up the ocelot collar. Her spirits dropping with the temperature, she got into her car and headed off wretchedly towards Chapelton.

25

'Thought you were going straight home tonight, boss?'

Tam MacNee was on his way off duty when Marjory Fleming came through the door of Police Headquarters. He changed his mind when she told him what had happened.

'Tactics, Tam,' she said as she preceded him into her office, switching on the lights. 'Where do we go from here? How do we nail the bastard?'

Sitting down, he told her about Charlotte Nisbet's latest piece of private enterprise. 'So we've his prints on the mask, anyway. But it'd hardly take a genius to come up with "I only wanted a look at it" as a defence.'

Fleming agreed. 'It could be corroboration, though. Circumstantial evidence is better than no evidence at all.'

'Can't see it going down well with the Super.' MacNee was gloomy.

'You think?' Fleming groaned. 'My neck's on the block tomorrow. And all I've come up with is getting a formal statement from Laura, recorded so we can analyse it piece by piece to see if he let something slip to her, some discrepancy that would give us a lever . . .'

He wasn't impressed. 'You want a bet? No? Och well, it's something, I suppose. High risk, mind – like giving a starving dog a dolly-mixture. Are you setting that up for tomorrow?'

'I'd wanted to do it tonight, but I can't get hold of her,' Fleming complained. 'She told Bill and my mother she'd be in for lunch, but she's disappeared—' She stopped, as if she had only just realised what she was saying.

MacNee, too, had gone very still. 'Wonder where she might be?' he said, carefully not sounding alarmist.

'I don't know. I'd like to know. Suddenly I'm feeling very uncomfortable.'

'Did she say where she was away to?'

'Burnside Cottages. She'd left stuff there – she was going to move it out to the farm. When my mother said she didn't come for her lunch I just thought she'd taken the keys back to Jessie MacNab and been given it there.'

'Do you want me to contact Jessie?' He got up. 'I could look in at the cottages too—'

'No. I'll get someone on to that. You come with me, and let's approach it from the other end. Play the man not the ball, to quote the Thoughts of Chairman Bailey. I've changed my mind about bringing Max in tomorrow for questioning. Let's go and get him tonight.'

It was a strange thing about being cold. At first it was painful, dreadfully painful, but then it wasn't. In fact, Laura could hardly even feel the pain in her hands and shoulders now. She was beginning to feel drowsy, almost comfortable . . .

There was a name for it. She struggled to think what it was but her mind seemed reluctant to respond, sluggish. Hypo-something.

At last it came to her. Hypothermia. It made you sleepy, but you were meant to struggle against it. If you let yourself go to sleep, you wouldn't wake up again.

That sounded good. She closed her tired, sore, swollen eyes.

Max had been sitting at the window of the restrained, elegant sitting-room, which so uncomfortably reminded him of his mother's personality, for hours now. It was to the side of the house with a view down to the first corner of the drive; he watched as darkness stealthily soaked up the light and the wind began first to tease the needles of the pine-trees, then assault whole branches which were now bending and swaying. At first he had been in a mood of exhilaration, excitement, even, but he was beginning to feel coldly afraid, afraid and angry. His brilliance was no defence against the whims of a fat, silly bitch who had gone off somewhere and hadn't returned yet.

And what if she didn't? What if she'd decided that she couldn't bear it here without Conrad and had gone to stay at the hotel? What would happen to his superb, meticulous plan? *And what would he do with Laura?*

The sky was a black backdrop for the cold, sparkling pin-points of the stars and a pale moon, almost at the full. With a wind too, the temperature outside would be dropping like a stone; he wasn't at all sure she could survive a night's exposure. And if she died – well, he'd read enough crime novels to know that you couldn't fake the scenario he had in mind with a body that was dead already.

He could go and fetch her out, of course, bring her into the house. He'd been going to kill her inside anyway – for who would ever believe Brett would go out trotting round the policies on a winter night? – but to have her spend any time at all on the premises was high risk. She'd be missed soon, and the police had a search warrant for the place which they wouldn't hesitate to use.

Chewing his lip, he looked out from the unlit room, scanning the skyline for any sign of headlamps in the distance. Nothing. He swore, and despite the warmth of the room he could feel beads of cold sweat on his brow. His whole future was on the line, thanks to that . . . He used every ugly word he could think of to describe her, but it didn't change the fact that the sky remained obstinately dark.

Soon he'd have to make a decision. Let her die – just leave her there? They'd never find her. They'd never have found Di, if she'd been left there. Or even if he'd known where she was, it would have been easy enough to divert the dig elsewhere.

It would have been the Minotaur who moved her to a burial place, of course – the Minotaur driven by pathetic guilt. Max despised guilt. As if it could eliminate his father's responsibility for Di's death! Still, he was paying for it now, a living vegetable, probably not even living much longer. Sometime soon they'd come to ask Max for permission to switch him off. Unless, of course, they found his mother.

Hardly likely, by now. She might even be dead. Strangely, he didn't want that. He'd been shocked to discover how much it had affected him when he'd believed Di's body was hers. He wanted his mother to be alive, but to be as she was in his mind, as he remembered her when he was a little boy and she was the most beautiful woman in the world. He didn't want her disapproving, controlling, criticising, saying terrible things about him, her own son. At least his father hadn't betrayed him – then. He scowled. Everyone let you down in the end. Everyone. You had to be your own person, supremely invulnerable.

He was vulnerable now. He felt sick, thinking about the terrifying decision he was going to have to make. He stood up, his hands to his temples as if pressure there would help the quality of his thought. Then he saw it.

A beam of light, from the direction of the drive, uplighting some low, thick cloud that was gathering over to the west. He stood very still, unconsciously holding his breath, watching it come closer and closer. Brett, or someone else – the police, even . . . ?

Brett. Her little car lurched round the last corner of the

drive and he shrank back into the shadows as the headlamps' beam crossed the darkened room. The car disappeared round the front of the house; he heard the engine stop, the car door slam, the outer front door open and close again, the inner front door do the same. He heard Brett's footsteps cross the hall and click-click up the uncarpeted stair, then another door close, then silence. She was, he could safely assume, in the upstairs flat on the other side of the house. He must move quickly now, and quietly. Silently, in fact, because Brett herself was going to be his alibi.

He steadied himself. Think it through: there must be no mistake. Fetch Laura. Take her to the study. Kill her. Leave the house. The jeep, with its luggage – that was concealed round the side of the house so that Brett wouldn't see it when she arrived, but not hidden, which would arouse suspicion. So far so good.

Walk down the drive. Walk up the Glen road to the field gate where he'd parked his hired Peugeot. Drive into Kirkluce, phone Brett from a pub to warn her to lock up because he'd decided not to come back that night. When the police questioned her, she'd be quite certain that he hadn't been at Chapelton. From his observation of his aunt, innocence would make her indignantly honest and she was so stupidly arrogant it would never occur to her that she was incriminating herself.

His confidence soared. How many of that tiny elite, the killers too clever to be caught, had ever used the psychology of their fall guy to give them an alibi? Not many, he was willing to bet. Sadly, by definition he would never know who they were.

Smiling, he fingered the knife in his pocket in its plastic wrapping, then stepped noiselessly out of the room and into the silent hall.

*   *   *

'She didn't go to Jessie's,' MacNee reported as he switched off the phone. 'And she's not at the cottages. The jeep's not there, but she hasn't arrived back at the farm either.'

Unconsciously Fleming's foot pressed down more heavily on the accelerator. 'What's gone wrong, Tam? Why would Max – do anything,' she gulped, 'to Laura, when as far as he knows Conrad's our suspect and he's safely locked up in jail?'

'We don't know he's done anything,' he pointed out, but without much conviction. There didn't seem to be much else to say after that.

The house, as they approached it, seemed to be in darkness, the main front door shut. 'Maybe there's no one here,' MacNee was saying as they reached the front, but as they got out they could see a light on the upper floor.

'Brett's flat. She must be in. Oh, great!' Fleming said hollowly as MacNee rang the doorbell.

For a moment, the only response was its echo. Then, unexpectedly, the fanlight above the door lit up as the hall light was switched on. They heard locks being turned and the door swung open.

There was a pause during which you could have counted to ten. Then Max Mason said in an attempt at his usual offensive drawl, 'Oh God, not the Fuzz again. Am I entitled to tell you to piss off, or will that mean you arrest me?'

That made it easy. 'I think we just might, Mr Mason.' Fleming stepped into the hall.

Under the light, she thought he looked very pale, his eyes darting uneasily from one to the other. 'I should tell you,' she said with calculation, 'that I've been having a word with your father this afternoon.'

The result was gratifying. 'My – my father?' His jaw had gone slack; he was staring as if, like Hamlet, his father's ghost had suddenly appeared in front of him.

'Oh, and your mother. It's all been very, very interesting, and I feel we have this and that to talk about. Just for a start, where's Laura Harvey?'

He was most evidently shocked and struggling not to show it. 'Staying with you, as far as I know,' he said with a ghastly attempt at jauntiness. 'Don't tell me you've mislaid her, Inspector?'

Absorbed in their confrontation, none of them had heard the movement on the upper landing until Brett Mason's voice hailed them from the top of the stairs. 'Oh, you're there, Max. I didn't see your car – I assumed you were out.'

Watching him minutely, Fleming noticed a curious half-smile cross Mason's face as Brett turned her attention to the visitors. 'And what, pray, are you doing here? Haven't we suffered enough?'

Catching a histrionic tone in her voice, Fleming tried hastily to reassure her. 'It's all right, Mrs Mason. Our business is only with Max.'

It was an annoying distraction. Fleming had used her shock tactics to considerable effect; now that advantage was being lost as Max visibly recovered himself. Turning her back, she went to the door of the study and held it open. 'In here?' she said pointedly.

But Brett hadn't finished. 'Max!' she called peremptorily. 'Max, is there someone else here? There was a jeep parked round this side when I got back a few minutes ago and went to draw the curtains – a rather battered-looking vehicle. I think you should check – it could be anyone.'

Max couldn't control an expression of pure rage but his voice was impressively level as he said, 'In a moment, Auntie. In here, Inspector?'

Fleming and MacNee didn't move. 'A jeep?' she said. 'Tam—'

'I'm on my way.'

Everything stopped, Fleming thought afterwards, as if you'd pressed the freeze-frame button on a video. Brett, oblivious, at the top of the stairs; herself, struck with horror; Max – well, Max had his back to the wood panelling of the hall and his expression was unreadable.

It all jerked into movement again as MacNee erupted through the front door. 'Your jeep,' he hurled at Fleming, then, 'What have you done with her, you bastard?' he snarled, advancing on the cringing Max.

'I – I haven't the faintest idea what you mean. Really, officer,' he tried to laugh, 'I think you'd better ask my aunt.'

MacNee, his face two feet away from Mason's, went very, very quiet. 'Oh, playing games, are we? That's good. We've a rare sense of fair play, in Glasgow. Heads I win, tails you lose.'

The menace of a thousand kilted 'ladies from hell', who had put the fear of God into the enemies of Empire, was in Tam MacNee's voice. Max's face, white before, turned grey. 'Inspector—'

Normally, she would have let Tam have his bit of fun. She'd other things on her mind now. 'Don't waste your time, Tam. I know where she'll be. Hold him and I'll get back-up.'

Then she was running across the hall under Brett's affronted gaze, talking into her radio phone, and was outside before Tam had said, 'Against the wall, arms spread!'

The stars had vanished now, blotted out by the wind-driven clouds scudding across the sky. It was almost surreal, like time-delay camera-work, and Fleming took a moment to get her bearings as she came out of the shelter of the house and staggered in the force of the blast. There was a roaring in the trees like a high-running sea and a huge, ancient pine on the edge of the path groaned and creaked as she passed; she cast it a nervous glance.

There, beyond, was the entrance where the bulldozer had made its brutal assault, scooping away the ground so that the wrought-iron gate, almost off its hinges, was blowing violently to and fro with a rhythmic, metallic clang. She made no effort to find a path to the centre, shouldering her way through wherever she thought she saw a weakness in the hedge, ignoring the rips in her clothes.

Laura was here. Her mind was unclouded by doubt on that score. But Laura – in what shape? Laura still, by some unlikely chance, alive, terrified, and waiting for rescue? Or – and here the shadows were dark indeed – Laura dead, as she felt in her bones that she must be?

She had reached the still heart of the maze now. It was very sheltered here out of the onslaught of the wind, with only the mysterious, uneasy rustling and whispering of the hedges and the long grass and the distant clanking of the gate like a tolling bell to break its unnatural peace. The moon appeared suddenly from a rift torn in the clouds and glittered on the metal plaque, highlighting the etched figure with its horns, its gaping mouth a complicit sneer.

The moon vanished and it was dark again. 'Laura!' Fleming shouted desperately. 'Laura, are you there?'

There was only wind sound, then faintly and still a long way off, the familiar, reassuring sound of sirens approaching. No voice, though, no sign of life from within the rough walls of the monument.

Pulling a torch from her shoulder-bag, Fleming shone it round – and there was the confirmation. Round the steps were chips of the mortar which, when last she had been here, had been securing the massive top stone into its place.

Her heart pounding, still calling Laura's name, she seized the corner of the slab and tried to slide it across. She prided herself on having, if not quite masculine strength, certainly more physical power than most women, but this she couldn't move. She swore, grabbing at it, breaking her nails; it was only when she heard the sirens stop close by, the flashing blue lights brilliant against the livid grey of the cloudy sky, that she gave up, running out to call for help.

It took three of them to shift it. At last the stone was off, toppling on to the paving below with an almighty smash. The dank smell of wet earth and masonry rose from the shadowy cavity within as the moon came out again, bathing it in cold, sickly light.

They lifted out the huddled body, bound and gagged, with infinite tenderness. She was limp, her eyes closed and her face in the moonlight a ghastly clay-white.

Fleming said stiffly, 'Is she dead?' but they couldn't tell her. The officer who was wrapping her gently in his great-coat couldn't feel a pulse.

Another officer appeared behind them. 'They're sending a chopper. It's on its way.'

Numbly, Fleming followed the cortège back to the house. As she crossed the sea of mud by the entrance to the maze, the gate swung violently forward into her path. Giving vent to her feelings, she wrested it violently off its rusted hinges and flung it to the ground.

They were escorting Max Mason out, his hands hand-cuffed behind him, as Fleming reached the front steps. His head had been bowed; as she drew level with him he raised it to look her full in the face, arrogant and unrepentant.

Still in the grip of helpless, murderous rage, she thought suddenly, *I want to spit in his face. Like Susie did to me.* With sudden appreciation of the other woman's depth of emotion, she watched as Max was pushed into the police car.

She could hear the helicopter now, going in to land in the

field beyond the maze. Satan's field, where Diana Warwick's sad, disinterred remains had exposed the sins of pride and jealousy and unwise love.

Paramedics were running up to the house now. Fleming stood in the bitter cold, her hands in the pockets of her badly ripped jacket, and watched them go in, then followed, her head bowed.

But Tam MacNee, coming towards her, was beaming. 'They've found a pulse. And now we've the paramedics to start working on her, she'll be fine. They're the wee boys!'

Laura was still looking very white and weak, propped up on pillows in her hospital bed when Marjory was allowed into the side-ward to see her two days later. She had developed pneumonia and been acutely ill; her hands were still bandaged but, she assured her visitor, she was on her way to recovery.

Marjory set down a huge bunch of pink lilies on the bed. 'These are from Bill. Conscience-money. He's feeling terrible because he told Max where you were.'

Laura looked stricken. 'Oh no! I hope you told him it wasn't his fault?'

'Well – only sort of,' Marjory confessed. 'It seemed to be having quite a good effect – realising that his own problems weren't the worst in the whole world.'

Laura smiled. 'Poor Bill! It's hard to keep a sense of perspective in a situation like that. If he's able to recognise it, that's a very good sign – in real clinical depression you can't just choose to snap out of it. Even so, don't expect too much too soon. He'll take time to forgive himself for giving way.'

'I can be patient. I'm just so grateful to see signs of the man I know and love coming back. It's going to take time for the community to heal too, but at least this dreadful epidemic seems to be over at last. What with that, and the Mason case, it feels as if the sun hasn't shone for weeks.'

'I don't think it has, has it? Anyway, tell me what's happening out there. They won't let me have the newspapers yet.'

Fleming pulled a face. 'You haven't missed a lot. It's the usual disgusting frenzy of speculation, hype and downright lies, and you can imagine what they made of the were-wolf angle.

'Max hasn't been charged with your sister's murder yet – we're still questioning him. Forensic tests are just starting but they've found some clothes left in the wardrobe of Max's old bedroom, including a black cloak he might just have used, and they're hoping they might manage to match up fibres. And we've got his fingerprints on the silver mask.'

'He put it on and – and gored her with it, didn't he?' Laura's mouth quivered. 'He described it to me as if Conrad had done it – and mentioned a black cloak, actually – and I was fool enough to react. I can't think why I didn't realise before. I'd been right there and seen Conrad *being* a bull – he didn't need to dress up.'

'I see!' Fleming was pleased to have a major question answered. 'We went round and round it – couldn't think why he should have decided to take such a risk as to attack you.

'Anyway, he's pled not guilty to attempted murder but he'll probably be advised to change his plea given that you'll be able to testify and that he had a knife in his pocket in a plastic bag with someone else's fingerprints on it—'

'Brett's,' Laura said with a shudder. 'That was the plan. He couldn't resist boasting about it to me, showing off how clever he had been.'

Fleming listened to her account, fascinated. 'Is he a psychopath?'

Laura wrinkled her nose. 'Loose term. You could hardly say he was normal – but after that you get into difficult territory.'

'That whole family is stark raving mad,' Marjory said firmly. 'Another loose term, but it does it for me.'

'What about Jake?' Laura asked suddenly. 'You know, while I was in that – that place, I kept thinking about Dizzy and about him. What sort of man was he? Was she in love with him? Did he love her?'

Marjory sighed. 'Piecing things together, I think he was an arrogant, hot-tempered man who was taught a terrible lesson. I think he still loves his wife, who is a woman of remarkable strength of character who made a sad miscalculation which she's been paying for ever since. Whether, after she left him, he and your sister – we're never going to know, are we?'

She told Laura about the success of the experiment she had suggested. 'That saved your life, you know,' Marjory said soberly. 'But I was talking to the consultant yesterday and now Jake looks to have given up, quietly slipping out of life. Rosamond's spirit seems broken; she hardly talks to him any more, just sits holding his hand. She's put in a request to go and see Max in prison but he's refused to see her.'

Laura sighed. 'So terribly sad! And Conrad – what about him? I – I really liked him, you know. He was nice to me – kind and funny.'

Marjory gave her an old-fashioned look. 'Oh aye,' she said. 'Charming enough when it suited him, right enough. Bit of a hunk too, I'd have to say. But take a wee bit sandpaper to the surface and he was an ill-tempered bully. Took it out on anyone too weak to hit back.'

'Oh dear!' Laura looked dismayed at first, then started to giggle. 'So much for my talents as a psychologist!'

'You won't get me saying a word against psychology,'

Marjory declared, then, as Laura's laughter turned into a cough, looked alarmed. 'Here – I'd better go. I've one ward sister who'd poison my tea given half a chance. I'm not needing another.'

'Wait,' Laura said taking a sip of water, 'what's the scary Mrs Mason doing in all this?'

'Keeping very, very quiet, I'm happy to say. Conrad will probably be released before too long and then it's my guess they'll sell up and disappear. Now, I'm away to leave you to rest.'

She went to the door, then paused. 'And you, Laura? What are you going to do? Is it back to London?'

Laura hesitated. 'I don't know, Marjory. You know, when I was in that awful place, waiting to die, I felt that the tragedy of Dizzy's disappearance had shadowed the past fifteen years, imprisoned me almost. Now – well, I suppose in psychological jargon you could say I've had closure, and I'm free. I don't think I've made the most of my life, and that's going to change. When I'm an old lady I want to be able to look back and say, "Well, I enjoyed that!"'

'Sounds good to me. Kick up your heels – paint the town red – steal traffic cones – oh well, maybe not the traffic cones.' They both laughed, then Fleming said more seriously, 'I never thought we could do this, you know – get at what happened after all these years. Max must have felt quite safe with his secret.'

'Yes, he probably did. But he should have remembered about truth and oil.'

'Truth and oil?'

'Dizzy used to say that.' Laura's eyes were wet. 'It's a Spanish proverb. *Truth and oil always come to the surface.*'

Postscript

Marjory Fleming stood in the orchard in the May sunshine, watching her chickens pecking hopefully in the long, lush grass. They were acclimatising well; the new rooster, Tony, was a quieter type than his predecessor Clinton and somewhat in awe of the alpha hen, inevitably christened Cherie.

Above, there was pink apple-blossom in the gnarled old trees while below the home meadows were bright with daisies, buttercups, white clover and soft blue speedwell. The white starry clusters of cow-parsley edged the margins of the field like sea-foam, making an idyllic picture for a lovely spring morning.

But there in the pastures, when you looked closer, were rank grasses, nettles, docks and sorrel, the ungrazed land rapidly succumbing to the stranglehold of weeds. It was happening in every field, on every hillside: the pretty, 'natural' landscape with its velvet-soft green contours, so beloved of visiting town-dwellers, was produced by its flocks of sheep and no more natural than a shed of battery chickens. She was reminded of the old gardener's reply to the minister who had congratulated him on what a good job he and the Almighty together had made of his garden: 'Aye, but you should have just seen it when the Almighty had it to himsel'!'

It could all be reclaimed in time, of course, just as their community life could be. It wouldn't be easy for these wounds to heal and there would, even years later, be areas which hurt when you touched on them. Marjory sighed. She was sadder and wiser, certainly: that was always talked up as being a good thing, though she wasn't convinced.

A thin, demanding bleating suddenly made itself heard, a sound once so familiar that she would barely have noticed it. Now she smiled; she had shamelessly used her contacts to have Mains of Craigie chosen as one of the farms to host 'sentinel' animals – sheep which would be regularly monitored to ensure that pastures were clean of the foot-and-mouth virus – and had even managed to find a black lamb for Bill, an engaging, leggy replacement for the one they hadn't saved.

The children idolised Hope, as they had christened it, and it was rapidly becoming thoroughly above itself. Silence had fallen again so it must be getting its bottle now; she'd better get back and tell the kids to hurry up. Even the conscientious Cat was inclined to be offhand about schooltimes when there was a lamb to play with.

They'd settled back with surprisingly few complaints about not having their friends round the corner and being offered Mum's cooking instead of Granny's. Her father, on the other hand . . . When she had phoned, after the high drama of Laura's rescue and Max Mason's arrest, to apologise for her non-arrival, he had said harshly, 'Oh, no doubt it's fine for you. But Cammie missed his rugby, with you being too busy strutting round being the big shot – what sort of mother does that make you?'

Foolishly, she had allowed her anger to speak for her. 'And you think I was happy, every time your work made you let me down? What sort of father did that make you? That was different, somehow?'

He hung up on her. Despite Janet's best efforts the atmosphere was still frosty and the GameBoy she had given him remained untouched. The television, to his wife's distress, was once more permanently switched on, to the accompaniment of his endless complaints.

It was time she wasn't here. She picked up the empty mash pail and the bowl of eggs and walked to the gate, then stopped for an affectionate look at her chookies. It was good to hear that warm, comforting clucking and crooning again.

And perhaps it was childish to wish that Bill had thought of buying her the replacements. Laura had warned her she'd have to be patient, and patient she would just have to be.

Read on . . .

Discover the next book in the DI Marjory Fleming Series

THE DARKNESS AND THE DEEP

The wreck of the Knockhaven lifeboat with the loss of all three of its crew is a hard blow for the small Scottish town. But it's harder still when DS Tam MacNee discovers that it isn't simply a tragic accident.

Was it just the act of vandals, bored in a fishing port stricken with unemployment? Could it be linked to the drugs trade which has taken root in the locality? Or is there someone who, in their determination to kill one person, is callous enough to take two innocent lives? And if so, who is the intended victim?

As DI Marjory Fleming and her team investigate multiple murders, with a whole community hungry for justice, the pressure – professional and personal – is on.

Out now in paperback and ebook.

HODDER